★ ★ About T͟ ...

First edition.

Rose Marie Ryder's favor... rowed from the great Te... put the jam on the lowe... it." She made a name for herself by becoming the first female State Comptroller of Texas—and by making sure that the rich paid their fair share of taxes. Now "Red" Ryder is running to become the first woman U.S. Senator from the Lone Star State. She's made a few enemies along the way, from country radio d.j.'s to the highest echelons of monied society.

Joe Holley's novel takes us inside the almost always politically incorrect world of 1980s campaigning in Texas. Red Ryder's team is a lone-star potluck: a has-been evangelist's son who once ran a string of mobile massage parlors, veterans of the civil rights struggles, Austin lesbian activists, old-school political operatives with sterling motives and shady morals . . . and then there is Wily T. Foxx. Until he joined the campaign—almost entirely by accident—Wily's passion in life had been cock fighting. Now he is literally the candidate's "purse bearer," a combination body-guard/campaign worker, privy to information that makes him a target for the intrigues of the other side and a magnet for at least one very sexy lady.

Texas politics are generally roisterous, often absurd, and occasionally deadly. Ballot boxes can grow fat in counties with more cattle than people, the dead can rise and walk to the polls, and the votes of common folk can be disqualified on a whim. Lawyers and lawmen, politicians and preachers, cow punchers and cattle barons all can come down on, well, both sides of the Law. Red Ryder's right-wing opponent, rancher and banker Jimmy Dale Sisco, is his own worst enemy when it comes to a thoughtful debate, but his minions will stop at nothing short of murder to ensure victory.

Other Works by Joe Holley

My Mother's Keeper (1997)

*Slingin' Sam: The Life and Times
of the Greatest Quarterback Ever to Play the Game* (2012)

THE PURSE BEARER

A Novel of Love, Lust
and Texas Politics

JOE HOLLEY

San Antonio, Texas
2014

SUMMER—FALL
1980

Let it be a day in August, deep into the grip of summer. And let it be a small Texas town, a town with a domed limestone courthouse from an earlier century, a sturdy structure set in a shady courthouse square. Commercial buildings on the square, also from an earlier century, are brick, one- and two-story, most of them still occupied. The sidewalks around the square are raised a couple of feet off the street. Old horsehead-topped hitching posts still stand every 100 feet or so.

And let there be a woman, a red-haired woman in late middle age, standing on the courthouse steps in a bright yellow, sleeveless dress. Her name is Rose Marie Ryder, but most people call her Red. She is giving a speech.

Her audience, what there is of it, is gathered in the shade of a tall magnolia tree, its long green leaves dry and wispy. They resemble a scraggly herd of cows, standing statue still under a tree, as if they're trying to wait out the brutal heat. Outside the circle of God's good shade, the grass is yellow, sparse. The ground is hard, cracked like ancient lava.

Standing behind Red on the courthouse steps, his blue eyes squinting against the sun and scanning the crowd, is a young man in his mid-20s, not too tall, but handsome, people say, with curly brown hair, rosy cheeks on a sun-tanned face, a ready smile. Heavy in his hand is a big purse, a woman's purse.

He is thinking, and the thought he is thinking is this: "Sparrows pick THE LETTER U, Pat Sajack!" Okay, so that doesn't make sense, unless you could see the abandoned building across the square that has prompted the thought. "Squire's Cafe," the faded old sign says. Sparrows have built a nest in the crotch of the letter U.

The deep thinker is Wily T. Foxx. Purse, they call him. Short for Purse Bearer.

He is halfway listening to words he has heard a dozen times before. He can't help it; his mind begins to wander on these campaign stops. Next door to Squire's Cafe, he notices an abandoned two-story building that maybe once upon a time was a boardinghouse. Wood weathered down to a silvery gray, it has a long front porch across both floors. The top floor sags a bit.

In his mind's eye Purse sees an inviting, whitewashed building and salesmen, drummers they were called back then. They're wearing seersucker suits and lounging in big wooden rockers at the end of the long day. Legs crossed, they're slowly rocking, fanning themselves with their straw boater hats. Some are sipping glasses of iced tea, a sprig of mint from the hotel's garden out back in the cold glass. They're telling tales about the day's customers.

On this day, though, the heat shimmers off the stone steps. It's one of those days when your shirt sticks to your back—like you've just stepped from a steam bath and somebody's stolen your towel. You feel grimy and wet, and the sun's beating down so hard the hair on the top of your head is hot when you touch it.

Ordinarily, it's pretty in East Texas—trees, flowers, deep green St. Augustine grass in shady front yards. But not in August, not this August. Hottest on record; that's what all the weathermen are saying. Newspapers are running red arrows up the side of the front page, showing how hot it is.

Purse recalls a story he had read about a turbaned fellow in India who self-combusted, just caught on fire and burned up for no reason. In August you feel like something like that may happen again, although in East Texas you'd more likely melt, like those tigers chasing Little Black Sambo. When it's the dog days of summer over here, you feel like you're running the risk some afternoon that you'll just slowly syrupify into a puddle on the hot Texas ground.

Purse bounces back to the joke Red is trying to tell, one she borrowed from a Hollywood comedian friend of hers. "Now, you may not believe this," she is saying, "but I can remember the first time I was in Sulphur Springs, the very first time. "I couldn'ta been more than six years old, though my mama says I was big for my age."

With a flat Texas twang that reminds Purse of bob wire and tumble weeds and dust storming in under the door, Red's voice pierces. It's a good voice. Once you've heard it, you won't forget it, and you won't mistake it for anyone else's.

She has red hair and laser-like blue eyes and, as people say, once she gets you in her sights, she won't let you go. Aboy told Purse that the first time he met her those eyes nearly hypnotized him; he couldn't look away. He said they were at the Chili Parlor in Austin, and she was drinking a diet Coke out of an ice-filled glass. When she lifted the glass up and drained it, he could still see those eyes, magnified, boring into him through the ice and through the bottom of the glass.

Another thing about Red: She never lets people see her sweat. Just like the old saying. How she does it, Purse hasn't figured out. It's a talent, he assumes, one he doesn't have. Certainly one Aboy doesn't have.

That's Aboy out on the street, his moon face red and shiny, the sun glinting off his glasses. He's leaning against a white Ford station wagon with the red 'RED RYDER' sign plastered on the side. He has his feet crossed and is intent on the task at hand—picking his substantial nose with a large index finger. He thinks no one is looking his way. His white suit coat is lying on the hood of the car, and even from where Purse is standing he can see half moons of sweat spreading out from under his arms. Aboy, a little husky, you might say, keeps a handkerchief stuffed under each armpit to try to control Niagara. Purse has seen him take the handkerchiefs and wring them out; it's not something he wants to see again.

★ ★ ONE ★ ★

They were nearly an hour behind schedule when they left Sulfur Springs headed for Lone Star. The speedometer needle was flirting with 90 as Aboy drove toward the steelworkers' gathering he had set up for noon. Why noon, and why on the side of the road, in the middle of a day as hot as Hades, Purse couldn't figure out. And neither could Red.

Purse could tell Red was none too happy, and what made it worse is that Aboy, with his labor connections, had pushed for it. It wasn't something Olene Whitten, Red's scheduler, had set up. Neither had Bobby Ray Evangeline, the campaign manager who had just come on board a month or so before. Fortunately for Aboy, they got to Lone Star before Red could really vent her spleen.

Coming over a rise, they could see—in the wavy distance like a mirage—a dozen or so diehard supporters in a gaggle on the side of the road. Apparently they had nothing better to do than risk getting run over or laid low by a heat stroke or breaking out in the screamin' meemies. They were milling around on the side of the road. Their blue work shirts, sleeves rolled up past the elbow, were sweated through, and their gimme caps were pushed back on their flushed, dripping foreheads. Purse was thinking they might be delirious already.

Across the highway a big battleship-gray mill loomed up out of a pine forest. It was quiet as a graveyard these days, its parking lots empty, its smokestacks cleaned and scrubbed. The men had nothing better to do, because they were out of work. Every last man of them had been laid off for months. Every one of them was standing in the heat because he was desperate. They needed help, and Purse ached for them. He remembered his dad being in the same situation when the farm went bust.

Maybe, just maybe, Rose Ryder as senator could figure out something to do for them. They sure as hell knew the other guy wouldn't do anything. They were bugs on the windshield of the speeding capitalist Cadillac, mere collateral damage in the free-trade war. That's how Aboy put it.

Aboy pulled up beside them in a cloud of red dust. The hard-charging Ford motor pinged and smoked when he switched off the ignition. Red got out and talked for about 10 minutes, shook everybody's hand and then got back in the car. She didn't jack around with them. She knew they were hurting. She told them she'd do what she could if she got to DC, and she hoped they'd vote for her. Purse figured they appreciated her honesty.

They drove on into the little town of Lone Star and stopped at a Dairy Queen. This is where it will happen, Purse was telling himself as he climbed out of the car, stretched his arms above his head and trudged to the smudged glass front door.

Purse went up to the red formica counter and ordered the usual—a fish sandwich for Red, mayonaise on the side, a cheeseburger for himself—while Red went to the ladies' room. Aboy walked up to the counter beside him and ordered what he called "the works": steak finger basket with country gravy, an order of onion rings, a chocolate malt to swish it down, a DQ Dude for dessert. They sat down and waited for Red, waited for what was coming, at a table near the window.

Sitting across from them, two older couples were having cheese burgers for lunch and sharing a large order of fries drenched in ketchup. "I'm telling you I've worked hard as a mule all my life," one of the women was saying, "but what I'm sayin' is I'm not gonna keep on workin' that hard if these little Meskin girls ain't goin' to pull their fair share.

"I went into Lloyd Stenholm's office the other day, and I told him, I said, 'Lloyd, I've been here way too long and seen way too much just to take what's goin' on without havin' my say. You know me, Lloyd. You know I'm the type that when I see somethin' that ain't right, I'm not gonna keep quiet about it.'"

Red, apparently unrecognized by the Dairy Queen diners, came to the table. Aboy stood up to pull out her chair. Purse walked up to the counter for their order. He could hear the couples at the nearby table.

"You reckon those boys gonna have two-a-days this year, hot as it is?" asked the old man sitting next to the woman who must have been his wife. He was asking the man across the table, a tall, skinny fellow in a faded John Deere gimme cap who was working hard on his burger.

"'Lloyd, you gonna have to get your little BE-hind out from behind that desk and come out on the floor and see what's goin' on,' that's what I told him," the woman said to whomever was listening.

Purse distributed the food. He noticed Red stare at Aboy's bounty. She didn't say anything as Aboy poured a stream of ketchup on the meat and French fries, the red sauce swirling into the grayish-white gravy.

It was quiet at the table, a kind of calm-before-the-cyclone quiet, and Purse caught himself staring at the pictures of DQ-sponsored Little League teams on the walls, while the voice of the woman at the next table droned on. He was just about to reach for the ketchup himself when the storm set in, when Red lit into Aboy. The couples nearby stopped talking and started eavesdropping. Purse wasn't sure they knew who Red was, but when she started lambasting Aboy before he could even get one of his steak fingers down, they started listening. You can bet it made their day.

Purse kept his head down and waited for her to finish with Aboy about his piss-poor scheduling, about his advance work, even about his driving. He figured she was mad enough that he would be the next punching bag.

"But Red," Aboy tried to say, his voice beginning to whine. "You harbor a fundamental misunder..."

"Stuff it, Ewell," Red said, in a voice low and powerful like a mama tiger's rumble.

Ewell was his real name, Ewell Suskin, and when Red got mad, that's what she called him. "Stuff it this minute. If I told you once, I told you a thousand times, I don't want to hear your lame-brained excuses when things go haywire. And I'll tell you another thing: Too many things have been going haywire lately."

Red took a quick sip of water. Her lipstick left a red print on the side of the glass. Purse was thinking that if she got elected senator, that glass would be a souvenir.

"Let me get one thing straight, Aboy," she said, "and I don't care if Purse hears it. You make damn sure you know who you're working for and why. You make damn sure you clear things with me before you go to setting them up. I'm telling you, I'll bounce you all the way back to that little 'medical facility' where you were when I rescued your sorry ass. You understand me?"

Purse noticed a rosy flush rising from her neck.

"But, Red," Aboy started to say—before Red slammed the table with the flat of her hand. The ketchup bottle skittered off the table and came to a stop underneath another table. The two couples stared, wide-eyed and open-mouthed. Purse glanced back at the counter. Three girls in white DQ uniforms stood staring, as well.

Aboy didn't notice. He just stared at Red, a baby-Huey 'bout-to-bawl look on his face. Cream gravy from the steak finger he held halfway to his mouth dripped down the side of his ham-sized hand.

Purse got up and walked over to the nearby table, crouched down and retrieved the ketchup bottle. He noticed that one of the men was wearing black socks with a pair of sandals. "Sorry, folks," he said.

"Well, I'll swan," one of the women said.

Back at the table, Red had sort of softened, and Aboy looked down at his plate. He got a napkin out of the dispenser and blotted at his hand. The storm was over, and it had passed Purse by.

Actually, Red never got on the younger man the way she got on Aboy. He wondered what he would do if she did. Sit there and take it, he guessed. That's what he did in the Army when some fat-ass mess sergeant got on him for not peeling enough potatoes. And then he would lie in his bunk at night thinking of things he should have said, or making up schemes in his mind about how he would get even. But he never did.

Aboy, who was closing in on 50, was the same way, Purse had come to realize, maybe because Aboy still considered himself a man of the cloth, and men of the cloth weren't supposed to have a temper. Or maybe he was just a big chicken-shit. Whatever he was, on this day at the Dairy Queen, he sort of sulled up and his face turned plum-red. He looked like he was on the verge of talking back or tossing his steak fingers on the table and walking out, leaving Red and her purse bearer in lonely, little Lone Star, but he didn't. The heat and the campaign drudgery were getting to him too, but he had apparently decided he would see it through to the bitter end.

They finished eating with nobody saying much. "Y'all have chock-fulla-cherry blizzards?" a weary-sounding female voice coming through the scratchy drive-through microphone wanted to know. Purse could hear kids in the back seat squabbling and whining.

The day had started out badly. Only a handful, maybe 30 or so, had turned out in Sulphur Springs, despite the signs local folks put up on the highway and the ads the campaign bought on K-S-U-N, "The Country Giant." The ground was so hard at the courthouse, Purse and Aboy had to lean the "Red for Senator" signs up against the trees instead of jabbing them into the ground. Even East Texans had enough sense not to venture into the blazing sun unless they had to. On the courthouse grounds they edged in closer, tracking the perimeter of the shade, as the candidate unspooled her funny story. At least, she hoped it was funny.

"Here I was with my granddaddy and my grandma," Red was saying, her voice a bit drawlier than usual. "They were in Sulphur Springs for a gospel singin'. I was just a little freckle-faced kid, but I loved the singing. Lord, I remember those golden-throated, God-lovin' voices filling the First Baptist Church with heavenly strains. Liketa lifted the roof off. We stayed at a big hotel across the street from the courthouse here, and after we climbed up the stairs to our room and got settled, Pa went back to the singing. Mama and me, we decided to rest up a little and then go get something to eat in the dining room."

Purse had seen old photos of Red as a little girl. A freckle-faced tomboy, that's for sure. She reminded him of a tough little girl with squinty eyes and balled-up fists he had seen on "The Little Rascals."

Red glanced across the square at a ramshackle red-brick building, four stories, nothing but an empty shell now. Above the front door, in faded block letters you could barely make out "HOTEL."

"Now, what you need to know," she said, "is this was the first time I was ever in a hotel. First time I ever was in a town any bigger than Prairie Hill or Dripping Springs. First time, I reckon, I ever wore shoes. Just a little ol' country girl, I was, from the blackland prairie over in Hill County. Folks decent, God-fearin' dirt farmers. Didn't have much, but they were as hardworking and honest as the day is long. But as I was saying, we saunter out into the hall, and I see these brown steel doors down at the end of the hall. Mammy sees 'em too.

"There was this old fella standing there staring at the doors. Now, I'm sure he was a good, upstanding old timer, but to tell the truth, he'd seen better days. You know how it is when time's wingèd chariot sorta knocks you down and runs you over. I can tell you, it happens to the best of us. Well, he'd been knocked down and run over, maybe even drug a bit down the bumpy road of life. But those doors opened up all of a sudden while me and Mammy watched. He kinda shuffled on in to a little closet, and the doors closed him up in there."

Purse scanned the crowd. Some of them were looking up at Red, half smiles on their faces, waiting for the punch line. Some of them were wiping their faces with handkerchiefs, glancing at their watches.

"Well, in no time the doors opened up again," Red was saying. "I had not the foggiest idea what happened in that little closet, and neither did Mammy, but when that ol' man come out, he looked like Charlton Heston in *The Ten Commandments*. Yall've seen that movie, I bet. Tall, blonde, strong. Just a real man's man. And he was a lovely golden color, not sort of reddish-tan with that white line on his forehead where he's been wearing a hat out in the pasture, and then sort of red on his cheeks and arms. Not like some of you good-lookin' fellas, God love you. He was the same shade of golden brown all over. You could smell his after-shave just waftin' down the hall. I'm tellin' you, he was a hunk; I hope that word doesn't offend you, 'cause that's the only word I know to describe what we saw that afternoon here in Sulphur Springs. Who knows, maybe he's here today.

"Mammy and me just stood there staring. She looked at me, I looked at her, and then she says, 'Quick, Rosie, run on down to the church and get your granddaddy. That brown box there done worked a miracle on that ol' coot. Just think what it'll do for Pa!'"

Red, her face a bit flushed, chuckled at her own story. The old men in khakis and straw hats laughed with her. A few secretaries who had been herded out of the county clerk's office clapped their hands, then left their hands clasped together and pointed in a V beneath their chins.

Purse laughed, loudly, even though he had heard the joke before—in Clyde and Gladewater and Cumby, in every little burg in Texas that might have had a hotel with an elevator at one time or another. He had heard it that very morning in Greenville. Reporters covering the campaign gave her a break on the repetitions. Every politician does it.

Red glanced down at her navy-and-white pumps. From where he was standing a couple of steps behind her and over to the side, Purse could see the veins of red sand in the creases of the white buck leather. He knew she didn't like getting her shoes mussed. When they got back in the station wagon and Aboy got behind the wheel, she would take them off, hand them over the seat to Purse and he would go to work on them with a little brush he kept in a box on the back seat floorboard. For now, she favored the crowd with her smile.

"Let me tell you," she said, "I've come a long way up the elevator of life since those days, a long way. And with your help, I'm gonna go higher. In 66 days and counting, I'm gonna be your United States Senator—the first female senator this state has ever seen. I just wish my dear ol' mama and daddy were here to see it."

She looked down and shook her head, then looked up again. "It's a high office," she said, her voice quieter than usual, though still carrying, "but I give you my word, I won't be high and mighty. It's a high office, because it's the people's office—and that's something my esteemed opponent can't understand."

Red could see the crowd shuffling and sweating just as Purse could. He noticed a man in boots and a short-sleeved white shirt, buttons straining across a belly splayed over his football-shaped western belt buckle, take off his glasses and wipe his brow with a sweaty forearm. Red began to wrap things up.

"Now, this morning I don't want you lingering out here in the hot sun any longer than need be," she said. "You know better'n anybody what this great state of ours needs. You know why I'm running, and if you don't, Wily here will give you all the information you could ask for.

"Yay, Wily!" some guy in the crowd shouted. Everybody laughs, and Purse's face turned red.

"That your boy?" someone else yelled.

"No, Wily's not my son," Red said, looking back with a grin. "I don't think he'd claim me; I'm too hard on him. Folks, this handsome young man holding my purse is Wily T. Foxx, the pride of Elm Mott, Texas, and I want you to know I couldn't do without him. He's a gem, I'll tell ya. And all you single girls out there? He's unattached. Wily, take a little bow."

Purse felt ridiculous, but he put one hand on his stomach and one on his lower back and took a bow, like a French waiter he had seen in a movie. People clapped and whistled, so he took another one. "Go get 'em, Wily!" somebody shouted. He lifted Red's purse above his head like it was the Stanley Cup, and shook it once or twice. People laughed, but he noticed Red frown. He pulled it back down. He knew not to get on the wrong side of Red.

"Now, Wily's gonna circulate out among you with our campaign literature," Red said, "and I want you to read it, and then I want you to put it in your neighbors' mailboxes. I want you to stand next to the preacher when he's shaking hands at the back door after Sunday-morning service, and I want you to put one of these brochures in every hand he shakes. I want you to tack it up on the bulletin board at that big Piggly Wiggly we passed coming in to town. And then on election day I want you to call everybody you know. If you know folks who're laid up at home due to age or infirmity, or just plain ol' laziness, I want you to carry 'em to the polls. I wanna be their senator too. The people's senator. That's what I intend to be."

He hung the shoulder strap of Red's purse over his shoulder

and draped her white suit jacket on the stone wall of the courthouse steps. Weaving his way through the small crowd, he handed out every brochure he had. People looked at the cover with her no-nonsense face and her helmet of curly red hair and knew she meant business. *This* was the State Comptroller, by god, the woman who shut down businesses big and small if they weren't paying their taxes. And then, if they turned it over, they saw the friendly, heart-of-gold Red, frolicking in the yard with her little grandkids and with Waylon, an old beagle.

"ROSE MARIE RYDER ('RED')," the words said. "A DOER, NOT A TALKER."

Joe Frank Golden wrote the words. He was the campaign press guy, and would have been on the East Texas swing, but he tended to get carsick on long trips. Purse knew the words by heart:

WHAT WILL SEN. ROSIE RYDER DO FOR YOU?
SHE WILL:

- GIVE THE LITTLE GUY A SAY IN WASHINGTON.
- EDUCATE THE KIDS THE WAY YOU WANT THEM EDUCATED.
- MAKE THE BIG BOYS PAY THEIR FAIR SHARE.
- FORCE THE FEDERAL GOVERNMENT TO WORK FOR THE UNDERDOGS, NOT THE TOP DOGS.
- PUT THE JAM JAR ON THE BOTTOM SHELF, SO GOOD, HARDWORKING TEXANS CAN HAVE A TASTE.
- BE THE PEOPLE'S SENATOR.

Purse was learning. He knew the claims were long on sentiment and short on specifics—that's what the *Dallas Morning News* said—but like Red told him one night at the Wagon Wheel, the voters would be choosing a person, not a program. A vote for Rosie Ryder would mean they trusted her to do what's right.

"By God," she said, slapping the table that night, as well, "that's what I intend to do."

Only problem was—and Purse didn't find it out until they got on the campaign trail—what he heard an ol' boy say at the cattle auction in Cumby earlier: "Rosie's fine, I like her as a COMP-troller; I mean it's the little lady in my house that pays the bills. But ain't no way in Hades I'm votin' for her as a senator. This state's not ready for a woman in the U.S. Senate. That's a man's job."

And that wasn't the first time he had heard somebody say it. It was always a man, but he suspected there were women who felt the same way.

"Any questions?" Red was asking as Purse finished handing out brochures. He was hoping the answer was no, since they were already late for the roadside meeting with the out-of-work steelworkers.

"How you feelin' 'bout your chances, Red?" a weather-beaten old man in khaki work clothes wanted to know. That's what people always called her—Red, never Mrs. Ryder or Madam Comptroller. They felt easy with her. The old man had a green DeKalb Feed gimme cap pulled down to shade his eyes. He scratched the back of his pant leg with one of the red K-Mart running shoes he was wearing.

"I feel good, real good," Red said. "Course, we can't be taking anything for granted. Anytime you run against a wheeler-dealer like Jimmy Dale, you're running against the fat cats, and they can make it awful hard. They've got pockets so deep...."

She paused, and a grin lit up her face, like she was about to be naughty and wasn't sure how these God-fearing, flag-waving East Texans were going to take what she was getting ready to say.

"You know what they remind me of?" she said. "They got so much money weighin' 'em down, they remind me of an ol' Piney Woods mama possum, her saggy tits draggin' the ground, if you'll pardon my French. They got money for TV, and we don't. They got money for big ol' signs out on the Interstate, and we don't. They got money for pretty ads in the newspapers, and we don't.

"But you know what we have?" She looked around the yard, as if waiting for an answer. "What we have is the people. We have the people on our side, and thank goodness there's more of us than there are of them. Like I say, I feel good. But I'm gonna need your help. So dig deep—and vote right."

"And vote often!" some fellow in the crowd yelled out.

"That's the Texas way," Red shouted. She crinkled up her face and laughed, and so did everybody else.

Red surveyed the crowd for any more questions, then started edging toward Purse and her purse and jacket. Another old-timer started shouting a question. ""What you gonna do about the house?" he said, looking a little wild-eyed, like an old hound about to get plopped into a tick dip. "What you gonna do about the house?"

At least, Purse thought that's what he was saying. It sounded like he had a mouthful of mush; maybe he had lost all his teeth. He had on one of those short-sleeve, see-through sport shirts, light blue, with little puckered squares all over it. Purse remembered wearing one when he was a kid; he was surprised they were still made.

"What's that, young fella?" Red said, looking back over her shoulder as she retrieved the jacket.

"What you gonna do about the house?"

Red looked at Purse, who could only shrug his shoulders. Did the old gentleman mean the House of Representatives? His own house?

"I'm sorry, friend, I'm having a little trouble getting your drift," Red said.

"Oh, don't pay no mind to Simon, Red," a stocky man in a blue seersucker suit shouted. He wore a snap-brimmed straw hat pushed back from his round, grinning face. "Don't pay him no mind a'tall."

The man in the suit put a hand to his mouth and said in sort of a pretend whisper, like this Simon fellow wouldn't hear what was being said about him, "You know how it is with some folks." He was making little curlicue designs around his ear with his index finger. "Ol' Simon here means well, but you might say he's one enchilada short of a combination plate."

Some of the folks still standing around laughed. With a last name of Simon, Purse could imagine what they called him around town. All in good fun, of course.

The suit, he figured, owned the local hardware store, probably president of the Chamber of Commerce, a pillar of the community. For years, he and his daddy and his granddaddy, no doubt, had been Democrats. But these days, you couldn't count on it. As the pros said, these little small-town businessmen were in play, and Red had to have them, if she was going to have a snowball's chance in hell of getting elected, or just making the race halfway competitive.

Mr. Chamber of Commerce smiled his salesman's smile and put his arm around the agitated old gent, who kept mumbling and grimacing, carrying on a heavy conversation with the only person who'd really listen to him—himself. Mr. Pillar of the Community started nudging him out of the crowd.

"Just a minute there, hon," Red said. She walked down the courthouse steps, red head held high and toes pointed like a model. Smiling and looking concerned, she began to make her way back to where Simon stood. "Maybe I can help a fellow Texan in need," she said, patting shoulders and shaking hands as she went.

The man in the suit took his arm away, and Red put a hand on Simon's shoulder. "Now take it slow and easy, young man," she said, patting him on the shoulder, "and tell me what seems to be the trouble."

The old man had his head almost on Red's shoulder. He glanced up out of the corner of his milky old eyes at the clean, fresh-looking woman standing beside him. What he was saying, it turned out, was that the little house where he had lived for years, this little house on the outskirts of town, had burned. Not down to the ground, but enough so that the fire department or the health department or somebody had to move him out. So he didn't have a place to live, and while he was away, somebody was stealing him blind. Furniture and keepsakes and stuff that hadn't burned.

"Dagnabit, last night they bust in there and got my chester drawers!" Simon spluttered, jerking away from Red at the thought of it. His face was red, like a tomato so ripe it's fit to burst. A little blue vein was pumping like mad at his temple. "I don't know who in tarnation you are, lady, but you look like you might could do somethin'," he told Red. "I'm telling you, I want you to do somethin' about it!"

"Well, who I am," Red said in a kindly voice, "is Rose Marie Ryder. My friends call me Red, Mr. Simon, and you should too. My job is being the Comptroller for the state of Texas—that means I keep tabs on the taxpayers' money—but I'm running to be your U.S. senator. And what I'm going to do right now is help you get the justice you so rightly deserve. Let's walk on in the courthouse here and talk to Sheriff Moody. He's a good friend of mine."

Red and the old man walked slowly up the courthouse steps. The rest of the crowd followed. A camera crew from K-N-O-W in Tyler scrambled to get in front of the gaggle.

The dim first-floor hallway of the old courthouse was cool as Longhorn Cavern. The crowd headed in a herd past a bulletin board outside the county clerk's office. Purse glanced at the auction notices for foreclosed farms, an agricultural extension service bulletin about a blackberry jelly-making class and the wanted posters for scary-looking dudes. They came to a halt at the door marked SHERIFF in black lettering across frosted glass. Jim Ned "Hossman" Moody, the high sheriff himself, stepped out into the hall and surveyed the crowd.

"Good to see you again, Madam Comptroller," Hossman said, his thin mouth—the only thing thin on him, as far as Purse could see—stretched into a tight smile. He wrapped up Red's dainty hand in his ham of a hand and leaned down to kiss her on the cheek.

Hossman Moody was big. Not just fat. And not just tall. The sheriff was tall and wide, "big as the side of a barn," Purse's mother would say.

Purse remembered him. Before he moved back to Sulfur Springs and ran for sheriff, he wrestled professionally in Big D. Any night the Wild Hossman of the Osage was on the bill at the Sportatorium, that old tin-can arena would be packed like a popcorn popper. The Hossman would come into the ring in his black tights, black high-top boots, a black vest like Wyatt Earp wore and a black cowboy hat, and before you know it, he would go berserk. He would pick guys up and toss them out of the ring, go after folks up in the bleachers. Purse saw him once or twice, back when he was staying with his Uncle Clyde, delivering eggs for Martinez Produce. Right before he went off to basic training.

Aboy told him later that Moody ran a bail-bond business near the courthouse square for about ten years after he retired from the ring. Used some of his old wrestling buddies as bounty hunters. Had been sheriff for a couple of terms.

Purse also knew how the Hossman met Red. Except for Aboy, he didn't know if anybody else in the crowd knew about Red breaking up a cockfight near Blooming Grove one Sunday morning. Aboy talked her into it. She raided the place, not so much to break it up, but to make sure the promoters paid taxes on their proceeds. And for the publicity.

What she didn't expect to find was the Wild Hossman of the Osage fronting a few banties himself. Red let him slide out of the crowd, didn't confront him. But instead of feeling grateful to her, Moody resented her for what she saw. He figured Aboy put her up to it, so he didn't have any use for Aboy either.

Plus, he had something else he didn't like about Red. He had gotten religion since he got to be sheriff, and the religion he got believed in a woman being man's helpmeet; that's what he and fellow believers called it. "Let the women keep silent in the church," the Bible said. Or, as Aboy said, Hossman was one of those God-fearin' Christian men who believed it was a woman's God-given duty to have her biscuits in the oven and her buns in the bed. A woman running for public office was against God-given human nature, as far as the good sheriff was concerned. "Eve was shaped from Adam's rib," Purse had heard a preacher say one time, "not the other way around."

"Y'all come on in," Hossman said. He ushered Red and the old man into his office and shut the door. Everyone else waited in the hall.

It was a good 10 minutes before they came back out. Red got everybody arranged so that the old man, grinning and looking a little wild-eyed and bewildered, was standing between Hossman and herself.

"What Sheriff Moody has agreed to do," Red said, holding on to the old man's bony, chicken-skinned arm, "is to have a deputy drop by Mr. Simon's house now and then, just to check on things. And he's pledged to track down the perpetrators of these dastardly crimes. He has a suspicion maybe some kiddos with too much idle time on their hands—and you know about idle time being the devil's workshop—anyway, he thinks these little devils've been finding a way to furnish their clubhouse in one of these venerable buildings on the square."

Some of the secretaries in the hallway began to clap their hands and cheer, but Red held up her hand. "That's not all," she said. "Members of Sheriff Moody's church have volunteered to rebuild Mr. Simon's house this weekend. Paint it and everything."

Now the women really did cheer, and the sheriff broke into a genuine grin.

"What church is that, Mrs. Ryder?" asked an earnest-looking young woman wearing glasses. She waited to write down her answer in one of those skinny, little notebooks reporters carry. No one else can get them, Aboy had told Purse.

Sheriff Moody spoke up. "It's the Sulphur Springs Primitive Holiness Church of God. We're not perfect, just protected. Shielded by the mighty hand of God."

"Sheriff," Red said, looking up at his big red face, "you're a big man in more ways than one. And young man," she said, looking the old man square in the eye, her hands on his shoulders, "I hope what you've seen today restores your faith in your fellow man. And in government of the people, by the people and for the people. And that means the good people of Sulphur Springs and Hopkins County!" She gave him a kiss on his wrinkled, liver-spotted cheek.

Everyone clapped and cheered. A photographer from the *Sulphur Springs Citizen* squeezed off a flash of Red, the sheriff and the old man. He had to turn his camera sideways to get the Hossman in the picture.

Red gave Purse a quick nod toward the door, and he politely extricated her from the women in the hallway. The two of them walked toward the door, Purse with her purse under his arm like a halfback carrying a football, Red walking backward and waving, calling out farewells to the sheriff and to the good people of Hopkins County. Aboy was waiting at the curb, the station wagon running and the air conditioner on high.

Two months out, and the crowds weren't showing. Part of it was the heat. You'd drive through neighborhoods in these little East Texas towns, and you'd see panting dogs in scooped-out holes in dried-up flower beds. Folks felt the same way. They were tired and draggy, just worn out, They were ready for summer to be over and done with. Ready for football and fall and feeling a breeze at night, so you had to pull a sheet over you when you sleep.

You could say it was still a little too early, that voters usually didn't start paying attention until after Labor Day, and that may have been true. It reminded Purse of when he played junior high football for the Elm Mott Screamin' Eaglets. He could tell even when they were behind—and they were behind a lot—when there was a spark or a spirit or something you couldn't quite put your finger on. And pretty soon they would take off, sometimes anyway. That wasn't happening with the campaign.

Even though this was his first election, he could tell that Red's run for the U.S. Senate, so far at least, was like a little Piper Cub bouncing across a grass runway trying to get off the ground, It was bumping along, bumping along, with no spirit to it at all. It was like they knew there was no way they could beat Jimmy Dale Sisco and all his millions and all his power people, the people who ran the state and knew how to get what they wanted, no matter the cost. It was like they were toying with Red, who was just playing out the string.

It didn't help any that right outside Lone Star, on their way to Paris after the DQ fiasco, they passed a huge billboard on the side of the road with the grinning face of Jimmy Dale Sisco underneath his big white cowboy hat. "BORN TO LEAD," the sign said. "JIMMY DALE SISCO—THE MAN FOR TEXAS."

"Why?" he asked Aboy. Red was dozing a bit in the back, her red head leaned up against the window.

"Why what?"

"Why is Jimmy Dale Sisco the man for Texas?"

Aboy glanced toward the back to see if Red was still dozing. "You poor child," he said. "So naïve, so trusting. What you must come to realize, Master Foxx, is the Calvinistic inclinations of the esteemed Mr. Sisco and his ilk, the bastards that have their greedy, grasping paws on the tender scrotum of this state. They may not know it, but they believe in what Calvin—John Calvin, that is—called predestination. Our boy Jimmy is rich, he's powerful. He runs a big Texas bank, and on his ranches oil pulses up out of the ground as regularly and incessantly as a John Wayne wet dream. Those are all signs of God's favor, don't you know. Wily, my son, Jimmy D. is predestined by God to be a U.S. senator and then president. It's in the stars, you might say."

"Oh," Purse said.

Although he didn't say anything at the time, Aboy had another theory about why things weren't going well. He blamed the new campaign manager. Aboy said Red hadn't really wanted him but that the party bosses forced him on her. It was Bobby Ray's idea that Red had to come across as a "man of the people." That's what he said, even though Red was an accomplished politician—a woman, by the way, not a man—with a master's degree from the London School of Economics. You didn't read anything about that in her campaign literature, and she sure didn't bring it up in her speeches.

Purse had been thinking. He didn't know whether Aboy was right or just jealous—jealous that he wasn't running the campaign. What he did know was that you didn't see much of Bobby Ray; in fact, he had never seen him. From what Aboy said, he would drop down from the sky, issue a few cornpone pronouncements and collect his paycheck. What Purse knew too, despite his inexperience, was that the campaign wasn't working.

In Paris that evening, maybe 30 people showed up at the Colonial Cafeteria. Olene had reserved a private dining room, but four or five tables in the main room would have been enough. Folks who showed up seemed more interested in their chicken-fried steak and fried okra and blackberry cobbler than in listening to Rose Marie Ryder. And, Purse had to admit, the cobbler was very good, particularly with a little half-and-half poured on top. Tasted homemade.

The county Democratic chairman, a slump-shouldered little man, bald head, long sideburns, stood up to introduce Red. He tapped his water glass with a knife, but when he got everybody quieted down, the microphone on the portable rostrum didn't work. You could hear the buzz of the crowd in the main dining room and the women on the cafeteria line shouting "M'elp you please?" but you could hardly hear the mealy-mouthed chairman. He introduced her as Rose Ann Raider.

"I 'preciate y'all comin' out tonight," Red was saying. She knew how to talk loud, so you could hear her, if you were listening. She tried to break the ice, so to speak, with another joke, one that Aboy had told her. At least, Purse had heard him tell a much nastier version than he figured Red was going to tell.

"So I was talking to this cattle rancher over close to Clarksville," Red was saying, "and he was telling me about this Santa Gertrudis bull he bought from the King Ranch. Oh, he was a handsome beast, deep red color, big, muscly shoulders. This rancher couldn't wait to get him unloaded, put him to work."

Red paused and took a sip of water. She was a pro; she could tell the crowd wasn't with her yet.

"Only thing about it, though, after a few days, the rancher could see his new bull was more interested in grass than ... well, let's just say he wasn't performing his manly duties, if you get my drift. His vet come by, and Rancher Smith says to him, 'Doc, what can I do? I got too much invested in this animal to just let him loll around in the sun.'

"So the vet says to him, he says, 'Mr. Smith, I got just the thing. It's called Vim-n-Vigor, and you put a spoonful in his water trough every day, and I'll guarantee you, he'll be performing in no time.'

"Well, Rancher Smith, he gave it to the bull, and it was amazing. That bull was at it all day, every day, even jumped the fence and had his way with the neighbor's cows. Rancher Smith couldn't believe it. He was over at the auction barn one morning, and he was telling his friends about it, and they wanted to know what it was.

"One of 'em asked him, he said, 'Whaddya think's in that there Vim-n-Vigor?'

"And Mr. Smith says, 'Well, I can't rightly say, but it tastes like licorice.'"

Red hesitated a moment for the laughter she expected.

"Tastes like licorice," Aboy repeated, and laughed his rumble-throated laugh, like when a boat runs aground on a gravel-bottomed stream. A few folks, some of the men anyway, chuckled a bit, but the sound of knives and forks was louder than the laughter. Some of the women just looked down at their plates.

"You gonna eat that piece of fish?" Purse heard a man ask his wife.

★ ★ TWO ★ ★

Purse didn't know it until Monday morning, but things had changed over the weekend. Red had not been resting.

"Go get the keys to the van from Aboy—and head on out to the airport," Joe Frank said to Purse. "The Ragin' Cajun's coming in."

"Who's the Ragin' Cajun?"

Joe Frank gave him that disgusted look he had come to know well—down-turned mouth, wrinkled brow. "He's the man who's running this campaign," he mumbled. "Bobby Ray Evangeline." He flipped through a stack of message slips in his hand.

"How will I know what he looks like?"

"Don't worry, you'll know him," Joe Frank said.

Purse was still worried, standing in the terminal and eyeing the folks filing off the plane from New Orleans. He thought about making one of those little signs that chauffeurs hold up, but he didn't have any cardboard. A couple of times briefcase-carrying important-looking guys—blue suits, white shirts with cuff links and distant, worried looks on their faces—got off the plane. Each time Purse tried to catch their eye, thinking they might be Bobby Ray, but both of them had wives and kids meeting them.

Aboy had told him about Bobby Ray. Aboy said he was *supposed* to be the smartest political hired gun in the business, said he was *supposed* to be a brilliant strategist and a fine campaign manager.

Aboy said he had found a formula for making underdogs top dogs. He said he had dropped out of Louisiana Tech maybe 15 years earlier to run the state senate campaign of a complete unknown, a cousin of his from Ponchatoula or some such place, and when the fellow squeaked through to victory, other candidates across the South came calling.

How he did it was something of a mystery, Aboy said, but what Bobby Ray called the "Griot's Gumbo—a little of this, a little of that and seasoned with hot red peppers from Evangeline—

worked more often than not. Nobody expected Red to win, of course, but if Bobby Ray could make things respectable, he would come out okay. If he somehow worked a miracle, then the big boys, the future senators and the would-be Harry Trumans, would be making pilgrimages to Bobby Ray's little swamp-side fishing cabin in Plaquemines Parish.

Purse kept waiting. The stream of disembarking passengers slowed to a trickle. He was beginning to panic, afraid that he would have to call Joe Frank and tell him he had missed the great man.

Just then, he saw two stewardesses. They were walking fast, talking to each other in low, worried-sounding voices and looking back over their shoulders as they came into the terminal.

Behind them, three men were walking down the gangway. Actually, two men were walking, two men in black suits and wearing dark shades. The man in the middle, in ragged jeans and a faded New Orleans Saints t-shirt, had his arms draped over their shoulders. His booted feet were dragging like a marionette's. His head lolled to one side, and he was mumbling something in a slurred Coon-Ass voice. Bobby Ray Evangeline was drunk as a Louisiana skunk.

Purse drove the Ragin' Cajun and his keepers to the Austin Hotel, an old establishment a few blocks beyond downtown that was one-half star above a fleabag. The Austin was where Bobby Ray always stayed when he came to town, his buddy and caretaker number-one, Duce Doucet, explained. Doucet, riding shotgun, glanced toward the back seat, where his sleeping boss sprawled against caretaker number-two, Andre Batiste.

Staying at the Austin had something to do with the first winning election he had ever managed in the state, back in the late 1960s, Doucet said. He stayed at the Austin that time, and that's where he had stayed ever since. He was a superstitious fellow, being around New Orleans voodoo and all.

He hated flying, Doucet said. As a little boy growing up in Plaquemines Parish, he had seen a small plane plunge into Lake

Chicot, Doucet told Purse. He never got over it. He had a big bus, like a musician's bus, that he usually took, but Red's call was spur-of-the moment, and he couldn't drive over to Austin in time.

Once his handlers got him to his room on the fourth floor, the same room he always stayed in, Doucet held him up while a silent Batiste went into the bathroom and turned on the shower. With the water running, they undressed Bobby Ray, took off their own clothes and dragged Bobby Ray in.

Purse trailed along, thinking they might need his help, until he saw the three naked men, their skin shockingly white, in the shower. With Boby Ray propped up against the wall of the shower stall, they seemed to have the routine down. Aboy had told him Cajuns were different.

Bobby Ray began to sputter and shout and try to fight off his handlers. "Goddamn it, it's cold!" he shouted. "Let me outta here!"

"Few minutes more," Doucet told him.

Batiste had Bobby Ray's bag opened on the bed and was laying out a dry outfit—pressed jeans, a clean black t-shirt and a fringed leather jacket Buffalo Bill would have been proud to wear. He also pulled out a well-shined pair of black boots. Aboy had said the jeans and t-shirt, and the jacket with the fringe on the sleeves, were Bobby Ray's uniform, his trademark. He hadn't said anything about his drinking. Maybe he didn't know.

Purse went down to the dim lobby to wait. At a scuffed wooden bar, a man wearing a gray Fritos Corn Chips shirt bent over his Lone Star. Purse leaned against the wall. A young blonde-haired woman, eyes closed, stood on a little raised platform and sang "Me and Bobby McGee" while she strummed her guitar. Nobody was listening but Purse. She was actually pretty good, he decided.

When the song was over, she propped her guitar against the wall, ducked under the waiter's entry leaf next to the cash register and fixed herself a Seven-and-Seven. Ducking back out, she slid onto a stool at the opposite end from the Frito guy. She glanced over at Purse, but neither of them said anything.

Twenty minutes later, the elevator opened and out stepped Doucet, Batiste and a transformed Bobby Ray Evangeline. He had on the clothes Batiste had picked out for him, including the pointy-toed black boots. With his long, crow-black hair, still wet from the shower and slicked back from his high forehead, with his razor-sharp nose and thin lips, he reminded Purse of a bird—a hawk maybe or a falcon, a bird of prey, for sure.

The man walking toward him was ruthless, Aboy had said. Purse was a little nervous, but Bobby Ray put him at ease. "Take me to your leader, ey, T-Bub," he said, eyes twinkling. At least, that's what it sounded like. He smiled, sort of. His mouth stretched wide, almost ear to ear, without opening, and his nose bent down over his lips. The smile, if that's what it was, disappeared as quickly as it came.

"Thanks for coming, Bobby Ray," Red said, standing up from behind her desk in her bare office at the back of campaign headquarters as Purse ushered Bobby Ray into the room. Sue Bee, Joe Frank and Aboy were waiting with Red. They stood up from the folding chairs they had dragged in.

The look on Red's face resembled the look Purse had seen at the Dairy Queen in Lone Star, the look she shot at Aboy. He figured it was because they were about 15 minutes late. He hoped she didn't blame him.

Bobby Ray didn't seem to notice. He smiled his strange smile—like a shark, Purse suddenly realized. He bowed before Red, took her hand and kissed it. "Mon cherie," he said. "So good to see you."

He kissed Sue Bee's hand and embraced Joe Frank and Aboy, clapping them on their shoulders. Purse stood in a corner, eager to find out about Bobby Ray's Cajun campaign magic.

The guru turned a folding chair backward, straddled it and launched right in. "I'm under no illusions, my dear friends," he said in his deep Cajun drawl. "I know we's in trouble. Dis fais-do-do we've got goin' is quick becoming a boucherie."

He saw Sue Bee's look of perplexity, a scrunched-up forehead and cocked head. "A community hog-butchering, mon cherie. Dey's great fun down on the bayou—less'n you're de little piggy." He smiled and glanced around the room. No one smiled back.

Something was up, but Purse couldn't tell whether Bobby Ray recognized it.

He glanced at Red. She sat straight up in her chair, hands folded on her desk, ice-blue eyes lasering into the Ragin' Cajun.

"What we have to do, my beb," he said, turning his attention to Red, "is to return to Phenomenology 101, just like dey done tried to teach me down at dat dere Louisiana Tech. Like I tol' you when we first tied da knot, mon cherie, all dat exists in da voter's mind is da perception of Red Ryder. Dey don't know de real Red Ryder. Dey don't care, mon cherie. We have to create da consciousness. Like Husserl would tell you, like Marcel, dat great Frenchman from de old country, all dat exists is in da mind. All dat exists is da idea of Red Ryder. And we got to propagate de perception. Propagate de perception."

Bobby Ray looked at each of them, one by one, the smile lingering as he slid from one face to another, before turning his full attention back to Red. He got no response.

"So!" he said, slapping his thighs and leaning toward her over the chair back, "what you say 'bout dat?"

Red stared at the guru, just a hint of a smile on her face. Bobby Ray, chin out, the thin-lipped smile still stretched across his face, stared back.

"As a good Cajun, Bobby Ray, I know you'll pardon my French," she said, after what seemed like minutes of awkward silence, "but I think you're full of shit—mon cherie. I thought so when we first met. I think so now."

"Ain? What did you say, mon cherie?"

"I said you're full of shit, Bobby Ray—with all due respect. I should never have listened to all those great D.C. minds that insisted I hire you in the first place. Here we are four months into this campaign, and you still haven't come up with a workable strategy. And you walk in here talking about propagating the perception. It's bullshit, Bobby Ray."

The shark smile stayed on Bobby Ray's angular face. He unwound himself from the chair and stared at Red. "But, mon cherie, what do you expect? You want to be da boss, but you're like an old gar fisherman I knew back in Pointe a la Hache. Without Bobby Ray, you up a creek without a paddle.

Scheduling? Budgeting? Finances? What you know 'bout dose tings?"

Bobby Ray looked at Joe Frank, then at Sue Bee. They stared back at him. He looked back at Red. "So whatta ya say, mon cherie? Jess a little ol' misunderstanding? Shall we get back to work?"

Red stood up from her desk. "I'm sorry, Bobby Ray," she said. "I'm cutting you loose."

And so she did. Bobby Ray continued to protest, threatened to call Red's donors, threatened to call the national campaign committee, threatened to sue, but Red was unbending. She promised to pay him what he was due, and that sort of settled him down. By the time Purse got him and his buddies back to the airport, he had already started drinking from a pint bottle of Old Crow that Batiste had pulled out of his briefcase. Between slugs, Bobby Ray was talking about some race in Tennessee. He was stumbling when Purse dropped the three of them at the terminal.

★ ★ THREE ★ ★

"Say Wily, I been meanin' to ask you," Willis Seymour was saying one Saturday morning when Purse dropped off his rent check. "How'd you get yourself mixed-up with that red-headed woman you work for? What people tell me is, she's so blindered, so deluded, I guess you'd say, she can't see how hopeless the election is. What's the deal?"

"It's a hoot, Willis," Purse said, signing his name to the check. "I'm having a ball."

"And you get paid for this? Is it a job, or you one of them volunteers?"

He had heard the questions before. Jo Lynne asked him the same thing when she called late Friday night after Red and company got in from East Texas. Actually he had asked the very same question of a real political insider—namely, himself.

He told her pretty much what he always told her when she complained about him being in Austin and working with folks she didn't trust, "gallavantin' about the state like you're Mr. Big"—that's what she said her mother called it.

"But honey," he said to Jo Lynne, "Red can be senator. A United States Senator. And it don't really matter what you think about her or what I think about her—you know, whether you like her or not, whether or not she's somebody you'd want to have over to the house for Sunday dinner. What matters is that she ought to be senator. She cares about people like you and me, like your mama and daddy. Just because she's a long shot doesn't mean you roll over and die. And besides, for cryin' out loud, she's a woman! Don't that mean something for someone like you, someone of the womanly persuasion?"

There had been a woman governor years before, not a senator, but she was governor only because her husband had put her up to it. He had gotten in trouble selling penitentiary pardons, gotten himself impeached, so she ran and got elected in his place. Everybody knew when they voted for her who they were really voting for. Sometimes he would be talking to the press, and he would forget he was not the governor, but the governor's old man. He'd say something like, "Now what I'm gonna do on this piece of legislation...."

This was different. Red would be the first woman U.S. Senator from Texas—ever.

He thought about that when he and Red and Aboy were driving through the little town of Athens right after dark, on their way back from Sulphur Springs and Lone Star. He happened to notice a woman on the front porch of a little frame house just off the square, a gray frame house with the light on in an empty living room. She had the front door propped open, and you could see a naked light bulb hanging down from the ceiling, and she had a pickup truck backed up across the beaten-down dry grass to the front porch. Just a middle-aged woman, maybe in her 50s, gray hair and glasses. She had on jeans rolled up to her knees, a man's blue work shirt.

Purse didn't know who she was, would never know who she was, but it didn't really matter. He felt something that night about who she might be, the life she lived, her hopes and dreams. Maybe he saw his mother standing there on that front porch, or Mammy, his grandmother all those many years ago, when she had the Red and White Country Grocery and Gas Station to run all by herself, after her husband died of pernicious anemia. Maybe something like that had happened to the Athens woman. Maybe her husband had just died after lung cancer crept up on him, after he had been smoking those Pall Malls his whole life. She had warned him—oh, she had!—about that hacking cough, but he never paid her any mind. Or after he had one of those heart attacks where you're going about your business one minute and you're dead as a door nail the next, something neither one of them had counted on.

And here she was starting over just at a time when most folks were thinking about spending more time with the grandkids or going fishing whenever they felt like it or strolling through the flea market offerings on First Monday up the road at Canton. She had rented this little house in Athens, and she was putting in a gift shop. She would have little black-eyed pea trinkets and canned preserves and inspirational sayings painted on little pieces of wood you would put up on the wall of your kitchen.

Or maybe she had run off from a low-down drunk, abusing husband. He was a long-haul trucker, who came home tired and angry and ready to hit someone. If it wasn't some stranger in a bar after a couple of shots, it was her.

Now she had finally gotten the gumption to leave him, to divorce his sorry ass and start over. She was just moving in, and she had been working all day to get her stuff in before dark, while the June bugs buzzed around the light bulb in the hot front room and the locusts whirred like hard dry paper blowing in the wind.

She was nobody, like himself, Purse was thinking. Like Mama and Daddy, like Jo Lynne, and maybe he and Aboy and Red and all the people who believed in her and were helping her—maybe they could help that woman in Athens some way. Maybe not, but at least they could keep her in mind, she and all the thousands of people like her. If, that is, Red ever got to go to Washington.

Red cares about the little people; she used to be one herself. That's what he told Jo Lynne. That's what he told everybody who asked, and he believed it—most of the time. But driving in from East Texas, he had been down. Tired, lonesome, the doubts drifted in like the dirty yellow smog they had seen settling over the Houston Ship Channel near Pasadena the week before. He couldn't stop them. Things weren't going well; that was easy enough to see.

Like what happened with Aboy at the Dairy Queen. He had seen it happen before and not with Aboy. Once he saw Red light into her son Richmond, who was helping out in the campaign. Richmond was a grown man, a manufactured-homes salesman in Fort Worth, but that didn't stop Red from jumping all over him when he had forgotten to do something she thought he was going to do. Call some money bags in Houston, if he remembered correctly.

Usually, she apologized later, said she hated herself when her temper got the best of her, but what with the heat and the polls and everything else going wrong, it had been happening more often than usual.

Still, Purse stayed with her. It was like he started to tell Jo Lynne but didn't. He liked it. He liked learning things—from Red, from Aboy, from the political crowd in general.

Since he had been traipsing around the state with Red, tending to her every mood and whimsy, he had become a purse expert, just to give a little example of what he had learned. He would put himself up against Christian Dior, Gucci. He had learned the difference between a tote and a clutch, a satchel and a shoulder bag. He knew a hobo when he saw it, not to mention a short shoulder swagger tote. Ask him about a peau-de-soie double handle box, and he could tell you all about that too. Cox's Department Store could have put him to work behind the purse counter.

For the record, he liked it better when Red carried a clutch, because he could fold it in behind his wrist and nobody noticed the curly-haired young man carrying a woman's purse. Unfortunately, she usually didn't carry a clutch unless it was some kind of dress-up deal—maybe a beer-distributors' reception at Armadillo World Headquarters or a trial-lawyers' fundraiser at the Driskill Hotel. To tell the truth, a shoulder bag was easy to deal with, because you could just hang it around your neck, but was a little too obvious for his taste. Whenever he carried a shoulder bag, he tried to swagger a bit, arms out to his side, legs spread when he walked. He wanted to look manly, as if he had a pistol under his coat on the other side.

She had another purse she didn't carry all that often, but he liked it. It was made of tiny chain-mail, sort of a tarnished-silver color, and the metal clasp was two narrow snake's heads with red glass eyes. She said it came down through the family from her great-grandmother.

The absolute worst purse he had to carry was when some old lady in Nacogdoches sent Red a purse she had made herself out of a cigar box, and Red figured she had to carry it in public just once, so as not to insult the old biddy. It had a little clear plastic handle the old lady had screwed on, and the "Hav-a-Tampa" label was still on the box. He felt like a fool carrying it around. Good thing Red didn't like it either. As far as he knew, it resided on the back of some shelf in her bedroom closet.

Anyway, he didn't tell Jo Lynne about his purse knowledge; she would think he had moved to wild and crazy Austin and, just like her mama warned, was moving toward what Aboy would call a gay sensibility. Aboy teased him about his "purse-picacity."

To tell the truth, he wasn't turning gay, but he had learned a whole lot more about how women think. It wasn't that much different from how a man thinks. And what kept eating away at his mind was that the voters were just too backward, too damned ignorant, to choose a woman. And he could say that, because he might have been just like them not long before.

And there was something else, something he would never, ever tell anybody. Aboy was his mentor. Not Red, not Joe Frank, not Sue Bee, but Aboy. The man was teaching him things about politics and about people. Sure he played the fool a lot of the time, sure he had "sinned and fallen short of the glory of God," as Aboy often reminded him. But he had been around. He knew things, and he was more than happy to school the younger man.

Purse was too tired to sleep, even though it was nearly midnight by the time he and Jo Lynne said good night and hung up. He cooled off in the cramped plastic box Willis Seymour called a shower, got himself a cold Lone Star out of the icebox and went out and sat on the steps of the trailer. It had been a hard day, a discouraging day, and not just because of the heat.

He heard Shoogy scuffing around in his little A-frame pen out by the utility pole. Seemed he couldn't sleep either. He had scratched himself out a little sandpit in front of his shed, and Purse could hear him ruffling his feathers, clucking and settling into the sand to shake out the mites. Shoogy Red, his prized Allen Roundhead fighting cock, now retired undefeated, had something to do with his being mixed up with Red Ryder.

The truth is, he had never cared a rat's ass about politics until that day he and Aboy had met up. And through Aboy he met Red. It would be two years next April.

Purse had taken his bird to a match in an undisclosed location near Elm Mott, his home town. Cock fights were illegal, of course, although Aboy thought they had a chance of getting a toned-down version legalized if Red could lobby enough members of the legislature.

He remembered climbing out of bed early one Sunday morning and driving through a deserted downtown Elm Mott and across the Katy Railroad tracks and into some cedar breaks just east of the Heart O'Texas Speedway. The morning sun flashed off dozens and dozens of cars and pickup trucks parked every which way—along the road, in a pasture, nose down in bar ditches.

Families with little tow-headed kids were having picnics on the tailgates of their trucks. Some of them had set up their portable barbecue cookers. You would smell that wood smoke, and your mouth would start watering and your stomach would feel like it was hollowing out, getting ready to make room.

Lots of them were barbecuing chicken, and Purse remembered wondering if a chicken had a beak that could tell when one of her own was getting cooked. They were smart, he had read, smarter than people gave them credit for. He had read, in fact, they could identify 26 different individuals and could tell from a warning squawk whether danger was coming from the land or the sky.

He walked through the raised dust and trampled vegetation of a cow pasture toward a dirty-white circus tent, open on all sides. Inside were rickety wooden bleachers grouped around a dirt ring, actually a square, of planks of wood about three feet high. Outside the tent Little Jimmy Swinson was sitting at a rickety wooden desk. An ex-jockey, the wee little man made a living raising fighting cocks and organizing matches. Purse had heard he did a little whiskey business as well. Moonshine, that is.

"How're the odds running on my match?" Purse asked him.

"Eight to seven in your favor, Wily," he said, counting out bills as he talked.

Shoogy Red that morning was matched against one of Emmett Wayne Easley's birds—Easley's Pharaoh, a breed called Thompson's White Hackles. Purse agreed they were nice-looking birds, but they didn't have enough gumption for his taste.

Purse and Emmett Wayne were in high school together, grade school too, but they never liked each other all that much.

They shook hands, and Purse could see the sort of wary look in Emmett Wayne's eyes, like a turtle peering out of its shell, as if he knew his Pharaoh had met his match. Chickens may be smart, Purse thought, but he was never too sure about Emmett Wayne.

He was right about his cock meeting his match. The two young men hardly got them in the pit that morning before Shoogy put the gaff to the Pharaoh's scrawny neck. Pharaoh got loose and hit the fence and tried to climb up it, but Shoogy was on him like a hawk, legs flying, gaffs flashing, his beak probing for a soft spot. He got his gaffs in again, and this time they hung in. Three, four minutes, that's all it lasted.

The crowd of people gathered 'round the pit four-deep were going wild. The referee yelled "Handle!" and there was Emmett Wayne with that bird's head in his mouth, trying to breathe some blessed life back into him. He cleared the blood out of its throat, but it was no use. The bird died in Emmett Wayne's mouth. What a way to go, Purse remembered thinking.

About the time of the Pharoah's demise, Purse noticed a tall, hefty fellow with curly, sort of dishwater-blonde hair and pink cheeks hovering around the edge of the crowd. He was tall enough to see over the heads of most folks, and he stood out, even though he seemed to be trying to look inconspicuous. He had a diamond stick pin in his tie that caught the light and threw it back in a mesmerizing way. Purse saw him bending down over Emmett Wayne and the Pharoah, as if he were Emmett Wayne's dad, or maybe the chicken's.

Purse knew why he was so concerned. He had seen the roll of bills he had laid down on Emmett Wayne's no-count bird. Purse glanced down at the brown and white wingtips he was wearing—for a big man he had little feet—and there was blood splattered on the white part. He didn't seem to mind, didn't try to scrape it off on his trouser leg or wipe it off with a hot dog wrap.

He came over to Purse afterward, and the two got to talking. "An impressive bird you got there, a real gladiator's heart," he said. "What's his moniker?"

"Shoogy," Purse said. "Rhymes with boogie-woogie. It's short for Sugar."

He held out his big pink hand. "Ewell Suskin," he said. "That's my given name, but I humbly request you don't address me by that appellation. My friends and family, and yes my mortal enemies too, call me Aboy, so you might as well too."

His initial impression of Aboy: A decent enough sort, in a smarmy, jack-leg preacher way. Someone you might enjoy being around, in short doses.

He was in politics, he said, worked for Comptroller Ryder. Purse had never heard of Comptroller Ryder, and he didn't know what a COMP-troller did. He just assumed that it was a MR. Ryder this fellow worked for; he never even gave it a thought.

Aboy Suskin told him that some folks in the comptroller's office had expressed concern about Sunday cockfighting. The comptroller had sent him out to see what the fuss was about. He said he didn't know he'd have to come all the way up to Elm Mott to do his boss's bidding, but when you were in state government, the whole state was your domain. One day you might be in Dallas, the next day in Dalhart. You just never knew.

Purse didn't say anything about the wad of bills he had lost, though he could have told him that Emmett Wayne's birds had about half Dominicker in 'em. Never did have much gumption. Sort of like good ol' E. Wayne himself.

Mr. Suskin—"Aboy"—pretty quick in the relationship got to where he would come by the house whenever he was around Elm Mott, and they would talk birds. He would ask Purse about breeding Roundheads with Connecticut Strawberries or Georgia-Shawls with Brown Reds, or he'd want to know how much money he had made off Shoogy. He knew quite a bit about birds.

Purse remembered one hot evening after work they went over to the NiteOwl, the old beer joint and night club that had been on the Dallas Highway for as long as he could remember. Aboy got to talking about fighting cocks and about Rose Ryder and her big plans.

"I can tell you this," he said, after a big swig of Lone Star, "but you've got to keep it to yourself. It's off the record 'till she can marshal some legislative mavens, but what she has in mind is to legalize the ancient sport of kings."

"Horseracing?"

"No, not horseracing," Aboy said, his tone impatient. "Cockfighting. The venerable sport with a royal pedigree just as old and just as esteemed as horseracing. She wants to legalize cockfighting."

"Come on, Aboy," Purse said. "That's ridiculous. Why would she want to do something like that?"

"I'll tell you why," Aboy said. He glanced over both shoulders, like he was checking to see if the waitress or a couple of old Czech farmers at a table in the corner had an interest in listening in. "Not only does she like the sport, but she wants to prove her rural bonafides. And she can do that with a state-option-only cockfighting bill that cuts the rug out from under all the bleeding-heart liberals."

He drained his beer, motioned to the waitress for another one and kept talking. "And how would she do that, my skeptical young acquaintance wants to know? Well, I'll tell you. What we're looking into at the moment is, first of all, miniature muzzles sort of like falcons wear, so the birds can't peck each other to death. TV audiences don't like real blood, real killing, just the pretend stuff. Also what we call chicken booties, so they can't claw each other to chicken fricasee. We'll get rid of the gaffs too, of course."

"But Aboy," Purse said. "What's the use of fighting if the birds can't hurt each other?"

"Good question, my young sportsman. What's the use of boxing, if the fighters can't send each other to that great Madison Square Garden in the sky? It's the sport of it all, the manly art, or in this case the poultry art, of self-defense."

He reached into his inside coat pocket and pulled out a folded-up piece of white paper with a bunch of drawings on it, chicken scratches Purse wanted to say, because they were pencil-drawn illustrations of the equipment. He pointed to what looked like little leather masks.

"These muzzles here are no sweat," he said, "but the booties are a real challenge. They'll be weighted, with buck shot or bb's or something, so that when the birds fly into each other, they'll feel the punch. Since we're getting rid of the blood, that's where the sport comes in. The problem is, these booties have to be heavy enough so they'll have a little kick to them, but not so heavy the birds can't get up in the air."

Purse drained his Lone Star. He had no idea whether Aboy was joshing or serious. He didn't try to hide his skepticism.

"Like I say, it's a challenge," Aboy said, "so the other day I took it upon myself to go by and see an acquaintance at the Agriculture Department. He said he was in frequent consultation with a poultry expert down at A&M who could probably help me. Sure enough, this guy said the booties we're considering had enough heft so that a direct blow to the breast might cause a coronary thrombosis—that would be like a knockout in boxing— but not so heavy that the birds couldn't get back up in the air."

The better Purse and Aboy got to know each other, the more they would talk about other things, not just birds. Aboy told him one afternoon about how he got his name. He said he was the tenth of ten kids, all of them boys. When he was born, somebody asked his daddy what the baby was, and his daddy said, real disgusted like, "A boy." That became the name everybody knew him by. Even people in his family had to stop and think sometimes about what his real name was.

A couple of times, out on farm-to-market roads Purse had seen old, tattered signs tacked up on abandoned billboards advertising "COME HEAR GOD'S WORD PROCLAIMED BY THE REV. EWELL SUSKIN—FIVE NIGHTS ONLY." Ewell was his given name, but almost everybody in his latest line of work, politics, knew him as Aboy. It's like he was born-again, but going the opposite way, and he needed a new name for his new life.

"Accentuate the A," Aboy liked to say. "That's what I take it to mean—gen-u-wine Grade A, nothing but the best."

Purse remembered asking him one time when they were driving to Cameron to have a burger at Tex Miller's why he had never run for office. "You've got the tools. You know the state, you like people, got a good voice."

He laughed, pleased at the flattery. "Well, son," he said, "you don't know me all that well, or you doubtless wouldn't ask that question. But the short of it is, I know my place."

"I don't understand. What is your place?"

"It's not unlike Moses' place. You know Moses, don't you?"

At first Purse thought he was referring to a beer joint by that name, Moses Place, on Marlin's Wood Street. Then he realized he was talking about Moses in the Bible.

They were coming into Cameron. Aboy pulled up in front of the burger joint right off the courthouse square.

"Moses," he said, "led his people out of Egypt, but he didn't lead them into the Promised Land. That was for his buddy Joshua to do. I'm not comparing myself to Moses, although the metaphor still stands. I can lead a candidate to the Promised Land, but I can't go in myself. My mission, my political place, so to speak, is on the edges, on the dark side, whatever you want to call it. I know my place, and so does Red Ryder. She knows my place. She knows that folks like me are indispensible, even though she doesn't always want to know exactly what it is I'm up to."

It was the first of many lessons Purse learned from Aboy—about politics, about people, about life.

Occasionally, even about chickens. Now and then he would come back to his cockfighting plan. "Wily," he said one evening when they were sitting on the front porch, "I wouldn't say this to just anybody, but I'll say it to you because I know you're heavy with sagacity, despite your youth." He looked at a bottle of Shiner he'd brought with him out to the house. "I'm drunk on a dream," he said. "I'm possessed of a vision, and it's one I think Red Ryder—bless her heart—shares. We're gonna bring cockfighting out of the shadows into the sunlight, out of the byways into the highways, out of the cedar breaks onto silk-stocking row. We're talking respectability, urban revitalization."

He stood up and looked out over the pasture across the road. "I can see it now," he said. "Hordes of good, common folks, good, family people, flocking to a Chickendome in Big D, a Roosterena in Wichita Falls, a Pectrum in the Panhandle."

Purse took a sip of Shiner and looked across the road too. He couldn't see it, not yet at least.

★ ★ FOUR ★ ★

One day, out of the clear blue, Aboy asked him if he wanted to work for the comptroller in Austin. He didn't know it at the time, but Aboy knew his Uncle Joe. They had met at a gospel singin'. His uncle had asked him to look after the young Wily, now that his daddy was dead.

Wily reminded Mr. Ewell "Aboy" Suskin that he already was a state employee, thank you kindly, that he was riding shotgun on a big yellow litter truck for the Texas Highway Department.

Aboy laughed that tight, short way he had of laughing—sort of like a red-faced fat man gasping for air—and told Wily he could take that litter truck and shove it.

"Come with me," he said, "and you'll go places—and not just to the county dump every evening. Yessiree, you'll go places. You'll learn things."

Wily thought about it. Thought about it for a couple of weeks off and on. He liked his work well enough. He would get to the maintenance barn about six every morning, and ol' man Hanna would come in and read out the work details for the day. There would be guys doing bridge maintenance and somebody else putting up road signs. Cat, a wiry, feline sort of fellow who had been with the department for years, would have his dozer out somewhere in the county pushing dirt and gravel around. There would be patching crews filling pot holes on farm-to-market roads with hot, black asphalt. And every day, without fail, Rufus Cuttrell and Wily would be on the litter truck.

Butch Hathaway, one of their occasional helpers on the litter truck, called Rufus "the picker of the litter." Trying to get a rise out of Wily, he called him Little Rufus.

Rufus, weak-chinned, with a high voice and a bobbing Adam's apple under his floppy-brimmed straw hat, the kind an old lady would wear in her flower garden, had been on the litter truck every single working day for nine straight years. Working for the state was the only job he could find after he went broke trying to farm a little worn-out patch of blackland prairie east of West. He was conscientious, almost to the very end, and he had his job down to a science.

The two of them would start out driving along the shoulder as slow as a funeral for a head of state. They would be looking a long way up the road for telltale lumps. Wily would have his foot propped up on the dashboard, eyes half closed, half asleep, and Rufus would be droning on about what he was going to do when he retired in 13 years. And then one of them would see it. A dead dog, or maybe a sheep, or—heaven's to betsy, as Rufus would say—a skunk. Rufus would pull up beside the carcass, Wily would hop out and with the trained eye of a litter engineer determine whether he could pick it up by the hind legs and fling it into the back of the truck or whether he needed a specialized tool, that being a wide-mouth spade. He would do it himself unless the carcass was in pieces. If it was, Rufus would climb out to help, either watching for traffic or using his own spade.

And then, off they would go. If the carcass was all of a piece, they would look for some tall weeds off the road to fling it into; if it was smashed up, they would take it to the county dump.

One of the happiest days he ever had with Rufus was one day when he hopped down out of the truck and retrieved the carcass of a little brown puppy that was lying on the shoulder of the road. He must have gotten hit just before they came upon it, because he hadn't had time to stiffen up. Wily grabbed him by the hind legs and tossed him in the back. About half an hour later, when they passed some tall weeds, Rufus stopped, and Wily climbed up in the truck to get the carcass. He couldn't believe it. There was that little dog, tail wagging, tongue hanging out like he was grinning, running around back there in the empty truck bed like nothing had happened. Apparently he had just been stunned.

Wily was so happy, he nearly cried. Months later he could still see that little white-tipped tail wagging to beat the band. They gave the little guy to the fellow who ran the county dump. He took him home to his kids.

That's the only time something that happy ever happened. Every other day, after their dead-dog duties, they would spend the next eight hours picking up trash along the road. Wily recalled driving through Oklahoma on a family trip when he was a kid and seeing convicts in their black-and-white stripes doing that kind of work, but not in Texas, although the great state of Texas wasn't paying him and Rufus much more than you would pay convict labor.

Rufus had it down to a science. They would pull up under an overpass, climb out and take a piss and then haul out their broomsticks. They kept a file behind the seat and would use it to sharpen the nail Rufus had jammed into the end of the stick. Then Rufus would drive off, and Wily would start trudging up the road toward where Rufus would leave the truck. Wily would spear crumpled-up napkins smeared with mustard and ketchup, crumbly sun-yellowed newspapers, hamburger wrappers, the occasional dirty magazine. He would glance through its pages all curled up by the sun.

He would spear 'em and toss 'em in the tow sack he had looped around his neck with a rope that always rubbed him the wrong way unless he remembered to keep it outside his shirt collar. Spear and toss, spear and toss, as he walked through the dusty, brittle grass beside the highway, the traffic whizzing by just a few feet away. Sometimes a big 18-wheeler would rush by like a Katy locomotive, and the back draft would nearly blow him over. He could imagine getting hit by one of those behemoths, getting splattered like a bug against the radiator screen, like the dogs they picked up on the road.

Occasionally he thought of a joke Butch liked to tell. "Old truckers never die," he would say. "They just get a new Peterbilt."

Sometimes he would spear an unopened can of brew, and the smell of the beer that made Milwaukee famous spewing out, hot though it was, made him so thirsty he would want to scream. Once he was so thirsty, he let it spew into his mouth. It was about like warm piss.

It was horribly, horribly boring—so boring, he would try not to look at his watch to see how much of the day he had used up. And if he looked at it and it was, say, 3:20, the sun boring into his head and shoulders, he would keep telling himself it was 3 o'clock. And then when it got to be 4, he could say to himself, "Hot damn! Another hour's passed! Only two more to go."

When he got to the truck, he would dump the sack, get a drink of cold water out of the big jug they carried on the running board, and then drive slowly up the road to where Rufus was. He'd been walking away from the truck while Wily was walking towards it. Wily would see him far ahead in the shimmery glare, his big straw hat bobbing up and down like a sunflower, ambling along from one piece of trash to another like a man gathering shells on a beach. A truck would whiz by, and he would reach up to keep the big straw sunbonnet on his head. The hat had a string that went under his chin, but he didn't like to keep putting the hat back on his head. They would leapfrog like that all day, until it was time to drive to the county dump.

"But I don't know anything about politics," Wily told Aboy when he was at the house one Saturday afternoon. They had the radio on, sort of listenng to the Rangers playing the Detroit Tigers on WBAP.

"But you know about people," Aboy said. "That's the thing. You're a good judge of humanity, Wily. You're just like me. I'm uncommonly discerning when it comes to humankind. Both of us, we're perspicacious. And that's more important than politics at this point in your career. The politics you'll gradually imbibe, like a lion cub sallys forth with its doting mother and imbibes the lay of the African veldt. I'll be your doting mother, of course."

Wily assumed he meant he would pick it up OTJ.

"What would I be doing?" he asked.

"You'd be the comptroller's factotum."

"Fack what? You mean like I'd be totin' things?"

"Factotum. In more colloquial terms, son, you'd be the comptroller's jack-of-all-trades, utility infielder, personal valet. That's what it means. You'd be an official factotum."

"I guess you could say I'm the honorable Rufus Cuttrell's factotum on the litter truck, right?" Wily said.

Aboy laughed. "Something along those lines," he said, "only you won't be a disposer of disgusting rural ofal—genuine Lone Star road kill to you, my boy—while you're in the employ of the comptroller of the great and glorious state of Texas."

They were sitting at the kitchen table. Aboy had a bowl of Mama Foxx's cherry cobbler in front of him. It was just out of the oven and swimming in melted Blue Bell ice cream, home-style vanilla. He had eaten all of Mama's crust—the recipe she had inherited from Wily's Great-Aunt Opal—and he was scraping at the sides of the bowl, trying to get the last glop of cherry juice and ice cream all swirled together in red and white. Mrs. Foxx was on the back porch folding clothes. She wasn't saying anything, but Wily knew she was listening.

"So you think I ought to do it?" Wily asked her after Aboy had left.

She was quiet for a moment while she smoothed out a towel and folded it over twice. "Do what you think best," she said, handing him the corner of a fitted sheet while she tucked the other end into it, "but you know about Austin. From what I hear, people down there are not like you and me. They're different."

She put all the sheets in one stack. "And Wily," she said, "I don't know how much you can trust that Mr. Suskin. I know, I know, your uncle liked him, but I've seen his type before."

So he wasn't sure. After a couple of years knocking around after high school, after the time he gave to Uncle Sam, he finally had a steady job, with room for advancement. He wasn't convinced he wanted to bet his future on some politician he had never heard of.

And he had plans of his own. He wasn't telling anybody just yet, not even Jo Lynne, not even his mother, but he sort of had a crazy notion that he wanted to be a teacher. Someday. He wanted to let kids in on what you could find in books and stories and writing. He would use his GI bill, go to junior college first, and then get his degree in something that would let him teach. He figured anybody who knew him would laugh his head off, like Aboy did when Wily first told him about Rufus and the litter truck.

But Aboy stayed after him. "Let me escort you down to Austin," he told him one day while they were putting Shoogy through his paces. "We'll have a little tête-à-tête with the comptroller."

So one day in August, he took a sick day, and Aboy drove him in his turquoise '69 Cadillac convertible down to Austin to meet Red Ryder, state comptroller.

The comptroller's office was on the sixth floor of a tall pink-granite building. Aboy had to josh with the secretary a bit—Ilene McDonald, Wily would come to learn—and then they walked into Red Ryder's inner sanctum. That was the first Wily knew that Red Ryder was a woman.

Every time Aboy mentioned Red Ryder, Wily had this image in his mind of a man. Actually, he told Aboy later, he had an image of the comic-book cowboy Red Ryder, with his chaps and his red bandana and his trusty sidekick Little Beaver, one of his heroes when he was a kid. Aboy seemed to realize he was confused, so he had made it a point not to let on. He got a kick out of Wily being embarrassed at meeting Rose Marie "Red" Ryder, comptroller for the great state of Texas, but he didn't make him look bad. Wily was obliged to him for that.

What most people noticed first about Red Ryder was that puffy helmet of curly red hair. It was her trademark. And it was bright red—actually orange—even though she must have been close to 60 years old.

What they noticed next were the blue eyes, icy blue eyes that stared right through you past a patch of freckles on her face. But what Wily noticed the first few times he was around her was how clean she was, no matter where she was or what she was doing. It was air conditioned in the building, of course, but outside it was hot and everybody's clothes were all wrinkled and damp. Not Red's. When she came from around her big desk to meet him, Wily noticed she had on a white skirt that showed off her legs and a navy-blue short-sleeve jacket and blue-and-white high heeled pumps. She may have been 60, but she didn't look a day over 50.

"So this is the esteemed Mr. Foxx!" she said, taking his hand in a tight grip and giving it a manly shake. "Do you mind if I call you Wily?"

"No ma'am, I wish you would."

She took him by the elbow and led him over to a brown-leather couch in the corner of the room. He sank down into it so far he thought his knees were going to bump his chin. He reached down and pulled his socks up as quickly as he could.

Aboy stood biting his nails and fidgeting over by the door, while Red sat in a straight-backed chair on the other side of the coffee table. She crossed her legs, lady-like, and Wily heard the whisper of her nylon hose. The toe of her high-heeled shoe pointed to the floor so that her calf muscle flexed nicely, like a Kilgore Rangerette's. She laced her fingers over her knees. Her white skirt rode a ways up her thigh. Wily looked away, but maybe not soon enough, he feared.

Behind her was a big picture window where he could see the Capitol dome rising up, as if listening in on their conversation. On a table at his elbow, a large fish tank with all kinds of bright colored creatures swimming around in it whirred quietly.

"Mr. Suskin's told me a lot about you, Wily," Red said, "so I was eager to meet you in person, but he didn't tell me you were such a good-looking kid.

He grinned and sort of ducked his head. He figured his face was as red as a number-three billiard ball.

"He tells me you want to come to work with us," Red said.

Well, that was news to him, but he didn't let on. "Yes ma'am," he said, not wanting to contradict her. "I've been giving it some thought."

She stared into his eyes without saying anything for what seemed like five minutes. He was so uncomfortable under her steely gaze he finally had to look past her, out at the dome. On top of the dome, Lady Liberty, bright white in the morning sun and the bright blue sky, her sword lifted high over her head, stared out at the Hill Country.

"Wily, can you keep a secret?" she said at last.

"I like to think I can, ma'am," he said. "I've never been one for gossiping."

"I have no doubt, but what I'm going to tell you has to stay in this room."

She glanced over at Aboy. "Will you quit that fidgeting and come over here and sit down?"

She looked at Wily and gave him a wink and a grin. "I always feel better when I have our friend Aboy in my sights," she said. "Know what I mean?"

He didn't—not at the time, anyway—but that didn't matter. What she had to tell him was so interesting, he wasn't noticing Aboy.

"As you no doubt know, Wily, the state comptroller is responsible for making sure that the people of this great state get the money that's due them from the taxpayers of this state. You may think people owe too much taxes, I don't know, but the fact is, the tax rate is set by the people's representatives, and once it's set, everyone's obligated to pay."

"Only some people don't think the law applies to them," Aboy said, grinning, "and what Red—I mean Comptroller Ryder's fixin' to do is..."

"What I'm FIXIN' to do, as Mr. Suskin so elegantly puts it, is travel the length and breadth of this state and collect what the hard-working people of Texas are owed."

As she explained it, she was about to set in motion a series of raids around the state on businesses that collected sales tax money from their customers and then just conveniently forgot to send the money on to Austin. She had a list—cafes, department stores, auto dealers.

"What I'm going after, for the most part," she said, "is these big, multi-state businesses that aren't paying their share. It's a matter of fairness, pure and simple."

The raids, she said, would be "high-profile." She would notify the media in whatever locale she was going to, and then she would swoop down with a Texas Ranger or two and either get the business owner to pay up on the spot or shut the place down.

"And what I need from you, Wily, is a smart, level-headed young man to accompany me on these raids and, in essence, think for me. I won't have time to anticipate all the little details—who we talk to, what I carry with me, how much the place owes, sometimes even the name of the town we're in. You'll be my..."

"Her factotum," Aboy said, grinning, his eyes glinting behind his glasses, pleased like a kid in a spelling bee who knew the word before anybody else did.

Red glanced at him, her mouth straightening out for just a second like an old-maid librarian's. "You'll be my assistant, my right-hand man" she said. "I'll come to count on you."

She told him the raids wouldn't start for a few months, that he would work around the office until then and get to know the department, get to know her.

"By the time we go out in the field," she said, "I want you to know me so well I won't even have to ask for something. We'll be in sync, totally, and you'll just know."

She stared at him again, for a long time. "So what do you think?" she said at last.

What did he think? What did he think? He thought, "What am I getting into?" although he didn't say it. He had never been in sync with anybody, certainly not a hard-driving, demanding red-headed woman. On the other hand, it was inside work, and he wouldn't be scraping the steaming carcass of someone's ol' dog Trey off the asphalt. Leastways, he didn't expect to be.

So he said he would think about it. Second thoughts had cropped up during the past couple of years, but for the most part, he was glad he took the job, especially after Red got drafted to run for the U.S. Senate.

To tell God's truth, though, he probably wouldn't have done it had it not been for Rufus Cuttrell's crack-up. It was one of those hot August afternoons and he and Rufus were headed out to the county dump with a full load of smelly, awful trash under the tarp. Wily was about half asleep as usual, Paul Harvey was on the radio, his staccato voice praising the president's secret plan to bring peace to the Middle East, and Rufus was droning on about a little cottage for sale on the shores of Possum Kingdom Lake. Possum Kingdom was 200 miles away, so Wily don't know whether he and his wife had driven up there one weekend or what. Maybe he had seen an ad in the paper. Or maybe he was just dreaming.

Rufus was driving funeral-slow along the shoulder, so the trash wouldn't blow out from under the tarp, when, out of the blue, he floored it. The old yellow truck groaned and shuddered, and Wily had to catch the armrest to keep from sliding onto the floorboard.

"Rufus!" he shouted. "What's the matter?" He thought he might have seen a wreck or something, was speeding up to go help, but he didn't say anything. When Wily looked over at him, he was leaning over the steering wheel, his chin almost touching the horn in the center. He was staring straight down the road, his mouth white around the edges.

He glanced over at Wily, his blood-shot pale-blue eyes under the floppy straw hat looking wild and scary. "It's the End Times, Wily boy," he said, his voice pitched even higher than usual. "The End Times. Rapture's coming. You and me, we got to get ready."

Wily knew Rufus was religious; he was always telling him about how God had a plan for his life—and for Wily's if he would just let Him in. But it seemed to Wily this wasn't religion talking. It seemed to him the heat had finally bored through that old straw hat and fried his brain. That, and years and years of Cat and the guys jeering, laughing, calling him "picker of the litter," calling him "Old Maid Cuttrell" and worse.

Picking up speed, Rufus jolted onto the pavement, and then he reached down and jerked on the lever that raised up the bed of the truck.

"No! Rufus!" he shouted, but it was too late. Looking out the big rectangular rearview mirror just outside his window, he saw white exhaust smoke billowing out behind them and trash streaming out along the road. Cars following were getting pelted with stinking garbage. They were veering off the road, into the other lane. Wily saw cars with their wipers on, trying to scrape off old newspapers. They were honking, flashing their lights. A couple of cars passed them, the drivers leaning over on the front seat, their passenger windows rolled down, so Rufus could see the middle finger jutting up at him.

"What the hell are you idiots doing?" one guy shouted. But there was no stopping Rufus. He was staring straight ahead, waiting for the moment when God would pluck him up to Heaven's reward.

Wily tried to stay calm. "Rufus, why don't you pull over and let me drive?" he said. "Don't you want to stop and get a cold drink of water?"

But Rufus wasn't hearing his partner; he wasn't even seeing him. In his high, thin voice, it sounded like he was quoting Scripture—Revelation, it seemed to Wily. The rear end was still tilted up, but all the trash had blown out. Now and then the tailgate would bounce and scrape on the pavement with a huge clangy sound, and in the rear-view mirror Wily would see a shower of sparks dancing along behind them.

He thought about jumping out, but Rufus was sailing down the highway, just sailing; they were going 70, maybe faster. Wily would hear him mutter the word "kingdom" now and then, but he couldn't tell whether he meant the kingdom of God or Possum Kingdom. Maybe they were one and the same, Wily thought.

He was desperately trying to figure out what to do. Was there some way he could get a cop's attention, take over the wheel, knock Rufus up the side of the head? They passed Red Ball Freight Lines and the Old Hickory Motel, and he realized that in a few minutes they would be passing Crittendon's Trailer Court, where Jo Lynne lived. Was there some way she could help?

Even though Rufus had seemed to settle down a little bit—he wasn't quoting Scripture anymore—the plan Wily had was a long shot, but he concluded he had to try it.

"Rufus," he said, "Let's go to Possum Kingdom. I'm ready, but I'm desperate to take a piss. I can't wait much longer. How 'bout stopping up here at Crit's? Just for a minute."

Wily was afraid Rufus would tell him to just pee on the floorboard, but he didn't say anything at all. Wily started trying to think of some other scheme, but when they got even with Crit's Rufus pulled off the road and stopped not far from the gas station where Mr. Crit himself was usually sitting behind the counter.

"Two minutes, son," Rufus said.

Wily flung open the door, jumped down to the ground and ran toward the back of the station where the restrooms were and kept on going to Jo Lynne's trailer. She had to be there, had to be there, he kept telling himself. He banged on the front door, hard, and Praise the Lord! she was.

"Rufus has gone crazy!" he shouted. "No time to talk. Call the Highway Department and tell 'em we're headed up I-35. Ask for Woodrow."

He left Jo Lynne standing in the door with her mouth open while he hurdled the little picket fence around the trailer and headed toward the road. Then he stopped. "Call Mr. Suskin too," he shouted. Tell him we got trouble."

People asked him later why he went back to the truck. Wily would say he guessed he wasn't thinking beyond the fact that Rufus, daft as he was, was his friend, and he figured if he headed up the road by himself there was no telling what he might do. Hurt himself. Hurt somebody else. He might be able to stop that from happening.

They drove for about an hour, the windshield speckled and flecked by the winged life that had smashed into them. Rufus quoted scripture for a while, and then he got quiet. That worried Wily, so he got him to talking about the little house on the lake, about his son Cletus who had died years before and how he wished he had been able to see the place.

"What about chickens?" Wily asked him. "You and Lou Dora gonna have chickens?"

Rufus said they were.

"And what about a garden?"

He'd put in some tomatoes, he said, maybe some Kentucky Wonder green beans, some black-eyed peas. Maybe some watermelon and cantaloupes.

"You like them yellow-meated watermelons" Wily asked him.

He said he did, but he preferred a good Black Diamond melon, if you let it ripen.

They were almost to Waxahachie before they stopped. Rufus pulled off the side of the road, got out and wandered into a cornfield, the ground cracked and hard, the stalks yellowed and dry and leaning every which way. Wily opened the door but stayed in the truck and watched Rufus as he staggered into the field, pulled down his jeans, his skinny, old legs white and wrinkled. He squatted, until all Wily could see was his red, worried face. He leaned back across the seat and pulled out the keys. From down in the field he heard an explosion of bowel noise that went on and on.

Wily happened to glance in the rearview mirror and saw a black and white highway patrol car, red lights flashing, pull up behind the truck. A patrolman, his pistol drawn, got out of the car and aimed down at him from behind the door.

Wily opened the truck door and got one foot out on the running board, before he heard the cop shout, "Don't move 'til I tell you to, you little bastard. Get that leg back up in there 'fore I blow it off."

He came up to the door and jerked it open. He reached in and grabbed Wily by the shirt collar and threw him down on the griddle-hot gravel, his revolver pointed at his head all the while.

"What'd you do with the old man?" he yelled. "Where'd you dump the body?"

Wily looked up at the cop towering over him and could see his curly hair reflected in his shiny silver sunglasses. He looked scared, and those sunglasses made him hate the cop all the more.

"He's right out..." he started to say, but the cop kicked him in the ribs with the toe of his shiny black boot. He knocked the breath out of him. Lying on the gravel trying to make his diaphragm work, Wily remembered that it was the first time that had happened since Jerry Stirling tackled him too hard playing football at recess in the fifth grade.

Still lying there, trying to keep the hot gravel from grinding pits into his face, he heard Aboy's Cadillac skid to a stop behind the cop car. The cop looked back, and Wily raised his head up enough to see Aboy in his white suit come hurrying up to where the cop was standing. Wily felt really proud of him. He looked big, bad and official.

"Put the weapon away, you brown-shirted miscreant," Aboy shouted at the cop. He flashed some kind of State of Texas ID card, and the cop backed away.

"Look out there in that corn field, you fascist fuckhead!" Aboy yelled. "There's the pathetic SOB you're seeking to apprehend."

They looked out in the cornfield. There was Rufus, standing up with his legs spread out, smoothing down his shirttail inside his jeans and buckling his belt. He started walking toward them, a big grin on his face, liked he'd done what needed to be done. The cop pulled his gun again.

"He's harmless," Wily said, his voice shaking he was so angry. He swiped at tears in his eyes.

He stood up and walked over to Rufus as he came out of the field. He took him by the arm. The cop put his gun away, even though he looked like he didn't want to.

They stood there on the shoulder of the road, Wily with his hand on Rufus' arm, traffic whizzing by, while he told the cop what happened, Rufus smiling all the while, murmuring to himself some verse from Paul's letter to the Ephesians.

By the time Wily finished his tale, the cop was willing to believe he was telling the truth about how Rufus had snapped, although he still seemed a little disappointed there wasn't somebody to beat the shit out of. He let Wily go with Aboy, and Aboy got him to put in writing that Rufus would go to a mental health facility and not to jail. An ambulance, its siren blaring, drove up about then. Aboy and Wily helped the attendants put Rufus in the back.

By then reporters from Channel 8 in Dallas had pulled up in their big white van, and a newspaper reporter from Waxahachie was also there asking Wily questions. Seeing the van, people driving by stopped. Wily had to tell his story several times, and each time he told it he noticed Aboy standing off to the side smiling like a proud papa.

By the time the cop had driven off with Rufus in the back seat, and a highway department wrecker had come for the litter truck, Aboy and Wily were left on the road by themselves. To the west the sun was a big, orange ball going down behind a field speckled white with cotton. Aboy looked out over the field and then back at Wily.

"Well, young man," he said, a big grin on his face, "that was a snafu of the first order you got yourself into. Wouldn't you agree?"

Wily grinned.

"Ready to come to Austin?"

★ ★ FIVE ★ ★

For some reason Purse had Rufus Cuttrell on his mind when he woke up one morning not long after the East Texas trip. He had been by to see the old man a couple of times at the state hospital. The doctors had let him tend a little garden plot at the back of the property, and the last time Purse saw him he was growing Big Boy tomatoes. Purse wasn't sure Rufus knew who he was, or where, but he seemed happy. He hoped the old man thought he was at Possum Kingdom.

Purse thought about how he could have said no, even after Aboy had come to his rescue. But that wouldn't have been the end of it. With Red, it was never the end of it. She would just work on you and work on you and wear you down like a carpenter planing a piece of loblolly pine. She just didn't quit until she had her way. That's probably what drove off Howard, her ex. She wasn't mean about it, necessarily. Even Howard would have agreed. She was just stubborn and bloodhound-persistent and self-obsessed. Whatever she had achieved in life, that's how she had gotten it.

Purse stumbled into the shower, then wandered into his narrow little kitchen, drying off. He fixed himself some coffee and unwrapped a sweet roll from Mrs. Baird's day-old bakery store. On the radio, two morning DJs were laughing about Red.

"I'm tellin' you, she don't have a snowball's chance in hell," Sammy Redd said in that wheezing fat man's voice of his. Purse never had seen Sammy Redd in person, but from his voice he pictured a fat, greasy-haired fellow busting out of a pair of bib overalls. He would have a red face that sweated a lot, and he would be cramming a donut or two into his mouth while he blathered about things he didn't know squat about.

"Why doesn't she just concede and save the taxpayers the cost of an election?" his buddy Bob Swit suggested in his deep, syrupy radio voice. Bob was a country-club conservative who was always trying to sound reasonable. When he wasn't doing his morning show with Sammy Redd, he was peddling boats and trucks and barbecue over the airways. In between the country-and-western classics, here would come syrupy Bob Swit offering his up-close-and-personal, ever-so-sincere testimonials about funeral parlors or diet plans or the plumber he used at his own house to swash out his toilet.

Purse had ironed a shirt the night before, so he decided he could go with his one-and-only J. C. Penney suit. He had gotten it on sale. Lizard green, came with two pair of pants. It was the first suit he had ever owned. On Sundays growing up, he would just wear a pair of slacks, a white shirt and maybe a clip-on tie. His daddy didn't wear a suit, so Purse didn't either.

What the radio boys said made him angry, and he thought about calling in, but he knew it wouldn't make a damn's worth of difference. Sammy Redd was not one to listen to reason. Instead of calling, he turned off the radio and put his mind to decision *numero uno*: to wear his suit coat or not. It was hot already, and they were headed to Junction, to an auction barn. It was going to be hot, smelly and dirty.

Shoogy stopped his morning grooming long enough to cock his head and greet the morning sun. Purse dragged his finger across the wire of his cage, and the bird looked up at him, his head cocked to the side like he was waiting for Purse to ask him something about the election. Maybe I should, he thought. He scattered some Purina pellets into his food tray, climbed into the Crusher, the aged Land Cruiser his Uncle Joe had bequeathed him, and headed across the river to campaign headquarters.

Aboy already had the station wagon gassed up, and Olene had their schedule typed out for the day. "Hayden Dalrymple will meet you at the Cattleman's Cafe right there at the cattle barn," Olene told them. "Mr. Dalrymple's the general manager of Junction Stockyard and Auction Barn. And Wily, don't you forget Red has a radio interview with K-S-A-T in San Antonio. She's on at 9, but they want her to be ready a little beforehand. You think you can remember that?"

He told her he could. Sue Bee Sealman, the campaign manager, drove up in her little white Volvo. She had Red with her.

"Morning, boys," Red greeted them. "Let me pay a visit to the little girl's room and get another cup of coffee, and we'll be on the road." She seemed to be in a good mood, Purse determined, which was a relief.

Out past the Y, on the outskirts of Oak Hill, the traffic began to thin, and Aboy started to sing along with George Jones on Pure Country K-V-E-T. "Well, the race is on," George sang, only Aboy sang, "Well, the race is on and it looks like Red on the backstretch, Jimmy D movin' to the inside; his tears are holdin' back, they're tryin' not to fall-ll-ll...."

Even Red, sitting in the backseat and going over position papers, chuckled at his silliness. "Now, Aboy, tell me again why we're going out here this morning?" she asked.

Outside, Purse noticed how new gravel roads and mobile homes and little ranchettes were punching into the pastureland and the cedar-covered hills. The Hill Country was being chewed up by city folks desperate for clean air to breathe and country schools full of little white kids that always said yessir and thank you, ma'am.

"You remember," Aboy said, glancing over his shoulder at Red. "It's all because of your nouveau riche, nouveau son of the soil, *viejo* amigo Jimmy Dale Sisco. How could you forget?"

"Well, God knows I tried," Red said. "I've had a lot of long, lonely nights in my life, but that's one night I thought would never end."

"Don't we go by his ranch?" Purse asked Aboy. The terrain looked familiar.

"No, it's out beyond Junction, fortunately," Aboy said, "but this is Jimmy Dale territory. Only reason we're coming out this way this morning's 'cause Judge Young called Olene a few days ago. Told her he thought it would do the comptroller a world of good if she'd show up on auction day and shake a few hands. He thought it might ease some of the bruised feelings, shall we say, over closing down Schott's Red and White Grocery in Junction 'til they got their taxes paid. So Olene penciled it in."

"They're open now, aren't they?" Red asked.

"Yes ma'am, they are," Aboy said. "My sources tell me it was Jimmy Dale who put up their recompense. Paid their taxes." He slowed down for a school zone as they pulled into the little ranching town of Dripping Springs.

"That man does have gall," Red said. She glanced out the window at the morning traffic and the new fast-food joints and the brand-new sprawling one-story high school with a big new football stadium out back. "Can you believe this place?" she said. "When I first started coming to Dripping Springs, I bet there weren't 500 people. And now look at it. First thing you know, it'll be an Austin bedroom community."

"It's happening across the length and breadth of the blessed Hill Country," Aboy said, speeding up as they hit the outskirts of town. "People desirous of their own little bit of rustic paradise."

Just like Jimmy Dale Sisco, Purse was thinking. It had been about a year ago when he and Aboy and Red had visited his ranch. He remembered Red saying she had no idea at the time Jimmy Dale was even interested in politics, didn't know whether he was Republican or Democrat. Purse recalled that Red had a speech to make at a 4-H Club convention in San Angelo, and when that was over the three of them drove back the two hours to Sisco's ranch between Sonora and Ozona. The "Jimmy D" it was called.

Purse remembered Red saying she had never heard of him, and neither had Aboy, but Lee Roy Bodine, the lobbyist for the sheep and goat raisers, had told Red that Sisco had enjoyed a stockmarket windfall and was looking to support candidates if he found them worthy. Red promised Bodine—against her better judgment, she said later—that she'd pay Sisco a visit.

"Remember that gate?" Red asked, laughing. Driving along, it was like all three of them were still thinking about Jimmy Dale Sisco.

"Goats rampant!" Aboy said, laughing. "Beat anything I'd ever seen."

At the entrance to the Jimmy D Ranch, just off the highway, was a huge limestone gate—probably 12 feet high—with the letters spelled out in cursive wrought iron, "The Jimmy D," across the gravel roadway. Purse remembered what Aboy had said: old Hill Country ranchers, honest-to-God ranchers, didn't go in for that kind of ostentation; they'd have a barbed-wire gate and a little wooden sign out on the road. If you didn't know where you were going, you didn't need to be there. But guys like Jimmy Dale Sisco had what you might call a big-gate complex. They wanted you to know who they were and what they had.

But Jimmy Dale's gate wasn't just big. On top of the wall at each end were what Aboy was calling "goats rampant"—two huge cast-iron statues of horned goats on their hind legs, front legs stretched out like they were boxing, their goatly members—that's what Purse's Aunt Eunice in Corsicana would call them—sticking straight up, their scrotums hanging down like heavy sacks of beans. Red had said it was the stupidest thing she had ever seen.

"What I liked was his cowboy outfit," Aboy said, and they set in to laughing again. Aboy swerved a bit, and the station wagon kicked up gravel. "Keep your mind on your driving, Aboy, not on Jimmy Dale's outfit," Red reminded him.

Jimmy Dale's ranch was a long way up a rocky, unpaved road. Longhorn steers and buffalo grazed peacefully in a beautiful green pasture on one side of the road; on the other side were big white Nubian goats, hundreds of them.

Judge Bill Young told Aboy later that Sisco had drained a natural spring for his own use. That's why the pastures were so green in the middle of the hottest summer on record. All the ranchers down stream had run out of water because of Jimmy Dale. They went to court, but there was nothing they could do. That's the Texas way. Right of capture, it's called.

As they got closer to the house, the road became smoothed-out pea gravel, with tall date palms lining each side. The way they bent gracefully away from the road reminded Wily of super-slim models he had seen in women's magazines, like something you would see in Beverly Hills, not in the Hill Country. The trees alone must have cost Jimmy Dale a fortune.

Just when they could see the ranch house, a two-story white Spanish-style mansion with dark-green shutters and a red tile roof, they saw a horseman on a golden palamino cantering down the road toward them. Aboy slowed down almost to a crawl, and as the horseman got closer they could see his big white round-topped hat and the shiny parrot-green boots he was wearing, topped off by a sky-blue western shirt and long yellow bandanna. The shirt had a sort of panel that buttoned off to the side, like Roy Rogers, King of the Cowboys himself, used to wear.

The drugstore cowboy cantering their way wore his Levi's stuffed into his green boots. He pulled back on the reins, and the mighty honey-colored stallion with a white patch on his chest reared a little, and then the man hiked a leg over the saddle and sort of slid down the big horse's side.

The cowboy was a small man, not more than 5-feet-7, if that, with a bowling-ball belly and a shoe-polish black mustache. Bandy-legged in his tight jeans and bright-green boots, he walked up to the window of the car slowly, swaying like a sailor, like his feet were hurting him. He swept the Stetson off a bald head and introduced himself. "I'm Jimmy Dale Sisco," he said, grinning like a Fuller Brush salesman and holding out his hand to Red sitting in the back seat. She took his hand, and he kissed it.

"Welcome to the Jimmy D," he said.

They were passing through downtown Johnson City, past the old rock courthouse, and Purse glanced at Red in the backseat. She was going over a Legislative Reference Service report on agricultural price supports. This was LBJ's stomping grounds. Purse had never asked her what she thought of him. He was hoping she would tell LBJ stories, but she was deep into her reading.

"Remember that house?" Purse asked Aboy.

"Ha! El Rancho Gauche, ol' Jimmy D should have called it," Aboy said.

Jimmy Dale had taken them on a tour of every square foot. The rooms were big, high-ceilinged, and in almost every room the couches and the chairs and the hammocks were upholstered in dark-brown leather, the arms and legs crafted out of horns—deer horns, cattle horns, elk horns. On the high-ceilinged walls were heads of buffalo and deer and moose and oil paintings of goats and bulls and deer and bears, bobcats, coiled rattlesnakes, even armadillos.

In the hangar-sized living room off to the right of the entryway was a larger than life-size statue of a cowboy in 10-gallon hat, bandana, holstered six-guns around his waist and sheepskin chaps. Purse thought it was Jimmy Dale at first, but then Jimmy Dale himself said, "Ya'll say hello to Hoot Gibson, rootin'-tootin' cowboy of the silver screen, my hero since I was a little shaver. A real man's man." He tipped his hat to the bronze statue.

"That's mighty fine, Jimmy Dale," Red said, staring up at Hoot. "A mighty nice rendering."

"I thought it was you at first," Aboy said.

"Well, sir, you just paid me the highest of compliments," Jimmy Dale said. "If I was half the man Hoot Gibson was, I'd consider myself satisfied."

"Ain't that a Hoot?" Aboy said, looking around at each of them and waiting for a laugh. What he got from Jimmy Dale was a frown. Jimmy Dale didn't like anybody messin' with his Hoot.

Jimmy Dale led his guests back across the entryway toward the kitchen. "Sissy'll be sorry she missed you," he said. "She's in Dallas for the week. "I'm figurin' y'all know about Texas ladies and Nieman-Marcus," he said to Red as they sat down to supper. "We had that Mr. Stanley Marcus out here at the ranch for a barbecue one weekend a few years back. I told him, I said I figured I'd probably paid for a whole floor of his downtown store over the years."

"I was right sorry we missed Sissy," Red told Purse and Aboy later. "Any woman who could stay with Jimmy Dale longer than a day, I wanted to shake her hand."

At supper, at a rough wooden table with knot holes in it, a table so long you'd have to shout to anybody sitting at the other end, in a dining room where King Arthur would have felt at home drinking mead from silver goblets, with a huge limestone fireplace at one end, Jimmy Dale took an hour to tell how he had made his money. How he came from what he called "humble origins" in Helotes, Texas, and how, when he got out of high school, he had gone to work for a furniture-moving company in San Antonio but knew he was meant for something more and how he was browsing through *Progressive Farmer Magazine* at the barber shop one day and found out that Nubian goats from South Africa, prized for their superior size and the quality of the meat, couldn't be imported into this country. It was against the law.

Jimmy Dale had an idea. He figured out a way to have Nubian goat semen shipped in; the semen was legal. Once the frozen semen arrived, he and Sissy organized themselves an auction on the courthouse square in Sonora, taking bids from the back of a pickup. At the end of the day they were millionaires.

Jovita served them that night. She was young and pretty and spoke broken English, but that didn't matter. Her smile was so bright, you didn't mind just smiling right back and guessing what she had said. They all wondered whether she came with the ranch or was born in Mexico.

Aboy told Purse later he had heard from West Texas folks how Jimmy Dale had spent a lot of his younger years, and maybe not so young, drinkin' and whorin' in Villa Acuña on the border most every weekend.

The food that night was first-class—big, tender cuts of Nubian *cabrito* with green-chili salsa; baked potatoes swimming in butter and sour cream and chives; red beans and rice; corn on the cob with little wrought-iron Jimmy D holders to keep your hands clean; hand-made tortillas with guacamole; and apple cobbler with ice cream on top for dessert.

Purse remembered trying to cut into a round piece of what he thought was a gizzard of some sort, and Jimmy Dale noticed. "Know what those are, son?" he asked. Purse told him he didn't. "Them's goat fries, goat testicles for you city folks. Whacked 'em off myself."

They were pretty good, Purse decided, although not something he would order at Luby's Cafeteria on a regular basis.

When the meal was over, it must have been 10 o'clock. All Jimmy Dale's guests wanted was to get in the car and head for home, two hours away. But they couldn't leave. They had to sit and listen to the little man tell his stories about Nubian goats, while Jovita stood behind him and massaged his sloping shoulders. At one point, he pulled her around and had her sit on his lap and patted her slightly rounded tummy. It was only then that they realized she was pregnant.

"Goat's ain't the only ones around here with a high sperm count," Jimmy Dale said, giving a little chuckle down in his throat. Jovita's pretty brown face turned red.

"How's that husband of yours?" he asked her, as she got up off his lap and scurried into the kitchen. "César's the best hand I got," he told Red. "I got him over at the King Ranch this weekend making a Santa Gertrudis buy for me."

Just when they were hoping the evening was coming to an end, Jimmy Dale hit on the idea of showing off his new guest house and auction barn for goat buyers, who would fly in from around the country and land on Jimmy D's private air strip. The guests had to scuffle along in the dark down a road behind the mansion to the guesthouse, which was like a log-cabin resort at Yellowstone. He took them through every room, while they listened to more stories about the lives and loves of goats.

Purse got to wondering later whether that was a test of some kind that Sisco was putting Red through, or whether he was so full of himself he had to show off to everybody who ventured up that palm-lined road. Maybe, like Jimmy Carter when he was governor of Georgia, Jimmy Dale was measuring himself against politicians he came in contact with. Maybe, even then, he was contemplating a run for the U. S. Senate.

Jimmy Dale's ranch was about 50 miles farther west of where they were going on the campaign trip today.

"Did Jimmy Dale ever give us a dime?" Purse asked Aboy.

"Not as far as I know. Did he, Red?"

"Did he what, Aboy? I wasn't listening."

"Did we ever get any money out of that asshole, Jimmy Dale?"

"No, we did not," she said, "and it serves us right for prostituting ourselves that way. I'm downright ashamed of myself for letting you and Sue Bee talk me into something like that."

"He knew right then," Aboy said, "he was running for the Senate. He was just pumping us for information."

They drove through Fredericksburg, the old German town with its wide main street and its sturdy stone buildings. Aboy asked Red if she wanted to stop for a good German breakfast at a place he knew downtown. "Superb apple strudel," he said. Red said they didn't have time.

"They ought to hang on to these buildings while they have them," Red said as Aboy stopped for a light. "They're what makes this town so different."

West of Fredericksburg, they were in sheep and goat country. It was dry and rocky, not quite so hilly, with more mesquite and prickly pear and less cedar and live oaks. Purse noticed a lot of Nubian herds, all thanks to Jimmy D. Some of the herds had big white dogs from Spain guarding them. Purse had been told that Basque sheepherders put the dogs with mama goats as soon as they were born; the goats even suckled the pups. So the dogs grow up thinking they're goats, only the coyotes knew better. Even they wouldn't fool with those big dogs.

Purse liked hearing about stuff like that.

Junction was a pleasant little town. It was the outer edge of the Hill Country and the beginning of West Texas. They drove across the big iron bridge over the clear, running Llano River and into downtown. A lot of pickups were pulled in front of the courthouse and across the square at the Main Street Cafe. They drove past what looked like a Christmas tree on a vacant lot across from the courthouse. It had a silver star on top, but it was made out of sun-bleached deer horns all tangled together. The auction barn was a few blocks off the square.

They could smell the barn and hear the bawling and braying half a block before they got there. Dust-caked trucks and cattle trailers lined both sides of the road. Aboy pulled the station wagon into a parking spot between two well-used pickups, at the Cattleman's Cafe. A middle-aged man in a summer straw cowboy hat, a white, pearl-buttoned western shirt and khakis stood at the front door smoking a cigarette. When he saw Red, he tossed the cigarette down on the sidewalk and scuffed it out with his boot.

"That's Hayden Dalrymple," Aboy told Red. They got out, stretched a bit and tried to get used to the acrid smell and the off-key trombone tones of unhappy cattle in a maze of wooden loading pens beside the cafe. Red walked over to Dalrymple. "Hayden, you ol' so-and-so," she said, a laugh in her voice and her hand outstretched. He took her hand, and she reached up and gave him a peck on the cheek.

"Sure am glad y'all could come out here this morning," Dalrymple said. "Your secretary—Mrs. Whitten?—called to remind y'all about the radio show. Come on back here to my office, and we'll get 'em on the phone."

They followed the auction barn manager back to his little glass-enclosed office. He had Red sit down behind his desk, and he shoved the phone toward Purse. Red checked her makeup in a little mirror she kept in her purse, and Purse dialed the number Olene had given him. A producer for the Ricky Ward "Sound of San Antone" show came on the line. "We'll get her on right after the network news," she said. "It'll be about five minutes."

"Punch that button," Dalrymple said, "and you'll be on speaker phone. She did, and after the news and weather—"another scorcher in the Alamo City"—Ricky Ward was telling about Red and about the U.S. Senate race and saying "There ain't a whole lot of folks who give her a chance, but, hot damn, you gotta admire the little lady's pluck."

Red looked at Aboy and rolled her eyes. "Asshole," she mouthed.

"Red—you don't mind if I call you Red, do you?—I hear you're way out in Junction this morning, hobnobbin' with a passel of cattle ranchers and West Texas cowpunchers," Ricky Ward said, his voice a whiskey-drenched country drawl. "With all due respect, ma'am, I have to ask what a city gal like you knows about country folks and the problems they have to put up with in this day and age."

"Ricky, I'm glad you asked that question," Red said, her eyes on the cattle shed outside the glass window of the office. "I'll tell you what I do know. I know that if you eat you're involved in agriculture, and I know if these ranchers out here in the Hill Country and all over this great state can't get a fair price for what they produce, they won't be in business much longer. And we'll all be the poorer for it."

"Can't argue with that," Ricky Ward said, "but with all due respect what are you gonna do about it?"

"I'll tell you one thing we're gonna do," Red said. "We're gonna make sure the tax structure of this country doesn't unfairly burden the hard-workin', productive members of this society—

just like these cattle raisers I'm meetin' with this morning here in Junction."

"We'll hear more from Red Ryder, the little lady who wants to go to Washington," Ward said, "right after a word from KB Homes. Manufactured housing a senator himself'd be proud to live in."

Red put down the phone on the desk, rolled her eyes and took a deep breath.

"You're doing fine," Madam Comptroller," Aboy said. "You've got about 20 more minutes."

Hayden Dalrymple brought in a cup of coffee and a glass of water.

"Why don't you boys go on out to the cattle pens and do a little meetin' and greetin'," Red said. "No use all three of us hanging around in here; fact is, you're making me a little jittery. When I'm through here, I'm going to step into the auction barn, and then Hayden'll bring me out to the pens."

Purse and Aboy wandered through the auction ring first. An auctioneer dressed like Dalrymple, khakis and a white shirt, stood in the dirt-floor pit, microphone in hand, rattling off sounds faster than Purse could fathom, while a couple of young cowboys with electric cattle prods herded cows and calves in and out of the ring.

Men and women were sitting on steep wooden bleachers in a semi-circle around the little enclosure. In lawn chairs at ground level were half a dozen or so older men. With skinny old legs folded over knees, hats pushed back on their heads, they were talking to each other, didn't seem to be watching the auction at all, but now and then, one of them would raise a finger, and the auctioneer would jump to another number. Pretty soon he'd shout "Sold!" and the old men would make marks in little notebooks they carried with little, number-two pencil stubs.

Aboy and Purse watched for a while—"Make sure you don't scratch your nose or you'll own a herd of calves," Aboy warned— and then they went outside. Just as they stepped out into the heat of the morning, a veterinarian slammed the door on his big, red extended-cab pickup and walked over with his little black bag. "Boys, I saw a scorpion in the house last night. I'm sure that's a sign," he said in a jovial voice to a couple of guys standing next to the cattle pen. He glanced over at Aboy and Purse and held out his hand. "Larry Brooks," he said, "large-animal doctor extraordinaire."

"What's it a sign of?" Aboy asked him as he shook his hand.

The burly, red-faced vet laughed. "Sign it's gonna rain. Lord, if it don't, we might as well close up shop for good around here."

Aboy and Purse followed the vet through the maze of pens, the slats a dusty, peeling red, cows milling about in most of them. They stopped next to an empty pen, and the vet began to set up his equipment. He said he had a hundred fifty cows to check that morning.

"Hey, Donnie," he said to a tall, slender man leaning against the slats of the pen and smoking a roll-your-own cigarette. "How's it hanging?"

Donnie Bode tipped his hat. "Can't complain," he said. "Wouldn't do no good nohow."

Mr. Bode said he was 64 years old. Said he couldn't wait another day for the rains to come; he had to sell. "These calves ain't ready for market and the cows are gettin' thin," he said. Nodding toward a pen of brown and white Charolais calves he'd brought in that morning, he shook his head. "They needed another month or two to really be ready for market."

It was hot and loud and dusty in the dimly lit barn, and the old rancher's mood was dim too. "It's not easy, it's disgusting and it's not fun," he told Purse as he stood with one foot propped up on the bottom rung, his elbows propped across the top. "For the last four summers we've just burned up."

The vet had his needles and little medicine bottles set up on a portable table in the middle of the pen. He waited for a cowboy to herd the cattle into a chute so he could check them for cancer or brucelosis; meanwhile he talked to Aboy about his practice.

"See, y'all need to tell your boss that what we got out here is a trickle-down effect, and it's not good," he was saying as he stuck a hypodermic needle into the rubber lid on a little bottle of medicine. "If the rancher's not makin' it, the vet's not makin' it and if the vet's not making it, the merchants in town aren't makin' it. We've lost a lot of livestock in this county the past few years. Ranchers getting' older. Selling out, subdividing, turning their ranches into huntin' operations. I don't get to work on a lot of deer."

The vet's blue work shirt was already soaked through with sweat, and his big, open face was shiny red. He walked over to the first cow in the chute. While a cowboy with big, broken-looking hands forced open the cow's mouth and looked at the blocky yellow teeth to check to see how old she was, the vet stuck a needle into her hip to draw blood. Then he walked back to his little table and unrolled a long clear plastic sleeve.

"What's that for?" Purse asked Aboy.

Aboy grinned. "I thought you was a country boy."

The vet put his arm into the plastic sleeve, strolled back over to the cow, lifted up her tail and stuck his arm inside her clear up to the shoulder. The cow bellowed, and her eyes bulged out.

"Damn, what's he doing?" Purse asked Aboy.

"You've heard of a finger fuck? Well, what you're looking at is a shoulder fuck, only it's up her ass hole. Checking to see if she's pregnant. Wouldn't you like to have that job?"

Aboy and Purse watched him do the pregnancy test on maybe half a dozen cows before they noticed Hayden Dalrymple escorting Red through the maze of pens and chutes. She was like a cactus flower in the dirt and noise of the barn. An old, wrinkled man in a stained, broken-in cowboy hat and faded jeans stuck out his knobby hand. "I'm Joe Norris," he told Red, touching his hand to his hat. "It's good to meet you."

"Good to meet you, Mr. Norris," Red said, taking his scarred and knobby hand in hers. "How long you been out here?"

"Well, now," he said, "I've been ranchin' since '39, but my place—we call it the 4N—it's been in the wife's family since aught-8. And I want to tell you, I was with the Soil Conservation Service during the drought of the '30s, and this is as bad or worse. We need some help out here."

"I know you do, Mr. Norris," Red said, her blue eyes looking into his. "And we're going to see what we can do. That's why I'm here this morning, to see what needs to be done."

She walked on toward Purse and Aboy, then turned back to Mr. Norris. "I wish I could make it rain," she said.

"You and me both," Joe Norris said.

"What they're havin' to do," Dalrymple was telling her as the two of them walked up, "is sell off their herd gradually. Joe was tellin' me the other day, he said he's got his herd on a three-pasture system. Rotates 'em on a three-month basis, but he still don't have enough forage to go into the winter with. And he hasn't had enough the last three years. And Joe Norris isn't the only one. They're all having to cut back and cut back."

Aboy opened the gate, so Red could walk into the pen. The vet was just pulling his arm out of a plastic sleeve. It was slimy and wet. He used a new one for each cow. He wiped his arm on a grimy little towel, wiped his face with it, then shook hands with Red.

Three young guys about Purse's age, cowboys who helped herd the cows out of the trucks and into the pens, were taking a break and had sauntered over to see who the visitor was. They climbed up on the top rail and sat down, their boot heels hooked into a lower rail. Red noticed them. "How you doin' fellas?" she said. "Good to see ya."

"You oughtta try that, Ms. Ryder," one of the cowboys, a blonde-haired Dennis the Menace look-alike, said, a big grin on his freckled face. With a hand-rolled cigarette between his fingers, he pointed toward the doc, who already had his arm in another of the plastic sleeves. He plunged in, and the cow bellowed.

"I don't think so," Red said, shaking her head and grinning. "I know what.... Well, let's just say I'll leave it to the expert."

"Aw, come on," another of the cowboys on the top rail urged her. "You're not one of those scaredy-cat city folk, are you, Ms. Ryder?"

"You need to show a little respect to your betters," Aboy muttered.

"No, no, that's all right," Red said. She glanced at the doc, who shrugged, as if to say, "It's all right with me." He had a clean plastic sleeve already unrolled.

Red walked over to him, and he blew into the sleeve to open it up and then rolled it up Red's arm. A heifer was already in the chute having her teeth checked. The doc lifted up her tail. He did a little bow and gestured with his arm like a doorman. "Have at it," he said, and Red's arm sunk in up to the shoulder with a sucking sound.

At that very moment, with Red's arm in to the max, with a grimace on her face and her eyes bulged out like the poor ol' cow's, a white flash of light blinded them all. Aboy and Purse looked up to see Nabob Slidell hop down off the side of the pen and scurry toward the light outside. Normally Nabob scurried toward the dark, as Purse and Aboy well knew, but this time he knew they would be right behind him. He had a flash camera in his hand, and they could hear him laughing like a hyena.

Nabob Slidell, the other party's dirty-tricks guy-for-hire had tracked them down. Aboy and Purse both knew, and so did Red, that they would see that picture again, and soon. It would be all over the state by sundown.

Aboy and Purse glanced at each other, both thinking the same thing. They raced out of the pen through the confusing maze of chutes. Turning a corner, Aboy stepped into a pile of slick new cow shit, and they both bounced into Haydren Dalrymple who was coming around the corner from the opposite direction. "What the hell," he managed to grunt as all three of them tumbled in a heap in the dirt.

"Sorry sir, sorry," a huffing Aboy apologized as they untangled themselves and raced to the car. Slidell's dust lingered, but his red pickup was already a couple of blocks away. They climbed into the station wagon, and Aboy peeled out of the parking spot, just missing a young cowboy, who shot them the bird and shouted, though Purse couldn't hear what he had to say.

He could sure smell Aboy, though. He had slimy greenish cow shit all over the right hip of his white suit.

They caught up with Slidell at a stoplight. "Get him!" Aboy commanded. Purse hopped out of the car and raced up to the passenger side of Slidell's truck. What he was going to do, he wasn't really sure—maybe grab the camera—but the light changed just as he was reaching for the door handle. Slidell took off, truck tires squealing, and Purse caught hold of the sideboard and vaulted into the bed. They were already out of town, and Slidell had speeded up to at least 50. When he glanced through the rear window and saw Purse sprawled out in the back of the truck, he started swerving from one side of the two-lane road to the other, all the while picking up speed.

Aboy was right behind, horn blasting, as they climbed into the rocky hills beyond the Llano River bridge. Slidell had to have been hitting 75 or 80; the truck tires squealing, gripping for purchase, each time he hurtled around a switchback up the side of the hill.

Purse was thinking about trying to find something to hold on to, reach around through the side window and grab the camera and throw the film into the deep gulch on the driver's side of the road. For some reason, Slidell didn't think to roll up the window, probably because he was too busy negotiating the turns. Each time Purse tried to get to his feet, though, Slidell would swerve and down Purse would go, banging his knees on the truck bed. Each time Slidell glanced back through the window, Purse could see his nasty, little rodent face, the sun glinting off his thick gold-rimmed glasses, his forehead sweating beneath what was left of his yellow hair.

"I felt like I was staring at the face of pure political evil," Purse told Aboy later. Everybody knew he would do anything to get his candidate elected, legal or illegal, and he sure as hell wouldn't show any mercy to some little pissant pursebearer from the opposition. Purse could see the edge of the gulch each time he was slung toward the driver's side of the truck. Aboy was staying right with them.

Purse had just managed to crawl over to the edge of the truck bed, get to his knees and with his right arm begin to reach around and through the window when Slidell got to the crest of the hill. A cattle truck, an 18-wheeler, was making the long, slow climb in their lane. Slidell hit the brakes, and Purse tumbled out of the bed of the truck. He managed to get a foothold, briefly, on the running board, but he couldn't hold on to the window. Down he went into the dust and gravel. He landed on the heels of his hands and on his knees, bouncing a couple of times for good measure and ripping holes in his J. C. Penney suit pants and in the skin of his knees. Red blood mingled with the lizard-green fabric.

Slidell jerked his truck around the cattle truck, barely missing a pickup coming down the hill. Aboy pulled up beside Purse, who was getting to his feet and surveying the damage to his hands and knees and his torn and dusty clothes. Both he and Aboy were soaked with sweat.

"Any broken bones?" Aboy asked.

"Not that I know of, but my knees sure smart." He tried to brush the dust off his pants, but the sweat had turned the dust into mud. He rubbed his dripping forehead, and his hand came away muddy too. He couldn't catch his breath.

"Well, let's get on back," Aboy said, his red face making him look like he was on the verge of tears. Both of them knew they might have just spent their last day in the employ of the Rose Marie Ryder for Senator campaign.

Aboy drove down the hill slowly, every window down because of the stench. By the time they got back to town they were pretty much resigned to whatever their fate would be. Aboy was chuckling. "You looked like a pinball bouncing around in the back of that truck," he said.

It reminded Purse of the time he'd found Aboy in the back of a pickup, an El Rancho to be precise, driven by a mother and daughter blonde tag team. Only Aboy had been sprawled out dead drunk.

"I'm tellin' you, that fucking little miscreant is lucky I didn't apprehend him," Aboy muttered. "I would have wrung his goddamn little chicken neck."

"So why was he out here?" Purse asked. "I woulda figured a big-time campaign whore like Nabob Slidell would have better things to do than be lurking around a West Texas auction barn."

"I don't know," Aboy said. "Maybe it's a sign of respect. Maybe he wanted to see for himself what Red's up to, and maybe he just couldn't help himself when he saw the photo op. Makes me think about when Elijah and the sons of Baal went at it trying to get the attention of Jehovah, 'cept we're going up against the son of Beelzebub. I guess you see now what we're up against. There's nothing that little four-eyed cockroach won't do."

They knew they had to get back to the cattle auction as quick as they could. Red was waiting, and she didn't like to be kept cooling her heels any amount of time, much less 20 minutes in a smelly old cattle barn.

They parked in front of the cafe, and Purse got out of the car. He looked down at his torn pants, his scraped and bloody hands. Aboy still smelled like shit.

"Let's go," he said, the way you'd say let's mosey on over to the gallows. They found Red in Dalrymple's office leaning back against the edge of his desk, her arms folded across her chest. They stood before her like Abbot and Costello, like the Three Stooges with one missing. Dalrymple was not in sight.

Red pursed her lips and shook her head. "I won't even ask," she said in a low voice.

★ ★ SIX ★ ★

The campaign staff, if you could call it that, had breakfast most every morning of the week at Alma's, a little hole-in-the-wall Mexican cafe on South First. Most mornings, Red would join them, and so would Sue Bee, the campaign manager, but on this morning, the day after the auction-barn ambush, the busy little Sue Bee was doing an interview with the *Fort Worth Star Telegram*. Alma herself, in her white, puffy-sleeved peasant blouse and turquoise-and-yellow striped skirt, was a slow-moving, easygoing, seen-everything *mamacita*. Alma loved Red. Told her she didn't eat enough to keep a bird alive.

"*¿Como esta, mi Almita?*" Red greeted her. "*¿Como esta su esposo, y los hijitos?*" She put her arms around the hefty Alma and kissed her on the cheek. The staff took that to be a sign Red was in a good mood, despite what had happened. Purse took it for a sign to order a full breakfast—Alma's homemade *chorizo*, refried beans, hot flour tortillas, strong coffee, a big glass of fresh orange juice.

While they ordered, Red made the rounds of the cafe, shaking hands with the working men sitting in the booths, with a few government workers who knew about the place. Everybody knew Red, wanted to say hello, and that was purely because of the raids. Before the raids, not one Texan in ten, not even in Austin, could have told you who their comptroller was. Now, the campaign had people coming up almost every place they went with that famous picture from the Houston paper, the one where Red has her chin right in the face of a good ol' boy who ran a big no-money-down, pay-by-the-month furniture store in Greenville. Red was so little and he was so big, her chin came about to his chest, but he was raring back like a big backward parenthesis. Purse was hoping they wouldn't be coming in with another picture pretty soon.

While Red strolled from table to table, Aboy was telling Olene about how he and Purse had come close to tearing Nabob Slidell apart limb from limb and smashing his camera into tiny, little pieces. His version of the story was absolutely true, except for the part about how the two of them caught up with Slidell on the mountain top just outside town and would have gotten the camera with the incriminating film if he hadn't pulled a gun on them and knocked young Purse down in the dirt when he, Aboy, tried to disarm him.

It was a good story, even if nobody believed it. Actually Aboy and Purse were amazed. Although she wouldn't let Aboy back in the car until he had gone to the men's room and tried to wash the cow shit off his shoe and pants, Red blamed herself. She said she shouldn't have let the young cowboys get to her the way they had.

They ended up going by a western-wear store in Junction, where Aboy bought a pair of jeans from the Big and Tall department for the ride home.

"You know why that happened?" Aboy said that night. He and Purse were sitting at an outside table under the big live oaks at Otto's Biergarten, a pitcher of Shiner Bock on the wooden table. "Testosterone, or the lack thereof, is the reason that happened. The only reason she felt compelled to reach up that cow's ass is because she's not a man. She felt she had to prove her manhood, and now she's going to pay the price for it."

Aboy at breakfast still looked a little down-in-the-mouth. He ordered *menudo*, but Purse decided that was a sign he still hadn't recovered from Saturday night at the Poodle Dog, not Friday in the auction barn. Every Saturday night he was in town, you'd find Aboy at the Poodle Dog Tavern, a dark little stale-beer-smelling den with a shuffle board game and no windows. It was way out on Burnet Road. Maybe even Sunday night if Don Walzer was yodeling at the Poodle Dog. Aboy loved that yodeling. He called Don Walzer the Caruso of Comanche County.

Olene Whitten took little bites of her usual, dry toast, and washed it down with a small glass of orange juice. Olene was tall and skinny with short black hair fading over to gray. Olene was the campaign's official worrier. She was the one who had to figure out how to get Red from point A to point B, not to mention reading her mind when there really wasn't anything in Red's mind to read about where she needed to go. She already had her little black notebook out, plotting times and schedules and planning events between now and election day. Purse noticed the furrow between her eyes. Like a new-plowed field, it was deep and headed up toward her hairline.

"Anybody see the polls?" Red wanted to know. Her big mound of refried beans, courtesy of Alma, was disappearing fast. (What Alma didn't know was that Red ate a lot, and often, only her metabolism was so speeded up, food didn't have time to settle into fat.)

Purse had seen the polls in the Sunday *Morning News*. They had Jimmy Dale at 56, Red at 30, with 14 undecided. Normally Joe Frank Golden, Red's press secretary, was on hand to give the poll figures, as bad as they were. This morning, Joe Frank was recovering from some kind of stomach virus, or something. Aboy told Purse he thought he had ulcers.

"I saw 'em, Red," Purse said. "They're not bad for this far out, with all that TV he's been doing. Once we get our spots up and running, we can make up a lotta numbers."

That's what he had heard Aboy say. He felt proud that he was the one to answer, but no one else seemed to notice. Aboy was trying to get the waitress's attention. He wanted a glass of ice water. Olene was deep into her little black leather notebook.

"'Fraid not, Wily, my boy," Red said. "We're going back to the days of yesteryear, back before Beaver Cleaver and Hoss Cartwright and Ed Sullivan and Amos 'n Andy. Back to the days of Sam Rayburn and Harry Truman. In other words, what I'm telling you all is that there won't be any TV." She daintily dabbed the juice from her *juevos rancheros* with a corn tortilla.

Purse thought he had misunderstood until he heard Aboy choke on his *menudo*. His face was as red as the bowl of salsa on the table, and his gullet was working like a fighting cock after his first kill. "Food down the wrong pipe," he managed in a wheezy voice, wiping his red, sweat-beaded forehead with a paper napkin.

When he finally got himself pulled back together, Aboy stared at Red the way he probably stared at "the little woman," back when he had a little woman, like, "Precious, you may have the best of intentions, but you're a woman, and you just don't know what you're talking about."

They were all staring at her. Flaco Jimenez was ripping through a lively Tejano accordion tune on the jukebox.

"Don't you all go looking at me that way," Red said, her blue eyes flashing like sunshine off polar ice. She stared back hard at them, locking in on first one then the other around the table. It was hard to hold her stare, so Purse looked down and poured some more cream in his coffee cup.

"Listen," she said, "you all know as well as I do that there's no way in hell we can outspend this bunch," she said. A jangly gold bracelet banging on the table whenever she gestured. "I could be on the phone from hell to Sunday, every goddamn minute of the day 'til election day. I could be begging and wheedling and kissing some fat trial lawyer's ass to beat the band. I could climb in bed with Donald Trump and whoever his wife is these days, and I couldn't raise as much money as Jimmy Dale Sisco carries with him to the race track out at Del Mar every year."

Red took a swallow of coffee and motioned to Alma for a refill. "You all know what TV costs," she said. "We're just not gonna play that game."

She knew what they were thinking, every single one of them at the table. It's all well and good not to play that game, as she put it, if you wanted to lose, or if you had already decided there was no way you could win. Her winning was a long shot anyway, but none of them were planning to give it away.

Jimmy Dale had had his TV spots up and running for months. You could hear his little jingle everywhere you went, from the Panhandle to Port Isabel, from Texarkana to El Paso. It was like elevator music. Once you heard it, you couldn't get it out of your mind. He had somehow got the rights to the old Davy Crockett song, so now everywhere you went you would hear: "Jimmy, Jimmy Sisco, the man to lead this state."

It was like brain-washing, like they had done in Korea 25 years earlier, when GIs got captured by the Red Chinese and a few of them got so addled they wanted to stay over there and eat rice and pull rickshaws for a living. They should have called Jimmy Dale Sisco the Manchurian Candidate. Purse had come to the conclusion that their only chance was that the jingle would drive enough people stark raving mad before election day, they would start jumping out of office windows, wouldn't be able to find their way to the polls. They would be staggering around in the streets moaning and holding their hands over their ears.

But the fact is, even if people hated that commercial, they knew who Jimmy Dale was, just as they knew Charmin toilet paper or Coca-Cola. He was like Elvis; you didn't even have to call his last name. Purse, green as he was, wasn't sure enough of them knew who Red Ryder was. The tax raids had helped. She had built up enough name recognition that when the party fathers came looking for what Sammy Redd called a sacrificial lamb to run against Jimmy Dale Sisco, they picked her. "I'm pretty damn sure that won't be enough," he told Aboy.

It seemed to Purse that TV was the way you played the game, the way you had to play the game. This wasn't the 1800s anymore, when Abraham Lincoln and years later Sam Rayburn ran races where they went by horse-and-buggy from town to town campaigning, sometimes with their opponents.

No matter. No TV it would be. What Rosie Ryder wants is what Rosie Ryder gets, though what she wanted reminded Purse of the Aztec calendar Alma had taped up on the cinder-block wall behind the cash register. Here was a beautiful, nearly-naked Aztec princess splayed out, all set to be sacrificed to the Aztec gods. In his mind's eye, Purse saw a redheaded, freckled-faced woman— nearly naked, he was ashamed to admit—about to be sacrificed to the gods of political necessity. It was not a pretty picture.

Red turned to Aboy, who by now was swabbing up the last of his *menudo* with a flour tortilla. "Come up with anything yet?" she asked him.

Aboy's job, besides driving Red everywhere she went, was to do what the political pros call opposition research. He would snoop around state agency offices and courthouses around the state—like the one at Sulphur Springs—and see if he could come up with any nuggets of information, little incendiary devices that might blow up in a candidate's face at an opportune time. Like Mike Hammer, he was looking for any skanky little skeletons in Jimmy Dale's giant walk-in closet, stuff he had just as soon keep locked away somewhere tight, that is, if he hadn't been able to dispose of it once and for all.

From what Purse saw of Jimmy Dale that night at the Jimmy D, he was the kind of guy who must have had skeletons galore. As Aboy told him once, he said he was looking for dead boys or live girls that might once have shared the bed of the goat man from Sonora. As Aboy well knew, some things you can't flush away (like pretty little, pregnant Mexican girls, maybe?). Either they are buried in the public record somewhere or in somebody's memory, somebody who had just as soon let them out as long as Jimmy Dale Sisco couldn't find out about it. Chances are, Jimmy Boy had the money and the wherewithal to keep most of his dirty, little secrets locked away in the dark, but Aboy was on his trail anyway.

"So far, I have yet to uncover anything that every S.O.B in Texas doesn't know already," Aboy had to admit. "The man's filthy rich, he's got a show house in Highland Park, a second home in Aspen, half a million acres of ranchland in Texas and Wyoming and a J. R. Ewing-style show ranch in the Panhandle with a boot-shaped pool out back. And, of course, he's got the Jimmy D. He's also the proud proprietor of 11 working ranches, on which he runs more than 11,000 head of cattle, 2,000 of them purebred Brangus. His wife Sissy's two years younger, she went to Hockaday and SMU, daddy's even richer than Jimmy, and her real name's not Sissy. It's Seawillow."

"Is that all?" Red asked.

"Well, Sissy, or Seawillow, is not his first wife. When he was in high school, he got this little Mexican girl whose mama worked for his family pregnant. And I'm not talkin' about Jovita, although it could have been her mother. One afternoon they skipped school, drove down to Acuña and got married. Jimmy Dale Senior had it annulled."

"Anything else?"

"Well, he's got a third interest in a hospital in Amarillo, he flies around the country in a Sabreliner corporate jet he calls the Yellow Rose, that is when he's not in his helicopter or his Beechcraft twin-engine turboprop plane." Aboy chuckled. "Other than that, he's just like you and me."

"Is that all?" Red asked again.

Aboy reached for the tortilla basket. "Give me a few days, and a trusted acquaintance of mine over at the Railroad Commission may have something of value for us. He was hinting of skullduggery involving oil-well vacancy tracts out in West Texas."

"Give you a few goddamn days, and this election'll be all over but the shouting," Red said. "And you don't need anymore flour tortillas," she told Aboy, slapping his hand.

Her eyes snapped on Aboy and augered into him. Purse was afraid they were in for another Dairy Queen-style hooraw, but Red let the moment pass and looked over at Olene.

"Where you got me going this week, honey?" she asked. She pushed back from the table, took a little spray bottle of perfume from her purse, and waggled a finger at Alma to come fill her coffee cup.

Olene frowned and stared at her little black book. "I've got you in the office making calls this morning," she said, "then this afternoon, you've got a hearing to go to on brucellosis that's hit the Valley real hard. It's here in Austin—not the brucellosis but the meeting. And then tonight, you're supposed to go by the Wagon Wheel to meet and greet. The cattle raisers are puttin' on some kind of shindig."

It seemed like Olene's perpetual frown had flown across the table and fastened itself to Red's face. Purse knew why. It was the morning calls Olene had her scheduled to make. Calls for money. She hated with a passion to call up a person and be all friendly and then beg for money. Olene practically had to strap her in her chair and do the dialing for her before she would make the calls. Purse was well aware that even if they were not doing TV, they still needed money.

Headed back to the office, the sun bright but not yet burning, Purse was just happy they weren't going out of town. He spent most of the day in the campaign office, writing out some press releases and calling some supporters out in West Texas.

"When y'all gonna be gettin' your TV spots up?" Bill Young out in Floydada wanted to know. Bill was county judge in Crosby County and an old friend of Red's. Purse had to tell him the sad truth and then listen to him rant about this day and age and how times have changed and how Red must have her head up her ass. And Judge Young wasn't the only one he had heard that little sermon from, from every part of the state.

After Purse hung up, something popped into his mind, and he almost called the judge back. He was thinking about how, after the run-in with Nabob Slidell at the auction barn and after Aboy had bought his new blue jeans, they drove Red over to a residential section of Junction, where they walked through neighborhoods and knocked on doors. And people were friendly, although Purse was thinking they had to be wondering why he looked like a mugging victim from the big city. (Red told some of them he had to do some work on the car on the way over.)

They seemed to like her and wanted to hear what she had to say. That experience, Purse figured, just might have had something to do with Red's decision not to raise TV money.

Just about when they were finishing up their day in Junction, after their little adventure with Nabob Slidell, Hayden Dalrymple drove up in his pickup. He got out, walked around to the passenger side, and held the door open for a tall, slender woman with white hair and a very wrinkled face. She was wearing an expensive-looking light-green dress, probably from Nieman-Marcus.

"Ms. Ryder, I got somebody here wants to meet you," Dalrymple said. The woman was frail-looking with skin that seemed like linen, like you could see through it, but you could tell she had been a beauty in her day.

"This is Mary Ann Wright," Dalrymple said.

"It's an honor," Red said, taking Mrs. Wright by her wrinkled elbows and kissing her lightly on the cheek. Purse didn't know who she was, but Red obviously did, and so did Aboy.

"Mrs. Wright didn't know you were comin' to town," Dalrymple said, "but when she heard you on the radio this morning, she hopped in her truck and drove on in. It's what, 25 miles, Mrs. Wright?"

"About that," she said in a quiet, refined voice, "but I've made it so many times it's second nature to me."

She turned to Red. "I know it's presumptuous of me, Ms. Ryder, but the reason I made the drive in this morning is to see whether you and your friends might join me for lunch at the ranch today."

"I'd be honored, Ms. Wright, although I'm not sure our schedule allows it today, as much as I'd love to," Red said. She turned to Aboy.

"I think we're fine," he said, anxious to get back in the boss's good graces, "but why don't I borrow Mr. Dalrymple's phone when we go by the auction barn and I'll give Olene a call. I'm sure she can rearrange things if she has to."

That's what they did, although Aboy told Purse afterward Olene was none too happy. Anything that upset her carefully made plans put her in an even more foul mood than usual. Actually, Purse was thinking, you couldn't blame her. Keeping Red's schedule straight was a bear, plus she was going to have to call the state retail grocer's association and explain why Red wouldn't be showing up at their annual convention in San Antonio that afternoon.

Mrs. Wright was driving an older model International pickup, a faded orangish-yellow in color. Red rode with her, while Aboy and Purse followed. As they drove—on Highway 377 the first 15 miles, an unpaved ranch road the last 10—Aboy told the Mary Ann Wright tale.

Back in the early 1900s, when she was just a little girl, a tornado had come through the little nearby ranching town of Rocksprings, where she lived with her folks. It did a lot of damage—destroyed the house where Mary Ann lived, killed her folks and picked her up and blew her clean over the water tower.

"It's the God's honest truth," Aboy said when Purse looked at him with a cocked eyebrow. "I've read about it in old newspapers. Somehow she came down and landed safely. For years and years, she was known as Cyclone Mary, Child of Destiny."

Her destiny, for a little while at least, turned out to be a big rancher named Sig Wright, one of the largest landholders in West Texas. But not long after she and Sig married, the man died when his horse fell on him while he was chasing some cattle down a dry wash. The Wright clan figured the young widow would sign over her rights to the ranch and start a new life elsewhere.

"They didn't know Mary Ann Wright," Aboy said, following the white dust raised by Mrs. Wright's pickup. "She was still in her 20s, but she worked that gol-durned ranch like a man would. Year after year, decade after decade, the place prospered, especially after the biggest oil field in West Texas came in on the property. And she ain't tight at all. She's got museums, hospitals, college buildings—and they've all got the Siegfred Wright name over the front door all over the U.S. of A. Never married again. Close to 80, and she's still a working rancher."

After what seemed like 50 miles on the hard, dusty road through rough Hill Country ranchland, they came to a gate over a cattle guard. Mrs. Wright stopped her truck and opened her door, then closed it again when Red got out first. Underneath a wrought-iron sign that read "Cyclone Ranch," Red pushed open the heavy iron gate, motioned them on through after Mrs. Wright and then shut the gate.

They drove another couple of miles, through an oak mott and across shallow streams, one after another like the lines of a hand. It may have been summer, but these spring-fed streams were still running clear and fresh. Crossing the last stream, they pulled up before a large, two-story native-stone house sheltered by three gnarled live oaks. Across the front of the house, on both levels, were wide verandas, and on the lower level maybe a dozen large wooden rockers. It looked cool and inviting in the shade. Red flowers grew out of hanging pots on the veranda, and at a couple of them hummingbirds whirred and darted their tiny beaks into the blossoms.

"What a beautiful place!" Red said as they walked up to the porch. A big collie dog came loping up, tail wagging, from behind the house and rubbed up against Mrs. Wright. "Down, Jit," she said. "You be nice, now."

Walking slowly and a bit unsteadily, her hand on Red's arm, she ushered them into a large living room with bright Indian rugs on the floor, lots of books on shelves throughout the room and a huge fireplace at the far end. Above the fireplace was a large color portrait of two handsome people. The woman, dark-haired and beautiful, was Mrs. Wright; the man, slightly older with a distinguished-looking mustache, was, of course, her husband.

"That fireplace is absolutely magnificent, Mrs. Wright," Aboy said. "It's positively baronial."

"Sig built it by hand," she said. "He found some stones he liked on a ridge across the creek, and he carried every one of them home in a tow sack."

She glanced up toward the painting. "This house was his dream place. He found the site when he was ten years old, out herding cattle for his daddy. Told himself right then and there he was going to own it someday, build a house on it. And he did, years later. The tragedy is, he didn't get to enjoy it very long."

After lunch—chicken-salad sandwiches on triangles of toast, fresh tomatoes, lemon icebox pie—they strolled back out to the veranda and each of them took a rocking chair. "An older man named Ruperto, who seemed to be cook and sort of the ranchhouse manager, brought out a pitcher of iced tea and set it on a table near Mrs. Wright. She poured glasses for all. Purse would have dozed off it was so calm and peaceful, the sound of doves cooing in the big live oaks, a little breeze, but he enjoyed listening to the two women talk. Even Aboy was quiet, for the most part.

Purse was fascinated by the hummingbirds—he had never seen one up close—so he stood up and walked over to the edge of the veranda, just watching. They didn't seem to notice his presence. When he sat back down, Mrs. Wright was talking about politics and about why it was so important for Red to run the hardest race she had ever run in her life.

"It's not just for you, Mrs. Ryder," she was saying in the soft, refined way she had about her. "It's for the people of this state, and, in a perverse way, for Mr. Sisco himself."

She smiled and shook her head slightly. Purse stared at her, at the seamed face, the beauty of the bone structure underneath, the calm assurance of her voice.

"I know Jimmy," she said. "Know his family. They're even neighbors, you might say. I wouldn't tell this to just anyone, because I prefer not to speak ill of the dead, but Jimmy's father did everything he could to help some of the Wrights run me off this ranch. I won't say anymore about it. That was a long time ago. But what I will say is that Jimmy Dale Sisco has no business being a United States senator. And if he somehow gets elected, you mark my words, he'll live to regret it. We all will."

At that moment, just for a second, Purse could see the young woman underneath the fragile old lady she had become, the young woman with fiery eyes and a determined jaw, the woman who turned out to be tough as a boot when people tried to run over her. And won. He had a feeling that strong woman was still running the Cyclone Ranch.

A little bit later, when she walked her guests out to the van, Purse could tell that Red was close to tears, even though he had never seen her that way. The two women hugged. "You don't know how much this means to me," Red said. "I won't let you down."

Mrs. Wright patted her on the back and smiled. "You just keep working night and day, dear, let people get to know who you are and what you stand for, and good things will happen."

She shook hands with Aboy and Purse. "You boys take good care of her," she said. "She needs you."

On the way back to Austin, Red was quiet for a long time. Purse would glance back and she would be staring out the window at the passing countryside. After a while, she handed him the envelope Ruperto had handed to her as they left. He opened it up, unfolded a check from Mrs. Wright and handed it to Aboy. Made out to the campaign, it was for $10,000.

About five in the evening, Purse trudged out to the Crusher, rolled down the windows, gripped the blistering hot steering wheel with a towel and headed across the river to home sweet home. He fed Shoogy, made himself a baloney sandwich and got a Lone Star out of the icebox.

He called Mama, called Jo Lynne and told her about Cyclone Mary, Child of Destiny, then took a cold shower and put on some clean jeans and a short-sleeve plaid cowboy shirt with genuine imitation-pearl buttons. He sprinkled talcum powder into his boots and pulled them back on, even though it was too hot to be wearing boots. He thought about wearing his Resistol, but hats just didn't seem to like him. They make his ears stick out like Jethro in *The Beverly Hillbillies*, someone once teased him.

It was about nine when he showed up at the Wagon Wheel. Cars and pickups were parked in front, out back and up and down both sides of the road. Through the dust swirling up from the parking lot, he read the portable sign under the old live oak tree out front: "Tonight: Tex Thomas and the Dangling Wranglers!"

Purse liked Tex Thomas and the Dangling Wranglers. They were sort of cowboy hippies or hippie cowboys, whatever you wanted to call a band whose members had long hair, wore boots and sang cowboy songs.

Inside the Wagon Wheel it was loud and crowded and smoky. The place was full of big, red-faced men in hats and boots and western-cut suits, either talking politics with each other or making fools of themselves with young and pretty secretary types from the Capitol, women who had escaped little towns from across the state, drawn by the seductive smell of power and money. Most of the women had on tight jeans and bright-colored boots and western blouses, the shiny pearl buttons barely holding the blouses shut. They had a way of smiling and showing their pretty teeth no matter what it was they were saying. If they hadn't been so pretty, they would have resembled so many whinnying horses.

Purse made his way through the cafe portion of the Wagon Wheel and on back to the dance hall. The music was loud. Quite a few couples were doing the two-step, though a lot more folks were sitting at row after of row of picnic tables around the waxed pine dance floor. They were drinking and smoking and trying to talk loud enough to be heard over Tex and the Wranglers.

In a far corner of the big room, he caught a glimpse of Aboy. He was hard to miss. He had on his usual white summer suit—he had a closet-full—a turquoise shirt and a yellow cockateel tie one of his former lady friends had bought him in Nuevo Laredo. He never deigned to wear cowboy duds, no matter where he was.

Aboy was talking to Claude Small, a West Texas rancher turned lobbyist for the cattle raiser's association. Small was anything but. He must have been six-six, at least, and his belly hung out over his big belt buckle like a Rocky Mountain foothill. He'd written out a check to Red a couple of times.

Purse found an empty table, and Aboy made his way over, a waitress following in the wake he made through the crowd. "Honey, why don't you rustle us up a pitcher of cold Lone Star," he asked her, draping his meaty arm around her neck under the pretense of getting close enough for her to hear. She removed his arm like it was a dead copperhead and squirmed back through the crowd toward the bar.

"You seen the dastardly image?" he asked Purse.

"You mean from Junction?"

"Of course, that's what I mean," Aboy said. He reached into his inside jacket pocket and pulled out a folded-up brochure, pink with black letters. Sort of shielding it with his shoulder, he smoothed it out on a table.

On the outside, in big block letters, it said: CARE TO SEE WHAT ROSE MARIE RYDER HAS IN MIND FOR TEXAS?

Opening it, he saw the photo, a grainy black-and-white: Red with her whole arm inside the cow, her eyes—and the cow's—bulging so all you could see were the whites. If it hadn't been Red, he would have to concede it was about the funniest thing he had ever seen. In little letters at the bottom it said, "Paid for by a group of concerned rural Texans who believe that 'SISCO IS *THE MAN* FOR TEXAS.'"

" Red seen it yet?" he shouted.

"I don't know," Aboy said. "But she'll see it soon enough."

"Where is she?"

"Running late, as usual," he said. "And for that perhaps we should be grateful. Olene's gonna squire her over here when she gets through at some kinda 'women in communications' reception. Keep your eye out for her."

With the music playing, it was hard to hear yourself think, much less talk. Between songs, Aboy was telling him about how Olene had them going to Waco the next day for some kind of Baptist gathering, when he noticed out of the corner of his eye someone sidle up beside them. He turned to see a big brass armadillo-shaped belt buckle at eye level, and then his eyes drifted slowly upwards and landed on a beautiful olive-skinned Asian face. He forgot what he was saying. He couldn't stop staring at the beautiful girl's flashing black eyes. They were like nothing he had ever seen, unless, for anyone who knows coon hounds, it was the eyes of a proud little black-and-tan fyce with spark and sass and fire in them.

But she didn't have those eyes trained on Purse. She was looking at Aboy. He hadn't noticed her yet.

Purse turned his own frog-bulging eyes to the blouse—white silk and open to the armadillo. Over it, she wore a suede vest, burnt orange with lots of fringe that swayed when she breathed.

And then Aboy glanced up, his mouth wide open, his big fist holding a frosty mug of beer in midair. She held out a long and lovely hand to Aboy, and he took it, like he was hypnotized, mesmerized, martinized. Without saying a word, just with that mysterious smile on her face, she conjured him out of his chair and led him through the crowd to the center of the dance floor. She glided, like her feet didn't quite touch the shiny wood floor, like she was floating in slow motion. Aboy lapped along behind her like a big St. Bernard.

Purse stood up and stared. The whole crowd stared. He noticed her hair, like liquid ebony cascading down to her waist. He saw how it swayed against the white, very tight, silky-looking pants she wore. Her boots looked like white doeskin.

Tex and the Wranglers slid into "If I Said You Had a Beautiful Body Would You Hold it Against Me?" and like a cobra coming uncoiled, the mystery woman began to slink and slide and sway about Aboy like a flame.

Tex Thomas gave a "Yaa-ha!" and a big grin, the crowd yelled and clapped and the band kicked up the tempo with "Faking Love." The lovely young woman began prancing like a pony, tossing her shiny black mane and kicking up her white-booted heels behind her. For a big man, Aboy was almost graceful, and once he caught the beat, he ripped off his wide yellow hand-painted cockateel tie from Nuevo Laredo, slung his coat around his head and across the floor, and began grinning and galloping in little circles around his fine and frisky little pony.

Purse had never seen him in such a state, even though he had seen him kicking up his heels, so to speak. He remembered one cold night when the two of them were at the Golden Stallion in Amarillo. Red was back at the Days Inn, exhausted after one of her raids. Aboy got interested in two good-looking women at the next table. They turned out to be mother and daughter, though you couldn't tell which one was older unless you got up close enough to see the wrinkles around the mom's mouth and eyes and how her face was a bit furrier than her daughter's. That was the night that Aboy ended up sprawled out drunk in the back of the women's El Rancho pickup, and it was Purse chasing along a country road behind them, trying to get them to stop so he could rescue the big dope.

Tex and the Wranglers kicked it up yet another notch with "I'm Going Huntin'," the number Purse had heard Hank Williams Jr. do in person one night at the SPJST Hall in West. The other couples backed off to give Aboy and his lady room. Aboy's two-toned wingtips were a blur. His wiry hair was bouncing like a Brillo pad atop his big head. And then, quicker than a crow's wink, quicker than anything Purse had ever seen, the mystery lady flipped into a handstand right there in front of ol' Aboy. Her hair pooled onto the floor at his feet and somehow—it was the damndest thing—she hooked her heels over his shoulders, slithered down his back and ended up flailing and writhing on the floor between his splayed-out legs.

Purse glanced at Aboy's face. It was a deeper shade of red than ever, and he was rubbing his neck with the bright red bandanna he always kept in his back pocket.

"Is she having a fit?" Purse heard a woman standing nearby ask the man she was with.

"Naw, she's doing the Gator," he shouted back to her, never taking his eyes off the dance floor. "They do that over in Loosiana. What I'm wondering is whether that ol' boy she's with is fixin' to have a heart attack."

Aboy certainly looked like heart attack material. He was grinning and sweating and swaying at the knees like an elephant doing the limbo, and then he was pretending his fingers were six-shooters firing at the writhing woman on the floor. Then, suddenly, his mouth fell open like he had shot himself. Without missing a beat, he changed his hand jive so that he was aiming at Purse, a deer-in-the-headlights look on his broad beet face.

The crowd was going crazy, laughing and shouting and clapping their hands to the beat. It was so loud in there, Purse couldn't hear myself think, and he had no idea what Aboy's problem was. He thought maybe he was having a heart attack, until he happened to glance toward the back door, back in the shadows, and saw what had spooked his friend.

A guy with a TV camera was backing in through the door, about to plunge into the crowd, and just beyond him was Red herself, in a blue denim dress and tasteful black boots, with a red bandana scarf around her neck.

Purse didn't know which spooked Aboy the most, the camera or the comptroller, but he knew his friend was thinking about Junction and Nabob Slidell. In a flash he knew what Aboy was communicating with his hand signal. "Come on out here, boy, and get me outta this mess."

Purse knew he couldn't just walk out there and pull him off the floor; the crowd would have skinned them both alive. He would have to break in.

He got a funny feeling in the pit of his stomach, and he could feel lines of sweat dribbling out his underarms and down his sides, just like when Miss Ward back in eighth grade called him up to the front of the room to recite "Abou Ben Adam," and he hadn't memorized a line beyond "Abou Ben Adam, may his tribe increase, awoke one night from a deep dream of peace."

He didn't like to draw attention to himself as a kid and still didn't as a grownup. What's more, he would give anything not to have to venture onto a dance floor. That was one reason he joined the Church of God in Christ. They taught that dancing was a sin worthy of everlasting hell and damnation. "You'll be dancin', yessiree, when your feet hit those hot coals," Pastor Bud had said. "You'll be hoppin' like Hell, so to speak, looking for relief, endlessly."

If that wasn't excuse enough never to have to learn the shag or the mashed potato or the twist, even the cotton-eyed Joe, he don't know what was.

But like an old mama cow headed down a tick-dip chute, he didn't have any choice in the matter. He started snapping his fingers, and he got his neck gyrating in one direction and his hips in another, the way he had seen Rockabilly Ron Dawson, "the Blond Bomber," do one night at Geneva Hall in Falls City, Texas.

Bending down to pick up Aboy's cockateel tie, he slung it around his neck and strutted like Shoogy Red onto the floor. Aboy boogied past him, his face red, his turquoise shirt dark with sweat, and there was Purse, face to face with the most beautiful woman he had ever seen. She was swaying like a cobra, and he couldn't look away.

★ ★ SEVEN ★ ★

He couldn't tell whether his eyes had gotten so used to the dark that he could see like a cat or whether the sun was coming up over the trailer park. All he knew was that he had been stretched out on that bed, hands behind his head, eyes wide open, not being able to sleep a wink since he left Trieu's.

That was her name, Trieu Au Nguyen.

"Pronounce it like this," she told him. "True."

"True."

"Ow."

"Ow."

"Win."

"Win."

"Trieu Au Nguyen," she said with a laughing lilt in her voice. "True Ow Win."

He loved saying her name, and he kept saying it in his mind while he was lying there looking up at the trailer's tin roof. In the blue-tinted moonlight streaming in the little window above the bed, he could almost count the rivets running like steel bands above his head.

Whatever it was that was keeping him awake—excitement or guilt or just what J. Riley Hankins his preacher used to call pure-dee old lust—he knew his life had been turned upside down and shaken up, about like Trieu had turned herself upside down dancing with Aboy, God rest his soul once Red got hold of him for making a fool of himself yet again. (Purse himself didn't count. People didn't know him as well as they did Aboy, didn't connect him to Red.)

Like catgut stretched to the tightest twang, the nerves in his body were on edge and alive. He could feel it mainly in his stomach, and sometimes it seemed his skin sort of rippled of its own accord, like a horse shuddering away a fly. He liked the feeling, even though he wondered if he would ever see Trieu again after what happened.

What he was seeing was like one of those little plastic viewfinders his Uncle Clyde had given him one Christmas when he was a kid, where you look inside the little black box and pull down the lever and see a different color slide on the wheel. He would be looking into the beautiful brown eyes of Trieu staring back at him a couple of inches away, and then the slide would switch and there would be Jo Lynne looking at him with her cute little face all bunched up, like she knew what had happened and she couldn't decide whether to cry or hit him up the side of the head with her fists, or both. And then the slide would switch to Trieu. And then back to Jo Lynne, and he would see the tears spilling out of her ocean-blue eyes and running down her cheeks and plop-plop-plopping into the hair of the person who happened to be sitting in the chair at Hair Apparent. He had a feeling he was in a heap of trouble.

He and Jo Lynne James had been "an item" —that's how her mama put it—for going on two years. He had known her in high school, even though he was two years ahead of her. He would have asked her out back then, she was so pretty and bright and cheery, but she was always twined like a morning glory vine around Roy Towsen's arm.

Roy Towsen was a grade ahead of Purse, which made him three years older than Jo Lynne. Purse figured Jo Lynne's parents weren't too keen about her hanging out with an older man, especially an older man who smoked and drank and drove around town in a souped-up '53 Ford with modified Holley twin carbs. Maybe that's why she liked him, because her parents didn't.

She told Purse one time that whenever they complained she would remind her mama that she had been all of 15 when she married her daddy, Dewey James, and Dewey himself was 21. Anytime you saw Jo Lynne back then she would be wearing Roy's blue corduroy FFA jacket with the gold letters on the back, even though it drooped down nearly to her knees.

Strangely enough, Roy had a twin brother, Ray. They looked pretty much alike, both of them with black, wavy hair, greasy-looking hair that they combed back in a duck-ass, Elvis style. You could tell when they got older, they'd lose their hair, but now they just looked cool. The difference was Ray looked a little cleaner, a little smoother than his brother Roy. More refined. Ray might grow up to be a funeral director in a black suit and a skinny black tie and a name tag on his coat pocket, greeting the bereaved with an outstretched hand and a smarmy tone of condolence, while Roy would be out back changing the oil on the big Caddy hearse.

Purse always said that if he was a girl he would like Ray, but he wasn't and Jo Lynne was—or is—and she liked Roy. *Did* like Roy, that is. It was a long time before she would tell him why they broke up, she was so embarrassed. He had heard rumors, and they bothered him, but she never would say. Finally she did.

One Saturday afternoon in the fall, one of those beautiful times of the year that linger maybe a couple of weeks, Purse had to drive out the Old Wilson Road to talk to a fellow who raised banties. Jo Lynne rode out with him. What he remembered is that they had the radio on, listening to the Texas-Arkansas game. At least Purse was listening; Jo Lynne was talking about beauty school and how much it was going to cost.

On the way they had to pass the Towsen house. He remembered seeing an old hound under a chinaberry tree out beside the shed where Roy worked on his Ford. The old dog was sprawled in the dirt in a little sandy hole he had dug out for himself, and he had some kind of pink cancerous growths like turtle shells popping up on his back through the scratched-off fur. It was a sad sight, and after Jo Lynne had made little murmuring noises about the dog, it sort of irritated Purse that she knew his name was Puddin'. That's what they called him.

"What kind of folks call a dog Puddin'?" he teased her. "Here, Puddin', here Puddin'. That's dumb, Jo Lynne, just downright dumb."

"And this from a guy that's got a chicken named Sugar?" Jo Lynne said to the window, gesturing with her arm like she was a Jewish comedian on Ed Sullivan. "Who calls a chicken Sugar? Who calls a chicken anything?"

There was a smile on her face, but her eyes were flashing. Jo Lynne might be little, but she always gave as good as she got.

Purse couldn't scare up a decent answer, so he played the strong, silent Gary Cooper type and drove along for a couple of miles, all the while his questions about Jo Lynne and Roy rattling around in his brain. On the radio, Harry Jones, the Razorback speedster, broke loose for a long run before Duke Carlisle hauled him down from behind.

"Sooooooo Pig!" the Razorback crowd yelled on the radio.

"My sentiments exactly," Jo Lynne said

He was barely listening. Every time he tried to hook up the questions he wanted to ask to actual words, they hopped away like crickets. Finally, he asked her. Just straight out asked her. "So what about you and Roy?" he said, trying to make the question sound casual, like he was asking about the weather.

Arkansas scored, and the "Sooooo, pig!" started up again.

"What about me and Roy?" Jo Lynne said softly, all the while staring out the window like she thought bob-wire fences and flat, brown pastures were the most fascinating sights in the world. Her head was turned away from him, so all he could see were the wavy curls in her hair, light-brown and shiny. They had a lot of bounce and body, her friend Trudy at Hair Apparent told him once.

"You know, were y'all really wrapped up in each other? Really involved? Like, like did you spend the night with him and everything?"

He knew how he sounded. It made him want to grit his teeth, because he sounded so pathetic, like some lovesick teenager, like Wally Cleaver when his girl was two-timing him with that eel Eddie Haskell, but his throat was tight, and his stomach felt funny, and he wasn't sure he really wanted an answer. They were at the banty farmer's house, and he pulled off the road near the front gate and turned off the key. Neither of them got out, and Jo Lynne finally started talking in a quiet voice.

When he remembered what she told him that morning, he couldn't help but see row after row of little A-frame rooster sheds out beside that farmer's house on Old Wilson Road. Some of the birds were poking around inside the chicken-wire enclosures; there were others inside the sheds. One of them was atop his house, crowing like the sun's sentinel. He kept staring at them while Jo Lynne sat with her back against the front door of the car and told him about her and Roy. She had her left leg crossed on the seat between them, and while she talked she kept looking down and picking at the hem of her jeans and smoothing out a white bobbysock.

What she said was that one night Roy took her to his house and his parents weren't home. They had gone to visit Roy and Ray's older brother Elbert Lee, who was in Air Force basic training at Lackland Air Force Base in San Antonio. It was his first weekend furlough, and their dad was so proud. He kept telling people they were going down to San Antone to see Airman Towsen.

Of course, one of the reasons he was proud is because of how his boy ended up in the Air Force. He'd been given a choice: military or jail. He had gotten caught in the company of Jo Lynne's wild and crazy older brother, Weevil, robbing West Food Store. That was the time Weevil was trying to get to the grocery store office and fell through the ceiling onto the produce bin. He squashed whole bunches of purple grapes, and when Sheriff C. C. Maxey found him he thought Weevil had been shot in the back or stabbed because of all the red juice.

Weevil ended up with a two-year prison sentence, but Elbert Lee got off light, since he wasn't in the store at the time it was being burglarized. He was out in the parking lot in the car, said he didn't know what Weevil was up to. The two families weren't on speaking terms, since the Towsens believed Weevil had led Elbert Lee astray. From what Purse knew of Elbert Lee, he didn't need anybody leading him astray.

The folks would be gone all weekend. She and Roy hung around all Saturday evening, listening to records—Roy was a big Buddy Holly fan—drinking Lone Stars that Roy's daddy had in the ice box. Jo Lynne fixed supper for him—fried steak, fried potatoes and cream gravy, his favorite. After they finished eating, one thing led to another, and before Jo Lynne knew it, she said, they were in the parents' bedroom. It was dark, and their clothes were scattered on the floor and Roy was in the saddle, so to speak.

Now, Purse didn't enjoy thinking about it, and he sure didn't like looking at the picture in his mind, but Jo Lynne had to tell him this wasn't the first time. It wasn't like she was forced into doing something she didn't want to do. She had to tell him, or her story wouldn't have made much sense.

Her voice weak and trembly, she said Roy had this little scar on his left butt cheek, on the side. That's the first Purse had heard of it, had never seen it in P.E or anything, so he gave this nervous, little laugh. "If you want me to go on," she said, "you better not be laughing at me."

He arranged his face and kept on listening. What she said was that a two-aught buckshot—a buttshot, he had to catch himself from blurting out—had ol' Roy's name on it one night when he was a kid stealing watermelons out of ol' man Hazey's field down in the Brazos bottoms not far from the Towsen house. Jo Lynne said the scar was perfectly neat and round, and—this is where she stopped, like she couldn't go on, but then she went on— she enjoyed putting her middle finger into that little rounded-out pit and kind of getting a grip when he was mobilizing in the missionary position, so to speak. So this night, her finger went for the scar, like always, and it wasn't there. She knew he hadn't had some kind of plastic surgery. She knew it didn't just disappear like some kind of pimple.

In a flash she had a sickly feeling about what had happened. It wasn't Roy trampolining around at all; it was Ray, the smooth-faced, smooth-assed Towsen. Somehow the Towsen boys had pulled the old twin switcheroo on her.

Well, the way Jo Lynne told it, and Purse had no reason to doubt her, she tossed Ray off onto the hardwood floor like he was Puddin's old flea-infested blanket. She scrambled across the bed and switched on the lamp, and there was Roy himself sitting in a chair in the corner, naked, hands busy down between his legs and a shit-eating grin on his face. She said she grabbed up all her clothes and stomped out of the house, pulling everything on, hopping along with shoes half on and half off, as she headed across the front yard.

She got all the way to the road before Roy pulled up alongside her in his Ford. Purse could just hear those twin tailpipes chug-chug-chugging while he idled in low. He was crying and swearing on a stack of Bibles that Ray paid him to do it and he was short of cash that week and he would never do nothing like that again.

No way was she getting back in that car with him. Ever. She walked nearly half the night to get back home.

That was the end of Jo Lynne and Roy. Next morning she went out to the trash pile at the back of Crittenden's Trailer Court, where she and her folks and her younger sister Darlene lived, and burned his FFA jacket. Roy told her the national office was going to sue her for destroying Future Farmer of America property, but nothing ever came of it.

Wasn't too long after that Roy quit school and went to work as a mechanic at Schmedley's Garage. As far as Purse knew, he was still there. Somebody told him he handled the power lug nut wrench in the pit for E. B. Schmedley's Olds 98, when E. B. raced stock cars on Saturday night at the Heart O' Texas Speedway.

That's the story that came back to Purse in bits and pieces as he lay in his bed waiting for the sun to come up. He supposed he was looking for an excuse, any excuse, to make him feel better about Trieu, or what had happened. Almost happened.

It's not like he and Jo Lynne were married or engaged, or that they even had an agreement, spoken or any other kind, that they wouldn't be with other people. It was just sort of an understanding, and nobody had ever come along before—come along for Purse, at least—to bust a hole through that understanding.

But what had he done? What was he guilty of? That's what he kept trying to sort out every time the Trieu slide slid back to the old viewfinder in the brain. And then he was back at the Wagon Wheel.

That old saying about your life flashing before your eyes just before you drown is sort of what happened to Purse when the music finally stopped and the mystery woman swaying before him looked him square in the eyes, giggled and gave him a hug. She took him by the hand, and he followed her through the crowd of couples and happy gawkers. Like a smooth-sliding zipper, they parted. They were clapping and whistling and laughing, and good ol' boys were slapping Purse on the back. It was so loud, it felt like the ocean roaring at the beach. A big red-faced fellow was yelling "Encore! Encore!" to Trieu and clapping his hands Spanish-style above his head. She just smiled that beautiful, mysterious smile, but Purse's cheeks were red as a Coca-Cola box.

He was relieved to see that she was leading him toward an empty picnic table toward the back, relieved that Aboy and Red were nowhere in sight. As far as he knew, he had just danced his little toe-tapping self out of a job.

Tex Thomas and the boys launched into another number, and the crowd got back to dancing. Still, it was so noisy Trieu and Purse had to lean across the table toward each other just to hear a word they said. It was the damndest thing, he was thinking; as they leaned in to each other, their elbows on the table, their hands and arms naturally coiled around like mating sea horses he had once seen in a *National Geographic* magazine. They sat that way for maybe a minute, their hands coiled together, staring into each other's eyes, both of them smiling like fools, like they were in a wonderful just-waking daze. Trieu finally said something.

"What's your name?"

He had to think for a second, his mind was so addled. "Wily," he said. "Wily T. Foxx, but folks call me Purse. What's yours?"

"Trieu Au Nguyen," she said, their hands still wrapped together. "Where did you learn to dance like that, Wily T. Foxx?" she asked.

"Like what?" he sputtered, laughing because he was embarrassed to think about what he must have looked like hopping around on the dance floor like the village idiot, and when he laughed, a little droplet of spit shot out of his mouth and landed on Trieu's hand, just below her thumb. His ears burned, and he wanted to sink under the table. But Trieu leaned even closer, looked deep into his eyes, and with her eyes still staring into his, her tongue lashed out and licked that drop of spit off her smooth brown hand. She smiled, and he couldn't take his eyes off that beautiful mouth and the tongue behind her blinding white teeth.

Tex and the Wranglers launched into their version of the old George Jones classic, "I've Got the Hongries for Your Love and I'm Waiting in Your Welfare Line." They played it loud and they played it fast, and Trieu's smooth brown forehead wrinkled for a split second. Purse read her lips. "Let's go somewhere else," she said.

They untangled hands, stood up from the picnic table and eased their way through the crowd of dancing couples toward the back door. It was quiet outside—you could just barely hear Tex and the Wranglers—and the air was cool and fresh, and a big, yellow moon, like a fat wheel of longhorn cheese, was just coming up behind the live oak tree at the back of the unpaved parking lot. He felt like he could jump and land on a limb of the tree.

He took a deep breath, just as Trieu put her hands on his arms, stood on tiptoe in her white boots and kissed him quickly on the cheek. She smiled, and her teeth gleamed in the moonlight.

"My place is not far from here," she said. "Why don't you follow me." Her voice sparkled and danced like music, like a little spring-fed creek skipping over rocks in the Hill Country.

Purse walked her, or rather he glided beside her, to an Alfa Romeo Spider, a moon-reflecting red with a tan top. He helped her open the door and then shut it for her after she got in behind the wheel. She looked up and smiled as she started the engine, and then he walked back to his car. "Stay with me," she said.

He was embarrassed a bit by the ol' Crusher as he pulled in behind her on South Lamar, but then he thought, "What the hell, Wily! You are who you are, and that's good enough for most folks. It'll just have to be good enough for her."

The Spider bounced into a quick left turn just before the bridge over Town Lake and zipped up into the hills above Barton Springs, along a steep, winding road he didn't know. Branches of old, spreading live oaks met and mingled above the road and made it even darker than it was. They made lurid shadows in the moonlight. The Crusher grunted and groaned and shuddered as Purse shifted into overdrive, trying to stay up with the zippy little Spider on the hilly street.

She slowed a bit, flashed her signal and turned into a gravel lane lined with trees. They pulled up before an old stone cottage perched near the edge of a cliff. Behind the house Purse could see the Capitol dome all lit up and behind it the university tower, straight and tall and glowing orange. He got out. All was quiet except for the sound of happy running water.

Trieu took him by the hand and led him to an old carved Spanish-style wooden door in an aged limestone wall higher than his head. Inside the wall, a small rock fountain gurgled near the front steps of the house, and large gold fish slowly swam back and forth in a tiny pool at the base of the fountain. Trieu reached down for a small stone frog that squatted by the pool and pulled a key from the hole that was its mouth. At the front door, she leaned over and unzipped her tall, white boots. She left them on the steps. Purse did the same, glancing down as he placed his boots next to hers to make sure he wasn't wearing religious socks—holey ones, that is. He wasn't. That was when he realized he still had Aboy's cockateel tie around his neck, so to keep from losing it, he tied it in a loose knot around his neck, even though it looked a bit weird with his red-plaid shirt.

Inside, the house wasn't Spanish-style or Texas-style or American-style at all, the way he figured it would be. And it sure wasn't coed-style either. He had seen some of those places around town, with Pink Floyd posters on the wall and beanbag chairs on baby-puke yellow shag carpet, Beatles albums scattered all over.

It was Oriental. It was like nothing he had ever seen, except in a movie he remembered seeing at the Joy Drive-in when he was a kid; "Sayonara," it was called, with Marlon Brando. In the dim light of a wall lamp that was already on when they walked in, he could see that everything was clean and spare and perfectly neat. The floors were hardwood, polished and shiny. The wall that separated the living room from the kitchen was paper—rice paper, Trieu told him later—just like in that movie. The only furniture was a white couch-looking thing she called a futon and two big white cushions on the floor that you could sit on, though he discovered they weren't the most comfortable things in the world.

At one end of the small room, on a low stone shelf, was a jade statue of a Buddha, all fat and smiling and happy. Beneath the Buddha, in a shallow vase with water in it, three white blossoms floated. It was beautiful. She had three books on a shelf near the Buddha, and a long, narrow picture near the shelf of a long-legged crane, standing in water beneath the branch of a tree.

"I'm going to get comfortable," Trieu said softly, her hand on his arm. "There's wine in the refrigerator."

He watched her fringe shimmy and shake when she walked down the hall to her room. She was unbuckling her armadillo belt as she went; the belt made a slapping sound as she jerked it through the loops of her pants.

He padded into the kitchen, which was small and neat and spare as well. The only bottle in the refrigerator that looked like wine said "sake" on the label. He pulled out the cork and took a sniff. He hoped "sake" wasn't Vietnamese for "vinegar." He found two wineglasses hanging upside down in a little wooden rack above the counter and poured some of the clear, yellow-colored liquid. Music, Oriental music, began to float through the house. It was quiet and soothing, like the fountain.

He took a deep breath and tried to let the music relax him, but the tingly feeling in his stomach wouldn't go away. It was a nice feeling, but it made him a little nervous and jumpy, like a Jack Russell terrier. He was afraid he would spill the sake.

He wandered back into the living room with the two glasses and went over to the Buddha. He didn't hear Trieu when she glided up behind him, put an arm around his waist and with her other hand took one of the glasses. "Cheers," she said, and took a sip. So did Purse. The sake, he decided, wasn't half-bad.

She was wearing what looked like a thin, silk robe; she called it a kimono. It was turquoise-colored, with thin gold and red curlicues all over. When you looked closer, you could see the lines were houses and little tree limbs and little humpbacked bridges over a stream. He had never seen anything so pretty.

Trieu took one of the books off the shelf, opened to a page in the middle and began to read. "Fallen flowers rise back to the branch. I watch. Oh! Butterflies!"

She looked up and smiled. "Haiku," she said. "Do you know haiku?"

He had never heard of the guy, so to hide his ignorance, he took the book out of her hands and opened it. He thought he would read a poem back to her, remembering how Miss Ward told him one time he had a passable reading voice.

No such luck: The words looked like this:

ガク わ め . く あ ご　ガク わ め . く あ ご

Trieu laughed. "They're in Japanese," she said. "My minor was Japanese literature."

"Are you Japanese?" he asked.

"Vietnamese," she said. "I came with my parents to this country when I was 17. That was 10 years ago."

A thought like greased lightning, here and then gone: Should he mention he had been to Vietnam? Should he tell her he never ever shot anybody while he was there, that as far as he knew he never saw a gook the whole time, that the last time he had even touched an M-16 was back in basic training at Fort Bragg? Should he tell her about the whores in Saigon?

He let it pass.

Trieu took a sip of sake and moved over to the futon. "Come sit beside me and share a poem, Wily T. Foxx," she said. "I expect you know many poems." Her voice was calm and musical, with just the hint of an accent. It was like her voice was used to hopping and skipping up and down the musical scale, and when she spoke English she had to think about keeping it more of a monotone.

She sat cross-legged on the futon and tucked her beautiful robe into her lap. He couldn't help staring at her brown legs. They were long and slender and smooth.

Did he know a poem, he thought of a poem. "I think it's a poem," he said, "but it doesn't rhyme."

"That's all right," Trieu said. "Neither did mine."

He started reciting as he eased down beside her on the futon. "The size of that boy's brain on the edge of a razorblade? Like a b-b rolling down a six-lane highway."

Trieu laughed so hard she fell over on her side; she even had tears in her eyes. "Hick haiku," she said between giggles.

He loved to hear her laugh, and another poem from Miss Ward's class began coming back to him. He said it like this: "So much . . . . . depends upon a red wheel barrow . . . . . . glazed with water . . . . . . beside the white chickens." He said it in a low voice— he loved that poem—and Trieu was quiet, with a little smile on her face when he finished. "Do you know another?" she asked

He did know another. "I'm nobody, who are you?" he started saying. "Are you nobody too?"

"Then there's a pair of us," Trieu said, her face lit up with laughter. "Don't tell. They'd banish us, you know."

And then they recited together: "How dreary to be somebody! How public, like a frog! To tell your name the livelong June"—Trieu began to conduct them with her hands— "to an admiring bog."

They laughed and then they were quiet. Trieu put her hand on top of his; it was resting on his thigh. Both of them watched her thumb softly rubbing the back of his hand, tracing the veins that tracked their way through the sun-bleached hair. Neither of them looked up for what seemed like a long time. Her head was nearly on his shoulder, her silky black hair tickling his cheek. And then they both looked up at the same time, their lips nearly touching.

They moved their heads just a little millimeter each, and their lips were touching and her lips were soft and full, and then they opened just the littlest bit and he could feel her tongue touch his teeth and then her teeth taking little, tiny bites. He groaned, and she fell on her side on the futon, stretching her legs out full length. She moved back a bit, making room for him to do the same, and her lips never stopped touching. He wanted to press himself full-length into the long, beautiful body lying next to his, like new-churned butter into a mold. The sash on her kimono had come loose, and he could see her beautiful, soft breasts, and he took his lips from hers and began to kiss her neck and then her chest and then the top of her breast. He could feel her arms around him, one hand running up and down his back. Her hand went lower, and just as it cupped his butt, he suddenly thought of Roy Towsen and then Jo Lynne and without even realizing what he was doing he groaned again and rolled backward—off the futon. Trieu tried to grab him, but all she grabbed was Aboy's cockateel tie. With the tie in her hand, she struggled to sit up, as he was getting to his feet off the slick floor and stumbling and sliding toward the front door.

"Wily!" he heard Trieu cry out. "Wily, what's wrong?"

He didn't look back.

Out on the patio, he splashed into the fishpond. When he got to the front gate, he couldn't figure out how to open it. he reached up and grabbed the top of the stone wall, pulled himself up and leaped down onto the gravel driveway. When his sock-feet hit the ground, that's when he realized he had left his shoes at the front door. He thought about going back but ran to the Crusher instead. He drove home fast. The Tower was still lit up orange.

★ ★ EIGHT ★ ★

Leave it to Aboy to know something was up. "Whoa, Nellie!" he said when Purse dragged into the office the next morning. "I intended to be so presumptive as to inquire, whether you enjoyed a bit of carnal bliss last night, but from all available evidence, someone accompanied you to paradise and back. Good Gawd, Man! You must have had the veritable tiger by the tail and couldn't let go!"

Aboy had a quart carton of Oak Farms milk on his desk—sweet milk he called it—and a box of powdered miniature donuts. Fluffy powdered sugar flecked his navy blue tie. He leaned his head back, tipped up the milk carton and drained it. He belched, loudly, then grinned. "Oh, I meant to inquire," he said. "Didja git any?"

Purse's face felt hot as he sat down at his desk across from Aboy's. He knew it was going to be a long day, what with Aboy's teasing—and with his mind still wrapped around the night before. At some point he would probably ask about the tie.

On top of everything else, his feet hurt. He was wearing loafers he had bought at Kinney's, and they weren't broken in. He had read once about how LBJ had a black man working for him who wore the same size shoes, and LBJ would have him wear his new shoes two or three days to break them in good. Purse didn't have a black man.

He hated to think where his boots were at that very moment.

A copy of the previous day's newspaper clips were on his desk, along with half a dozen or so little pink message slips—Judge Young calling again, no doubt belly-achin' about the TV decision. Olene was calling to remind him to get his travel receipts in so he could get paid. Now that he was part of the campaign staff, not the comptroller's office, he tended to forget to do the paperwork.

The clips showed a new poll out, Sisco by 20. Still double figures. And with the presidential race a wash for the incumbent, it was hopeless. Now it was a Dallas columnist suggesting that Red drop out of the race, save the taxpayers of Texas the expense of an election. Heck, he was thinking, maybe the guy was right.

Nothing from Jo Lynne. He figured she was just leaving for Hair Apparent. She would be wearing her black rayon hairdresser pants that swished when she walked, and a black rayon top she called a smock. She'd be padding about in her white shoes, the kind nurses wear because she had to be standing all day. "I know you don't want me to be getting those ugly ol' varicose veins before I'm 30, do you Wily?" That's what she said one time when he was watching her lean over and tie her shoes one morning as she got ready to go to work.

Her partner Trudi Bulin would have unlocked the front door and gotten the coffee going, snapped on K-BOB radio, "the country giant that's deep in the heart of Texans." It would be on all day, Jo Lynne cutting, curling and setting to the bull-deep bass of Johnny Cash, teasing to the tunes of Tammy Wynnette, and—best of all to Purse, at least—dyeing and shampooing to the wonderful whiny wailings of his man Willie. Willie grew up just a few miles north of the Foxx place in Elm Mott, although he was a number of years ahead of Purse. His daddy told him he used to hear Willie at the Nite-Owl.

Jo Lynne would be getting all her clippers and scissors and sprays all set out. Purse had sat with her early in the morning sometimes, drinking coffee, watching her bustle about Hair Apparent. Sometimes she would send him to the back of the shop to get the towels out of the dryer. He would fold them. The thick, white towels would be so nice and warm he would hold them to his cheek before he brought them up to the front.

It was only a two-chair shop, she and Trudi, so she would sweep around each chair, sweep up around the front door, switch on the dryers to make sure they were working, put out the new "McCalls," "Good Housekeeping," "Redbook," "Silver Screen," throw away the old ones, old being five years or more with recipes torn out. She might spray some Windex on the mirror behind her chair and give it a good wipe-down, then she would scrub the sinks where she washed ladies' hair.

After all that, she would flip over the OPEN sign, unlock the front door and, since it was a Monday, wait for Mrs. Lillian

Beall to come in at nine on the nose for her weekly shampoo and set. At 8:59, Jo Lynne and Trudi would stop what they were doing and get ready. The big mystery every week was whether little ol' blue-haired Mrs. Beall, 90 years old and so tiny she could barely see over the steering wheel of her '58 Buick Century, would plow through the front window of the shop. She had done just that at Green's Pharmacy, where they had head-in parking, just like Jo Lynne and Trudi had. That was back when she was 75.

And Trieu? He couldn't imagine, though it was hard not to try. Maybe she woke up to calm, soothing Oriental music, that tinkly kind that never gets loud or raucous. Maybe she strolled out on the back deck where the hot tub was and did yoga, the UT tower standing straight and tall in the distance, doves and mockingbirds twit-twit-twittering all around her, while she twisted her beautiful body into all sorts of impossible positions. And then what did she do? Did she read, write? He could almost see her sitting down at a desk and writing poems in black ink with a brush, in calligraphy, the calm music still playing in the background. He could hear it in his head.

And then, on her way to class, did she step outside the front door and see them—a pair of broken-down old cowboy boots, the tops broken over like a coon dog's ears? His boots. They were like cow patties in the perfectly neat little Oriental tapestry he could see in his head, like an ugly brown coffee stain on that beautiful silk kimono she was wearing.

"Hey! I said. HEY!" A powdered donut came sailing across the room and hit Purse on the chest.

Aboy was staring at him, his face red from laughing and from having to shout. "My goodness gracious, man, you're seriously afflicted! I sought your undivided attention three times, and you weren't even cognizant of my presence. Man!" He was trying to brush the white powder off his tie.

"I uh, I was just going over the week in my head. You got any more of them donuts?" The wheels of his chair had just smashed the one Aboy had thrown at him.

"No, my good man," he said, "Consumed them all with an avidity intrinsic to a man like myself, a man of LARGE appetites. But I have a couple of quarters if you care to venture downstairs and extract them from the machine. You've taken a fancy, I presume, to sweet little things with holes in them?"

Purse knew there was no use trying to fend him off. That's what he wanted. He tried to change the subject. "So where we going today?" he asked

"My good man, you don't *wanna* know," Aboy said, leaning back in his chair and locking his hands behind his full head of curly gray hair. "Fact of the matter is, maybe that's why you are unaware. Olene sought to call you late last night and divulge the itinerary, so you'd dress for the occasion, so to speak. But I'm guessing you were out, indisposed, naked as a jaybird and not wearing any clothes. Am I correct in my assumption?"

"Could be," Purse said. "But just tell me where we're going, Aboy. I'm not in the mood for foolishness."

Aboy stood up from his desk and started singing, swaying his hips and leaning backward and forward like the Big Bopper. "Hit the road, Jack, and don't you come back no more, no more. Hit the road, Jack, and knock on doors some more."

Rats! It hit him where they were going. Fact of the matter, the no-TV campaign was hitting the road and hitting it hard. They would be knocking on doors all day, on a day that was shaping up to be even hotter than the East Texas nightmare from the week before.

Something reminded Aboy of the Bobby Ray Evangeline dust-up. "Red sent Bobby Ray packin', didn't she?" he said. "Sent him back to the nutrias and the 'gators over in Louisiana."

Just as he was about to voice his opinion about Sue Bee taking over, Sue Bee herself poked her perky, short-haired head around the edge of the office door.

"You guys ready?" she asked, perkily. Normally, Sue Bee was Red's deputy comptroller; she had a master's degree in accounting from SMU, something she mentioned frequently. During the campaign she had taken a leave of absence so she could be the deputy campaign manager. Actually she was the person who did all the work, since Bobby Ray Evangeline was usually off in Washington making appearances on "Meet the Press," and getting his name in the papers, sometimes in relation to Red, sometimes not. Now she had the title to go with it. This was her first campaign.

Purse was about to ask "Ready for what?" when Aboy spoke up. "Sue Bee, my little honeyed confection, young Foxx and I are ready, dare I say eager, to follow you to the ends of the earth, yea into the valley of the shadow of death."

He stood up and brushed donut crumbs onto the floor, took a last sip of coffee from a yellow mug with a label that read "Lulu's Cafe: Never Trust a Skinny Cook" and ran a forearm across his mouth. "You run right along now, and we'll be so close behind, you'll think you're being accosted by MEN. Oh, and by the way, Congratulations! I mean it."

"Thank you, Aboy," Sue Bee said. "You know where we're going, don't you, Purse?" she asked, looking over her shoulder as she hurried down the hall. She was wearing jeans and a blue work shirt with the sleeves rolled up and little blue low-top tennis shoes. The jeans made her ass look big as the side of a barn.

Aboy had told him where they were going. The TV-deprived campaign was venturing back out into summer hell to go door-to-door in some godforsaken little burg—Elgin, if he remembered correctly, 30 miles east of Austin.

Aboy didn't like Sue Bee, and the feeling was mutual. "I hold no grievance with homo-SEX-uals," he told Purse one time, drawing the word out like an old-time preacher on the radio, "but she affronts the nervous system, rubs me the wrong way, in a manner of speaking, and I'd rather not be rubbed in any way by Miss Sue Bee Sealman."

Sue Bee was part of what Judge Young out in Floydada called "the homosexual contingent." Purse already had seen how women flocked to Red's campaign, particularly gay women, and not just in Texas either. When she made a speech at the national convention, one of the country's most famous comedians, a lesbian, fed her lines that the newspaper commentators were repeating for months afterward.

Aboy and Judge Young were afraid the Sisco campaign would figure out a way to use the gay connection against her. Purse had heard them talking about it. He had a feeling Red herself was aware of it. Heck, he thought to himself, just him standing behind her holding her purse was probably a little subliminal message. And whenever she went out on the social scene, she was always with Axel Grenon, the ponytailed Frenchman who came to Texas to make a movie and never left.

She wasn't gay herself, as far as Purse knew. After all, she had an ex-husband and four grown kids. But she and the gays sure had made a connection.

But if she had some kind of lesbian strategy, she never said anything to Aboy and Purse about it. What she could say, and really mean it, was that some of her best friends were lesbians. And, as Purse had come to realize, they would do anything for her, had been with her for years.

That didn't make a rat's ass of difference to a crusty, old snuff-dippin' West Texas judge.

"Now, I've got nothin' against homosexuals," the judge had told Purse over the phone one day a few weeks earlier, "but I can guaran-damn-tee you, a lot of my folks out here do. If I had a dollar for every time one of 'em told me 'Tain't natural,' I'd be a rich man. Just yesterday, I was talking to Runt McAfee over at the gin. He was tellin' me his preacher stood up in the pulpit last Sunday and told 'em all that a vote for Red was about as close to God's original sin as you could get. You and me may not agree with 'em, son, but these are good, churchgoin' folks, as straight and narrow as a row of South Plains sorghum. You know that, Purse. It's just another damn albatross around our necks. And we don't need any thing else to tote; hellfire, we got a crap load as it is!"

As soon as they hung up, Purse went over to the legislative reference library and looked up albatross in the *World Book Encyclopedia*. He knew it was always around people's necks, but he had no idea it was a damned bird.

Aboy felt the same way about lesbians in general, plus he had a personal thing with Sue Bee and her friends on the campaign. They wouldn't put up with his shit, his smarmy good-ol'-boy ways with women. They would call him on it; hell, they might even sue him. Purse told him he ran the risk of being Sue-bee'd.

Take how Aboy treated Raenell Sitton, partly because she was pretty in a sad and lonely sort of way and partly because she used to work for him. Until about three months ago, Raenell was working as a carhop at the Stallion Drive-In on North Lamar.

Before that she had worked for Aboy when he had his fleet of mobile massage parlors over in Northeast Texas. He didn't know she was living in Austin until one afternoon he and Purse went by the Stallion for a couple of cherry limeades.

Aboy had told him about his massage business. He was living at Nash, near Texarkana, not long after he got defrocked. His massage parlors catered exclusively to the feet. At least that was his pitch. Raenell was one of his female foot masseuses; he only had women. They worked out of RVs up and down IH-30 between Texarkana and Dallas, and they plied their wares over the CB radio. The RVs were these big, long Winnebagos, painted cherry red with big white lettering: "SUSKIN'S SOLE TRAIN." It showed a picture of a well-endowed young Daisy Mae type in blue-jean shorts and a halter top tweaking a pair of oversized toes.

He'd had a "SUSKIN'S *SOUL* TRAIN" as a traveling evangelist, so when he got into the foot business, all he had to do was change a couple of letters and morph Jesus into Daisy Mae.

Truck drivers swore by the foot massage, Aboy told Purse—more than once. Nothing like a patented Suskin foot massage to relieve the dreaded "clutch foot," the bane of over-the-road haulers the world over.

Anyway, Raenell had been a waitress at a cafe in Texarkana, right on the state line. She would serve one meal in Texas and the next one in Arkansas, depending on whether her customers were sitting in one of the booths up front or at one of the tables near the back.

"He come in," Raenell told Purse one evening at the Wagon Wheel, "and told me all about his business. I remember he kept on saying, 'We're bonafide, absolutely bonafide. My young ladies are required to have in their possession an associate of arts degree in podiatrical therapeutics, preferably from Ouachita Valley Christian Junior College, just outside Arkadelphia, Arkansas, where I take great and humble pride in serving on the board of regents.'"

"I remember he was eating a big, juicy bacon cheeseburger," Raenell said, "couple of 'em, as a matter of fact. And I'm saying, 'But Mr. Suskin, I don't have a college degree. I'm still working on my GED.' And he's saying, 'Never you mind, little lady, we'll get you qualified under the provisional arrangement I've arranged. You'll do just fine.' He kept saying, 'You'll be bonafide.'"

Raenell took a long draw from her Lone Star. It was funny how she could imitate Aboy. She was a born mimic. Purse watched her long, slim neck and how her throat palpitated like a little bird's when the beer went down. She put the bottle down and, like a truck driver at a roadside dive, wiped her mouth with the back of her hand.

"Well, Purse," she said, "I knew then and there I never ever wanted to look down at a platter of chicken-fried steak with cream gravy crawling up my arm, so I was sore tempted. But I have to admit, I had a little bit of an uh-oh feeling about this gentleman. If you know what I mean."

Purse knew what she meant, for sure. The image of Aboy passed out drunk in the back of that El Rancho station wagon was what popped into his mind.

"Anyway, I managed to tell him I was a little worried about some things. He said, 'Miss Sitton, I want you to know and I want your dear mama and daddy to know that if any above-the-ankle hanky-panky goes on, I'll bounce your lovely little watusi right out the back of those Winnebagos. No offense intended, but I get quite exercised about such base accusations. We're a mobile massage parlor, pure and simple.' That's what he said." Raenell giggled.

To make a long story short, Raenell, age 27 at the time, six feet tall, with long, straight blonde hair and legs that looked like they could stretch across two states, went to work for Aboy. Stayed with him about six months.

"All that stuff he said about no above-the-ankle hanky-panky, Purse? Let me tell you, it was *all* hanky-panky. Let's just say truckers aren't my cup of tea, even though it took a trucker to rescue me. Caught a ride with one of 'em headed to Austin, I guess it's been five years now. Went back to waitressing and hated it a hundred times over. Oh so much more than I did before. But I couldn't stir up anything else. That's why I jumped at the offer when you and Mr. Suskin came by the Stallion that day. I figured if he was working for Red, it must be okay. She's a hero of mine, always has been."

So Raenell sorted mail and delivered it to all the different divisions of the comptroller's office and came over in the evenings and volunteered on the campaign. That's when Aboy treated her like a combination geisha girl and peon—like she still worked for him.

Purse liked having her around, because she was pretty, but also because she was nice—and fun to be with. She was always saying something funny without knowing it was funny. If she was with them knocking on doors in Elgin, she'd make the day go faster.

But instead of Raenell, they would be with Sue Bee, perky Sue Bee, and her band of short-haired, dead-serious gals, who wouldn't know a joke if it bit them on the butt. Purse had even heard Red tell them to lighten up a little.

It took them maybe 40 minutes to drive over to Elgin in Aboy's pickup, both of them swearing every 10 seconds or so at some idiotic crap Bob Swit or Sammy Red spewed out over the airwaves. Just as they were pulling into Elgin, Sammy got off on the governor's race.

"Oh, she's got the people behind her," he was saying in his tight, little fat-man's voice—"that is, if honest-to-Gawd Texans count liberals and lesbos and welfare queens as real people, real Texans."

"Now, Sammy, you be nice," Bob Swit said in his deep, sorghum-syrup voice. And then he launched into a commercial about something you could drink at night and lose weight while you were sleeping.

"Goddamn those idiotic caterwauls, these hydrophobic hayseeds!" Aboy yelled, his face glowing red as he hit the tuner button and switched to a country music station.

"Watch the speed limit," Purse warned him. Hunched over the steering wheel, he was still going 80, in his mind and in the truck.

"This little bedeviled burg, they used to call it Hell-agin," he said as they drove past a new state prison on the outskirts of town, the razor wire at the top of the high chain-link fence glinting in the sun. "Had a gang of thieves sort of like the Hole-in-the-Wall Gang, took refuge in a hackberry thicket not far from here. Train comes through, and like brigands of yesteryear they would waylay it."

They stopped for a light. "Still resembles a denizen of the devil," he muttered, looking around.

Purse looked around. He wouldn't call it hellish, he decided, so much as ragged, down-at-the-heels, like a lot of little country towns. The highway still passed pretty close to downtown, what was left of it, so you saw a lot of gas stations and little run-down frame houses. About the only thing new were the fast food joints. Downtown itself, they noticed, still had its old brick streets and its crumbly red-brick buildings, most of them empty if they hadn't been turned into junk shops and antique stores with names like Elgin Marbles and Whatnot, Ye Olde Elgin Antiques, and Auld A-Quaint-ance.

Across the brick-paved street from a building that used to be the First State Bank of Elgin, now a store called Second Time Around, they pulled into the parking lot of the Elgin Market, the town's only claim to fame since the hole-in-the-wall gang was subdued. Ask anybody who knew anything about meat, and they would tell you that the Elgin Market cooked up what may be the best barbecue in the Lone Star State.

Maybe half a dozen other cars and trucks with red-and-white "Red Ryder for Governor" signs and "Ride With Red" and "Red Hot for Texas" bumper stickers were already there. A knot of people, locals and campaign volunteers, were standing around the back of a flatbed truck lined with bales of hay.

"Red alert! Red alert!" Sue Bee was shouting into a microphone as Aboy and Purse sauntered up. She had clambered up into the bed of the truck and was having trouble getting folks' attention. The microphone screeched, and people stopped talking to their neighbors long enough for her to launch into her little speech.

"On behalf of the next U.S. senator from the great state of Texas, Rose Marie Ryder, I want to thank y'all for being here on this glorious morning. Your time and your effort and your energy are the reason why this state is gonna send a great lady to the Nation's Capitol in a couple of months, a great lady that's gonna make every Texan proud as punch."

Sue Bee paused for applause, her mouth pursed in a satisfied, expectant smile. The folks clapped but not too enthusiastically. Out of the corner of his eye, Purse saw Aboy grimace and kick the ground with the toe of his boot. "Proud as punch" was not something that tripped off the tongue of the Elginites gathered around them. Aboy, who considered himself something of a student of oratory, hated that "Red Alert" thing too, but Sue Bee used it every chance she got.

Sue Bee went on to lay out the day's schedule for the small crowd of locals. She had the volunteers divided up two by two—just like the disciples, Aboy said—and each team had a street they were supposed to cover between where they were downtown and Elgin High School on the edge of town. Red would join them in a couple of hours and knock on doors herself. Then about noon there would be a barbecue picnic at the Old Settlers' Park near the school, with catered Elgin Market chicken, ribs, sausage and pork loin.

Aboy and Purse were paired up to cover Ash Street, a potholed street with no curbs and no sidewalks, lined with scraggly houses that backed up on a cotton field on Purse's side of the street. They parked the truck under a withered cottonwood tree at the end of the street. It wasn't even fall, but brown, burned leaves crunched under their feet. Aboy got out and stretched a bit, and instead of walking up to the house on his side of the street, he started walking, fast, around the truck—once, twice, three times. Purse stood there and watched him, watched his face getting red and his breath coming in heaving gasps as he did his speed-walking.

"Aboy!" Purse shouted. "What are you doing, man?" He was afraid the sun had gotten to him, afraid he was having a kiniption fit.

Aboy stopped and leaned on the front fender on the driver's side. He fished his red bandanna out of his back pocket, took off his glasses and wiped his face. "I'm gathering momentum," he said between gasps, "calling on the power of centrifugal force to propel me into the fray."

Purse shook his head. "Whatever works," he said, and grabbed a handful of "Jam on the Bottom Shelf" brochures and walked up the sidewalk to a little frame house, its yellow paint peeling in the sun.

A sun-faded plastic Big Wheel and a tricycle with a missing back wheel lay on their sides near the small cement-slab front porch. What grass there was in the yard was yellow and brittle. Purse moved the tricycle out of the way, stepped up on the porch and rapped on the doorframe. After a while a woman came to the door, at least he thought it was a woman. He couldn't see her all that well, because the sun reflected off the screen door.

"Yes?" a tired woman's voice said, none too friendly. He heard a baby squalling inside the house somewhere. He could hear Bill Cullen and "The Price is Right" on a TV in the living room.

"Good morning, howdy do," he said. "Ma'am, I wanted to take a few seconds of your time, and talk to you about the upcoming election. Would that be ok with you?"

Now here's where he made his mistake, he realized later in the day. Because he was nervous and mainly because he couldn't see who he was talking to through the screen door, he started, without thinking about what he was doing, trying to open the door. The woman saw what he was doing even before he realized, so she pulled it to, hard, and latched it. "I don't think so," she said. She shuffled away from the door, what must have been house shoes scraping across the linoleum.

He left a brochure in the screen and walked across the dried-up yard to the next house, grinding his teeth at how stupid he had been. He glanced across the street. Aboy and a chunky middle-aged woman in shorts and a floppy straw garden hat were sitting in lawn chairs under a pecan tree, and Aboy was talking away and wiping his face with his bandana while the woman looked at one of the brochures. They both had glasses of iced tea in their hands.

"Why can't I be like that, all natural and easy?" he was asking himself, and he was like that, sort of, at the next couple of houses. He would say good morning, they would take a brochure, he would say thank you kindly and then he would go on to the next house. But he still wasn't striking up a conversation.

At his sixth house, an old, historic sort of house with peeling white paint and a huge crepe myrtle bush growing up onto the sheet-metal roof over the front porch, he turned a rusty little knob in the middle of the front door. A bell rattled behind the door. He stood there for a while, and nobody came. He tried again, and still nobody came. He was about ready to leave a brochure in the front door and walk on when an elderly gentleman came around from the side of the house. He had a hoe in his hand, and his khaki pants and shirt were sweated a darker shade of gray. He still had a full head of hair, snow-white and matted down from wearing an old straw hat.

"Good morning, howdy-do," Purse said, holding out his hand. "My name is Wily T. Foxx."

The old man took his hand and shook it. "I'm Truman B. Lawson," he said, his gold-rimmed glasses glinting as he looked Purse square in the eye. "Won't you come on in?"

Purse followed him inside the house. It was hot and musty and dark in the living room, and the furniture looked like it was a hundred years old. He could hear a grandfather clock ticking from back down the hallway and then it rang, a deep, sombre sound, 11 times. A paint-by-number watercolor picture of a palomino horse, unframed, was thumbtacked to the wall. It made him think of Jimmy Dale Sisco. That was the only decoration in the room. He wondered if Mr. Lawson had painted it.

"You go ahead and have a seat, young man," he said. "I'll go get us a glass of ice water."

He switched on an oscillating fan on an end table in the corner, then went into the kitchen, where Purse heard him breaking ice out of a tray.

Purse sat down on an old splayfooted sofa. It was wine-colored and looked like it had been velvet once upon a time, before the velvet got what appeared to be the mange. About the only sign of a woman's touch was an age-yellowed doily across the rounded back of the sofa. Purse figured Mrs. Lawson had passed on, leaving her husband to batch as best he could. An old upright piano with yellowed ivory keys was up against one wall; a songbook, "Great Songs of the Church," was propped up above the keyboard.

Mr. Lawson came back in with two Howdy-Doody jelly glasses filled with ice water. He sat down in a rocking chair across from the sofa. He crossed one leg over the other and let it hang down the way old men do, his heavy, brown work shoe dangling as he gently rocked. A baggy, white sock bunched at the ankles, revealing a hairless, corpse-white shin. "You'll have to speak up, young man. I don't hear too good," he said, smiling

"Yes sir," Purse said. "I will. The reason I'm here, Mr. Lawson, is to tell you about Rosie Ryder, who's running for the U.S. Senate. Do you know Ms. Ryder?"

Mr. Lawson, still smiling, nodded.

"As you know," Purse said, as loud as he could, "Ms. Ryder is the State Comptroller, and I think you'd agree she's done her best for the people of Texas. She's done a fine job. You probably know about how she went around the state getting businesses to pay up on taxes they didn't want to pay. That's money that goes for schools and highways and PO-lice and health benefits for senior citizens like yourself, stuff we really need. Did you hear about all that?"

Mr. Lawson, gently rocking in his chair, nodded. He was still smiling.

"Sir, the reason I'm here today is because I have not a doubt in the world that's the kind of senator she'd be too. She'd be out there working for the people, the working people, not the people up in Dallas or somewheres who sit in those big, air-conditioned office buildings and have more money than they know what to do with. Rosie, uh Miss Ryder's one of us. Only difference is she has the experience in state government and the willingness to serve the people that we need in a U.S. senator. I think you would agree with me, we don't need a big oil man that's out to serve the fat cats and not you and me. Isn't that right, Mr. Lawson?"

Mr. Lawson rocked and nodded. He was still smiling. Purse's voice was getting tired from all the shouting, and then he realized: Mr. Lawson hadn't heard a word he had said. He was stone deaf, and just being nice to sit there and listen while he yammered.

Purse stood up from the couch, grinned at the kindly old man and took his water glass back in the kitchen. He walked over to Mr. Lawson and shook his hand. "Thanks for the water, sir," he said, loudly, making a show of smiling real big and rubbing his stomach. "It hit the spot."

Mr. Lawson clambered up from his rocker and walked his visitor to the door. "You come again now, you hear," he said. Purse nodded and grinned and said he would.

★　★　★

So was it him or was it the campaign? Somehow they just didn't seem to be getting through. Voters weren't getting the message, and not because they were deaf as a doorknob. He was thinking about that, waiting on the corner for Aboy to come by in the truck. Of course, Aboy seemed to be doing okay, so maybe it was just him, Purse was thinking. Then he thought about how Aboy and Red and Sue Bee and everybody else could be doing okay, but look how long it took them just to walk a couple of blocks. There was no way they could cover a whole city, much less a whole state. Was it pure-dee ol' pride not to take TV money? Stubbornness? Didn't she want to win?

Aboy pulled up at the curb. "Nice folks," he said, as Purse climbed in. "I'll have to revise my prejudicial presumptions about this fair city. And this may be of minimal interest to you, my boy, given your current state of *hormonus interruptus*, but I encountered a comely widow back up the street who definitely deserves a little personal campaign attention from yours truly. I'll be trekking back to Elgin town this Saturday night anon."

"Aboy, you beat all," was all Purse could say, as they headed out to the Old Settlers' Park on the edge of town. Purse was surprised once they got out there. They both were. Cars and pickups lined the road three and four blocks away from the park. You could smell the barbecue from out on the road. "Somebody's done a good job of enticing the *hoi polloi*," Aboy said, as he slowly looked for a place to leave the truck. "Could it have been our busy little Bee of a Sue?"

"What's Sue Bee doing?" Purse said, pointing to where she stood at the edge of the park, one hand shading her eyes, peering up and down the road. Before Aboy could make a crack about her, she spotted them and scurried out into the road with her arms outstretched like a school-crossing guard. "Aboy, where have you been?" Sue Bee said, her voice in a panic as she ran up to Purse's side of the truck. "Never mind," she said. "Purse, you have her speech?"

Her panicky voice nearly threw him into a panic—What did he do with it? What did he do with it?—and for a second he had to think whether he had it with him. Then he saw the blue box they always kept Red's speeches in, there on the floorboard between him and Aboy.

"It's okay, Sue Bee," he said, "I got it right here."

"Well hurry, young man. Hurry," she said, opening the door for him even before Aboy had fully stopped.

"Hurry, young man," Aboy mocked her in a Dolly Parton voice, as Sue Bee and Purse jogged over to the gazebo where Red would talk, and Purse would hold her purse.

Was it the meat or the madam that had brought them out? That was the question as they sidled through the large crowd. Red was moving along slowly, shaking hands, hugging people, kissing plump, sweaty babies. Sam Wheeler, the big Department of Public Safety guy assigned to her, his handsome black face wet with sweat, was gently trying to clear a way through the crowd. He had been Sammy Wheeler, an all-conference quarterback on the Prairie View A&M football team, but with Red he was more like the lead blocker. When he saw Purse, he raised his eyebrows, like he was saying, "This is something different; I'm having to earn my keep for once."

Purse tried to help Sam part a path through the crowd to the old-fashioned whitewashed gazebo where Barefoot Boyd Chesser and his Country Cuzzins were playing a lively fiddle tune. Barefoot Boyd, he noticed, had on his striped overalls, as usual, and, as usual, he was barefooted. When he saw Red coming his way he switched the band into "Deep in the Heart of Texas," and people in the crowd gave out with rebel yells. She handed Purse her purse, he handed her the speech on blue sheets of paper, and she looked out on the crowd.

"Yee-ha yourself!" Red shouted, her arm around Barefoot Boyd's beefy, sunburned shoulders. She kissed him on his sweaty cheek, and people laughed and hollered.

Red had never been better. She looked great, in a kelly-green short-sleeved suit and a bright-white blouse, and once she got past all the introductions of county commissioners and jp's and city councilmen she sounded great. Standing behind her and just to the side, hobo handbag in his hand, he could see her hands on the railing of the gazebo, leaning out to the crowd, reaching out to them, and they were leaning in toward her. They were laughing with her, feeling sad with her, nodding their heads and answering back when she had a question for them.

She had the speech in her hand down by her side; Purse wasn't sure she even looked at it. Red was talking from the heart in a way he had never heard on the campaign trail, and the folks were responding. He saw Sue Bee standing at the front of the crowd. She was looking up at Red, a big smile across her face and tears running down her cheeks. Purse felt the need to swallow a little lump in his throat himself.

Afterward, he wasn't sure he could even remember what she said. Probably it was pretty close to the written speech, but the words weren't as big a deal as the feeling.

"I can't win this race," she told them near the end, and from the crowd you could hear groans and shouts of "No, no!" and "Yes you can, Red!" Red held up her hand. "That is, I can't win it without you," her voice a little rough, like she was about to cry. "Every one of you. All you mamas and grandmamas and grandpapas and daddies out there. I need you all. It's up to you. Are you with me?"

People went crazy. Purse saw an old farmer rip off his sweat-stained straw hat and throw it into the air. He saw women hugging each other and little kids jumping up and down. He saw one little girl with bright yellow hair who was just learning to walk fall on her back in the dry grass and lay there like a beetle waving her arms and legs. People were too excited to notice her.

Red held her hands up in the air, and the crowd quieted a bit. "What I'm going to do," she said, "is have me a little barbecue from this wonderful Elgin Market"—the owner was standing at the edge of the gazebo with a double-layered paper plate piled with barbecue and beans and slaw, and he reached up and handed it to Red—"and then I'm gonna go knock on some doors and talk to your neighbors. I do wish you'd join me."

The crowd stood in three long lines at tables covered with white butcher paper and connected end to end for barbecue and all the fixins'. Purse ate so much, he wanted to lie down in the shade of a tree and take a nap, but Red was ready to go. They cleaned up a bit with little Handi-wipes and headed back on foot into the neighborhood on the edge of the park—Purse and Red and Sue Bee and many of the volunteers who had started out with them downtown.

As Red walked up to a little yellow frame house on the right, Purse happened to glance back. He couldn't believe what he saw. Much of the crowd was following them, like Red was the Pied Piper, and they stayed with them all the way back to town. It beat all he had ever seen. Here Red would be knocking on a front door, talking to whoever answered, sometimes for 10 minutes at a time, and crowds of people would be out on the sidewalk, spilling into the street, all abuzz about Red Ryder knocking on their door, in their little town.

Purse got to thinking afterward that it might have been Junction, but it was probably that afternoon in Elgin that he first noticed it—the women, that is. They were out there with her, young and old; black, white and brown; middle-class and not-so-middle class. There were men too, of course, but a lot more women than men. Aboy mentioned that he wouldn't have been surprised if some of them were out there in spite of their men. Maybe they hadn't taken an interest in politics before, but now they were standing up for someone they believed in. Something was happening.

TV crews from Austin and Houston and San Antonio showed up the middle of the afternoon, and Red, from what they heard later, led all the 6 o'clock newscasts. Here was the TV coverage they would be getting—free coverage, coverage that was honest and real.

Of course, none of them got to see the 6 o'clock news. They were still out there with Red, knocking on doors, talking to voters. They were on the streets long after the sun went down, long after the streetlights had come on.

The Elgin Tigers football team had just started two-a-days, and the good-natured crowd urged her to drop by the practice field. The stadium lights were on, and dust from the dry field swirled up around the tired, sweaty players. She talked about education to parents on the sidelines watching, had her picture taken with the red-faced, dirt-streaked team captains and posed for a picture holding a football with her arm cocked back like a quarterback. Folks loved it.

And then they knocked on more doors. When the crowd finally began to head back to their homes for supper at about 8, Red was still talking, and the man she was talking to was old Mr. Truman Lawson, only Red had sense enough to get up right next to him, throw an arm around his shoulders and shout like a railroad conductor into his left ear. Mr. Lawson was still grinning and nodding, but you could tell that Red was getting through.

"So what do you make of it?" Purse asked Aboy as they drove back toward the lights of Austin.

For a minute, Aboy puffed on a cigar, not saying anything, which wasn't like him at all. And then he said, real slow-like, "Wily, my boy, I think the red, red Rose of Texas found her glow today—found her voice, to be precise." He picked up the can of cold Budweiser between his legs and with his cigar in his steering-wheel hand, took a long swig. "On this day, you and I may have seen Texas political history in the making," he said.

He started singing in his soothing baritone voice: "Now the day is over, the sun's behind the hill. The birds are in the tree tops, I heard a whippoorwil." Purse heard that song often. Aboy wrote it and was trying to sell it to Nashville.

Purse poured a stream of beer down his own parched gullet and wiped his mouth with the back of his hand. "But why Elgin?" he asked. "Why was she so different in Elgin than she was last week in Sulphur Springs, all those other little places where we've been. You know as well as I do she bombed over there."

Aboy chuckled. "Well, I could say it was merely an inconvenient time of the month, if you catch my drift, but I'm afraid the menses are a mere fond memory, so there must be another explanation." He tapped his horn and pulled around a car on the two-lane road. "If you ask me—and you did, my callow protégé—I would hazard a guess that she's a free woman. She's emancipated herself from the merciless manacles of the money god, from Bobby Ray Evangeline, the wild man from Nachitoches, even from our own little Sue Bee and her textbook-culled campaign strategy.

She's free of expectations. Free to be herself. And what you saw today was the result."

They drove along for a few miles without saying anything. Purse was thinking about calling Jo Lynne when he got home, trying to explain yet again what he was learning. Aboy started in to singing: "Trust and obey, for there's no other way, to be happy in Jeeesus, but to trust and obeyyyy."

He gave Purse a little backhand across the chest. "You know what I'm sayin?"

"I guess so."

"I'm saying you have to trust yourself, your real self. You have to obey what your heart's telling you to do. That's as true in politics as it is in life, boy. And don't you forget it."

Aboy started in to singing again. His voice was beginning to put Purse to sleep, and as they drove along, Purse in a kind of a tired and pleasant daze, he was thinking about what Aboy had said. It made sense. What he saw that day reminded him of fighting cocks he had known, the ones with brave hearts. If they were going to go down, they were going to go down fighting. At least they would have their self-respect—and they would have a good time doing it. Sometimes that fighting spirit carried them through. They rallied, and they won. He had seen it.

Aboy dropped him off at the Capitol. The moon was shining, and he glanced up at the pink-granite dome. It reminded him of way back when he had just starting working for Red, and Raenell had just gotten there too. One night it was nearly midnight when they finished up, everybody else had gone home, and when they came out it was a night just like this—moon shining behind the dome, the sky a deep purple, Lady Liberty gleaming white in the moonlight. They looked at each other and started laughing, just out of the pure joy of it all. Who would have guessed that an East Texas waitress and a Central Texas chicken farmer would have ascended to the very pinnacles of power? They gave each other a hug and walked to the parking lot arm in arm, like Dorothy and the Cowardly Lion in the "Wizard of Oz" prancing up the yellow brick road. They couldn't stop grinning.

Purse switched on the radio. "I'm just an old chunk of coal," Billy Joe Shaver warbled, "but I'm gonna be a diamond some day."

He thought about going by the Wagon Wheel, he was so revved up, but he was afraid Trieu Au Nguyen might be there. He thought about going by to see Raenell, tell her what had happened in Elgin. But then he decided he would go on home and call Jo Lynne, share with her this most amazing day. It had been nearly a week since they had talked. He wasn't sure he could trust himself talking to her after what had happened the night before. She could always read him, hear things in his voice that he had no idea were coming through. But tonight, feeling good about Red, he figured he could control the conversation.

Willis Seymour, his landlord, was sitting in his saggy lawn chair in front of his trailer. He had his porch light on and his bug light too, the zapper, he called it. As usual, he was wearing his beat-up old sea captain's cap, a Hawaiian shirt and a pair of baggy khaki shorts. He waved at Purse with a cigar, sort of like he wanted him to stop, but Purse knew he had paid his rent on time, and he didn't particularly want to sit and shoot the shit with him, so he just waved and kept on going back to the trailer.

He parked the Crusher, said hey to Shoogy, and noticed something on the concrete block at the front door. He couldn't see what it was in the dark, until he got closer. When he saw what it was, his stomach got tight, and his head got swimmy. He stared down at his boots, all cleaned up and shined, some kind of wooden shoe trees inside keeping them erect.

He picked them up and sniffed the good smell of shoe polish. He unlocked the front door. It was dark in the trailer and quiet, except for the whir of the air conditioner, which was funny, because he rarely turned it on, trying to save on his electric bill. He bumped into the kitchen table, then walked slowly, feeling his way into the bedroom. In the moonlight through the little window above the bed, he could see her, asleep, her black hair and dark shoulders beautiful against the white sheets. It looked like all she was wearing was Aboy's cockateel tie around her lovely neck. It was glowing in the moonlit dark.

★ ★ NINE ★ ★

On the very first glorious weekend of freedom from basic training at Fort Bragg, that most glorious weekend way back when, he had strolled through the loblolly pines over to the base library. After getting jarred out of sleep at four every morning by a dickhead D.I. blowing a whistle in his ear, after marching and shooting and running in formation from way before sunup to sundown, he was just looking for some nice, easy way to pass the time. He browsed through sports, browsed through history, and found himself in the religion section. He suddenly realized that he was a kid away from home for the first time, and he had this curiosity about other religions. At his church, the Church of God in Christ, thinking about other beliefs was the work of the devil. It was old smooth-talking Satan messing with your brain, taking advantage of an idle mind, setting up his dangerous little workshop. Thinking about any religions but the one true religion was right up there with dancing when it came to awful sins.

But here he was at Fort Bragg, where he was Uncle Sam's recruit, not Jesus'. He wasn't sitting in Bailey Jordan's Sunday School class looking at the little coal-black curls on the back of Alice Snowden's snow-white neck while Brother Watkins warned about lascivious thoughts. He was out on his own in the world. He looked down at the buck private stripe on his heavy-starched, short-sleeved khaki shirt. It was time to be a man.

He was skimming through the few books the library had about the Jews and Muhammad and Christ Jesus Himself, about Billy Graham and Norman Vincent Peale and Mary Baker Eddy, and pretty soon he was in the section about Eastern religions. There was the chubby old bald-headed Buddha and the Hindu god with arms like a package of pretzels. He didn't know his name.

And then there was a book down on the bottom shelf with other oversize books, with the words "Kama Sutra" written in wavy, decorated letters on the cover. He started turning the pages, and his arms and legs started trembling. Some gland started pumping, and down below things started happening—trainees, of course, hadn't even seen a girl for six weeks—and he looked around to see if anybody was watching. He was afraid John Puffenbarger or Clyde Graham or some of his other basic-training buddies might be lurking, but there wasn't much chance they would be in the library. They had been deprived of booze for six weeks, as well, so most likely they were over at the NCO Club guzzling down ice-cold cans of 3.2 beer.

He spotted an overstuffed chair. Holding the book down at his waist and shuffling sort of Hunchback of Notre Dame-like, he went over and sat down. That was one time he was glad new, heavy-starched khakis that made him look like a doofus were too baggy. Hey, he was thinking to himself—or maybe he thought it many years later: How do you keep 'em down on the egg farm once they've seen the *Kama Sutra*?

So what he and Trieu did that night in the trailer, or what was left of the night, was just about as close to the Kama Sutra as anything he could imagine, and like Jo Lynne used to say, he had a fertile imagination. He felt just as jumpy, just as excited, as he felt that morning in the base library. Heck, with a Kodak, he told himself, they could have made their own *Kama Sutra*. And it all came naturally, to both of them.

It didn't start out that way. When he ventured into the bedroom and in the moonlight saw her there in his bed, her long black hair streamed across the pillow, it took just a moment for him to realize what he had to do. He started to touch her luscious shoulder and shake her gently and wake her, but then he said to himself, "Man what in heaven's name are you thinking?"

He took off his clothes real quiet-like, let them drop in a heap on the floor and slipped into bed beside her. She sort of smiled, her eyes still closed, and murmured "Hi, Wily. I'm glad you're home."

They slipped right into each other, like those creatures in the Greek myth that had always been looking for their other half and weren't complete until they found them. They were complete, like them. Everything was nice and slow and easy, as in a dream. Neither of them said a word; there were just the creaky bed, these little murmurings and the soft sounds of their bodies enjoying what they were doing. What had happened the night before at her house, he gave not a thought.

And then they slept for a while, and just as the sun was coming up, just when it was getting light enough to see, he woke up to find Trieu in a position sort of like she had been in on the dance floor with Aboy that night they first met. Her movie-star body—naked except for Aboy's tie—was writhing, arching and twisting into one Houdini position after another, only this time, lying on his back to begin with, he was into the dance. They turned and they twisted and they tangled, and in his own mind the background music was Willis Alan Ramsey's "Muskrat Love." Randy little muskrats they were, with bright eyes and sharp little teeth, and they couldn't get enough of each other. They were one being, and it was the most excruciatingly wonderful feeling he had ever experienced.

All morning they stayed tangled up in the light blue sheets on his narrow bed, sheets his Mama had washed and ironed, he realized at one point. They were wrapped up in each other, getting up only to go to the bathroom or to get a drink of water and then once for him to call Sue Bee to tell her he wasn't coming in. Even though it was the first day he had missed since the campaign began, he could tell she wasn't pleased. He told her he had some family business to take care of.

"Are you prepared for Houston?" she asked, her voice sort of snippy. he could see her with a checklist in the crook of her arm, pen in hand, like a school marm in "Little House on the Prairie." By Houston, she was reminding him that Red was scheduled to make an appearance on Sunday at the Mighty Spirit Flame Church of God in Christ. With 5,000 members, it was the largest black church in the state. He told her he would be ready, then reached across a sleeping Trieu and hung up the phone.

A little after noon they both agreed they had to have something to eat. Trieu sat up on the edge of the bed, slipped on the kimono he had seen the night before—those were banyan trees in the design, she told him—and padded into the kitchen. He heard her open the refrigerator.

"Oooh my! Wily," she said, laughing, "there's nothing here."

"I'll tell you what," he said, sitting up in bed as she leaned against the doorframe, yawning, one foot lazily rubbing the smooth brown calf of her leg. "Let's go over to Grungy's for burgers and fries, and then head to Levi Springs."

"Levi Springs I know. And love!" she said, "but Grungy's? What's Grungy's?"

"You'll see." He bounded out of bed naked, took her in his arms and lifted her off her feet and, with her legs locked around his waist, they twirled around the narrow room. She tossed her head back and giggled, and he couldn't believe she was so light and flexible—until he remembered the night before. He put her down on the edge of the bed and pulled on a pair of faded old jeans and a cutoff Waco Lulacs baseball sweatshirt. Trieu had a little drawstring canvas bag she had brought with her. She put on khaki shorts and a dark blue t-shirt that showed off her shape and her dark skin. Around her neck she wore a gold necklace with a tiny arched dolphin.

"Get your swimsuit," she reminded him as they stepped outside, the noonday sunlight nearly blinding them. He went back in and got a pair of old cutoff jeans. They decided they would drive by her house to pick up her suit on the way to Grungy's. He pulled the front door to and reached under the front porch for Shoogy's pellets.

"So who's this?" Trieu asked, bending down beside Shoogy's cage. "He's a banty, isn't he?"

She knew enough to keep her fingers out of his cage, but she admired him just the same. And he did look good, the red and orange and green feathers iridescent in the sun. "He's beautiful!" she said softly. "Do you fight him, Wily?"

For a split second, he couldn't decide whether he knew her well enough to confess. "He's had his moments," he said. "Retired undefeated." He poured the pellets into the tray and filled Shoogy's water bowl. "How'd you know about banties?"

"I lived in the Philippines. Cock fighting is almost the national sport in the Philippines."

"But I thought you were Vietnamese."

"I am," she said, laughing and taking him by the arm and dragging him around the back of the trailer to where she had hidden her Alfa Romeo from him the night before. "I'll tell you all about it over lunch."

She opened the door and got in behind the wheel. He walked around to the other side and vaulted the passenger-side door into the tan-leather front seat.

"Grungy's? Is that what you call the place? So alluring! And so romantic! Our first meal together. At Grungy's." She laughed that lovely, tinkling laugh he already had come to love. They gave a wave to Willis Seymour, who was puttering around the front porch of his trailer. Purse glanced back and saw him staring as they turned on to Levi Springs Road.

Grungy's was on the Drag a few blocks north of the university. It was a dingy white stucco building with faded orange lettering —"Grungy's Come-Back Burgers," it said—and from the outside looked about as inviting as the name suggested. Once it had been a drive-in, with two young black men as the carhops. These days you went inside to order, and Raymond, one of the original carhops, now old and gray, was still there to wait on you. Back in the '40s, varsity cheerleaders used to climb up to Grungy's flat roof and hold big pep rallies the night before a game, with thousands of cheering people in the parking lot below. Grungy's had a history. It also had some of the best cheeseburgers west of the Mississippi. Grungy's was to burgers what the Elgin Market was to barbecue.

The old place was already crowded with its usual lunchtime crowd—students, businessmen, a table filled with firemen from the station up the street—but they found an empty booth in the noisy back room. Raymond, in his usual black slacks and long-sleeved white shirt, a neatly folded white dish towel tucked into the waistband of his slacks, came over, his order pad at the ready. Ray Charles was on the jukebox singing about Georgia being on his mind. Raymond, with his Brillo-pad gray hair and ready smile, looked a little like Ray Charles.

"How's the campaign, my man?" Raymond asked.

"It's looking good. I have a feeling we turned a corner the last few days."

"And you, my dear, welcome to Grungy's," Raymond said, putting down paper napkins and silverware.

"Raymond, this is Trieu. This is her first time."

"Again, welcome, my lovely," he said. He and Trieu shook hands. "You chirren ready, or do you need more time?"

"We're ready," he said. "Two double-meat chicken cheeseburgers, two orders of french fries, two chocolate malts. We're hungry as dogs."

"What ch'all been doin'?" Raymond asked.

Trieu giggled and looked down at her lap. He let the question pass.

Ordering, he had this sudden memory of being in high school and taking Cherrie Wallace to the Triple AAA Drive-in on their first (and only) date, before he met Jo Lynne. He was worried he didn't have enough money, so as they drove along Bellmead Drive he felt in the pocket of his jeans and ascertained that he had just enough for two burgers and two cokes, just enough and no more. That's what he ordered for the both of them as soon as the carhop roller-skated up to the car and chirped "Take your order?" And that's when Cherrie leaned over and said in simpering words he could still hear, "I'll have the same."

Trieu did no such thing, and besides, he wouldn't have felt bad with her about not having any cash. With her, he didn't feel bad about anything. They looked at each other and grinned. "You go first," he said.

"Go first where?"

"I want to know about your life," he said, leaning across the table and taking hold of both her wrists, sliding his hands up her smooth, honey-colored forearms. "I want to know everything!"

Trieu looked off over his shoulder. He glanced back to see what she was looking at and realized that she was looking far, far away, at nothing and at everything as she summoned her past. She looked up at Grungy's grease-dingy ceiling and then at him. She took a deep breath. "Ok," she said, "here goes."

She told him she had been born in a village a few miles up a little river from Tua Hoa, that she had two older brothers and two older sisters. Her father was a rice farmer and fisherman. Her mother took care of the house and helped out in the rice paddies at harvest time.

"It was a wonderful life, Wily. Vietnam is a beautiful country, so green and so lush. And the lovely river sustained us. We were poor, but we always had enough to eat, and our hut was spacious enough for our large family, also for my grandparents. My older brothers worked in the fields with my father, and my sisters were working in Saigon. And I would work in the fields too, when I wasn't in school. My grandmother helped my mother around the house, but I was outside as much as I could be."

Raymond brought their food and set it on the graffiti-scarred wooden table. "Anything else?" he asked, but Purse barely heard him he was so caught up in Trieu. She stopped talking for a minute and handed him the ketchup. He shook the bottle and let the sauce flow over the hot, salty fries. Trieu, he noticed, didn't use ketchup.

"Do you know what my favorite job was?" she asked, smiling. "In the summer, and even when I got home from school if my father was working in the fields, my job was to bring our water buffalo in. He was like a member of the family. I'd lead him into his pen, scratch his huge back with a wire brush, put his hay in the hay rick for his hard day of working.

"Oh, Wily," she said, taking a deep breath, her eyes sparkling, "I remember how wondrous it was coming in from the fields, me perched like a little myna bird behind his big head as he ambled slowly down the path, my bare feet hanging down behind his big ears, the beautiful banyan trees a tall canopy above us, the birds singing and flitting about. Sitting up so high, I loved pretending I was Trieu Au."

"But you are Trieu Au," he said.

"Not really. Every Vietnamese person knows there is only one Trieu Au. She is the Vietnamese Joan of Arc. When she was in her early 20s, this was 2,000 years ago, she led a thousand men into battle against the hated Chinese. She wore golden armor and rode a giant elephant. The Trieu Au *you* have come to know was wearing shorts and riding a lowly water buffalo, her beloved father walking alongside."

"I wish I could have been there," he said, thinking of what he had seen of Vietnam. It wasn't the Vietnam Trieu described.

She took a sip of her malt. "Do you know what we called him?"

"Your father?"

"No," she said, giggling. "My water buffalo. We called him Tibo."

"What's that mean?"

"Big balls," she said. Both of them laughed so hard, they nearly sprayed chocolate malt all over the table.

Again, he thought about telling Trieu that he had been in country for 13 months, but he thought better of it. "So when did you leave?" he asked. "And why?"

"My father was the village elder," she said, "even though he wasn't elderly. It is just that he was smart and practical and everyone looked up to him. They expected him to know what to do, especially when the war began coming closer to our village. Many times we could hear the sound of guns firing and we'd look up and watch the American choppers flying overhead and the men with guns in the open doors, but for a long time we were left alone. We were village people, and we wanted nothing to do with war."

The lunchtime crowd was leaving, and it was easier to hear Trieu's soft voice. Joni Mitchell was on the jukebox recalling life's illusions. "I really don't know life at all," she sang.

Trieu daintily picked up a french fry with her fingers and bit off half. She got back to her story. "One night," she said, "the VC came to our village. They were like ghosts in the night. They just appeared, silently. My father went out in the darkness, and I remember pushing back the curtain and peeking out the door of our hut. I saw him talking quietly to three men in black pajamas. One I recognized; he was my cousin. They had guns. After a little while, my father came back in and lay down on the mat beside my mother. 'What did they say?' she wanted to know. He whispered 'Hush. We will talk in the morning.'"

And so they did. The VC wanted her brothers, Trieu said, but neither the young men nor their father felt the VC's fight was their fight. The family started the day as usual, but instead of going down to the rice fields, they made their way to the inlet where the family fishing boat was tied up. They brought as much with them as they could without making it obvious that they were fleeing. And then they cast off into the river, headed toward the open sea and, they hoped, to the relative safety of the Philippines.

"It was very, very difficult, Wily," Trieu said in a soft voice. "We left behind our friends, my grandmother. We left behind Tibo," she said with a little smile.

He took her hand. Leaning across the table, he kissed the back of her wrist. Her brown eyes glistened.

Levi Springs was crowded, even though it was the middle of the week. The giant natural pool of cold, clear spring water drew people from all over, almost year 'round but especially when it was so beastly hot. It was Purse's favorite place in town, maybe his favorite place anywhere, he told people. All he had known growing up was the brown, old Bosque River. He would go with his dad and his Uncles Joe and Clyde to the river to swim during the heat of the summer. He would swim; they would noodle for catfish. Only once was he brave enough to do any noodling himself.

It was the last time he went with the three of them, just before he shipped out. His basic-training buzz cut still hadn't grown out, so his head looked like a brown tennis ball with ringlets. He was home on leave, on his way to Fort Lee for supply-school training and then to 'Nam. Normally he would stay on the bank fishing with a cane pole, a real scaredy-cat, while his dad and uncles would walk out into the water, wade down a ways toward a high bluff and then start reaching in under that bluff, into little hollowed-out dens. That's where the catfish liked to hole up. He could imagine them lurking, big and fat and wise, their long whiskers like sharp gray whips. His Uncle Clyde liked to tell about the time when he was a boy that he reached into a hole and found himself a no-shoulder. The snake left a crook in his right forefinger he still had. J. Pott Rolland, their boyhood buddy, had been attacked by a mean mama beaver while he was out noodling. She sliced into his arm, his Uncle Joe said, like it was a steamed weenie.

Some noodlers use gloves, but not the Foxxes. They say they have to be able to feel what's in that hole. "Iffen it feels smooth like a rock, you got yourself a turtle," Uncle Joe will tell you. "Smooth and slick, then it's a catfish."

This time, just to prove he was a man, just to prove he was tough enough to defend his country, he waded out with them. They waded down river a ways, water up to their bellies, the bottom sandy and shifting, until Uncle Clyde picked out a place where the bank had been scooped out by rushing floodwaters.

"I'll go first, son," he said, "just to make sure there ain't no gars or cotton mouths lying in wait for Uncle Sam's finest." He grinned and winked at his nephew, then crouched down until the water was chest deep. Wily could barely make out his right arm waving back and forth among the slimy roots and murky water. His hand was up in that hole.

"You try it," he said.

He bent down, his hand splay-fingered, moving his arm back and forth. Oh, man, he hated what he was doing. He realized that his fingers were wriggling, almost asking for a bite.

"Can't you feel him?" his uncle whispered in his ear, all excited.

"No," he started to say, but then that's when he realized he couldn't feel him, because his hand was all the way down his mouth. That's about when that catfish caught on too. The creature tried to yank free, and then it was all a big blur of splashing and thrashing, his dad and Clyde and Joe falling all over each other trying to yank Wily's arm out and get a hook in that big old Moby Dick mouth.

They had a good day, that day on the river. He proved he was a man, sort of, even though he did give a scream when that fish bit down on his arm. Who would've known his dad would be dead six months later? Dead from cancer.

No noodlers at Levi Springs, that's for sure, but there were luscious college girls, topless on towels laid out on the soft St. Augustine grass. He could smell sun tan lotion and fresh-cut grass, and it was intoxicating, Down the hill, in the glistening green water, serious swimmers in tiny black trunks, bathing caps and goggles, made their way slowly back and forth, back and forth, like trolling sharks, across the wide pool. Little boys in baggy swim trunks lined up at the diving board, bouncing on their toes and hugging skinny arms to their chests, waiting to take their turn to do their cannon balls and somersaults off the board into the cold water. Just outside the chain link fence, where the cold spring water narrowed into a white-water stream over the low dam, a gaggle of stoned hippies, their big Heinz 57 dogs decked out with red bandanas around their necks, cavorted in the cascade. Levi Springs was a glorious place.

He found an empty spot on the hillside half in and half out of the shade of a big live oak and spread their towels on the grass. He felt the hint of a breeze, gently shaking the limbs of the live oak above, and then, just as he knew he would, he breathed in the sweet insinuating scent of marijuana.

He watched people tossing Frisbees and spotted one of the Levi Springs regulars. Scotsman Hillatop was here as usual; that's what one of Purse's buddies called him. Tall and bony, strolling the limestone bluff above the shallow end of the pool, he wore his baggy black Speedo, rimless glasses above a long gray beard, and a plaid tam o-shanter. Purse had never been to Levi Springs without seeing him, though he couldn't say he had ever seen him so much as get a toe wet.

Across the pool, he saw Trieu emerge from the dressing room in a black one-piece bathing suit that fit her like a dolphin's skin. She had her long, black hair pulled back in a ponytail. He watched her stride to the side of the pool. Without even sticking her toe in the frigid water, she skim-dived in. She swam like a dolphin too. From one side of the wide pool to the other she never came up for air, just occasionally flapped her arms and legs until she was all the way across to Purse's side.

She bobbed over to the ladder, climbed out of the water and with a quick flick of a finger pulled the edge of her suit down over a lovely buttock. She was beautiful; there was no other word to describe her. The water dripping off her perfect olive skin, her long leg muscles shifting like a dancer's as she walked—he couldn't stop looking at her. And neither could a lot of other people, guys and gals.

"Are you going in, Wily?" Trieu asked as she knelt on the towel.

"In a minute," he said. "I want to get good and hot first."

She picked up the tube of sunscreen, squeezed a dollop into her hand and without even asking began spreading it across his shoulders. He was a bit embarrassed at first but then leaned back on his elbows and, like an old dog with his stomach being rubbed, relaxed and enjoyed.

He was thinking about her legs. "Where'd you learn to dance like that?" he asked, his eyes closed, echoing her question for him at the Wagon Wheel. He couldn't see her face, since she was behind him, but she stopped massaging his back and shoulders.

"Like what?" she asked softly.

He glanced around at her. "Like at the Wagon Wheel," he said, grinning. "It was pure-dee amazing."

She looked off toward the water, the hint of a smile on her face. At least he thought it was a smile; it looked like she could just as easily have burst into tears. "Go in the water and cool off, my fine young friend, and I'll tell you when you come back."

The third day out into the South China Sea, pirates intercepted the crowded, leaky boat the Nguyens paid a fortune to take passage on. The family, along with everyone else on board, lost everything they had. Still, they were grateful that Trieu and other young women weren't kidnapped. Eight days later, they limped into Manila where they were told to stay in the bay. They stayed on the boat for another 11 days, with hardly any food and water and then lived for months in a refugee camp. At 15, Trieu found a job first as a waitress and then as a dancer at a disco in Subic City's Barrio Barretto.

"First I worked at a place called Cherry Boy," Trieu said, "then a friend of mine—her name was Mowladon—got a better job at a place nearby called Devil's Inn, and I tagged along with her. For three years I was one of the girls of Olongapo. You know what they say about the girls of Olongapo, don't you?"

He was afraid he did. He had spent his R-and-R in the Philippines. "'Nothing more beautiful, nothing more fine.' That's what they say anyway."

He had listened to the lovely Trieu without saying anything. He was trying to take it all in. She was quiet for a moment, and, still without saying anything he went down to the water and dived in, the cold forcing a gasp out of his skinny chest. He splashed across and back, then climbed up the grassy rise and flopped down beside Trieu on the towel. She was lying on her back, her feet crossed, her hands resting on her midsection. She had her eyes closed.

"Did my story upset you?" she asked quietly.

"Not upset me exactly. It's just, it's just a lot to take in."

"You do what you must do to survive," she said. "Someday you will learn that, my dear Wily."

When they got back to the trailer late in the afternoon, they were beat, probably from being in the sun so long. They collapsed onto the bed and slept, waking up only briefly to make a slow, sleepy kind of love, and then immediately fell asleep again.

The next time Wily woke, it was dark, and the quiet sounds of evening drifted in through the window. He raised up and peered across Trieu's back at the clock; it was close to 11. "I'm starving," Trieu mumbled into the pillow. "What time is it?"

She shuffled into the bathroom to take a quick shower. He waited for her to come out before he took his shower. Suddenly, it seemed, they were a bit shy with each other; he didn't know why. When it was his turn, he noticed that the tiny, steamy bathroom smelled of mysterious female potions and lotions. The shower spray pricked his sunburned skin.

They decided to drive over to the Magnolia Cafe, a hippie kind of place across Town Lake with pancakes and omelets at all hours, plus a lot of humus and tofu and all kind of vegetarian delights. In one of the booths, a kid in a wrinkled white dress shirt and black-rimmed glasses, his wiry black hair piled high, leaned his head on the palm of his hand and read from a book called *The Symbolism of Evil*. The Magnolia stayed open all night and was a gathering place for night owls and students and local musicians after a gig.

A young woman with short, pink-colored hair showed them to a table. She was wearing tattered jean shorts, hiking boots and a tie-dyed t-shirt knotted under her braless breasts. Above their heads, hanging on wires from the ceiling, was a pink papier-mâché pterodactyl. The creature wore red high-top tennis shoes.

Trieu yawned. "I have to get home and get some shut-eye," she said. "Sleep does not seem to be on the menu when you're around." She smiled.

"What is it you have to do?"

"I have to be in court," she said, waiting for his eyebrows to rise in surprise. "No, no, it is not what you think. I do work for the Catholic diocese, whenever someone in the judicial system is Vietnamese and needs an interpreter. This one should be interesting, maybe even a little scary. It's a young man from my hometown on trial for murder."

Once she mentioned it, he remembered reading about the case. A young Vietnamese fisherman from Minerva, a little town on the Gulf Coast, had had a run-in with the local Ku Klux Klan. Ended up shooting some guy, a Klan member who was also a shrimper, and now he was on trial for murder.

"You have to drive all the way to Minerva?"

"No. Fortunately, there is a change of venue. The trial's in Seguin."

"You know the guy?"

"Yes. I do. Even though he's a bit older. He used to work for my father."

That was the first time Trieu had mentioned her father, since her story about the Philippines. He assumed the man was still over there. Just when he was about to ask her about him, Red and Axel Grenon walked in. Red in a casual skirt and t-shirt with sequins across the front, tall, slim Axel, his gray hair slicked back in a ponytail. White bell-bottom jeans, leather sandals, tight black t-shirt—he looked exactly like what he was, a French film director. They were an odd couple, you had to admit, especially when you compared Axel to button-down Howard, Red's ex, a lawyer and the father of her four grown kids.

A few people spoke to them, some stared, but most paid them no mind. It was like that in laid-back Austin. Big-name folks could pretty much go where they wanted without anybody bothering them. Of course, if they were together in a place like Lubbock or Amarillo, it would be a different story. Red's relationship with a Frenchman, a French filmmaker at that, might turn out to be as big a deal as her lesbian buddies.

Axel noticed Purse and nudged Red. Smiling, they made their way over to the booth. Purse introduced them to Trieu, and she asked them if they wanted to sit down. Purse hoped they would say no, figured they would say no, but to his surprise they accepted. Trieu slid out and came around beside Purse. She patted his thigh as Red and Axel slid in across from them.

"This is the first night in ages we've had absolutely nothing to do," Red said. "It's heavenly."

"Tonight was also my night in the kitchen," Axel said in his deep Yves Montand English, his brown eyes flashing in their nest of wrinkles. "So I decided c'est une bonne nuit for le Magnolia!" He smiled.

"You guys want to order?" the pink-haired waitress asked. Red ordered a Caesar's salad and a cup of Earl Grey tea, Axel a short stack of pancakes, bacon and coffee, real coffee, not decaf, he told the waitress.

"Ms. Ryder, it is so very much a pleasure to meet you," Trieu said, smiling. "And Monsieur Grenon, I want you to know that I love your work."

"And what do you love the best, ma cherie?"

"There's no question," Trieu said. "'Je mange les enfants.'" I've loved it ever since I saw it at the Waverly in the Village. I love the intensity of it, the subtle sense that something's wrong long before the denouement. But still you let it build and build until—until the suspense is almost unbearable."

"Mon Dieu!" Axel exclaimed, slapping the sides of his head with the fingertips of both hands, a big grin on his face. "This girl knows her cinema."

"And what is your critique of—let me see, of 'La Danse de la Llama Nue'? He sat back from the table as the waitress plopped down his pancakes.

Red and Purse watched Trieu look over Axel's shoulder, fashioning a thoughtful response. Axel reached for the pitcher of maple syrup. Purse was surprised a Frenchman would use syrup, not only on his pancakes but on his bacon too.

"To be quite frank, Monsieur Grenon, it troubled me,' Trieu said, a slight frown on her face.

"And you will tell me why, sil vous plait?"

And they were off. Red looked at Purse and shrugged. "Hey, you ran out on me today," she said, with Trieu and Axel so caught up in their film conversation they were oblivious to anyone else.

Purse had learned to look into her ocean-blue eyes. If they looked like steel, if they bored right through you, you knew you were in trouble. If they seemed to be dancing, everything was okay. They seemed to be dancing, sort of. He could tell she wanted it to sting a bit. He knew he wouldn't get too many chances to displease her.

His face felt hot; he was sure he blushed. The Dairy Queen blowup flashed through his mind. "Everything go okay?" he asked quickly.

"It was pretty routine. Speech to the Abilene Rotary Club this morning on property taxes and hospital beds for drug addicts, walking the streets in Abilene and Buffalo Gap this afternoon. It was a pretty good day, all in all. People seemed receptive. And your pal Aboy says hey, by the way."

"You have him all to yourself today?"

She grinned. "No, Raenell was with us. They did ok together. Both of them seemed to be on their best behavior."

Their waitress came by to collect her tip. "Midnight shift change," she said, yawning.

Arms crossed atop the table, an index finger tapping, Red tuned back in to our companions. She didn't like it when she wasn't the center of attention.

"But it was a political statement, a subtle geopolitical statement," Axel was saying, eyes flashing, arms waving. "Perhaps it was too subtle? I am a European, after all, not a gauche Texan—but it's there nevertheless. It's embedded in the characterization, in the setting! Mon dieu, in the bloody era itself!"

"Political statements? What do you know about political statements?" Red teased, pushing into Axel with her shoulder. And that brought Purse and Red back into the conversation. She started telling about how Axel found Texas-style politics so bizarre, what with Ma and Pa Ferguson and W. Lee "Pass the Biscuits, Pappy" O'Daniel and Cactus Jack Garner, so bizarre he was thinking about making a movie. He'd have to wait for Red's political fate to be decided, of course, but he was already making inquiries with some guy named Dino, one of his wealthy European backers.

"The only problem," he said, "is that real life here is so unbelievable it's *tres difficile* to make up something that tops it. Where else do you find a politician who shoots himself in the arm, so people will think—how do you say?—the Ku Klux Klan is after him? And where else would you find a man elected judge simply because he has the name Gene Kelly? My dear, did your beloved Texans think he was going to don his black judge's robe and tap dance into the courtroom everyday while singing 'Singin' in the Rain'?" Axel shook his head and laughed. "I love it, I fucking love it!"

"And what about when Red wins?" Purse asked him (proud that he hadn't said if, like he was thinking). "Can you still make the movie?"

"Oh, I fully expect her to win. And, yes, I believe I can make the movie."

"We'll have to see about that," Red said, frowning slightly as she took a sip of tea. "And what about you, *ma cherie*?" Axel asked, ignoring Red's comment and flashing a grin at Trieu. "Do you believe she can win?"

Trieu was silent for a moment. "Please understand that I am still new to this country, Monsieur Grenon," she said slowly, "as are you, so I do not understand all the idiosyncrasies of the American system. But yes, I think you can win, Ms. Ryder. Please forgive my effrontery, but I think voters here are, in some very basic ways, not unlike voters in my own country, in any country."

"In what way, dear?" Red asked. "I'm intrigued by your insights."

"I know literature more deeply than I know politics. May I be so bold as to recite a poem?"

"By all means," Red said, smiling the way you smile when a little kid is about to say her A-B-Cs.

"Beneath three tall trees, inviting spring shade, and, oh! glorious flowers."

"A haiku, no less!" Axel exclaimed, reaching across the table and squeezing Trie's hand.

"That's lovely, Trieu," Red said, "but what in hell's half acre does it mean?"

Trieu smiled, shyly. "Perhaps it means nothing," she said. "Or perhaps it means that the people, all people, are interested in themselves, their children, their security. That is the way it was in my family. A candidate wise enough to address those three concerns—taxes, schools, security—allows other concerns to blossom on their own."

Axel had his mouth open, his eyes wide open above the coffee cup held halfway to his lips. Purse already knew he was in love, but suddenly, at that moment, all three of them seemed to be.

Later that night, after Trieu had gone to her home and Purse had gone to his, sometime in that nocturnal moment between deep sleep and groggy wakefulness, he drifted into a dream. He was lying on a daybed on the screened-in porch of a fishing cabin. A woman lay beside him. It wasn't Trieu. It wasn't Jo Lynne. It was Red. Her hair was a bright burning flame against the pillow, her smooth skin a dazzling white. And then they were riding double on a mule, Red holding the reins, as they descended a narrow, rocky trail into the depths of the Grand Canyon. Red wore cowboy boots with spurs, nothing else. He locked his arms around her waist. It was taut, like Trieu's, and slippery with sweat. Suddenly, she spurred the mule, hard, and the animal leaped forward just as the trail twisted back on itself. All he could see was blue sky as they went sailing over the edge, and the sinking-stomach sensation of falling jarred him awake.

★ ★ TEN ★ ★

Tall and skinny, with just a little bit of a fat man's paunch, Joe Frank Golden reminded Purse of the Tin Man whenever he saw him. Joe Frank was hunched over a pay phone in the lobby when Purse walked through the doors of Cox Air Service on Sunday morning. He had a paper cup of coffee in one hand and a cigarette in the other, the phone receiver wedged between his neck and shoulder. That's how you usually saw Joe Frank, hunched over a phone, smoke from a cigarette curling around his head, a cup of coffee within easy reach.

Joe Frank tended to get air sick, so he would be staying behind, which was a good thing as far as Purse was concerned. He liked Joe Frank just fine, but he had been with him one time when they flew through a summer thunderstorm on the way to Longview. What happened on that flight was not pretty. He had come out to the airport on this morning to make sure Red got off okay, and she would want to talk to him about the Houston media. It sounded like he was on the phone with a guy from the AP.

Purse was early, so he got a cup of coffee and a powdered-sugar donut from a table in the lobby, happy he got to them before Aboy showed up. He sat down on one of the orange plastic seats in the waiting area. Somebody had left pieces of the Sunday paper scattered on the seat. He glanced at the sports section—Red Sox and Carl Yastrzemski making yet another, probably futile run at the American League pennant; Longhorns cutting back on two-a-days a week before their first game of the season with the Houston Cougars.

The sun was streaming through the big plate-glass windows. Far across the airfield, he saw a big silver jetliner taxiing out to its takeoff point. The plane shimmered in the glaring heat. On the tarmac just outside the window, the six-seat Cessna 640 they would be flying on to Houston was being gassed up and serviced. The spiffy little brown and cream-colored plane belonged to a trial lawyer in town named Merlin Pitts. Merlin had made a load of money hauling sawbones doctors into court and winning millions of dollars in settlements for people who had come out of surgery to find the wrong leg amputated or with a sponge sharing space with their spleen. Purse had never met him, but Aboy said he was a real smooth character; he would have a jury in tears and writing a blank check for the victim before closing arguments. Red relied on him for a lot.

There on the front page of the paper was the goofy grin and big white hat of Jimmy Dale Sisco. It was a huge spread—Jimmy Dale on a charging quarter horse, his lariat looped above his head as he chased after a steer on one of his West Texas ranches; Jimmy Dale at the head of a long, polished table in a high-rise boardroom, the Dallas skyline thrusting up behind him through the floor-to-ceiling windows; Jimmy, Sissy and their three daughters and a son relaxing in what must have been the family room of their Highland Park mansion. "THE SISCO KIDS," the headline read. A sidebar on the governor's race had the headline "LOCKED UP?" At least they threw in a question mark.

Purse was just starting to read about how 54-year-old James Dale Sisco, Jr. could have rested on his laurels running the family ranching operations throughout West Texas and Argentina, just like his daddy had done, but he wasn't satisfied. No-sirree-bob! He geed and hawed the family business into oil and banking and insurance and racehorses; the company had been a rip-roaring success in every single venture Jimmy plunged into. And now that he had climbed every mountain and forded every stream, now that he was richer than Jett Rink himself, he had decided to take his old-fashioned horse sense, his supreme self-confidence and his mystical Midas Touch and set his sights on Washington. It was his bounden duty as a fourth-generation Texan, he proclaimed with all due modesty, to get things running right for the good people of his beloved state—and then, as Calvin Locke noted, Jimmy Dale, like Cincinnatus himself, would retire back to the land, back to the simple ranching ways he loved so deeply and so well.

That's what the story said, anyway. From what Purse could tell, Jimmy Dale was dumb as a stick. All hat and no cattle in the brains department. What he was, as Red herself said, was a stalking horse for the monied interests that ran the state.

Before he got to the jump page, Sue Bee and Red came rushing in. Red was already in her Sunday-go-to-meetin' clothes: a swishy blue dress with tiny white polka-dots, white patent-leather pumps and a white patent leather purse—it had a strap, he noticed. Her flaming red hair just peeked out from under a broad-brimmed white straw hat with yellow daisies—real ones, they appeared to be—curlicued around the brim. Snappy. She looked snappy, his Uncle Joe would have said. Sue Bee was dressed up too and had a blue speech box in her hand. He was glad he was wearing his lizard-green suit.

While Red conferred with Joe Frank over in a corner of the waiting room, he scooped up the papers and ambled out to the plane. It was already hot outside; waves of heat from the pavement felt like an oven. Standing around on the tarmac talking to Gene Ray Donovan, Merlin Pitts' full-time pilot, he saw Aboy hurrying through the glass doors, a cup of coffee in one hand, what looked like half a dozen donuts ring-tossed on two fingers. He was wearing his own Sunday-go-to-meeting clothes: white suit, white suspenders, light-blue shirt, pink tie, and white patent-leather loafers. "Good Sabbath to you, Deacon Foxx," he said. "May the Lord bless you and keep you as we gambol into His heavenly azure pastures."

"Morning, Aboy," he said. "Any of those donuts for me?"

Sue Bee and Red were right behind Aboy. "Mornin', Gene Ray," Red said. "Let's go to Houston."

"Yes ma'am," Gene Ray said, tipping his navy-blue pilot's cap and doing a little bow. They all climbed, hunched over, into the plane, Purse and Aboy in the two seats next to each other facing forward, Sue Bee and Red sitting across from them. Red carefully took off her hat and handed it to Purse, who twisted around and laid it in the luggage compartment behind their seats.

Gene Ray glanced back at his passengers. "Seat belts fastened?" he shouted as the propeller started spinning and the roar of the single engine filled the cabin.

Once they got airborne and leveled out, Aboy commenced consuming his donuts. Purse spread out the papers on his lap, while Sue Bee handed Red the speech. She had her silver Mont Blanc pen at the ready, tracing line by line what she would be saying at the church in a little while. Every once in a while, Purse would hear her give a little snort, like a pig would do, glance at Sue Bee and grumble, "I can't say that." She'd slash a line through the offending words, while Sue Bee's face bloomed red. Knowing Sue Bee, and knowing Red's disdain for Sue Bee's infernal high-mindedness, the stuff she was knocking out was probably something that made her sound like a cross between the kindly, old nun in *The Sound of Music* and a pissy hair-in-a-bun high-school librarian. Sometimes Red would write in something to replace what she'd marked out; sometimes she'd go on to the next line.

It was a little trickier than usual this time, for two reasons. One, her speech was in a church, on a Sunday morning, so it had to be a combination speech and sermon. And two, it was a black church.

Here was this planeload of white folks headed over to Houston, where more black people lived than any place in the state, and they had nary a black face among them. Now, there were a few minorities in the campaign—Winsome Yarbrough, the finance chairman, was one of them—but none were part of the inner circle, and there was rarely any reason for them to travel with her. Even though she had always carried the black vote every time she ran, it seemed to Purse that Sue Bee was right on this one. It was time to give colored staffers higher profiles; that's what she told Joe Frank Golden. Joe Frank said he would talk to her about it. On this trip, Red was hoping that the two black city councilmen who were expected to be at the church, plus Eddie Owens, would be considered part of the campaign entourage.

Purse handed Aboy the funny papers—he followed the adventures of Mary Worth, girl reporter—while he turned to the state/local section. The first story he noticed was about the trial in Seguin, the Vietnamese guy's murder trial that Trieu was a part of.

The story, as he read it in the paper, was pretty much what Trieu had told him. Tran Kim Tuyen was 35, although the picture in the paper made him look about 15. The local Catholic church had helped bring him and his family to Minerva some years earlier, and they had managed over the years to scrape together enough dough to buy a boat. Once they started catching shrimp, some of the locals tried to drive them out of business—burning crosses, vandalism on their boat, that kind of low-down, dirty dealing. Apparently Tuyen and a local fisherman, a guy named Leonard Silsbee, had some kind of confrontation out on the water and Silsbee ended up dead. And now the Vietnamese guy was on trial for murder.

Sue Bee and Red were still going over the speech. All that was left of Aboy's donuts was a sprinkling of white crumbs around his seat. The drone of the plane had put him to sleep, his big, red face slumped against Purse's shoulder. He looked out the window at the clear blue sky and, far below, the patches of brown and yellow sun-parched fields squared-off by straight gray lines of highway. The trial, murder, Trieu's past life in Vietnam—it was all a different world to him. He liked being above it all at the moment, maybe get a little bird's-eye view on the matter, but he still missed Trieu. He couldn't stop thinking about her.

There was a feeling that came over him now and then. It was hard to explain. In fact, to try to grab hold and think about it, to try to understand it, was enough to make it go away. It started in what people called the pit of your stomach and was sort of like when you're in a car and hit a dip in the road or you're on a roller coaster and you come over the top and start heading down, just before it gets too scary. It was a wonderful feeling, like your belly's filling with air or helium or something and you feel like you can float right off the earth. He remembered feeling it in a class at school, when he was really interested in the lesson, or when someone with a good, soothing voice was telling a story, or, when he was a little boy and had been put to bed late at night and he would hear the adults, their voices droning as they sat talking around the kitchen table, until he drifted off.

He didn't feel it often, and he could never summon it, but he loved it when it appeared. These days, just thinking about Trieu, which he did way too much for his own good, he realized, was almost like that pit-of-the-stomach feeling. He had fallen for her, hard, and he wasn't sure what to do about it. And he damn sure didn't know what to do about Jo Lynne.

"Eddie going to be at the airport or at the church?" he vaguely heard Red ask Sue Bee.

"I don't know, I think at the church," Sue Bee said. He saw Red wince when Sue Bee said 'I don't know.' She didn't like leaving things to chance. Sue Bee looked up at him; she didn't seem to notice Red's impatience. "You know, Purse?" she asked.

"Church is what Aboy said." He nudged Aboy with his shoulder.

"The church. Eddie, the Washington brothers, Councilman Steves, Councilman DuJonge—they'll be waiting at the sanctuary," Aboy said, eyes closed. He began rousing himself and folding up the funny papers. "Eddie's going to introduce you."

"We're in for a treat, no doubt about it," Sue Bee said. "I can hardly wait!"

"How 'bout C.T.?" Aboy asked. "He going to be there?"

"I doubt it," Red said. "I hear he's in real bad health." She capped her pen and put it in her purse and pulled out her compact. She shook her head and smiled. "But wasn't he something in his prime?" she said, looking in the small mirror and powdering her nose. "Cornelius Thaddeus Washington." Her freckled face wrinkled into a wide grin and she looked at Purse and Sue Bee. "Aboy'll remember this, even if you youngsters don't. Remember Lee Otis Ravenal, Aboy?"

"Indeed I do," Aboy said, cocking his head and laughing. "He was the . . . ."

"He was the epitome of the outside agitator," Red said. "Scraggly goatee, big Afro, combat boots, mean scowl on his face— just a real scary-looking dude. From New Orleans, I think—this is going back 25 years—and he showed up in Houston to lead these demonstrations against the Houston School Board because of their bullheadedness on integrating the schools. Well, young Mr. Ravenal ended up getting himself arrested for having one marijuana cigarette on his person."

"And the judge set his bail at $300,000," Aboy said. "But then his attorney, Dave Kotke, got so mad, he said, 'Judge, why don't you just make it a million?' Said it real sarcastic-like. And the judge, he said, 'Okay, it's a million.' Remember that, Red?"

"Indeed I do," she said, laughing. "So there was this big demonstration downtown, organized by the Rev. C. T. Washington himself. Howard 'n me drove over from Austin. I think that's the first time I met C. T. He got us organized out at Mighty Spirit Flame, and then we all marched downtown singing and shouting, C. T. playing the Pied Piper. It was a glorious day. I bet there was 5,000 people holding up signs and yelling 'Free Lee Otis! Free Lee Otis!' Well, it just so happened that the right honorable Governor Leo Kite happened to be in Houston to open the Houston Fat Stock Show and Rodeo, and he comes bumbling out of the Rice Hotel where they were having a press conference. . . ." She started laughing all over again. "Anyway, here's all these people shouting 'Free Lee Otis! Free Lee Otis!'"

"And Governor Dimwit," Aboy broke in, "turns to one of his dimwitted aides, and he says, he says. . ."

Red had recovered. "Are these hungry people? Is that what're hollering about? Can't somebody get 'em some government-surplus frijoles?"

They were all laughing as the plane began its descent, even Sue Bee, until Aboy reached over and slapped her on the knee. She grimaced and crossed her legs, her nylons making a swishing sound.

Purse swallowed to open up his ears and glanced out the window. The downtown skyscrapers were thrusting up so close he could almost reach out and touch them. He could hear Gene Ray talking to the control tower.

"Purse, there's gonna be a crowd," Red said. "You're gonna have to stay with me, but be polite about it. Knowing the Washingtons, it's gonna be choreographed down to the last amen, and that's good, unless the service goes on and on. Are we coming back right after the service, Sue Bee?"

"Yes ma'am, that's the plan."

"Anyway, Purse, stay with me. You'll be sitting on the front row with Sue Bee and Aboy; I'll be up on the rostrum with Shad and Eddie."

They landed a few minutes later, and a beautiful, chocolate-skinned college student met them at the plane in a shiny black Lincoln Continental. Her name was Coque Wilson; she pronounced it ko-kwee. Once they got in the car Aboy pointed to a little metal sign on the back of the front seat: "Williams & Fell Undertaking."

Red sat up front with Coque Wilson. Driving down Airline Road into the Fifth Ward, Purse heard her tell Red she was a marketing major, but she was taking the fall semester off to work in the campaign.

"That's wonderful, dear," Red said, "but you've got to promise me one thing. Promise me you'll get right back into school just as soon as this race is over. You hear what I'm sayin'?"

"Yes ma'am," Coque said with a cheery smile and a marketing-major kind of voice. She was very pretty. "Pastor Abednego told me he'd help me get college credit for my experience."

The neighborhood they were passing through looked bad, depressing. Everywhere you looked there was graffiti, grimy pawn shops, boarded-up storefronts, liquor stores with bars across the windows. Aboy nudged Purse and wiggled his eyebrows as they passed the Dew Drop Inn, a beat-up tourist court that advertised rates by the hour, plus free adult movies in your room. They passed a sad-looking little grocery store; a handwritten butcher-paper sign in the window advertised a special on chicken necks and gizzards. In the shade of a Walgreen's sign a legless man was sitting on the sidewalk selling pencils; he had scuffed leather coverings over his stumps. About the only people out and about on this Sunday morning were winos and bums hanging around the liquor stores. They were drinking what Purse guessed was cheap wine or Big Boy malt liquor. They hid the containers in brown paper bags.

Coque turned into a tumble-down residential neighborhood, little frame houses with junked cars out front, a lot of tall chinaberry and pecan trees that made Purse think of the Old South. Some of the houses had well-kept yards, were obviously tended to. Others, little shotgun houses on cement blocks, looked like a strong wind would flatten them to the ground.

A few blocks into the neighborhood, they began to see cars parked everywhere and families in their Sunday best walking along the rutted street. The men wore dark suits and hats, despite the heat, and almost every woman wore a big hat and wobbled in high heels through the dirt and gravel beside the road.

He could see the church itself a couple of blocks away. Little boys in white short-sleeve shirts and suspenders, their dark dress pants pulled high up on their waist walked along holding their mothers' hands, and little girls in frilly pastel-colored dresses with stiff petticoats held hands with each other. He liked the little pigtails that stuck out from their heads.

The church was a big, brown-brick box, two stories, with stained-glass windows and on the roof a squat round dome. Aboy pointed to the sign at the corner of the property: "THE MIGHTY SPIRIT FLAME CHURCH OF GOD IN CHRIST, A.M.E. "FOUNDED 1903, THE REVS. SHADRACH, MESHACH AND ABEDNEGO WASHINGTON PRESIDING, THE REV. C. T. WASHINGTON PASTOR EMERITUS."

"People call them 'the Three Revs' because of that sign," Aboy said as Coque came to a stop in the middle of the jam-packed street. "Shadrach's the pulpit minister, Meshach's the education minister and Abednego's the minister of music. They're triplets. C. T. was the pulpit minister here I'd guess 50 years. A towering presence during the Civil Rights Movement. The boys took over about a decade ago. I'm tellin' you, they're powerhouses in their own right. Not much happens in Fifth Ward without their okay."

Wide concrete steps across the front of the building, the steps bounded by brick walls, led up to a bank of bright-red doors into the sanctuary. Spread out like an inverted peacock's tail on each step from bottom to top were choir members in electric-blue robes trimmed in gold, a bunch of them at the bottom, fewer at the top. Presiding over their flock at the top of the stairs were The Revs, three movie-star handsome men in their mid-thirties, maybe a little older, with pencil-thin mustaches and shiny, slick-backed hair like Nat King Cole. In identical white suits, white bow ties, white shoes, with little red rosebuds in their lapels, they glowed in the morning sun like three ebony Gabriels.

Down on the sidewalk and spilling out into the street, a huge crowd of people in their Sunday best, their good-natured faces glistening with sweat, were waiting for the special guest. They began applauding as Purse hopped out and held the door open for Red. She swung her legs out, gracefully, and handed him her purse. He tried to carry it like a man, strap around his forearm, hand gripped underneath like it was a schoolbook.

Red straightened her dress, touched her hat and turned toward the crowd, smiling and waving. A big, sturdy-looking black woman in a green silk dress, middle-aged with short, curly hair, came striding toward them, a smile on her face, her broad, matronly arms reaching out toward Red. "Goodness gracious, if it isn't Eddie!" Red said, laughing. "How are you, Sugar?" Eddie laughed a deep man's laugh, and the two women hugged each other tight. The crowd at the bottom of the stairs kept on clapping.

Red quickly introduced them to the legendary Edwina Victoria Owens—Congresswoman Owens, the most famous black politician in the state, maybe the whole country. Everybody knew Eddie Owens, knew that voice, "the voice of God," some people said. Once you heard it, you never forgot it, as plenty of politicians hauled before her House Judiciary Committee had learned to their great discomfort.

Eddie took Red by the elbow and began to usher her old friend up the stairs. The moment the two women started up, the choir broke into song—"Oh, happy day!/ Oh, happy day!/ When Jesus washed/when Jesus washed,/ he washed my sins away." They were rocking and swaying and singing in four-part harmony, and Purse had never been a part of anything like it. People in his church, the Elm Mott Church of God in Christ, sang on Sunday mornings, but it was more like a heavenly obligation, a drone and a mumble as they stared down into their hymnals. It surely wasn't anything like this, something that was truly a joyful noise unto the Lord. He felt like they were walking up toward the gates of heaven itself.

At the top of the stairs, Congresswoman Owens introduced Red to the Washington brothers, who each gave her a kiss on the cheek. He heard Red ask Shadrach Washington how his daddy was. "He's doing a might poorly," the reverend said, "but as you can imagine, the power of prayer among these good folk has been known to work glorious wonders. The Good Lord willing, he'll be back amongst us soon." Then the Rev. Shad Washington took her by one arm and Eddie took her by the other, and they escorted her into the sanctuary.

Meshach and Abednego Washington ushered the rest of the entourage into the jam-packed building. Extra folding chairs narrowed the red-carpeted middle aisle. Everyone was standing.

Purse glanced up and back and saw that the balcony was full to overflowing, as well.

As they walked down the aisle, an orchestra up front broke into "Walking to Jerusalem," and the singing, swaying, hand-clapping choir began filing down the outside aisles and up to their choir loft in wide rows behind and above the pulpit. Behind the loft was a huge watercolor painting of the biblical Shadrach, Meschach and Abednego, wearing floor-length white robes and standing tall and proud in King Nebuchadnezzar's burning fiery furnace. The bright orange and red flames were licking all around them, but in the picture they hadn't even broken a sweat.

Purse remembered his Sunday school lesson, back in the fifth grade, when Miss Ocie Lambright had her students memorize one of her favorite verses: "The hair of their heads was not singed, their mantles were not harmed and no smell of fire had come upon them. Daniel chapter 3, verse 27." That's the way they had to say it. Full and complete.

Red and the congresswoman, along with Reverend Shad, sat themselves down on tall, white-cushioned, gold-trimmed chairs on the rostrum just below the choir. Aboy called them Empire chairs. The Reverend Meshach took his place before the singers and musicians, and suddenly his arms were gyrating, his hips bouncing, his toes tapping as he conducted.

Reverend Abednego strode over to the pulpit, raised both arms out in front of him and lowered them slowly, the signal for everyone to sit. As they took their seats on the red-cushioned front pew, Purse glanced over at Aboy. He had a blissful smile on his face; tracks of tears glistened on his red cheeks. He still thought of himself as a man of God, or at least he wished he were. You could tell he loved and appreciated professional presentations.

After the welcome, after two more songs and a prayer, after a rollicking version of "When the Saints Go Marchin' In" from the orchestra, the Reverend Meshach introduced his brother Abednego, who introduced Eddie, who told the crowd that Red was God's emissary, that she was doing God's work by looking out for His people. "Elect this woman," Eddie said. "Send this woman to that big granite edifice in Washington, and justice and mercy can't help but rain down on His people. Can't help it!"

Just listening to that deep, thunderous voice gave Purse goose-bumps. She flung out her right arm. "Brothers and sisters," she said, "I give you the next United States Senator from the great state of Texas! My friend and yours, the honorable Rose Marie Ryder!"

The congregation broke into applause and amens; the orchestra gave a drum roll and the choir held onto one long note in four-part harmony.

Red walked slowly to the pulpit, gave Eddie a big hug and smiled out over her audience. "I thought y'all were my friends," she said, laughing, "but now I'm not so sure. I learned a long time ago there's no winning when somebody has you follow Edwina Owens. Isn't that woman a treasure? Isn't she something?"

"Amen! Amen!" scattered voices shouted, and the congregation broke into applause again.

Red thanked Eddie again, thanked the congregation, thanked the Washington brothers, thanked the two city councilmen and thanked the Lord for a glorious Sunday morning. "The only thing missing this morning," she said in her Texas twang, "is my dear friend C. T." She glanced over at Shad Washington. "I know one thing," she said. "He's with us in spirit, just as he has been for well nigh half a century."

"Praise the Lord!" voices shouted. "Praise Brother C.T.!"

Shad put his hands together beneath his chin, gave a little bow and then looked down like he was praying.

Red paused, and the audience got quiet. Then, with just a hint of a smile on her face, scanning the audience right and left, back and front, she said. "Beware of Greeks bearing gifts." She paused for a beat, expectant faces hanging on her words. "Or whites who claim to understand blacks."

A loud, lone voice shouted "AMEN!" and Red did sort of a double-take, a wide grin on her face. The audience exploded with laughter.

Everyone quieted down, and Red continued: "A famous New York congressman, Adam Clayton Powell, said that, and I have lived long enough on God's good earth to know that he was right. And you have too. I would never presume to say that a little ol' white girl from the blackland prairie can put herself in your shoes or empathize totally with the plight of many of your brothers and sisters here in Houston and across this great state. But never no mind about that. There's one thing you and I have to keep on remembering: We are all one in the eyes of God. We are all one."

"Amen!" voices shouted.

"We all want the same things for ourselves and our families, don't we now? You know it as well as I do. We want the respect of our fellows, a decent job, good schools. We want bountiful opportunities for these beautiful children with us here this morning. We want to be safe and secure in our own neighborhoods, and we want to be able to worship the good Lord when we see fit and as we see fit."

"You tell 'em, Sister!"

"And I'm here to tell you this morning, those blessings of the Spirit can be ours. If—if we keep on working together, working as one, and if we keep on praying together, praying as one. As your dear, old daddy would say, Shad, we got to be pullin' those traces together."

"Amen!" people in the congregation shouted. "Amen!"

Purse was proud of Red. He could tell she was speaking from the heart. "You figure Sue Bee wrote that?" he whispered to Aboy, who didn't answer. He was mumbling to himself, under his breath, in words Purse couldn't understand.

Red talked for maybe 15 minutes about what she wanted to do in Washington and how she needed their vote, all their votes. Then it was time for Shad's sermon.

He started slow and low, like a locomotive gathering speed, like a mighty riverboat pulling out from the ship channel not far from where they sat, the big wheels turning, picking up steam. Once he got going—Purse had never heard anything like it, never seen anything like it. Tall, handsome Shadrach Washington became James Brown—pacing, light on his toes, like a panther from one side of the stage to the other, back and forth, back and forth. And then he was kneeling, dancing, microphone in hand, words tumbling out like a cataract. And then he slowed, came to a stop. "Pray with me," he said after a moment.

He lowered his head into the microphone. "Lord," he said in a low voice, "thank you for this glorious, blessed day. And we beseech you, Lord, for the strength and the wisdom and the energy to use it for your glorification. We don't want to be TV stars, Lord, we want to be 3-V stars—vessels in your glorious church, vassals in your glorious kingdom and victors, Lord, in your heavenly battle with that split-tongued serpent we called Satan!"

A cascade of amens from the congregation and a swish of snare drums from the orchestra poured down on the preacher. The man was up and pacing again, now with a swirling white-silk handkerchief in his free hand. Ever now and then he would wipe his glistening forehead. Shad pivoted into something about women in travail.

"Where's that?" Purse whispered to Aboy, who was listening intently to the sermon. "Is that in Texas?"

"No," Aboy whispered back. "He's talking about women in labor."

That made sense, sort of. Labor unions were vital to the campaign.

Aboy leaned over again. "Not organized labor," he said. "Women having babies."

Purse nodded and shifted his attention back to the preacher.

"For Jesus says, 'I'm gonna CRY like a woman,'" he shouted, and Purse was hearing James Brown on a high note. "A pregnant woman in labor. Like a woman delivering a child!"

Shad came to the edge of the stage and peered out. "Now, you ladies know what I'm talking about"—"Amen!" smiling women shouted, nudging their husbands sitting beside them. The men shook their heads and laughed—"and *I* know what I'm talking about." Shadrach stopped in mid-step and pivoted toward the congregation. "But what was *He* talking about?"

"Tell us, preacher!" the people shouted. (Purse was hoping he would, because he sure didn't know what *He* was talking about.)

"Now, He didn't say He was pregnant. He said he was going to cry out *like* a pregnant woman. Our Lord is being metaphorical, so to speak."

He went on like that for a while, about being in travail and so forth, and then he began winding down. "Now the time has come," he said in a low voice. Now in a louder voice: "The time has come to deliver up unto God Almighty, your toil and your troubles, your sins and your shortcomings. The time has come, right now, this morning, this glorious birthday morning! The time has come for *your* birthin', the time for *you* to be born again! Born again into a new day! Into a new life! Into Heaven's everlasting light."

Meshach had glided back in front of the choir, and as he raised his white-suited arms the choir started singing softly, "Just as I Am," as background sounds to Shadrach's words.

"Feel the PAIN!" Shadrach shouted. The pain of travail. The pain of broken lives, broken promises, broken hearts."

"We feel it, brother!" people shouted.

"Just as I am without one plea, but that thy blood was shed for me. . ."

"But then don't you feel the GLORY, don't you feel the JOY, feel the miracle of new life, new birth. Won't you come?"

"And that Thou bidd'st me come to Thee, O Lamb of God, I come! I come!"

Purse could feel chills running down his spine, the beginnings of a lump in his throat, and he could sense a shuffling behind them. When he glanced around, it seemed like the whole congregation was moving toward the front, slow and purposeful, like a mighty wave heaving toward a Galveston shore. Ushers leaned in to their rows and courteously motioned for them to move over toward folding chairs in the side aisle to make room for the multitudes coming to rededicate their lives, to be born again, to be baptized.

He glanced at Aboy. He was staring up at Shadrach. Tears were flowing down his big red face, and his gold-rimmed glasses were all fogged up, and he was still mumbling words to himself Purse didn't understand. He pulled on Aboy's sleeve to get him moving toward the side, but Aboy wasn't there beside him anymore. His eyes had seen the glory of the coming of the Lord, so to speak, and he had to follow. Slowly, he started moving trancelike up the steps toward Shadrach. Red saw what he was doing about the same time Purse realized what was happening, and she was trying to talk with her eyes, the corners of her mouth, her clenched-tight hands, that Purse was to pull him back—back to earth, so to speak. It was too late. This wasn't beautiful dancing Trieu leading him on; this was the Lord Jesus Christ himself.

Slowly Aboy climbed the steps to the stage. Slowly he walked to Shad Washington's side. And suddenly Shad realized that a big, bawling white man in a blinding white suit was standing beside him. Like a karate master, Shad whirled, and his arm flashed out and the heel of his hand collided with Aboy's broad forehead. He smote him. The sound was like slapping a side of beef, and Aboy fell backward like a lightning-struck tree. His head bounced once on the red carpet, and then he was still. Instantly, Shad crouched beside him, his hand in the air beseeching God. "HEAL, this man!" he commanded God in a loud and confident voice. "HEAL this man, and send his devils in a rush to everlastin' perdition! Send 'em in a rush, Lord, send 'em on a mighty wind!"

Others began crowding the stage, the ushers trying to form them into some semblance of a line. The same thing happened to each of them as happened to Aboy, and after five minutes or so, there must have been a dozen or so men and women stretched out like cord wood on the floor beside the white beached whale. Now and then, some of their legs would tremble or they would moan. The choir and the orchestra and the audience broke into another rendition of "Oh Happy Day, Oh Happy Day, When Jesus Washed, He Washed My Sins Away."

After the sinners and the born-aginners had come to, after more singing and more praying and money-collecting, after admonitions from Abednego about the God-given duty to vote, the service finally came to an end. It was after noon, and Purse felt stray-dog famished, but he had to get up to Red, surrounded by well-wishers, and to Aboy, who was in the middle of a huddle of choir members with their arms around each other. He saw Coque Wilson walk over and give him a big hug. He wondered if the hug felt more sisterly to Aboy now that he was born again—again.

He finally made it to Red, who was surrounded by church members. She saw him on the edge of the crowd and reached out to him. He managed to get her going down the steps until they got to an escort of older women in white gloves and white dresses with green sashes across the front and red straw hats shaped like rimless flower pots. They were to take Red and Congresswoman Owens into the Education Annex for a brunch with the Eunice

Guild, a women's group that did the bidding of the Lord and the Washington brothers.

Purse went with Aboy to Shad Washington's office behind the sanctuary. The plan was to meet with the three Washingtons, to go over how the church might assist Red's campaign. After meeting with the ministers, they would get the elders of the church to ratify their decision. He hoped Aboy had come back to earth, because he figured they were in for some hard horse-trading.

"Gentlemen, as you can see from the outpouring of love and affection this morning, the brothers and sisters here at Mighty Spirit Flame feel a bond with Ms. Ryder," Shad was saying in his smooth, mesmerizing voice. He sat behind his big desk in a high-back swivel chair upholstered in leather the color of a ripe plum. Purse and Aboy sat in soft, velvet-feeling high-backed chairs in front of the desk. Meshach was on one side of the room, sort of lounging against a kind of bay window that looked out on the parking lot behind the building. Abednego was sitting on a couch in a corner of the room smoking a cigar. (At least Purse thought it was Abednego; he still had trouble telling them apart.)

"Yes, there's no denying it was a mighty outpouring," Shadrach continued, a gold watch on his left wrist reflecting light from the chandelier above them, "and I expect the collection this morning will reflect the affection our people have for the good comptroller. But in all candor, Mr. Suskin, Mr. uh, Foxx, am I correct?"—he paused and nodded at both of them—"we have to give equal opportunity, and, of course, equal consideration, to Ms. Ryder's opposition. Again, being candid, I must report to you that Mr. Sisco's ambassador, Mr. Calvin Locke, was here last Sunday, and the reception he received was quite warm, quite warm indeed."

Purse had heard about Calvin Locke. He was the silver-haired Houston banker who would probably be the real senator if Jimmy Dale got elected.

"As Mr. Locke himself reminded us," the Reverend Shad was saying, "the black folk of this nation do themselves little good if one party assumes it can take them for granted."

He looked into the eyes of both his guests, first one, then the other. Purse couldn't hold his stare, didn't know what to say. He wasn't even sure why he was there. Joe Frank should have been there, he was thinking. Sue Bee, maybe. Somebody other than himself.

He looked down at the thick wine-colored carpet beneath his boots, looked over at pictures that covered one whole wall: C. T. Washington with Martin Luther King. C. T. Washington with the governor. The Washington brothers as Afro-headed teenagers, white suits even then, in the pulpit of some church. The Washington brothers, as adults, with Billy Graham. The Washington brothers meeting the president. Both of them flanking James Brown, up on a stage. Shelves filled with books covered two walls, floor to ceiling, and behind Shad Washington's desk was a painting of a black Jesus, with little children gathered around him. Purse had never seen a black Jesus.

Aboy was smoking a big cigar that Abednego had given him when they walked into the office. He took it out of his mouth, held it up in front of his face and watched the smoke curling toward the ceiling. It was quiet in the room.

"Shad," Aboy said finally, "I've been in the acquaintance of you and your brothers since your little brown asses were wrapped in swaddling clothes just like the baby Moses, just like the baby Jesus, come to think of it. I've known your daddy since way back when black people were colored, longer than you've been alive, my good sir. And, pardon my French, Reverend, but I'm not gonna sit here and let you bull jive my ass about what Calvin Locke or that hick of a Hopalong Cassidy he's got running for senator are gonna do for black folks in this state. You know as well as I do that the only black folks that ever darken the door of the Calvin Locke manse—and I mean the BACK door, Reverend, not the front—are the hardworkin' folks that cook his meals and swab his toilets and wash his dirty silk underduds. Calvin Locke, my foot."

Shadrach didn't move, didn't change his expression, just sat staring at the big man in the white suit spilling out of the chair in front of his desk. Aboy, it seemed, had come back down to earth. The preacher, Purse suspected, had underestimated him. So had Purse, who saw that his friend was a real political pro.

"I'll tell you something else," Aboy said. "You don't have to go back too far and you'll find some white-sheet wearin' lynchers in Jimmy Dale Sisco's woodshed. You want to cotton to that ilk, I guess you have a God-given right to, but I don't think the people of this congregation would be real happy about it, And I know how your daddy, bless his name, would feel."

Aboy put the cigar back in his mouth and talked around it, leaning one elbow on the edge of Shad's desk, legs crossed at the ankles and bent back, his belly hanging onto his lap. "Now, if it's walking-around money that you're talking about, just say so. We can talk about that. Fact of the matter is, that's what we expected. But we don't need any of this pie-in-the-sky, holier-than-thou, realpolitik bullshit."

He sat back in his chair, uncrossed his legs and grinned—to show they were among friends. It sort of eased the tension.

Meshach strolled over and stood behind his brother's desk, leaning toward Aboy slightly, the tips of his perfectly manicured fingers on the edge of the desk . "Fifty thousand dollars," he said in a low voice. "That's what the Sisco people are offering. I hear you folks runnin' this campaign on a shoestring. Y'all got that kind of money?"

Aboy took out his cigar again, pulled a lighter out of his coat pocket and snapped up a flame. "Well, let's talk about it," he said. "What do you think we'd be getting for our little Fifth Ward investment in good government?"

Before either of the Washingtons could answer, there was a knock at the door. Purse saw a look of annoyance cross Shad Washington's dark, handsome face. He nodded at Abednego, who walked over and opened the door. A very old woman in a flowery Sunday dress and a blue straw pillbox hat stood at the door. She was so small and bent, the pearl-looking beads around her skinny, wrinkled neck hung down almost to her waist; the big, white patent-leather purse on her arm seemed to weight her down. She reminded Purse of a kindly old turtle. Her stockings were wrinkly and crooked on her skinny, bowed legs.

"Sister Brewer," Abednego said. "We're having a little meeting right now. You'll have to come back later."

Sister Brewer's eyes flashed behind gold-rimmed glasses. This old turtle was snapping. "No, Brother Washington, I cannot come back later," she said in a strong, determined voice. Several other women had crowded into the hallway behind her. "Can't come back," they murmured. "Won't come back."

Purse wondered if they had been listening outside the door.

"We're here to tell you not to be playing no games with Ms. Ryder," Mrs. Brewer said. "The good women of this church won't stand for it. And neither would your daddy neither, if he knew about it."

"Don't be playin' no games," her chorus cautioned.

Mrs. Brewer shot out her arm with the purse on it and pushed her way past Abednego into the room. A dozen or so other women crowded in behind her. Shad stood up from behind his desk. "Now see here, Sister Brewer," he said.

"No, you see here, Brother Washington," she said. She plopped her purse down on his desk, put her hands on her skinny old hips and spread her feet slightly like she was getting good balance. She stared up into the young preacher's face. Purse and Aboy got up and moved over to the side. "The Mighty Spirit Flame Church of God in Christ is throwin' its support to Ms. Ryder, and that's final. The Eunice Guild has already made that decision, made it just now. It's unanimous."

"With all due respect, Mrs. Brewer," Shad said, "I don't . . ."

"With all due respect, Shad Washington, you better listen to this little lady." It was the voice of God out in the hallway. Actually, it was Eddie Owens filling up the door and coming on in to stand behind Mrs. Brewer. She put her big, mannish hands on the little, old lady's skinny shoulders. "You may be smooth as silk, all three of you brothers," she said, looking around at the other two Washingtons, "but I'm not going to let you sell the souls of black folk down the river of filthy lucre."

Purse glanced at Aboy. He had his mouth wide open in admiration of the show of force in their midst. All he had to do, Purse was thinking, was to keep quiet. He did.

"But, but, ..." Shad was trying to say, but Eddie Owens rolled right over him.

"So it's decided," she said, her eyes gleaming, a big smile on her face. "I knew the Washington brothers would see the light, as God gives them to see the light." She looked over her shoulder through the open door. "Come on in, Red," she said, "and tell that photographer out there to come in with you. We got us a picture to make."

"Picture time, picture time!" the chorus of women cooed.

Red was in a good mood on the way back home. She didn't even hurraw Aboy about his born-again moment. It was dark when they landed—Red had done a little door-knocking after church—and as they rolled toward the terminal he could see Joe Frank waiting inside. As soon as Gene Ray shut down the engines and let down the steps, Joe Frank threw down his cigarette on the tarmac and came hurrying out to the plane. "I hear it went real good," he said to Red, falling into step beside her.

"Tolerably well, tolerably well," Red said, walking toward the terminal, her big straw hat in her hand. Purse caught up with her, and she handed him the hat. She was pleased with herself, you could tell.

"Well, the fun's just beginning, Madam Comptroller," Joe Frank said. "*The Morning News* is leading with a story in the morning that shows you within single digits of Jimmy Dale. What's more, the bastard's agreed to debate—this weekend. We got him on the run, Red. Things're about to pop wide open!"

★ ★ ELEVEN ★ ★

Joe Frank and Olene were already at a table near the back when Purse walked into bright and busy Alma's on Monday morning. It was cool inside, the air conditioner running full blast. Olene had a cup of coffee on the table in front of her. Joe Frank had his coffee and a cigarette. He had newspapers from around the state fanned out before him. Jaunty *Tejano* music from K-MEX, *esterio latino*, filled the air. It was jaunty and fun, even though to Purse the guitar-accordian mix all sounded the same.

The two of them sort of grunted in his direction, their way of saying good morning. Joe Frank went back to the *Morning News*, Olene to her black scheduling book.

Purse tried not to take it personally, even though they both made him feel like he was a kid, a yahoo from Elm Mott who didn't know a whole lot about politics and how the world worked (which he was, of course). He knew it was just their way. Their social skills with everybody left a whole lot to be desired.

Most of the time he could take it, but sometimes it weighed him down. Here they were having a great time—at least he was—making some good progress in the campaign. Why wouldn't they be excited?

Alma was behind the counter. Her plus-sized daughter Lourdes, in a long skirt with wide stripes of yellow, turquoise and red beneath a low-cut white peasant blouse, came over and poured him a cup of coffee. Trying not to stare at the necklace with a gold cross that tumbled down the deep, dark canyon beneath her blouse, he ordered the # 2 breakfast, *chorizo* and scrambled eggs, coffee and a glass of orange juice. He slid the front page of the *Fort Worth Star-Telegram* out from under Joe Frank's coffee cup and looked for the story. There it was—it was under the fold, but at least it was on the front page. The headline said, "RYDER ON THE MOVE LATEST POLLS SAY.'

"Jimmy Dale Sisco and his supporters expected the rancher, banker and first-time candidate to waltz across Texas on his way to Washington, D.C.," political reporter Earl Mangum wrote, "So did the pundits. But Texans seem to be saying they like a little battle of the bands at the big dance.

"After jumping out to an early 25-point lead in the polls in the U.S. Senate race, Sisco has seen that number steadily dwindle over the past month. Polls now show him leading feisty Rose Marie Ryder, state comptroller, by a mere nine points."

Mangum, who had been around state politics for years, had several theories about what was happening. Some people were saying Sisco was too arrogant, too cocksure that a Senate seat was his just for the taking, or rather the buying. "This ain't no [expletive deleted] coronation," a cafe owner in Nacogdoches told him. Others said the more they saw of Rose Marie Ryder the more they liked her. They liked her energy and how she wasn't letting her underdog status discourage her. The fact that she was a woman was still a hindrance but maybe not as much as it first appeared.

Reporter Mangum quoted Jimmy Dale: "Brother, we been expecting a horse race all along. That's what makes politics more root-tooty-toot exciting than dominoes or quiltin' or canasta. But sure as shootin', when the good people of Texas take a long, hard look at that little lady's stand on the issues, they'll be happier than Howdy Doody to vote for the hombre that stakes his claim on limited government, no-new-taxes and gettin' corn-cob tough on crime."

Mangum also quoted Red: "We're going to keep on doing what we've been doing all along. We're talking to the folks face to face, listening to their concerns, and assuring them that a vote for Rose Marie Ryder is a vote for their interests, not the special interests."

The *Morning News*, the *Chronicle*, the *Express*—they all had similar stories.

Slow-moving Lourdes sauntered over with his *chorizo* and eggs just as Aboy pulled up a chair at the table. "I'll have the very same thing, Lourdes, *mi hija*," he said, "plus a side order of sliced tomatoes. If, that is, they're finger-lickin' fresh from the farmer's market." He stuck out his chest and gave it a couple of two-fisted thumps. "Top of the morning to you gents, Olene. This is the day the Lord has made. Let us rejoice and be happy in His presence."

Olene looked up from her notebook with an expression on her face like she'd bitten into a green persimmon. She didn't say anything, just dived back into her notebook.

"Oh, that's right," Joe Frank mumbled from around his cigarette. "Yesterday you was born again. Again. What's that make, Aboy, a dozen? Good thing we're not giving baby showers every friggin' time you get re-born." He chuckled and took a drag on his cigarette, then a sip of coffee.

"Scoff if you must, my good man," Aboy said, looking down on Joe Frank with a smile of papal patience and forbearance, "but the good Lord moves in mysterious ways."

"So do photographers, Preacher-man," Joe Frank said. He slid the Metro section of the *Houston Chronicle* over to Aboy. Purse leaned over and looked at it. There on the front page was their own beached whale sprawled out on his back, Shad Washington kneeling down beside him, his arm outstretched to God.

"Red's not real happy," Joe Frank mumbled as he lit up a cigarette.

"Followers of the Lord are accustomed to abuse and persecution," Aboy said, smiling a bit as he looked at the photo. "Besides, Josephus, any fundamentalist true-believer, Pentecostal, Holy Roller, any Hard-Shell Baptist, Church of Christer, Assembly of God, God-fearing Christian perusing his morning paper over a cup of Sanka this morning will know exactly what's transpiring, and he'll be proclaiming 'Praise the Lord!' Even if it is a preacher of the colored persuasion standing over me. That born-again Christian you see laying there prostrate before the Lord Almighty Himself, his sodden soul bared for all the world to see, he just might have picked up a few votes for the Redhead. Even though that wasn't my intention. Ever think of that, Joe Boy?"

Joe Frank caught Lourdes' eye, pointed to his empty cup of coffee and went back to his paper, as if whatever Aboy had to say was not worth a plug nickel. Sometimes Purse wanted to slap Joe Frank across his salamander-skin cheeks, wake him up a little, bring him alive. He would read sometime about how nonplussed Joe Frank always was, how he was the calm at the center of the Red Ryder hurricane, how he kept Red from fizzing off into the ether like an untied balloon, how that was his value to the campaign.

But what looked like calm, Purse often thought, seemed when you were around him every day like neuritis, neuralgia, the heartbreak of psoriasis, something. He could see why his first wife left him.

Joe Frank reminded Purse of a song he had heard on a country-and-western station in the Panhandle late one night, a song called the "Dead Willie Blues." The woman in the song is asking the undertaker about her husband Willie, "You sure he's dead? He don't seem no different now than he did every night for the past 20 years." And then she says, "You think maybe I could keep him around? That's the stiffest I ever seen him."

He could imagine that's what Joe Frank's ex-wife was thinking. (As he recalled, she was a pretty hot redhead herself. She had her own business working as a CFO for a big chain of discount stores.)

"Maybe he's right, Joe Frank," Purse said, but Joe Frank had nothing else to say about it to Purse either. He thought about mentioning to Aboy that his mama should have named him Joe Funk.

"And is the good Ms. Ryder dignifying this august gathering with her presence?" Aboy asked, a big smile creasing his round face. Nothing this morning was going to jar him out of his jaunty mood. "So, my little Mizz Olene from Moline, do you know?"

"She's downtown this morning," Olene said in her dull, monotone voice, never looking up from her black book. She took a tiny bite from a triangle of dry toast. "Meeting with some TV advisers from New York about the debate."

"What about this afternoon?"

Purse had almost forgotten that this evening was the opening day of dove season. It was another of those rituals that candidates had to go through, so they could show they were real men, even if they were women.

Sue Bee hurried in and sat down next to Olene. She shooed away a menu-bearing Lourdes. "Caravan leaves here at noon," she said. "Aboy, you'll drive the van to the homestead with all the equipment. Purse, you and Aboy will be gun bearers for the day. Joe Frank and I'll be on the press bus."

He glanced at Aboy. He could usually read his face, could tell from his expression whether he thought he was being shoved out of the circle, a drone on the fringes of the hive. Purse didn't care all that much, but Aboy did. He was touchy about such things.

Sue Bee was going on about the day. "The plan is to set up a press availability on the porch of the homestead by three and be in the pasture by five when the birds start coming in over the stock tank on the old home place. The press bus leaves here at noon. We even have Edmund Blumenthal coming in from the *New York Times* to go with us. Isn't that marvelous?"

"What about Red?" Aboy asked.

"She's gonna be on the bus with us," Sue Bee said. "She thought the press would appreciate a little face time on the way up to the old home place. I agree. You've heard those stories she tells about summers with the old folks. The out-of-town press'll eat that stuff up."

"Who's gonna be hunting?" Purse asked

"Red is," Sue Bee said. "She's the only one of us, 'cept for Sen. Raley, who's driving in from Lampasas with some of his constituents. I'd guess there'll be a couple of dozen ranchers from the area, maybe a banker or two from Liberty Hill, Lampasas."

Red ever been dove huntin'?" Purse asked Joe Frank. He didn't answer. He was still reading the papers, thinking his thoughts, planning his plans.

"She's been blastin' doves out of God's great firmament since she was knee-high to a bowlegged grasshopper," Aboy said, talking through a mouth full of Tabasco-laced scrambled egg, thin strings of melted cheese hanging down every time he lifted the fork to his mouth. "Her old daddy used to take her every year, I guess 'til she got in high school. She's a good shot."

"One more thing," Joe Frank said, "before you all scatter. I was talking to Red about this last night. She's worried we're not getting more traction on the issues. And one of the reasons we're not is because Jimmy Dale's doing a good job of checkmating us on our campaign themes. His people seem to be anticipating what we're going to do and what we're going to say, even before we say it. I don't like to be that predictable."

He took a drag on his cigarette, and through the smoke looked right at Aboy. "Now I know that Nabob Slidell is a goddamn genius when it comes to campaign intelligence, probably the best in the business, but he doesn't have to be that good if somebody's yapping. What I'm worried about, and what Red's worried about, is loose lips inside this campaign. Y'all are gonna have to watch who you're talking to, what you say, even when you think you're among friends. Another thing, I want every press query coming through me." He was still staring at Aboy. "Y'all understand?"

Joe Frank scared Purse. He was trying to think who he had talked to, what he had said, but nothing came to mind. He swore to himself that he'd be careful, though.

He finished up his breakfast, paid Alma his $1.50 and glanced at September's Aztec princess splayed across a snowy mountain on the calendar hanging on the wall behind the cash register. "*Hasta luego*, Señor Wily," Alma said.

Back at the office, he checked the pink message slips, called Mama at home, called Jo Lynne. Trudy said she was doing Mrs. Skinner, said she would have her call when she got done. He thought about calling Trieu at her motel room in Seguin, but he figured she was in court already.

He couldn't wait around for Jo Lynne to call back, so he drove back across the river to the trailer, fed Shoogy and changed into jeans and a pair of hunting boots he kept in the back of the closet, combat boots actually, leather on top, rough side out on the foot part. His dad had left them to him from his days in Korea. They didn't really fit, since wearing them for days at a time in the cold at Chosin Reservoir had molded them to the shape of his father's feet, but he could bear them. He liked the idea of wearing his daddy's army boots.

Willis Seymour was out watering the four withered tomato plants he had growing behind a little picket fence at the end of his trailer. Purse wanted to tell him the water would turn to steam before it hit the ground this time of the day, but that was Seymour's business, not Purse's. They just waved at each other, and Purse headed on back downtown.

At the office, Aboy looked like he was ready for an African safari. Purse laughed out loud. He had on khaki shorts, a pair of brown knee-high, lace-up boots, a short-sleeve khaki shirt and a red bandana around his neck. Perched atop his big head was a pith helmet like Ramar of the Jungle used to wear in those Saturday-matinee serials Purse took in at the Orpheum when he had an extra 50 cents and could hitch a ride into town.

"Where's your bearers?" Purse asked when Aboy pulled the van around to the front of the building and stepped out to check on the guns in the back.

Aboy thought he said bears at first. "Oh, bearers," he said. He threw his head back and laughed, holding on to the helmet. "You're usually not so jocular, old son. I'm pleasantly surprised. I presume my only bearer would be you, young Master Foxx. You know how to handle weaponry of the sporting sort?"

"I bought me a .410 the summer I was 15. Got the money baling hay for a neighbor," he said, settling into the front seat. "You may not believe this, Aboy, but fact is, I'm a pretty fair shot—I was a sharpshooter in the Army—but I never did much hunting. Didn't have time."

"As a man of the cloth, I myself am not the hunting sort," Aboy said, pulling onto the Interstate between two eighteen-wheelers whizzing by. There was a lot of traffic for this time of the morning. "Although I must say, the Holy Book is rife with mighty hunters. You've heard of Nabob, I presume."

He had heard of Nabob Swindell, but that's not who Aboy had in mind. He commenced to tell him that Nabob, son of Cush, was the first on earth to be a Mighty Man. That's what the book of Genesis said, but who knew what it meant to be a Mighty Man? Must have had something to do with dispatching creatures to the Great Beyond, Purse decided, because Aboy said the Bible also called Nabob a mighty hunter before the Lord.

"I presume the offspring of those multitudinous creatures old Noah saved from a watery grave needed thinning out," Aboy said, chuckling. And then there was Esau. Got in a bind with his brother Jacob. And Samson. You're acquainted with Samson, aren't you?"

He was acquainted with Samson. He remembered the brightly colored pictures they had at home in a big maroon-colored book called *Hurlbut's Story of the Bible*. He loved those pictures. He would stare at the long-haired Samson when he was a young man ripping a lion apart with his bare hands; this was before Delilah got hold of him. And then he would spend a long time looking at him lolled in Delilah's lap, and then he would turn the page and there would be the old man Samson, his hair grown out and straggly over his gouged-out eyes, straining with all his might against the round, white columns of the temple, pulling the giant edifice down on top of the Philistines and himself. Talk about a mighty hunter before the Lord!

"So the Good Book condones taking the life of other species," Aboy was saying, "but as a wee sprite of a lad, I was much as you; I never found the time for it either. My peers over in the Piney Woods went hunting for squirrels and rabbits and possum, for supper a lot of the time, but I was too busy at home, praising the Lord in song and spoken word."

Purse looked over at Aboy to see if he was joshing. He didn't seem to be. He hadn't completely gotten over his Houston born-again experience. He had his eyes on the road, although his thoughts appeared to be somewhere else, somewhere long ago and far away.

They passed the exit that would have swung them by Round Rock Donuts, one of Aboy's favorite places in all the state. The donuts were hot if you got there the right time of the day; sticky with glaze on the outside, and on the inside they were a bright yellow, from all the butter, presumably. Purse loved them about as much as Aboy. The fact that Aboy didn't stop, Purse took to mean that he really was born-again. How, in his born-again state, he would deal with the Poodle Dog Lounge and yodeling Don Walzer Purse would have to wait and see.

"So, Aboy, what is it with you and religion?" He slouched down in the seat and propped his foot on the dashboard, like when he was with Rufus Cuttrell on the litter truck. "No disrespect, you understand, but I just want to know. 'Cause, you know, I've gone to church all my life, but I can't say it gets to me the way it does you. I mean, I can't imagine falling out in front of all those people like you did on Sunday. I don't know, maybe I'm headed for hell in a hand basket and can't do a thing to climb out. I guess you could say I've got a ticket to ride."

Aboy didn't answer for a while, just concentrated on his driving. He looked like he was thinking what to say. "A long and arduous journey, my son. A long and arduous journey. That's the propitious way to describe my lifelong pilgrim's quest seeking to discern the footprints of the Lord and then walking therein. It certainly ain't no Interstate, all smooth and easy, and God knows I've strayed. Yes, I have strayed onto some mighty foolish exits. And not a few dead-ends."

He pulled around a Greyhound bus. A hand-lettered sign on butcher paper taped to the side said "Hyde Park First Baptist Church—Six Flags or Bust." Purse looked up at a bunch of kids, maybe junior-high age, guys and girls, peering down at them through the big, gray-tinted windows. A blonde-haired boy shot him the finger and laughed. Purse shot him one back. The kid began beating on the glass with his fist, making faces and shouting something Purse obviously couldn't hear.

"You're sanctified, aren't you?" Aboy asked.

Purse wasn't sure what that meant. "I'm baptized, if that's what you mean," he said. He started to tell him he wasn't sure his baptism took, because it was pretty much an accident. He was 11, had gone out of the sanctuary during a long, long sermon to go pee, get a long drink of water, waste a little time. When he came back in, the congregation was standing, singing "Softly and Tenderly," the invitation hymn. The preacher, Pastor Cloyd Reese, thought he was responding to the invitation, so he met him halfway down the aisle, bent down and threw his arms around him. He led the young Wily to the front, folks singing "softly and tenderly Jesus is calling" as they walked up the aisle. He was too ashamed to tell Pastor Cloyd he was just coming back from the bathroom, so he let him go ahead and pray over him and preach and sing and pray over him some more and then baptize him there in front of the whole congregation. He remembered being so light that when they pushed the maroon velvet baptistry curtain to one side and Pastor Cloyd put one hand behind his neck and one over his mouth and nose and laid him back in the chest-deep water, his bare feet popped up like two white fishing bobbers.

Afterward, his Mama and Papa were so proud, Mama crying and all, men shaking hands with red-faced Papa, him looking down at the floor while men clapped him on the shoulder. Wily didn't have the heart to tell them he had just gone out to pee. He didn't say anything to anybody about it. He knew from what he learned in Brother Bailey's Sunday school class you weren't supposed to be baptizing kids and babies like the Catholics did, because kids didn't know right from wrong, they hadn't reached the age of accountability. He figured he knew right from wrong, but he didn't feel much different than before he was buried in Christ by Pastor Cloyd.

"Sanctified," Aboy was telling him, "is when the good Lord plucks you from the *hoi polloi*, sets you on the path of righteousness for His name's sake, gives your three-score-and-ten divine meaning and purpose. You're one of the chosen, in other words."

He could see Aboy preaching in some lantern-lit revival tent set up in a lonesome Texas town, the dust rising up from the sawdust floor, preaching that sermon to the faithful. No doubt he had preached it many a time. "You sanctified?" he asked Aboy.

"Goddamnit! Would you look at that?"

Aboy nodded toward a giant billboard with Jimmy Dale Sisco striding down the steps of what looked to be the Capitol in Washington. He was wearing boots and a cowboy hat and one of those long yellow dusters like the gunmen in "The Wild Bunch" wore. You sort of had a feeling he had a double-barreled shotgun under that long buttoned-up coat. Squinty-eyed and determined-looking, like a man ready to rid the town single-handedly of the Clanton gang, the Jimmy Dale in the picture looked big and tough, not a bit like the little sawed-off wimp Purse knew him to be. "A MAN FOR TEXAS" the sign said.

"A gol-durned moron for Texas," Aboy said, shaking his head and gripping the wheel hard with both hands. "It's hard to believe the people of this state could be so fuckin' stupid, so gaggle-assed ill-informed, as to think that little pipsqueak could piss in a pot unless the directions were on the bottom, much less find his way around Washington."

A little while later, Aboy took a deep breath, leaned back, draped his left hand over the top of the steering wheel, his gold ring with a turquoise stone gleaming in the sun.

"Sanctification you were inquiring about," he said. He laid

his right hand across the back of the seat. "I never told you my story?" he asked, glancing over at Purse with a smile on his face.

"I guess not. Don't forget you got to turn left right up here. Joe Frank said it's the road to Liberty Hill we want to take."

Aboy took the Liberty Hill exit onto a two-lane farm-to-market road that curved up into the foothills of the Hill Country. Clumps of live oak here and there offered some blessed shade to cows standing still as statues. Scraggly herds of white goats grazed in parched, rocky pastures. Small farmhouses, beat-up old house trailers, brand-new manufactured homes, were tucked into hillsides. They passed another billboard, this one with red letters on a white background, no pictures. "GET **US** OUT OF UN," it said.

They were getting close to where Red's grandparents had homesteaded around the turn of the century, where Red spent many a summer as a little girl.

"Ever hear of Marlin Suskin?"

"Can't say I have," Purse said, but the name did sound sort of familiar. A picture from the past flashed into his mind. "Wait a minute! Yeah, I do know that name. Some kinda preacher, right?"

Aboy grinned. "That was my daddy," he said. He swerved to avoid a giant, red-beaked vulture that had been tearing into the half-eaten remains of a deer. The big bird flapped its wings and lumbered into the air as they passed. Without even thinking about it, Purse was going through the tools he and Rufus would have used to get a deer carcass off the road. Probably he would have just picked it up by its half-eaten hind legs and flung it into the back of the truck.

"You see that?" Aboy said, all excited. "That woulda been a challenge of monumental proportions for you and that old girly man you worked with."

Suddenly, it came to Purse where he had known Marlin Suskin. "You know, he came to our church one time. I was a little bitty fellow. He had some kind of Bible memory scam he was trying to sell us. I don't think it took."

"That's my dear ol' daddy," Aboy said. "Chances are, I was with him."

"I just remember an old man."

He didn't tell Aboy how his old man, as he remembered him, gave off a whiff of rotten fruit every morning he came in for Vacation Bible School, a little, bald-headed fellow in a wrinkled brown suit and an old, extra-wide tie spotted with food stains. He would be preaching at them, and the young Wily couldn't take his eyes off the tufts of hair, like little Brillo pads, spilling out of his ears, and how the light reflected off his bald head. He was always eating a banana or an apple, some kind of fruit, and while he was preaching to the youngsters, they would hear his stomach churning, and god-awful smells would permeate the room every few minutes. It was just the boys—the girls were studying with Miss Ocie Lambright how to be God's perfect helpmeet—and they didn't want to be there anyway, so it was hard for the old man to keep control of the class, or his stomach either. They would fall out of their chairs giggling, groaning, holding their noses.

"He was instructing you in the patented Suskin's Power and Might Method," Aboy explained. "Usually he just called it the Might Method."

"Might method?"

"Might—M, I, G, H, T. Mnemonics in God's Holy Teachings. Key words and mnemonic devices—you know, ways of remembering things. Those were the secrets of his success. 'God's power and Might!' he'd say. And, by the way, he wouldn't have appreciated your slanderizing it as a scam. He may not have told you, but he had the whole Bible memorized, every single word of it, from 'In the beginning' to 'I warn everyone who hears the prophecy of this book: If anyone adds to them, God will add to him the plagues described in this book, and if anyone takes away from the words of the book of this prophecy, God will take away his share in the tree of life and in the holy city.' That's Revelation, my good man. Pa liked Revelation."

Purse was impressed. "I remember he told us a joke, trying to break the ice with us, I guess. He said, 'What's the only state that's got its name in the Bible?' We didn't know, so he told us—it's in the book of Genesis, where it says 'Noah looked out of the ark and saw.'"

"He used that for years."

"Is that where you learned to quote Scripture? From your daddy's Might Method?"

"I think I've told you that I'm one of nine progeny; I was the whelp of the litter. By the time I came along, many of my siblings were out of the house and on their own. None of them had followed in his footsteps, to his great regret. None were young Samuel to his Eli. Fact is, they skedaddled away from home like cotton tail rabbits as soon as they could. I was Daddy's last, best hope. My mama died in childbirth, bringing yours truly into the world. Couple of my sisters helped raise me."

That was the first time he had heard about Aboy's mama. He wondered what it meant to a youngster to lose his mama like that—and to feel he was partly to blame.

"Even before I could toddle, Daddy had me learning the Bible. Instead of mother's milk, I suckled on the Holy Word. I was good, you bet your sweet bippy. I was a holy prodigy, if I do say so myself. And I wanted to please my dear old daddy. By the time I was five, he was taking me with him all over—up through the Ozarks into Missouri, out west to Arizona, all over the South. Just him and me. I was the closer, so to speak—this little golden-haired angel in a white suit and red necktie quoting scripture from Genesis to Revelation just like it was Jack and Jill went up the hill. People's eyes would pop out, listening to me preach the Word. I've seen old women set in to crying their eyes out, even while they had smiles on their powdery, old faces. I've seen grown men waving their arms in the air, shouting 'Praise God! Praise God!' Got a little older and they were comparing me to the boy Jesus in the temple."

"So that's how you got started?"

"That's how I got started, though, to be honest with you, it was something of a false start. After about 10 years, I wandered off on my own prodigal path. Before that happened, I never felt so alive. I never felt so on fire, so electrified with the juices of existence, as when I was standing up in a pulpit in some backwater church or standing on a chair in an East Texas brush arbor proclaiming God's Holy Word. Purse, my boy, I'm telling you, I'd have the audience in the palm of my little baby hand."

Aboy shook his head. "My Gawd, it was a heady experience! Nothing like it! Nothing like it, that is, until, lo and behold, one night up in Tulia, way up in the Panhandle, out behind the revival tent after the service, I discovered, dare I say uncovered, the mysteries of the fairer sex. Ilene Richards, mmm, mmm. You know about that delectable sensation, don't you, Purse? The feel, the fragrance, the allure. By the way, how is your little Oriental delectation?"

Purse sat up in the seat. "Slow down, slow down," he said. "The road where we're supposed to turn's coming up."

The old mailbox with the Ryder name was still standing on a rickety-looking post at the turnoff—someone, probably Sue Bee, had tied a red balloon to the post—and so were the barbed wire fences, although they were rusted and saggy. The road was dirt, hard enough because of the drought but rutted. Purse wondered if the bus would be able to make it. As soon as they turned on to the road, they scared up a chaparral, a road runner. It raced them a hundred yards or so before it veered off into the brush.

After a mile or so along the dirt road, past stony, hard-scrabble pasture on both sides, they made a right at the fence row and pulled up before what was left of an old farm house. It was the Ryder homestead. Swaybacked, high-pitched roof, ugly gray asbestos siding and a front porch about to fall in. About the only thing you could say about the old house was that it was still standing, sort of, but from the stories Purse had heard Red tell she had spent many a happy summer there.

They stepped out of the van and stretched. While Aboy walked over and took a piss on a prickly pear bush, Purse opened up the back of the van and took the guns out. Aboy opened a box of shells and slid several into the slots of a hunting vest he had brought along, and then they walked down to an old, unpainted barn, what was left of it. They found some old Coke bottles, and Aboy had Purse toss them up in the air while he shot at them. He was pretty good. Purse loaded a .22, set up a couple of bottles on a well cover and blasted them into smithereens.

The caterers showed up while they were shooting. They were driving a big black pickup truck with "Cooper's Barbecue, Llano, Texas" written on the side, and they were pulling a trailer with a eight-foot-long, black metal butane tank made into an oven. They parked down in the yard below the house.

Aboy and Purse strolled down for a look-see. The barbecue chef, a big-bellied, red-faced fellow in a gimme cap, jeans and blue work shirt hopped out of the truck and introduced himself. "Acie Cooper's the name," he said, "barbecue's the game." They shook hands, and Acie led them over to the trailer, where he lifted up a door to show off a mixture of oak and mesquite logs on which 60 pounds of brisket had been slow-cooking for the past 14 hours. It smelled good.

Farmers and ranchers in khakis and gimme caps began driving up in dusty pickups. One guy had a couple of bird dogs in the back. Feet skidding in the bed of the truck, noses and tails twitching, they were eager to jump out and start hunting.

A wiry, little guy named Chub used both hands to stir a caldron of beans with a five-foot-long spatula. Three Mexican guys in jeans and straw hats hopped out of the back of the pickup and began setting up long tables with red-and-white checkered tablecloths. Every once in a while, one of the Mexicans would break off his table duties and toss more wood onto a fire they were getting ready for the doves Red was sure to shoot.

Aboy wandered over to a big drink cooler filled with ice and fished out two Dr Peppers. He handed a cold can to Purse, who took a long draw. It tasted good. He burped.

I was just thinking," Purse said, wiping his mouth with the back of his hand. "When you were talking about your folks, I was wondering about Red's. What's the story? From what I heard, her dad died when she was a little girl, but what about her mom? When did she die?"

Aboy took a sip of his Dr Pepper. Sitting on the trunk of a dead tree, his legs sprawled out in front of him, he looked at Purse without saying anything.

"What?" Purse said. "What's the story?" He squatted down in the dirt across from Aboy.

"Well, my good man, the story's not what you've heard. And I'm sitting here cogitating on the question. Should I tell you the campaign tale, or should I tell you the real story? That's the existential dilemma at hand."

"They're not one and the same?"

"Well, not exactly. This is politics, my callow, young cowpoke.

You'll learn that truth and a campaign tale aren't always one and same." He took a deep breath and set his Dr Pepper can in the dirt beside him.

Not long after the barbecue guys started setting up, they looked across the pasture and saw the big blue and silver bus bouncing like a heavy boat on a billowy sea as it eased down the road toward the house, the sun glinting off its side. Several cars followed in the dust. The bus pulled up in the dirt yard beside the house, and reporters piled out like a circus spilling out of a VW. They yawned and stretched, looked around at the broken-down old house, the old barn.

Sue Bee chased after a guy who had to be the *New York Times* fellow, a tall man in a blue blazer and wrinkled khakis, his tie loosened around his neck. He kept looking around and over Sue Bee's head like he was bored and wished he could lose her.

Joe Frank stepped down off the bus, turned around and held out a helping hand for Red and then began rounding up the reporters and herding them toward the porch. Red spotted Purse and nodded. He walked over and she handed him her hand-tooled leather purse she had bought one year in Nuevo Laredo during the George Washington Birthday Celebration. Otherwise, she was wearing sunglasses, a khaki hunting outfit and a camouflage vest.

Purse heard a young woman reporter ask an old rancher who was standing around what he called the small yellow wildflower with the black center growing in a clump beside the house. "We call 'em nigger toes," the old man said.

Doyle Robison of the *Dallas Morning News* shouted, "Go on and start killin' somethin', Red."

"Gotta wait 'til the sun gets a little lower," Red said. "That's when the birds start coming in over the stock tank."

"You sure you can hit something?" Lloyd McManus of the *Houston Chronicle* shouted.

"I been reading your trash, Lloyd McManus," Red said with a grin. "You get too close, and I might shoot you."

"Why don't y'all gather over here at the porch, in the shade of the house," Joe Frank said, herding reporters over. Red stepped up on the rickety wooden steps, and Aboy handed her the .12 gauge. Photographers started shooting. Purse stood at the bottom of the porch, his sweaty fingers leaving dark spots on the leather purse. The window screens on the screened-in porch behind Red were rusted red and coming loose from their frames.

"I spent many a summer out here with my granddaddy and my grandma," Red told the reporters, who were standing at the foot of the porch scribbling in their notebooks. "And I just wanted y'all to have a chance to see how beautiful it is, how peaceful and nice, out here in the Texas Hill Country."

Purse saw the reporters sort of look around and grin at each other, wondering if Red was making a joke. He knew she meant every word.

"How'd you learn to hunt?" Clay Robison asked.

"It was my daddy and my granddaddy that taught me, right here on this farm," Red said. "Fact of the matter is, this .12 gauge I'm holding here belonged to my daddy. I treasure it."

Purse didn't know whether it really was her daddy's gun or not; Aboy hadn't said anything about whether that was part of his existential dilemma. But he guessed it could have been. She did handle it like she knew what she was doing.

Red answered a few more questions, then looked toward the pasture where the sun was beginning to sink behind a low rise. "Let's get on out there," Red said. "Y'all comin'?"

Like a gaggle of geese, with Red and Sen. Raley in the lead, they all walked down below the house, passed a big, old live oak where Red said her granddad used to butcher hogs, out past the broken-down barn, then sort of single file along a path through the scrub brush and mesquite and prickly pear. Purse watched Aboy try to angle up beside the *New York Times* reporter. It was hot, still, and everything seemed dried up and stunted, prickly and scabbed over. He was still carrying Red's purse for some reason. Aboy was carrying her shotgun.

They walked along the rim of the stock tank, the water line way down, you could tell, from where it usually was. What had been cow prints in mud were now like post holes in concrete. Although the sun was setting, it was still very hot.

Red and the senator set themselves up on the trunk of an old knocked-down bois d'arc tree. Red, you could tell, was irritated by the photographers who kept coming up to her and crouching down for pictures. "I'm afraid I'm going to shoot somebody's fool head off," Purse heard her tell Raley.

"They're just reporters," Raley said, chuckling. "Might as well fire away."

Raley and Red sat on the trunk of the tree for 10 minutes or so and not a single dove showed. "Senator, if you don't get some birds flying over, you can forget about an appointment in the Ryder administration," some reporter hollered. Just then, a bird flew over, and Red took a shot. She missed. She called back to Aboy to bring up the .20-gauge. It was lighter, he told Purse when they were walking past the tank, than the gun her daddy had given her. He took the twelve-gauge and crouched down beside her.

Another 20 minutes went by. The sun was going down, and it wasn't quite so blazing hot, but pretty soon it was going to be too dark to hunt. Joe Frank was getting worried. The reporters were getting restless, and the photographers were about to lose their light. A flock of birds flew over, headed for the tank. Suddenly Aboy, the great white hunter, rose up and fired. A bird fell, just short of the tank. It was a great shot.

The man handling the dogs sent them to retrieve, and they were off like a shot through the dry grass. One of them picked up the bird in his mouth, the dogs tussled over it a bit, and then the retriever brought the little creature back to its handler. The farmer took it out of the dog's mouth, gave the dog a pat on the head, turned the bird over in his hands and then yelled out, "This ain't no dove; it's a kildeer."

Lloyd McManus was the first to speak. "Aren't they endangered, Red?" he asked, pen poised over his notebook.

Red didn't answer. She looked at Aboy, shook her head and ordered him back to the house. She knew that kildeers were endangered, that the photographers were shooting and that the next day's papers would be all over the story. A kildeer just might have killed Aboy's career. Purse watched him trudge back up the path toward the house and thought about going with him.

About then the birds started coming in, and Red and the senator shot their share. She was angry, Purse was sure, but she couldn't just retire from the field. The dogs had a field day, rushing out to retrieve and bringing them back to Red, who stuffed the doves into her jacket pockets, making sure they actually were doves before she did.

Back at the house, Red laid a dozen birds on the table and began plucking. Reporters and photographers gathered around. Aboy was nowhere in sight. "What about that kildeer?" somebody asked.

"Y'all know Aboy, leastways most of you do," she said. "His zest and his zeal just get in the way of his good judgment ever now and then. I'm sure he's profoundly sorry for what happened, and we'll pay whatever fine the local game warden deems necessary."

She had 12 naked little carcasses laid out on the table. Blumenthal of the *Times* shuddered at the little dangling heads, the yellow beaks and scrawny wings. Red laughed. "My daddy always said, 'If you're not willin' to clean it, you shouldn't kill it. And if you clean it, you gotta eat it. And if you eat it, you gotta cook it first.'"

She handed the birds to Chub, who put them on the grill. Then she went back to answering questions about education funding and Medicare reimbursements and the situation in the Mideast.

Robison of the *Morning News* had a portable telephone back in the bus. He had been talking to his editors and sauntered back to the crowd of reporters around Red. "Hey Red," he shouted. "Hear what Jimmy Dale said last night?"

"'Fraid not, Doyle. I'm not in the habit of hanging on every word of the esteemed Mr. Sisco."

"Seems he was out on the land last night, Red, one of his ranches out around Fort Stockton. Had an AP reporter with him, maybe a couple of others. And, it's hard to believe, but it actually rained out in West Texas. So Jimmy Dale's sitting around the campfire with the press, rain drops fallin' on his head, and he says to everybody, he says, 'You know how it is, boys. When it looks like you're gonna be raped, ain't no use complainin'. Just lay back and enjoy it.'"

Purse looked around at Robison's fellow reporters. They were grinning and scribbling in their notebooks. He looked back at the house, at Aboy sitting on the steps. Maybe Jimmy Dale's big mouth just knocked Aboy's kildeer off the front pages.

★ ★ TWELVE ★ ★

Purse didn't really want to go, partly because he didn't particularly enjoy big gatherings with people he didn't know that well, partly because he wasn't sure he could get off, or should get off. But he had promised Jo Lynne long before he knew he would be involved in the campaign, plus he was feeling the weight of a guilty conscience. He stuck his head in Sue Bee's office and told her his dilemma. She told him to go ahead.

"Don't forget the party at Red's house tomorrow night," she reminded him. He told her he would be back in time.

He drove home Friday night, stayed all night with his Mama, and got Jo Lynne a little after noon Saturday. It already was hot.

"You wanna come in and help me carry this stuff?" she said as he got out of the car. She gave him a kiss on the cheek as he sidled by her into the James mobile home. Her hair smelled good, like she had just gotten out of the shower.

She looked nice too, even with the apron she wore around her waist. She had on a pair of khaki Bermuda shorts, a sleeveless blue T-shirt, white tennis shoes.

He followed the seductive scent of fried chicken into the narrow, little kitchen.

Jo Lynne slid past him to the stove and with a cooking fork began filling a big red mixing bowl with still-warm pieces of golden-brown chicken she had just plucked out of the bubbling hot grease in the skillet. On the TV in the den, the burbling voice of Julia Child, her voice like nobody else's, was talking about preparing lamb. He would put Jo Lynne up against Julia Child any day.

She covered the bowl of chicken with tin-foil and handed it to him, then got a Tupperware bowl of potato salad from the refrigerator and handed that to him, as well. Cooling on a metal tray on the kitchen table were frosted chocolate brownies, a pecan half in the middle of each. Jo Lynne tore off a sheet of tinfoil, scraped her little finger through the soft icing on one of the brownies and held it out to him. He licked it off her finger and then gave her a little kiss.

"Where's your folks?"

"They went on ahead," she said. "Daddy was gonna help with the chairs in the auditorium. Mama had to make sure all the tables were set up for the food." She smiled. "Why do you ask, Mr. Foxx?"

"Just wonderin'," he said. "Seemed a little quiet around the house."

"Hmmm," she said, putting her arms around his waist and her head on his chest, careful not to jostle the bowls he was holding. "I wish we had time to take advantage, but we really need to go."

The drive through the country took about 40 minutes. He tried to keep Jo Lynne talking about herself as best he could—about work and her mother's health, her father's job at the tire plant—so he didn't trip up with any information about his life on the campaign trail. It was sort of hard, since she wasn't one to dwell on her own life.

Maybe it had to do with being the younger child in a troubled family, but she was usually the one who tried to keep the peace, tried to make people feel better about themselves. He always felt like her family neglected her, partly because she never caused any problems, unlike her older brother, and partly because she preferred being outside the spotlight. You could see it in pictures of family gatherings. You would always have to look twice to find Jo Lynne. As pretty as she was, she always would be in the back row, maybe off to the side.

"So where is it we're headed to?" he asked as Jo Lynne had him exit the Interstate at Farm Road 313 toward Aquila.

"They call it the Allison-Blocker reunion," she said. "They've been having these gatherings every September, I would guess, for 50 years or so. It's these two families who all grew up around Aquila, all their kin, their neighbors, people they all went to school with. There'll be people there you know."

At Peoria—Pe-orry, Jo Lynne called it—they turned right on a gravel road that ran past sun-scorched cornfields toward Bethel

School. A roadrunner popped out of the Johnson grass beside the road and led them on a chase for a quarter mile or so. He speeded up, and so did the bird.

"Be careful, Wily," Jo Lynne said, her hand on his arm.

"I don't think he has to worry," he said, just as the bird veered off the road.

The road zigzagged along the right angles of the fields they were passing. "Be careful," Jo Lynne said again. "Monroe Hill's coming up."

He slowed down as they came over a rise and the countryside dropped away toward Big Aquila Creek. On the driver's side, where the road had been cut through the rocky side of the hill, travelers from years past had carved their names into the soft red sandstone cliff that rose up maybe 30 feet or so. He saw one name dated 1904.

They dipped down the rutted road, crossed a rickety wooden bridge over the creek and turned into the playground of old Bethel School.

Cars and trucks lined both sides of the grass lot that would have been the playground when the old, white-framed building had actually been a school. Once the school closed, years earlier, the building had become a community center. Youngsters chased each other back and forth, played on swings and a seesaw beside the building.

Two little girls, maybe 6 or 7, ran up to them, their faces red, out of breath, and giggling. Jo Lynne knelt and gave them a hug.

"Jo Lynne, would you come push us on the swing," one of the little girls begged. She held on to Jo Lynne's hand.

"Not right now, Ilene," she said. "Wily and I have to get this food inside. But you come find me later, okay?"

"Shirley Thomas's little girl," she said as they walked past knots of people, many of them elderly. "She's a cousin."

He sidestepped around two old ladies who had stopped to greet each other. "I'll swanny, you haven't changed in 40 years!" he heard one tell the other, holding her at arms' length and peering into her wrinkled face.

"Minnie, you always were a good fibber," the second lady said, laughing as they embraced.

He saw Dewey James, Jo Lynne's daddy, standing with three other men near the front steps. They were all smoking cigarettes. Dewey James motioned them over.

"Fellas, y'all know my little girl here," he said, giving Jo Lynne a hug. "But what about my future son-in-law, Senator Wily T. Foxx?" He grinned and shook Purse's hand, clapped him on the shoulder. A small, slender man, he had slicked up for the day—white dress shirt with the cuffs rolled up a couple of times, black suit pants, his wavy hair oiled and combed back. Purse could smell his hair oil, Three Roses.

"You don't expect that lady to win, do you, boy?" asked one of the men with Mr. James. He was a big man with a farmer's two-toned face—sunburned from the neck to just above the eyebrows, white as a baby's bottom from his forehead to his thinning hairline, thanks to a straw hat he always wore in the field. Purse knew him, sort of. His name was Barney Berry. He raised peanuts.

"Never can tell, Mr. Berry," he said. "She'll give it a good fight whatever happens."

"Ask me, it's a total waste of time and money," Dewey James said, stubbing out his cigarette in the red dirt. "She's got about as much chance of winning as Barney here has to be the next pope."

"Y'all excuse us," Jo Lynne said, smiling at each of the men in turn. "We got to get this food inside."

"Your mama's inside," Dewey James said. "She may need some help settin' out the food."

They climbed the wooden steps and added their food to all the other dishes laid out on long tables. Purse was ready to eat right then, but Jo Lynne said they had to wait.

The big, high-ceilinged room—it must have been the school auditorium at one time—was crowded with people, maybe a hundred in all. They all seemed happy to be there. On a stage at one end, a country-and-western band was playing. They were Calvin Boyd and his Brazos Valley Bounders, a banner on the wall behind them said.

They had just put the food on the table when Calvin Boyd and his boys launched into "The Chicken Song," one of Purse's all-time favorites. It was a song Uncle Joe had taught him when he was six years old. He began singing along under his breath: "C is the way to begin, H is the second letter in, C-H-I-C-K-E-N, that is the way to spell chicken."

Jo Lynne laughed and gave him a hug. She was happy he was happy.

After the chicken song, Leroy Vitek, a county constable Purse had met on a campaign trip a few weeks earlier, stepped up to the stage. He asked for a round of applause for Calvin Boyd and his band and told the crowd it was nearly time to eat.

He called on Brother Miles Goodrich, the local Baptist preacher, to come up and say the blessing. Brother Miles thanked the Lord for the good ladies whose hands had labored over the repast they were about to partake of.

After his amen, Mr. Vitek came back and told a story about how when he was growing up in the 1920s, all the young'uns had to wait for the adults to finish eating before they got to eat. "We was lucky if there was a scrawny, ol' wing left or maybe a gizzard by the time the old folks got through," he said. The older folks in the audience grinned and nodded at each other. "That's right" they murmured.

"We're not gonna do it that way today," Calvin Vitek said. "I know you youngsters are hungry, so y'all go head on and fill your plates. But just leave us a little something if you don't mind."

He needn't have worried. Two long tables were filled with fried chicken, baked ham, barbecued ribs, potato salad, pea salad, Jello salad, green beans, baked beans, black-eyed peas, fresh tomatoes from somebody's garden, cornbread, homemade rolls and more. For dessert, there were cakes, pies and—Purse's choice—blackberry cobbler. He filled his plate, grabbed a cup of sweetened ice tea with a slice of lemon and wandered outside with Jo Lynne.

Since the Crusher was in the shade of an old live oak, they spread their lunch on the hood.

"Did you get some of this ham?" Jo Lynne said. "Mrs. Collins brought it. She's kin to the Allisons somehow. It's really good."

"For a little girl, you sure can eat," he teased Jo Lynne.

She laughed, and about that time Shotgun Epps strolled by carrying a plate piled high. Shotgun was his old boss at the Highway Department. Purse introduced him to Jo Lynne.

"I been meanin' to tell this boy his job's still waitin' for him," he told Jo Lynne. "Haven't been able to find a fit replacement for ol' Rufus."

"I'll work on him," Jo Lynne said. "Nice to meet you, Mr. Epps."

Jo Lynne took a sip of iced tea and wiped her mouth with a paper napkin. "So tell me, Wily T, what is it you do all day?" She waved her hand at a bee that was interested in Purse's cobbler.

He told her about the campaign trips and the morning meetings. He told her about Joe Frank and Sue Bee and Aboy.

That's pretty much how my days go," he said. "Like Aboy told me when I first started out; he said, 'You'll be Red's factotum.'"

"And how do your nights go? What do you do at night?"

"Well," he said, just as Ilene and her little friend—Ilene called her Sissy—came running up. They were just finishing their desserts, and Purse was thinking about going back for a slice of Jo Lynne's pecan pie.

"You promised," Ilene said, cocking her head and wagging her finger at Jo Lynne.

"You sure you want to swing right after you've finished eating?" Jo Lynne asked.

"It don't matter," Ilene said. "I never get sick."

The girls led them over to the swings, kicked off their sandals and plopped down on the wooden seats. Purse and Jo Lynne pulled them up and back and let them go, their skinny legs stretched out toard the trees and blue sky

"I got sick one time," Sissy said as she swung back toward Purse and Jo Lynne. "It was when I went on the baby roller coaster at the fair. I threw up on a man's bald head. He was waiting in line with his little boy."

"Ewww, that's gross," Ilene said.

"Push me harder," Sissy squealed.

"Would you really go back to the Highway Department?" Jo Lynne asked as they pushed the creaky, old swings.

"I wouldn't want to," he said, giving Sissy a shove. She leaned backward and pointed her bare feet. "Would you want me to?"

She didn't answer for several pushes. He looked to see if she had heard his question.

"I want you to do what you want to do," she said. "I want you to do what you think is best for you."

"What about you?"

"Let's just say I'm not going anywhere."

From inside the building they heard the rippling sounds of the old upright piano, as someone played the opening chords of "When the Roll is Called Up Yonder." It was a little off key but loud and spirited.

"Girls, we have to go inside," Jo Lynne said. "Singin's started."

"Shoot," Ilene said. "Who wants to hear that ol' singin'?"

The preacher, Miles Goodrich, was at the piano. Jo Lynne's dad was standing beside the piano and singing with a quartet. A lot of people were still eating as they listened to the old familiar gospel tunes.

Jo Lynne had told Purse that her daddy sang, but Purse had never heard him. He sang bass, and for a little man he had an uncommonly deep voice. Purse couldn't keep his eyes off his Adam's apple as it bobbed up and down from one note to the next.

The preacher bent over the keyboard and banged out the opening chords of "Low in the Grave He Lay," and Mr. James really went to town on the chorus. The lead and the tenor pealed out "He arose!" and Mr. James echoed from down in the depths. And then all four would join in on "Hallelujah, Christ arose!"

They were actually pretty good. The audience thought so too. "Dewey James ought to be on Lawrence Welk," he heard one woman tell another.

Purse glanced at his watch and realized he needed to go if he was going to get back in time for the party. He told Jo Lynne.

"You go ahead, she said. "I'll ride home with the folks. Come on, I'll walk out to the car with you."

Standing at the car, they could still hear the music. Preacher Goodrich had the piano really jumping, and they could hear Jo Lynne's dad singing two-part harmony with the tenor, his brother, Hugh James. They were good.

Jo Lynne smiled and put her arms around him. "Love 'em or hate 'em, those are my people," she said. "Yours too. I hope you don't go off and forget that."

He kissed her. He promised he wouldn't forget.

★ ★ THIRTEEN ★ ★

Back where he was Purse and not Wily T., he found out
that Aboy not only had gotten knocked off the front pages by
the boorish Mr. Sisco—there was just a little item on the inside
about the kildeer—but also had made himself a hero of the first
order. Purse didn't know how much of a hero until Red had the
campaign staff out to the house Saturday evening.

Red's house was in West River Place, a hilly, cedar-covered
part of town on the other side of the river. It used to be where
livin'-hand-to-mouth cedar-choppers and scruffy hippie commune
dwellers built little homemade cabins, but now it was where a lot
of the lawyers and lobbyists and downtown bankers lived, not in
ramshackle cabins, but in big stone and glass houses that clung
to the edges of limestone cliffs, the chalky-white outcroppings
softened by the dark green of cedar .

The house was made of stucco, sea-foam green on one side
and sort of lilac-colored on the other. It was shaped like two
square boxes set cantilevered on top of each other at the base of
a chalk bluff. A narrow waterfall tumbled over the bluff into a
black-marble pool next to the house. From the second-story side
away from the water, you could see the dome of the Capitol above
the thick green trees. Howard, Red's ex, had hired a local architect
to design the place after his law firm won a huge asbestos-in-the-
schools settlement. Howard moved out when he and Red divorced.

These days, now that Red's kids were grown, Axel spent a
lot of time there, although he had a condo of his own in a funky
neighborhood near downtown. Called Downsville, it used to be a
black part of town but had gotten gentrified. Purse had never been
to Axel's house, but Aboy had told him it was nice.

He liked Red's place. When there was a crowd, it got kind of
noisy and echo-y inside; other times it was calm and restful, lots
of nice pictures on the wall, a lot of books on shelves and tables.
Her housekeeper, Josie Salmon, looked after things, so there was
always good food in the fridge.

Now and then when Red was out of town, before the campaign, she would have him drive out and feed Dog, her cat, and bring in the mail from the box at the road. Then he would pop open a cold beer and sit by the pool in a lounge chair listening to the waterfall until the sound put him to sleep. He had thought about bringing Trieu out, but he hadn't got up the nerve yet, even if he could find the time.

A pleasant purple dusk was settling over the hills when he showed up. Cars lined the driveway, so he had to park the Crusher on a side street a hundred yards or so down the hilly, winding road. Doves were soughing as he walked back up the hill to the house. Sue Bee answered the door, a big smile on her face. She gave him a kiss on the cheek.

Most of the campaign staff were there, plus some of the money people. They were standing around the big open living room with the view of downtown. Everybody was drinking beer or wine or margaritas with salt around the rims of their glasses. There were tortilla chips in big wooden bowls around the room, and Josie was fixing nachos in the kitchen. Through the glass picture window, he could see Red herself on the deck talking to Merlin Pitts, the trial lawyer.

He stood around for a while talking to Judge Bill Young, who had come in from Floydada. Aboy, his face red from being in the sun all day on the dove hunt, sauntered up. The judge kidded him about shooting the state's last dodo. Axel drifted by, a glass of red wine in one hand, a small cigar in the other. He wanted to know whether Trieu was going to be there.

Sue Bee scurried into the house from out on the deck with Red and walked over to a cypress stump in one corner of the room. The size of a manhole cover, about a foot high, the stump was a gift from the writer and folklorist C. L. Worthy. He had cut down a bald cypress tree on the banks of the Guadalupe River years ago and had bequeathed the stump to Red just before he died. Now, politicians who dropped by the house could deliver a stump speech whenever they were of a mind to.

Sue Bee kicked off her blue tennis shoes and stepped up on the stump. "Red Alert! Red Alert!" she shouted, banging a fork against her wineglass. Purse saw Aboy wince and glance over at

Judge Young. The judge gave a quick shake of his head and looked down at the floor.

"Thank y'all for being here tonight," Sue Bee said. "Y'all been working real hard, and Red thought everybody needed a little break. She has a little something to talk to us about, but first I wanted to share with you the latest news. I think you're going to like it."

"Don't tell us Jimmy Dale's pullin' out," Ricardo Zamora, a county commissioner from Eagle Pass, shouted from the back of the room.

People laughed, and Red shouted out from the other end of the room, "Good Gawd, I hope not. We've got to give that little bastard an old-fashion ass-whuppin' before we put him out his misery."

Everybody yelled and shouted "Hear! Hear!," and Sue Bee stood on the stump beaming, her eyes sparkling behind the big glasses she wore. "No, he's not pullin' out," she said, "but he mighta wished he had. The latest *Morning News* poll shows us within five, with a margin of error of three."

More shouting, and Sue Bee started to chant, waving her arms like a third-grade singing teacher: "Red Ahead, Red Ahead, Red Ahead." People sort of joined in until they began to feel slightly ridiculous.

Now Red made her way through the crowd to the stump, people reaching for her hand and patting her on the back. She held out a hand to help Sue Bee down, then stepped up herself, kind of bouncing on her toes while she got her footing. She looked good. She had on a pair of jeans and a white blouse and a t-shirt over the blouse with her own face on the front, her bicep flexed like Rosie the Riveter. Her red hair was pulled back with a blue ribbon.

"Thank y'all, thank y'all," she said as the chanting slowly died down. "What beautiful, beautiful people y'all are, every last one of you. And it's my ever-lasting privilege to be working with you in this great endeavor."

"We love you, Red," a young woman in the back shouted.

"And I love you too," Red said. "Thank you, Mary Nell, 'cause that brings me to what I want to say here tonight." She looked down at the floor, put both hands in the front pockets of her jeans, then looked back up at all of them. She looked like she might be about to cry.

"I know you can't always tell how I feel about y'all," she said in a quiet voice, "because sometimes I let my fears and my fearsome temper and my old tapes from long ago get in the way of how I want to be. I'm not easy to live with; I admit it. And if you don't believe me, you can ask dear old Howard Ryder the next time you see him. But I'm trying, Lord knows I'm trying, and I want you to know here and now and right through to the end, however it turns out, that I love and appreciate every single one of y'all more than you know."

Watching her on the stump, Purse was thinking about what he had seen the night before, when Aboy had taken him down to Annie's Alley. That's what it was called, the little side street off Barton Springs Road that a tiny, old woman with skin like beef jerky, a woman named Annie, had made her own. She was the mayor of Annie's Alley; her constituents were a dozen or so other street people who spent their nights in a hobo camp near the railroad track and their days on the street with Annie drinking malt liquor and cheap wine.

Aboy walked over and squatted down beside the old woman. She wasn't afraid of him; she knew him. "How's it goin', Annie,?" he asked. "Need anything?"

"Well, I could use a Cadillac Eldorado and a sirloin steak, medium-rare," Annie said, her smoker's voice a slur. Up close, Purse could see the dirt that had settled into the wrinkles on her hands and face. Her friends chuckled and nudged each other with their elbows. "You got those for me, Mr. Big?"

"'Fraid not, Annie," Aboy said. He stood up and reached in his pocket for a ten-dollar bill.

"Much obliged, kind sir," Annie said. "I'll put this down on the Cadillac, with your permission, of course."

His mind popped back to Red. Her blue eyes were glistening. Seeing Red cry, or almost cry, was a rare sight indeed, one he suspected not many folks had seen. She looked up and smiled and took a deep breath. "We can do it," she said. "Working together, we can win this thing. And that's exactly what we're gonna do."

It was like a rock concert again, so loud the noise seemed to vibrate in his ears. He was nearly crying himself. Even Joe Frank was excited. Purse saw him yelling, pumping his fist in the air.

Red held up both arms to try to calm the raucous crowd. "There's something else I want to talk to y'all about," she said, and they gradually got quiet. "I know, and most of you know, that the man who usually bears the brunt of a Red Ryder outburst is the big fella standing right over there next to Purse, the big fella with the nacho in his mouth and a Shiner in his paw. My old friend and traveling buddy, the Rev. Ewell Suskin. Or should we call him Sure Shot Suskin these days?"

Everybody laughed, and so did Aboy. He liked being the center of attention, even if he was the butt of the joke.

"But I'm here to tell you tonight," Red continued, "that Aboy Suskin has outdone himself, and every single one of us in this campaign are in his debt. Joe Frank, why don't you and Aboy come up here and explain to these good people what I'm talking about."

The two men made their way to the stump, and Red stepped down, then quickly stepped back up. "I almost forgot," she said. "You fellas mind?"

Aboy bowed toward Red, who looked out over the crowd. "Raenell, where are you?" she said. "Come on up here."

Purse saw Raenell in the back, smiling with an embarrassed look on her face and shaking her head no, but a couple of folks standing nearby gently shoved her forward.

"While she's coming up here, let me tell you what this lovely young woman has done," Red said. "Some of y'all may know her kinfolks live over in East Texas. What you may not know is that she's got a brother-in-law over at Rosharon that runs one of the biggest nurseries in the state. And Raenell has come up with a delicious little plan, and he's agreed to it, to provide little rosebuds to every newspaper delivery person east of IH-35. So when people go out in the front yard every morning to get their papers, they'll find a Red rosebud wrapped in a campaign note right there beside it. It's positively an inspired idea. And it comes from our own Raenell Sitton."

Red stepped down from the stump and hugged a blushing Raenell. Again, cheers. "Little things like that add up," Red said.

"Those flowers could be the tipping point."

Now it was time for the Aboy and Joe Frank show. What they had to say sent little chills down Purse's spine. For the first time, for him at least, it was beginning to seem like maybe, just maybe....

"Well, we have a friend in the treasurer's office," Joe Frank said. "Lot of y'all know Benita Hearn...."

"Where's she been lately?" Carl Castle shouted. Carl worked in Red's office with accounts receivable.

"Just hold on, and I'm going to tell you," Joe Frank said. "Benita is no more."

"What? Whadda you mean?" people were asking each other. Purse saw Raenell put her hand to her mouth and bite her knuckle.

"No, no, she's fine. I mean he's fine. Benita decided about a year ago—and I have permission to tell y'all this—that she's always been a man trying to break out of a woman's body. She's—or he's—what you call a transsexual. So she took off work for a while, got all the shots and the treatments and the—um, surgical enhancements, I presume. And now Benita is Bennett—Mr. Bennett Wayne Hurr."

There was all this murmuring in the room, as people looked at each other and tried not to laugh. In his mind's eye, Purse kept seeing guys in togas, racing chariots around the capital. He looked at Judge Young. The judge was not happy.

And he was truly not happy when Joe Frank looked over toward the corner of the room and spotted a big, blonde-haired guy, a shy smile on his face, in a lime-green Ban-Lon t-shirt and khaki slacks that sort of strained across his belly.

"Take a bow, Ben," Joe Frank said, and Ben Hurr took a step forward, gave a little girly wave and kept on smiling, his wide face turning red. People started clapping, and Sue Bee made her way through the crowd to give the new Ben Hurr a hug. Judge Young did not.

"We're happy things worked out," Joe Frank said. "But that's not the important thing, although I guess it is to Benita; I mean Ben. The important thing, as far as the campaign goes, is that she—I mean he—and Aboy—have been going over the books and investigating tax returns, and what they found—well, you tell 'em what you found, Aboy."

"What we have found, with Mr. Hurr's sterling support, and working solely on his own time," a proud and smiling Aboy announced, "is that our friend Mr. Sisco is a tax scofflaw. That little West Texas pissant hasn't paid Uncle Sam his due for yea the past ten years.

"It's absolutely true. Jimmy Dale Sisco, one of the richest men in this state, achieved that lofty pinnacle because taxes were for the little guy, not for him and his kind. He found a way, every year for at least ten years, to send in his tax return owing nothing, zilch, nada."

"No wonder he's easy talking about rape," Judge Young said to Purse and Aboy and Joe Frank as people were leaving. "Jimmy Dale Sisco's been screwin' folks for years."

They laughed and laughed.

"So what you gonna do with this bombshell?" the judge was asking the next morning over breakfast at Alma's. He pushed back his western hat, poured about half the sugar container into a spoon and then into his coffee and took a sip. He had decided not to make the long drive back to Floydada the night before, mainly because Red was going to need him later in the week. In her debate preparation, he was going to be Jimmy Dale. "You got a press conference scheduled, Joe Frank?"

"Not yet. I thought about it, but Red wants to play it cool. Build it through the week, then unload at the debate."

"What in the tarnation is she thinking?" the judge shouted, red-faced and leaning across the table toward Joe Frank. His cowboy string tie dangled across his *juevos rancheros*. "You can't sit on dynamite like this, like it's a day-old turd in a two-seat privy. You got to get it out there, let folks bring it up down at the Chat-and-Chew, give ol' Bob the Barber over in Corsicana time to mention it to his customers while he's clipping what hair they got left on their scrawny old noggins."

"Out in the West Texas town of El Paso ..." Marty Robbins

began to warble over the juke box sound system. Alma came by to fill their coffee cups. Judge Young held his hand over his cup, since he had the sugar mix just right.

"The debate's five days away," Joe Frank said, lighting up his first fag of the day. Ralph says wait. That's where Red got the idea."

Ralph was Ralph Wayne, the political consultant from D.C. the campaign had hired—at the national party's insistence—after Bobby Ray had been sent packing. He had won a few congressional races across the country, a governor's race or two. He had lost a bunch more, but somebody had convinced her—maybe it was Sue Bee—that he knew what he was doing.

Judge Young didn't. "Ralph Wayne's got about as much gumption as a gotch-eyed gazelle," he said. "And about as much sense, too."

By the time Aboy and Olene wandered in, the judge had cooled off a bit, but he still wasn't happy. He and Joe Frank started making a list of questions they thought Red ought to be prepared to answer, and Joe Frank said he'd be meeting with Ralph Wayne later in the day to talk debate strategy. Purse could see Young wanting to say something about Ralph Wayne, but for once the old judge with the perpetual scowl held his tongue.

Sue Bee scurried in just as they were about through. Thursday and Friday would be debate preparation days. Aboy and Purse would be going with Red to a Mexican American *pachanga* in the Valley on Tuesday evening and a "Clean Beach" ceremony in Galveston on Wednesday morning. He was wishing Trieu could go along, since her hometown was just up the coast, but she had told him the night before that the trial was just getting critical. He missed her.

When he got back to the office, he had a note that Jo Lynne had called. He called her back, but Trudy said she had stepped out. Trudy didn't seem too friendly.

The campaign events were fun. There were good crowds in the Valley, lots of mariachi music and *cerveza*, and even though Red mangled her remarks in Spanish, the folks were good-natured about it. At least she tried, and Mexican-American folks appreciated that.

The weather was great in Galveston, sunny, not too hot, and Red put on pedal pushers and tennis shoes and walked along the beach a few hundred yards picking up trash that people had left on the beach. It made you realize Texans were none too tidy.

Purse enjoyed the debate practice too, mainly because he didn't have to do anything but be part of the pretend audience and clap when Red scored a point against Jimmy Dale, aka, Judge Young. Ronnie Swigert, owner of Otto's Biergarten, let them rent out the music hall next door, an old frame building where the German choral societies and oompah bands had done their recitals and performances for more than a hundred years. They were still in that room, standing in rows, straight and tall, black-and-white photos all around. Broken chairs and tables and boxes of empty beer bottles were stacked in the corners. Red and Judge Young stood behind portable lecterns. Joe Frank, Ralph Wayne and Sue Bee were the fake reporters.

Wayne, slick as ever in his canary-yellow, perfectly pressed, oxford-cloth shirt, double-breasted blue blazer, gray slacks and tasseled loafers the color of calf's liver, was the director of the show. He knew better than to get too close to the judge, and toward the end of the second day he seemed to be getting a little wary of Red. She was never one to like things orchestrated and artificial, and her buddy Wayne was getting a little too close to the edge with all his strategies and debate tips and applause lines. As Bobby Ray Evangeline had learned too late for his own good, she just wanted to be herself and let the voters make up their own minds. Wayne didn't trust the voters that much.

If it came down to who knew their stuff, then Red would win hands down. She had been in public office a long time, and she could talk issues with the best of them. Plus, she had been a debater in high school. But what Ralph Wayne was saying is that you had to factor in the likeability quotient. People would vote for whoever they liked the best, whoever gave them a warm feeling, even if that person's tax policies or whatever walked right through their front door and snatched money out of their pocket.

Red finally blew up at him right after lunch on Friday afternoon. He was telling her something about how she had to work in a reference to capital punishment and being tough on crime, since that was what Jimmy Dale's latest ad talked about; Jimmy Dale had people in black-and-white striped prison coveralls bustin' rocks with sledge hammers. The ad said being a U.S. senator was a man-sized job for real men and real men didn't coddle criminals.

"I'm not a whore, Ralph, despite what you may have heard up there in D.C.," Red said. "I'm not goin' to prostitute myself before the people of this state simply to win an election."

Everybody was quiet in the room. The afternoon sun was streaming in through a front window; the dust motes were dancing. Ralph Wayne looked at Red for a moment, then began folding up his papers and putting them in his leather briefcase. "Have it your way, Red," he said. "After all, you're the boss."

"Goddamn right I am," she said, halfway to herself but loud enough for him to hear.

Red and Axel, Joe Frank, Sue Bee and Ralph Wayne flew to Dallas Friday night. Purse did his laundry, made sure Shoogy Red had pellets to last the weekend and that Willis Seymour would check on him. Trieu had told him over the phone that morning she was going home to Minerva as soon as the trial shut down for the weekend. She said she thought it would last maybe another week. Jo Lynne told him over the phone she was going up to Geneva Hall to play bingo and she wondered if maybe he could come home and go with her. He told her he couldn't.

"We need to talk, Wily," she said. "I need to see you."

"We will," he said. "But you gotta remember what I told you about the campaign. How it was going to be crazy? How you wouldn't be seeing much of me? We got three weeks to go, and then things will settle down again. I'll see you as soon as I can."

He heard Jo Lynne hang up. She didn't say good night, I love you, nothing. He went to bed early. He had an anxious feeling in the pit of his stomach every time he thought about her.

★ ★ ★

Purse and Aboy hit the road about nine, driving the campaign van. Folks honked and waved when they saw the big red sign on the side, and they saw more and more Rose Ryder bumper stickers. They were in a good mood. They stopped at the Village Bakery in West and bought two dozen kolaches, and Purse drove while Aboy ate a couple of prune kolaches before they pulled back onto the highway. He washed them down with a quart carton of milk. He favored the prune flavor, said they kept him regular.

Purse favored them too, simply because they tasted good. He would eat all around the middle, saving the warm prune and buttery sugar topping for the very last. Aboy ate them in maybe two bites, no putting off the pleasure for him.

Driving into downtown West, he noticed some morning newspapers still out in people's yards, with Raenell's rose bud right beside them.

"I thought they were supposed to be red, for Red Ryder," he said to Aboy. "Those over there are yellow."

Aboy glanced at a couple of yards on the right, both with yellow rosebuds. When he saw another one in the next block, he pulled over and stopped. He opened the gate on a little white picket fence, looked around for anybody at home and picked up the yellow rose bud, wrapped in a campaign flier. "Compliments of the morning to you," it said. "From your friend, Jimmy Dale Sisco, MAN of the people."

Aboy stuck the flower and the flier in his shirt pocket and came back to the car, all the while talking to himself. "You tell anybody about Raenell's plan?" he asked, starting up the car and pulling out without even looking back.

"Not me," Purse said. "Did you?"

"There's a worm in the rose," Aboy said. "There's a spy in the house of Ryder."

Aboy pulled into a gas station and called Joe Frank on the pay phone. For the next 20 miles all he and Purse talked about was how Nabob Slidell had been able to find out what they were planning, and who on the campaign staff might have loose lips.

"So how do we know it's not you?" Purse said in a teasing sort of way. "I've seen you talking to Nabob on occasion. Always sort of surprises me."

Aboy laughed. "Son, you'll find this surprising too," he said, "but I sort of like little ol' Nabob.

Purse stared over at him, trying to see if he was pulling his leg. He looked serious. Sounded serious. "What do you mean you like him? I can't imagine his own mother liking him! If he's ever even had a mother."

"I mean I like the fact that him and me understand each other. We understand our role in the grand scheme of things. No illusions, none whatsover. And I like to think we're good at our jobs."

"Your jobs being what?"

He pulled out around an elderly couple in a Ford station wagon and mulled over the question. After about a mile, he said, "Think of it this way. You ever see a maggot?"

"Sure I've seen a maggot. I've seen thousands of maggots, millions of maggots. Remember who signed my paycheck before you and I met?"

"Okay, then think about maggots this way. You know how maggots are just about the lowest of the low, but did you know they actually do some good on this earth. If you've got a wound, maggots actually clean it out for you, cut down the chance of infection."

Purse shook his head, trying to clear away the mental image of thousands of crawling maggots on somebody's injured arm. "So you're saying you and Nabob are campaign maggots?

"Precisely, my son. Precisely."

"I want to ask you something," Purse said a few miles later, just to change the subject. They were passing through Abbot, hometown of Willie Nelson himself.

"Fire away, my young swain," Aboy said, wiping his mouth with the back of his hand. "Interrogatories are the incendiaries of wisdom. Don't you agree?"

"I do, but what I was wondering is how come you didn't want to tell me about the old bag lady we went to see the other night? Annie, or whatever her name was."

Aboy rummaged in the kolache box like he hadn't heard the question. He had eaten all the prune kolaches, so he latched onto an apricot. "Mighty fine, son, mighty fine," he said, licking his fingers.

They passed a "men at work" sign, and Purse slowed down going past the orange cones and a huge yellow striping machine. He always looked to see if his old pals Buster Heaton or Shotgun Epps or Donny Ray Lehrman were on the work crews. This time he didn't know any of them. Aboy turned in his seat to face Purse, his arm laid out across the back of the seat.

"Occasionally," he said, "the burden of knowing is not worth the bearing. This may be one of those occasions. You've heard it said, no doubt, that ignorance is bliss. And if you don't believe me, just ask Jimmy Dale. I thought about telling you the other night, but I decided to give it more thought. I've decided that as someone intimately involved with this political endeavor, you deserve to know the truth."

"The truth about what?"

"The truth I'm about to tell you, but you have to swear to me that it never goes beyond the confines of this car. All right?"

"All right," Purse said.

"No, say it," Aboy said, squeezing Purse's shoulder, hard. "Say the words."

"Aboy," Purse complained, glancing over to see if he was serious. He looked to be serious. "Okay. I swear to tell the whole—oops that's the wrong one. I swear that I'll never tell anybody, not even my dear old mother, what you're about to tell me, even if my dear old mother wanted to know."

"It's not your mother I'm worried about," Aboy said. "It's those motherfuckin' bastards running Jimmy Dale's campaign. It's my bosom buddy Nabob Slidell." He threw back his head, took a final swig of milk and tossed the empty carton into the back seat. Purse waited.

"That woman you met the other night, Annie, is Annie Ryder. She's Red's mother."

He paused for Purse's reaction, and it wasn't long in coming. He stared at Aboy, slack-jawed. The tires veered onto the shoulder.

"But I thought her folks were dead," Purse said, steering the van back onto the pavement. "That's what I've always heard. That they were killed in a car wreck when she was a little girl."

"That's what she thought for a long time, all the time she was growing up. That her parents were killed in a car wreck and that her grandparents took her in and raised her like she was one of their own. But she found out different once she got to Austin and Annie tracked her down."

Aboy rolled out the whole story between Hillsboro and Waxahachie. Annie, it seemed was a small-town girl from Okmulgee, Oklahoma, her folks down-on-their luck Okies who never left for California. When she was maybe 15 or so, a traveling circus came through a nearby town and Annie got to go to a performance one Saturday afternoon. Hanging out on the crowded, lively midway outside the Big Top, wide-eyed at all the rides and sideshows and suckers' games of chance, she struck up a conversation with one of the circus performers taking a smoke break behind the tent between shows. He was a pole climber, a crazy, redheaded Irishman. His act was to shimmy up to the very tip of a tall, flexible pole, do all kind of acrobatics while he was up there and then get it to swaying. Once he got it swaying far enough, he would switch to a nearby pole that was the same height.

He gave Annie a pass into the show. Staring into the sky at the man 40 feet above her, she was mesmerized. When the circus left town, she left with it. It wasn't long before she was part of the act. Since she was from Oklahoma, they dyed her blonde hair black and stuck an eagle feather in it, put her in a short leather skirt and she was the lovely little Indian maid performing acrobatic feats at the top of a swaying pole.

"How come she wasn't afraid of heights?" Purse asked Aboy.

"The story they told fair-goers is that she was one of those Mohawks that built New York City. You know, working on skyscrapers, walking like cats up on skinny steel girders hundreds of feet off the ground. What I think is that she and her folks had been down so low during the Depression that being high up was nothing compared to that.

"So Annie toured the country with the circus, which finally made its way to Dallas and the State Fair of Texas. That's where she found out she was pregnant, with Red, who, in looks, apparently took after her redheaded Irish father. A pregnant pole swayer was a burden the man didn't want to carry, so he and the circus took off without her.

"A young fellow from Austin, a tow-truck driver by the name of Sam Ryder, who was showing his parents around the fair one Saturday, got to talking to Annie. She'd gotten a job selling corn dogs at a stand on the midway. After a while, she told him she was pregnant, but that didn't matter. Sam Ryder took her back to Austin with him and married her. Not long after Red was born, he was killed when a car out on the San Antonio Highway plowed into him while he was getting a broke-down car hitched up to his truck.

"Annie, in the depths of her widow's weeds, started drinking and cutting her skin with a Bowie knife, and that's when Red's grandparents took their little grandbaby in. Annie got worse and worse and ended up on the street. Even though her in-laws did all they could to try to get her help, she didn't seem to want help. She'd rather live behind the U-Tote-Em and drink malt liquor, with Mogen David wine for dessert, than get herself back together."

"So they didn't tell Red about her?"

"They didn't," Aboy said, "They thought it would be too traumatic for the little girl to know. They told her that her mother was dead. But Red told me one time she always had a feeling her mother was alive."

Purse took a deep breath. It was a lot to take in. "But why keep her a secret?" he asked. "It's nothing to be ashamed of, is it? Lots of people have loony relatives. Skeletons in their closets."

"Listen, my naïve, young know-nothing," Aboy said. "You and me are the proud citizens of a state where simply being a female of the species is well nigh reason enough to disqualify you from holding office. How do you think being the daughter of a homeless woman, not to mention a homeless woman that's plumb loco, would go over with the average Texas voter?"

"So, who knows?"

"Me, Joe Frank, probably Howard, maybe Red's kids; I don't know. She has me see after Annie's needs, as best I can. I've had her in the insane asylum, I guess half a dozen times, but they can't keep her. Says she not a danger to herself or others."

"So Red's father, her real father, could be alive too."

"Could be," Aboy said, "although I doubt the legs on the old actuarial tables for circus pole climbers run too far down the page."

The traffic was picking up as they approached the ragged outskirts of Dallas, mainly endless auto junk yards, used car lots and fast-food joints lining the highway, the tall, silver spires of downtown still shimmering in the distance. It was ugly, and except for the skyscrapers it didn't get much better as the Interstate swooped into town and crossed the Trinity River. Only the traffic got heavier and faster.

Aboy pointed to a giant billboard on a bluff high above the freeway. It was a beer advertisement—Pearl Beer, from the country of 1100 springs—and it showed tall green cypress trees and a clear running spring, with water pouring over some rocks. The water was real, and it never stopped running. Purse wondered how they did that. It was pretty neat.

He switched on the radio, to WFAA-AM. Suddenly he was a little boy again, riding in the backseat of his folks' Dodge on their way to Aunt Lola's and Uncle Lem's. The deep mellow sounds of WFAA always told him they were in the big city, although this time whatever mellow sounds he might have heard kept being drowned out every few minutes by "Jimmy, Jimmy Sisco, the man who loves this state."

He flipped off the radio, and while Aboy looked through his notebook for the address of the local public TV station, the debate site, he kept seeing a picture in my mind's eye. It was a little Indian girl, high in the sky, one arm and one leg attached to a pole, the other arm and leg reaching outward, like a cut-out piece of a paper doll. And then he would see her let go. She would fall straight down.

★ ★ FOURTEEN ★ ★

It was about six o'clock, the heat of the day just easing into a perfect fall evening, and already the parking lot of the public TV station was full. Cars were parked all through the residential neighborhood nearby, and that's what Purse and Aboy had to do with their rent car, as well. Big, white TV trucks with satellite dishes and antennas on top, their deep-throated engines idling, were lined up just outside the back door of the two-story stucco building; this one and only debate would be broadcast all over the state. This is big time, Purse was thinking, as he and Aboy walked into the parking lot.

Jimmy Dale and his head honcho Calvin Locke, the brains and the brass behind the campaign, didn't want even one debate, and it was easy to see why. When negotiations started back in the summer, Jimmy Dale was riding his double-digit lead, plus he and the issues were not exactly on speaking terms, so for him a debate was everything to lose and nothing really to gain.

And then there was Nabob Slidell, Jimmy Dale's chief trickster and campaign genius. The little rodent loved the dark, scuzzy corners, and the more he could keep voters in the dark about the real Jimmy Dale Sisco, the better his chances.

But, over time, the big newspapers shamed Jimmy Dale into it, questioned the size of his *cojones*, so to speak, by asking how he could be afraid of a little-bitty red-headed lady.

"You can only play possum for so long. Then you got to stand up on your own two feet and face the music," Red told reporters when she was down in the Valley. "Like a man," she added with a grin and a wink.

So Jimmy Dale—or rather his silver-haired handler, Calvin Locke—said yes, even over Nabob's objections, from what Aboy had heard. About the only thing they could be happy about was that a lot of folks would be watching the Longhorns or the Aggies or whoever was playing football on a Saturday evening. They might be thinking about whether their team should kick or receive if they won the coin toss, but not about elections.

Couldn't tell it by the crowds, though. Purse and Aboy sidled through a passel of folks trying to get into a big, white tent the station had set up on a corner of the parking lot. Although only 200 people would make up the live TV audience inside the studio, the candidates were scheduled to come out to the tent afterwards and speak to the media and to their supporters, so people carrying homemade signs and wearing t-shirts for their candidate were already jostling for space. A band called Ponty Bone and the Squeeze Tones was playing *conjunto* music inside the tent. It was a lively scene.

Aboy, in white Pat Boone bucks, a leisure suit the color of a robin's egg and his bad-ass cockateel tie, looked a little like Foghorn Leghorn. A couple of people figured he had to be some kind of senator or something, even though they couldn't quite place him, so they asked for his autograph. He grinned and winked and obliged.

They found Red and her entourage—Sue Bee, Joe Frank, Ralph Wayne and Axel—inside the office of the station manager. Red was sitting on a couch on one side of the room going over position papers with Sue Bee. From what Joe Frank had said the day before, she had her closing statement pretty much down pat, or at least the outlines of it. She would be able to adapt it to whatever developed during the debate.

Howard, her ex, had sent her a huge bouquet of red roses; they were in a vase on the coffee table in front of the couch. The smell reminded Purse of rich people in magazines.

A make-up man was fussing around Red's face with a brush and some powder. She motioned Purse over and handed him her purse without looking up. She looked great. Purse had heard Sue Bee earlier in the week tell a fashion reporter from the *Dallas Times Herald* what she would be wearing, and here it was in real life: a St. John suit from Neiman's, summer tweed in a periwinkle shade, with a bit of flare at the knees.

Purse liked how it showed off her legs, and, on the other end, how it made her red hair come alive. She had on a silk blouse the same color as the inside of an oyster shell and a necklace that her great-Aunt Eunice from Mexia had given her when she was a little girl. The purse she handed Purse, a clutch, was in a matching color. "Coach," he had heard Sue Bee say, "no faux."

Aboy bee-lined to a table in the corner that was filled with canned soft drinks, little meatballs on toothpicks and some other kind of cheese and cracker-type things, only fancier. "Where they got Jimmy Dale?" he asked Joe Frank, his mouth full of meatball.

"You didn't see his bus?" Joe Frank said. "Big silver blimp over in the Stoneleigh Hotel parking lot. That Roy Rogers picture of him raring up on his palomino on the side? Go back outside in a few minutes, and you'll probably see the Jimmy Dale Sisco grand processional."

"Wonder if the young Jovita's along," Aboy pondered aloud.

"Who?"

"Never mind."

After a few minutes Sue Bee shooed everybody out except for Ralph Wayne and Joe Frank. Aboy and Purse found their reserved seats on the side with the other Ryder people. Jimmy Dale's crowd sat on the opposite side of the studio.

Purse looked for Jovita but didn't see her. He decided she must be back at the ranch. He did see Sissy, the "little wife." Ruby-red lips, blonde hair piled high like the meringue on his Aunt Lola's coconut-cream pie, a silver necklace gleaming against her pale-blue silk dress, she was sitting with a couple of the Sisco kids. She had her purse on her lap, just like Purse. He thought she looked anxious, even when she smiled and greeted well-wishers strolling by on the way to their seats.

Purse was jumpy himself. He could feel it in his stomach, and he realized he was taking little shallow breaths and playing with a hangnail on his thumb. He got to thinking about how, just a few weeks ago, none of this would really have mattered, since everybody figured Red was about as likely to be the next U.S. senator as Purse himself was. Now, everybody knew that what happened on this night might decide the election—not to mention Purse's own little life.

The sounds of "Texas Our Texas" came wafting over the airwaves, and a pretty, young TV reporter from Dallas named Sylvia Sumatsu walked out and sat down at a table facing the lecterns. She would be the moderator, and after she sat down two other reporters joined her. The back wall behind the lecterns was a royal blue curtain with a giant state flag pinned to it.

Ms. Sumatsu warned the audience before the broadcast began not to yell or applaud, since it would take time away from the candidates, but Jimmy Dale's folks couldn't help themselves. When he walked out into the lights from the right side of the stage, striding sort of bow-legged, elbows out like he was Wyatt Earp about to reach for his gun at the OK Corral, his people not only stood up and clapped but whistled and yahooed like they were at a tractor pull.

Jimmy Dale, wearing his round-topped Hoot Gibson hat, along with a navy-blue suit, a string tie and shiny black boots, grinned, tipped his hat and cocked his finger at the crowd like he was firing a Colt 45 from the waist. He carefully took the big, white Stetson off his head and handed it to his daughter. When he bent down and gave her a kiss on the cheek, the crowd went "ooooooh," and the pretty little girl, blushing, hurried back to her seat and held her daddy's hat on her lap.

Jimmy Dale must have had powder applied to his bald dome; despite the TV lights, it wasn't as shiny as it had been when he and Aboy and Red had seen him at the Jimmy D. What Purse noticed was that his ears stuck out even when they weren't being mashed by his hat.

Once Jimmy Dale got settled behind his lectern, Joe Frank stuck his head out from the left side of the stage and did a quick hands-down kind of motion to the folks sitting on Red's side of the room. They knew what he meant—applause, yes, but don't go hog-wild like you're a bunch of fork-of-the-creek yahoos. Sort of like Coach Woody, Purse's eighth-grade football coach, used to say: "You little piss ants act like you've been here before."

And that's what happened. Red walked out smiling, her side applauded, she and Jimmy Dale shook hands midway between lecterns and Sylvia Sumatsu launched into the first question.

Both candidates were nervous. Jimmy Dale had that old deer-in-the-headlights look whenever Ms. Sumatsu or one of the other two reporters started reeling out a question for him. Usually he stumbled through some kind of answer, and when he couldn't think of what to say, he would repeat what he had said a few seconds earlier. Despite warnings from Sumatsu, Jimmy Dale's crowd applauded every answer like their man was in the isolation booth on "The $64,0000 Question."

It seemed to Purse that Red was being too careful, like when a pitcher gets to thinking too much and starts aiming the ball instead of letting 'er rip, not letting his arm do what it already knows how to do by instinct. She always had an answer to the questions, but her answers lacked life. There was no Rosie Ryder in what she had to say—until maybe halfway through the debate.

Glenn Roy Smith of the *Houston Post* had a question for Jimmy Dale about Proposition 1 on the November ballot. Jimmy Dale started nodding his head as Smith finished the question, but then, you could tell something was wrong. He opened his mouth, but nothing came out. He screwed up his forehead and cocked his head to one side like Shoogy eyeing a yellow kernel of corn, but still, nothing emerged. He glanced over at Calvin Locke, and the banker with the slicked-back silver hair had his eyes narrowed, his forehead wrinkled and his arms crossed, probably the look he gave some poor sap who couldn't make his payment on a 30-year mortgage. Purse saw him mouth something, but he couldn't tell what he said. Neither could Jimmy Dale.

"Now, uhhhh, Proposition 1, is which, excuse me?" he finally managed to say.

"It's the only one on the ballot, sir," Smith said.

Purse glanced over at Red. She was looking down at the lectern making notes, trying not to smile. Suddenly it was quiet in the studio. Jimmy Dale was living everybody's worst nightmare, naked in his ignorance in front of six million people.

"Oh, on the education commissioner."

"No sir, with all due respect, it changes the criteria for judicial appointments. I was wondering whether or not you were aware of the problem it causes?"

Damn straight, Red was. Purse had heard Red talk about it at Otto's Biergarten when Ralph Wayne asked her about her position. Ralph had to tell her not to go on so long about how it had been a major problem in Congress the year before, about how it hamstrung the judicial system. With Joe Frank's help, she had finally come up with a short, snappy answer in the final practice run that afternoon.

Jimmy Dale could only be so lucky. "Well, it ought to be fixed," he finally told Smith, like he knew all about it, "but I haven't taken a position on the mechanics of it all just yet."

"Excuse me, sir, but didn't you already cast your absentee ballot?" Smith asked.

Jimmy Dale looked at Sylvia Sumatsu and held his hands out like he was appealing to a referee. "I think that's what they'd call a two-fer down in Villa Acuna," he said with a nervous little laugh. "Does he get to ask a follow-up question?"

Ms. Sumatsu nodded her head.

"Well, Mr. Smith, the fact of the matter is I, uh, I did cast my ballot, in Sonora the other day, and, uh, well, I'm pretty sure I voted for it. I, uh, I recollect Sissy telling me how I ought to vote on that particular matter. Didn't you, Hon; don't you remember?"

He glanced over at his wife, and, from the monitor, Purse could tell the camera did too. He had noticed that during the campaign she had the adoring stare down to a tee, but this time it was a dumbfounded stare, like she was thinking, *what kind of idiot am I mixed up with?*

Like a crawfish burrowing down backward into a mud hole, Jimmy Dale kept digging himself in deeper. He looked straight into the camera. "I just want to say to the great people of this state," he said, his coat unbuttoned and hands on his hips, "that I ain't no politician—I been telling y'all that all along—but I do know how to read. You put that dadgum document, that there Proposition 1 or whatever it's called, you put it in front of me, it would take me all of about thirty seconds to give you my honest opinion. I don't go around tellin' everybody, but the fact is, I had the highest grade point of all in the school of agriculture at A&M my last semester."

A buzzer sounded, and Ms. Sumatsu called time. What Purse saw when he looked at Jimmy Dale was an addled Sonny Liston staggering back to his corner. He knew he had been staggered by a punch Red hadn't even thrown—by her rope-a-dope, you might say—and so did his folks in the audience. There was a little buzz of whispers in the room, but no applause.

Purse guessed that some of them were still whispering about the crack he made about the Acuna whorehouses that sort of slid by during Jimmy Dale's moment of terror. And, of course, what folks didn't know was that Red Ryder, like a young Cassius Clay, was just getting started. Her knockout punch was still to be unleashed.

It came right at the end, just as Ralph Wayne hoped it would. Bruce Dysart, a sad-sack and serious political columnist from San Antonio, launched into a wonky sort of question about property taxes. Even before he finished, Jimmy Dale jumped in with an answer.

"Dad-blast it, Dysart, they're too high!" he said. "They're too high! Any fool can tell you that." He leaned back on his haunches, grabbed hold of his lapels and stuck out his chest. "And when Jimmy Dale Sisco gets to Washington, he's gonna launch a holy war against waste, fraud and abuse, and high taxes," he crowed. "Like that old-time cowboy and my hero, Hoot Gibson, used to say, 'come hell or high water, it's nut-cutting time in the corral.' Folks, Jimmy Dale Sisco's gonna cut 'em til they squeal. How can a man do business in this state when he's paying taxes out the wazoo? And, uh, one more thing, Mr. Dysart: Too many folks in this state been sucking on the sugar tit way too long, and the rest of us have had it up to here. You're from San Antone, I take it, and with all those so-called poor people down there, you know what I'm talking about."

Jimmy Dale shook his head, grinned and hopped aboard a different metaphor. "The welfare Cadillac's grinding to a halt, folks, so what I'm saying here tonight is that if you been riding inside on those soft, plushy seats, you better get yourself ready to climb on out and start thumbin'."

Even before he finished his answer, Jimmy Dale's people found their voices. They were hootin' and hollerin', whistling, letting loose with rebel yells.

When the noise died down, Dysart turned to Red. "A response, Ms. Ryder?"

"I'm so glad you asked that question, Bruce," she said, again trying not to smile, "and I'm going to answer it with a couple of questions of my own. Question number one is this: What does a man that can write a personal check for $6 million for his campaign—which Jimmy Dale did just yesterday—what does he know about the tax burden most folks have to live with, in San Antonio and all over this great state?" She looked over at Jimmy Dale. "Maybe Mr. Sisco can answer me that," she said.

He started to, but Ms. Sumatsu held up her hand.

"And question number two," Red said, looking straight ahead into the camera, "how can a man who paid no taxes last year—and yes, you heard me right; I said NO taxes—what does a man like that know about you and me?"

She glanced back at her opponent. His face red, his neck stuck out and his Adam's apple bobbing, Jimmy Dale was staring right back. Purse thought he was going to charge across the stage and grab Red by her own neck.

Red kept twisting the dagger, her voice calm, shaking her head ever so slightly, like she was thinking, "You poor sap; somebody ought'a put you out of your misery right here and now."

"I don't care how much Jimmy Dale talks about the tax burden," she said, "the fact is, he does not represent nor does he understand what it is like to be among the working people of this state. People who pay their taxes and meet their payrolls. People who have to scrimp and save to send their kids to college."

That moment, that one awesome moment, beat anything Purse had ever seen in his short-lived life in politics. The Red light came on just as Red uttered that last word, "college," and the room exploded, at least her side of the room did. It was an avalanche of noise.

The debate format didn't allow Jimmy Dale to respond, so he stood there, his face still red, gripping the lectern with both hands until his knuckles were white. He tried to use his closing statement to respond to what Red had just said, but that just got him all the more confused and wopper-jawed. He said something like, "Well, dad-gummit, it was a bad year last year," and it came out like a Little Lord Fauntleroy whine. He stumbled through some of his campaign slogans, but ran out of things to say even before his time was up. He looked like a beaten man.

While his people clapped, Purse looked at Calvin Locke. The big-city banker was sitting up straight in his chair, staring straight ahead, his hands clasped around his crossed knee. Purse noticed Jimmy Dale glance toward Locke.

Red gave her closing remarks—talking plain ol' common sense to the folks who would be voting, it seemed to Purse—and then it was over. While the cameras rolled, everybody in the studio rushed to the front to gather around the candidates. Purse, his arms folded across his chest, purse in hand, leaned against the wall and watched as first Sue Bee and then Red's kids and grandkids hugged her, and then a lot of other people gathered round, laughing and hugging and shaking hands.

He saw Ben Hurr wrap her in his big, meaty arms. He saw Nabob Slidell, his angry rat face an inch away from the bland mug of Bruce Dysart, telling the newsman what a jerk he was for asking that unfair question about taxes. The cameras were still rolling.

Purse was about to make his way to the front to see if Red needed rescuing when he felt two arms enclose him from behind—they weren't Ben Hurr's; he knew that—and then he felt two lips on the back of his neck just above his coat collar. He turned and there was Trieu, smiling and looking into his eyes, her arms still tight around his waist, her laced fingers locking him in to the most wonderful prison.

At that moment, he had never been so happy. "Trieu, what are…" he started to say, but she put her hand to the back of his head and pulled him down to her soft, moist lips. She smelled faintly like apricot, like what he had smelled at her house in Austin. It was fresh and intoxicating. She kissed him for a long time, her tongue darting like a curious little coral snake into his mouth. With Red's clutch in his right hand, his arms were clutched around Trieu, and for the longest time the jostling crowd and the buzz of sound were far, far away.

They finally broke for air. "I wouldn't have missed this for the world," she said. "And I missed you."

They were still holding each other. "How'd you get in?" Purse asked.

"I just walked right in like I belonged here," she said, smiling, her beautiful black puppy-dog eyes flashing. "I sat in back the whole time, but you were so intent on Ms. Ryder you never looked my way."

He made up for lost time and looked at her, up and down. He could see why someone would let her in, no questions asked. She had on maybe the prettiest dress he had ever seen. It was sort of tight on top, sleeveless, cut low in the front, almost to her waist. He was no fashion expert, but he guessed you would say it was pink—maybe you'd call it raspberry—with tan leaves and darker pink blossoms all over. The skirt part was loose and swirled around her lovely legs whenever she turned. It was so thin, you could almost see right through it, and she wasn't wearing hose, Purse noticed. With her long, shiny black hair and her coffee-with-cream skin, she was so pretty he couldn't say a word. He just gave her another hug and breathed in her scent.

She licked his ear. "Can you put your purse down and sneak out?" she whispered.

"Maybe," he said, giggling. Jimmy Dale and Red both, he noticed, were still surrounded by friends and admirers, and Sam, his dark face calm and strong-looking, was standing nearby. The plan was for Red and the campaign team to head back to the Fairmount Hotel after the press conference outside, have something to eat and watch a video tape of the debate.

Purse wanted to be there, but he wanted to be with Trieu more, and he didn't want to share her. He waved at Aboy on the way through the crowd. Aboy gave him a grin and a thumbs-up.

It was a beautiful night, a yellow moon peeking out from behind the trees of a nearby park, the air almost crisp and with the leaves beginning to turn, smelling, finally, of fall. He felt like running and leaping down the dark street like a fool—a fool for love, he supposed.

The lights of the downtown skyscrapers, just beyond the neighborhood they were in, made him think of daggers, tall, shining daggers, their needle-pointed tops jutting into the night sky. They walked toward Trieu's little car in the hotel parking lot, their arms around each other's waists, stopping every few steps for long, slow kisses. When they kissed, she would take her finger and rub it softly and slowly around their lips.

She reached into her purse and handed him the keys. That's when he realized, in a panic, that he still had his purse, or rather Red's. "Don't go away," he said to Trieu. He raced back to the tent, handed the clutch to Raenell and raced back to the car, all in about two minutes.

Trying to catch his breath, he got behind the wheel of the Spider, and Trieu directed him toward a steak place, Baby Doe's Mine Shaft Number Three, on a bluff a couple of minutes from the TV station. She clung to his right arm, making it a little hard to shift gears. No matter.

"There's that sign," he said as they drove into the parking lot. The billboard with the flowing water loomed right above the restaurant.

"I adore that sign," Trieu said. "It's just like you're in a lovely mountain stream."

Once they sat down at a table next to the big, plate-glass wall, Trieu flashed open her purse, and he saw a stack of crisp, green bills. "My treat tonight," she said, smiling. "I just got paid."

He felt a little uneasy having the woman pay, but Trieu insisted. He ordered the broasted chuck-wagon chicken, with baked potato and a Caesar salad. She had the lady's bacon-wrapped filet mignon and a martini, dry, she told the waiter. Purse passed.

He stuck with a Lone Star. In fact, he had two, and then another.

It was crowded inside the restaurant, crowded and lively and dark, with little candles at each table providing almost the only illumination. Over the buzz of conversation around them and the clatter of dishes, he could barely hear what sounded like the music of Bob Wills and the Texas Playboys coming over the sound system. Looking through the window, once his eyes adjusted to the reflection, he could see the freeway at the base of the bluff, never-ending yellow streams of light coursing in both directions. On the other side of the freeway was a big Miami-looking hotel made of light-green marble, all lit up, with undulating architecture. The cursive letters on the front spelled out The Cabana. One day he would stay there with Trieu, he promised himself. Just like at the Wagon Wheel a couple of months earlier, they held hands across the table and couldn't stop smiling.

Purse couldn't stop talking about Red, about how well informed she came across, and likable, which was probably even more important. And both of them kept imitating poor old Jimmy Dale in his hour of need. Purse put his hands behind his ears, making them stick out, and tried to look as dumb and out of it as Alfred E. Neuman, as Jimmy Dale Sisco. Trieu could hardly stop laughing.

"So do you think the momentum shifted tonight?" she asked. She had taken a big, green olive out of her martini glass and had daintily bitten off a piece.

"Do I think it's changed?" he almost shouted. "Do I think it's changed! I think we won the election tonight! Like they say in Elm Mott, I think it's all over but the shoutin'!"

He told her about how he had been feeling the momentum shift just in the past couple of weeks when they were out on the campaign trail and how Aboy and Ben Hurr had come across the tax bombshell and about some other little things they had up their sleeve. He held up his beer glass, and Trieu carefully tapped it with her martini glass.

She smiled. "Perhaps too the shouting is over, no?"

"I hope so. Did you see ol' Calvin sitting up there tonight? I'd say Red wiped the smile off his face pretty quick."

"And who is Calvin?"

"Calvin Locke. He just happens to be one of the richest ol' geezers in the state. Fact of the matter is, he runs this state, and Jimmy Dale is his cowboy puppet—his Howdy Doody, you might say."

"Howdy Doody?"

"Never mind."

There was a lull in the crowd noise around them, and he realized that there really was a western swing band, live, in a far corner of the dining room. The band broke into "San Antonio Rose."

"Shall we dance?" Trieu asked.

He thought of the Wagon Wheel and her take-your-breath-away performance that night and started to say "no, thank you, ma'am," but she was already pushing her chair back and leading him by the hand past the closely spaced tables. On the dance floor, it was too crowded for Trieu to do anything spectacular, even if she wanted to, She snuggled up close, and he kept talking about the campaign. It had been a while since they had seen each other, so he told her about Aboy and the kildeer and the *pachanga* in the Valley. He told her about Red's mother.

They went back to their table and waited for dessert and coffee. "So is there anything, anything at all, that could trip her up?" Trieu asked. She reached into her purse, opened up a thin, silver case and took out a cigarette. "You don't mind, do you?" she asked.

He didn't mind, although he was surprised. He had never seen her smoke, never smelled tobacco on her breath or in her hair. She handed him a small, gold lighter and he managed to get Trieu's cigarette lit without singing her eyebrows, something he had actually done with a woman in a Filipino nightclub once. He didn't mention that.

"So can anything trip her up?" he asked himself, thinking out loud and playing with the salt shaker. "Overconfidence, maybe. Calvin Locke's TV money. Voters still antsy about a woman senator. I don't know, I'm trying to think of something."

"What about her mother?"

He sliced into his cheesecake and thought about the question. "Well, for one thing, hardly anybody knows about her. And for another thing, if Red gets a chance to explain it, then I think people'd feel sympathetic. Lotta folks have to deal with those kind of things. The problem is if Nabob Slidell gets ahold of it."

"Who is this Nabob person?" Trieu asked. She was holding a little mirror up to her face.

"Only the meanest, smartest, low-down political consultant in the whole country," he said. "And he's working for Jimmy Dale. Or I should say he's working for Calvin Locke. If he gets ahold of the story, he'll make Red sound like that woman who chopped up her folks with an ax. Lizzie Borden. Like Aboy said, I'm not sure she could survive it."

"I wouldn't worry," Trieu said, smiling. "Do you know this?" she said. She cast her eyes toward the glass wall behind me. "Stop thinking, and end your problems. What difference between yes and no? What difference between success and failure? Must you value what others value, avoid what others avoid? How ridiculous."

"Who said that?" he asked. "Sue Bee?"

"No," Trieu said, laughing. "That's the Tao." She picked up her wineglass and held it toward Purse. "Here's to Red," she said as they clinked glasses.

"Here's to the Tao," he said.

Their waiter brought Purse the check, and Trieu handed him her money, three brand-new twenty-dollar bills. He still felt funny about taking it, but she didn't seem to give it any thought.

Outside, they were walking arm in arm toward the Spider when Trieu noticed a narrow gravel road leading out of the paved parking lot and toward the giant billboard. "Let's see where it goes," she said.

They strolled along the meandering road toward the bluff for a hundred yards or so. It ended up underneath the sign, lit by spotlights situated on a catwalk at its base. The traffic down below was a dull roar, and he could barely hear bits and pieces of the music from the restaurant.

Below the billboard was a scooped-out pond, maybe 25-feet across, the water about four feet deep. Green grass and cattails about knee high grew at the water's edge. As the water flowed through a slit in the billboard, it spilled noisily into the pond, and then a pump lifted it back up to spill over again and again. It smelled a bit like a swimming pool.

Wow, this is neat!" Purse said, standing beside the pond. He imagined it was like being at some mansion in the hills above Hollywood, standing beside a giant hot tub and staring down at the streams of traffic far below.

He glanced at Trieu. Barefoot, she had her back to him and was bent over, her hands beneath her dress, peeling off her panties. Turning around, she grinned, handed the panties to Purse, and then let her beautiful pink dress pool fall at her feet. She took a little step out of her dress and leaped feet first, hands at her side, into the pond, her beautiful body knifing into a silver splash.

She turned to Purse and looked up. "Don't just stand there," she said, laughing, the water up to her waist. She held her arms across her chest like she was cold.

He looked all around, back up toward the restaurant and down toward the freeway. As best he could tell, nobody could see them, so he started tearing off his clothes and hopping first on one foot then the other, trying to yank off his boots. He stumbled, one boot on, one boot off, into the water beside Trieu. He shouted when the cold water hit bare skin, and Trieu, laughing, tried to grab his curly hair to keep him from going under.

She splashed water in his face and then ran her hands up and down her sides. They laughed at their goosebumps and her candy-kisses nipples. Purse pulled her to him, and she pressed into his body, her legs gripping his thigh. They kissed for a long time. Then she led him by the hand toward the edge of the pond. Hefting herself out of the water, she sat down among the cattails, her feet dangling into the pond. Shaking from the cold or the excitement or both, Purse stood a few feet away watching, worrying in the back of his mind that a Dallas cop was going to drive up and shine a spotlight on their shenanigans.

Trieu's shoulders tensed, her eyes closed tight. Her hand moved down to her belly, then lower. She pressed the heel of her hand into herself.

"You better get yourself over here, child," she said in a low voice.

Purse stepped joyfully between her lovely thighs, and she drew him gently in, sighing as they settled into each other. Tidal waves soon splashed over the edge of the pool.

★ ★ FIFTEEN ★ ★

They spent the night in Trieu's room at the Stoneleigh, a room with a high ceiling, a deep beige carpet and a big, wide bed. They were on the seventh floor, and, high up like that, Trieu liked sleeping with the curtains open and the windows raised a bit, even though it got a little cool toward morning. She said it reminded her of mornings on the Coast, just before the sun came up, when a breeze drifted in from the Gulf.

Purse reached down to pull up a light blanket from the foot of the bed and noticed she wasn't beside him. When his eyes adjusted to the dim light, he saw her at the window, naked, on her knees, watching the sun turn the sky peach-colored between the tall buildings of downtown.

He got out of bed, padded over and knelt down behind her and put his arms around her chest. Maybe he was interrupting some kind of Buddhist praying, he didn't know, but she didn't seem to mind. She leaned her head back onto his shoulder. Soon they were making love right there, on their knees, looking across the treetops when their eyes were open, at the tall buildings of Big D.

Afterwards they scurried back under the covers and dozed for a while and then ordered room service—bacon, eggs and hash browns for Purse, coffee, orange juice and a croissant with orange marmalade—in a little glass bowl, not a jar—for Trieu. He never had tasted marmalade. It was good, even though it had little bits of rind mixed in. Maybe not as good as his Mama's homemade fig preserves, but still good. The sun was streaming in the open window, and it promised to be an awesome Saturday morning. He felt like a real big-city boy.

The bellboy had brought the *Dallas Morning News* on the tray with breakfast, next to a silver pot of coffee, and the front-page story was just as scrumptious as the breakfast. "RYDER LOBS DEBATE BOMBSHELL," the headline shouted. "Sisco Campaign Takes Direct Hit," the subhead announced.

Morning News political reporter Sam Attles led with the tax charge and after a replay of the debate, he wrote that Ryder was in command of the facts the whole evening and that Jimmy Dale frequently had to resort to familiar campaign bromides. He wrote that Red's charge about Jimmy Dale avoiding his tax obligations appeared to be accurate. He quoted Nabob Slidell as saying that Jimmy Dale's tax return was ill-gotten information and that Red had taken complicated concepts of high finance and misunderstood and misused them, just like she would misunderstand and misuse complex national issues if, God forbid, she was ever elected U.S. Senator.

"Woooo, doggies! Nabob's in a snit," Purse told Trieu. He read to her about how Calvin Locke, on behalf of the campaign, was considering a lawsuit. A couple of people Attles quoted said there wasn't much chance such a lawsuit could prevail.

An Insta-Poll conducted Friday night had Red winning the debate 62 percent to 28 percent, with the rest undecided.

He and Trieu, in matching white terry cloth bathrobes they found on wooden hangers in the closet, were sitting at the table by the window. Trieu, her long black hair as shiny in the morning light as a king snake, a bare foot tucked under her legs, was sipping a cup of tea and writing in the leather notebook she usually had with her.

"Listen to this," Purse said. "It's from the editorial page." He read aloud to her: "Although we have long believed that the pro-business, pro-law enforcement and strong national defense positions espoused by Jimmy Dale Sisco are in the best interests of this state, we must concede after last night's one-and-only debate that Mr. Sisco did not offer voters an image to inspire confidence in his abilities. Unfortunately, the West Texas rancher, a political neophyte, seemed tentative and ill-informed, and his blockbuster admission under pressure from his opponent that he had paid no taxes last year was nothing short of devastating."

The editorial praised Red for her command of the issues, "even though we don't agree with many of them." It concluded that maybe Jimmy Dale, since he wasn't a professional politician, "had simply had an off night and his performance wasn't a reflection of his true competence and capability."

"Can you believe that?" Purse shouted, slapping the paper down on the table and rattling the silverware. "How could anyone with a brain in their head not vote for Red after last night? Even the *Morning News* is getting queasy about the idea!"

"Wily, dearest, I love to see you excited," Trieu said, looking up from her notebook and smiling. "So what about polls for the race itself? When does the next statewide poll come out?"

"I would guess early next week. Like the paper says, we're surging—surging, baby!—and I bet the polls'll show it."

Trieu crossed her arms and put a finger to her chin. "So tell me, Mr. Foxx," she said, "what will you be doing in a Ryder administration? Something transportation-related? Maybe agriculture? Federal poultry inspector, perhaps?"

She was smiling when she asked, but he couldn't tell whether she was teasing or really wanted to know, but he knew enough not to go skipping down that rabbit trail.

"Whoa, Baby," he said, getting up from the table and backing away, hands fending off the very idea. "Ooooh no. Don't ask me that question, Baby. You know—or maybe you don't know—but this is just like what happens in baseball. You never, ever, pack up the equipment until the very last out, I don't care how far ahead you are. It's like my old man always said, he'd say, 'Never count your pullets before the first norther blows.' I bet you got something just like that in Vietnam. I don't think I'm all that superstitious, but the fact is, you don't want to come anywhere near jinxing these things."

"You're absolutely right, Wily," Trieu said. "I apologize." She closed up her notebook. "Anyway, I have to get dressed. I'm going shopping at Nieman's. Anything I can get for you?"

"Nothing I can think of," he said, "unless they have those little things—whachamacall 'em?—oh yeah, an ascot. Buy me an ascot. One that matches my lizard-green suit."

Trieu gave him a hug, giggled, and pulled loose his sash as she backed away toward the bathroom. He chased her into the shower.

★ ★ ★

Trieu dropped him off in the circular driveway of the Fairmount downtown. A doorman in a white helmet, red jacket and white gloves opened the car door. Purse leaned over and gave her a quick kiss and hopped out of the car. Inside, just past the revolving doors, he stopped for a second and craned his neck at a huge golden chandelier hanging from the high ceiling and then ran smack into Aboy promenading through the busy lobby. He said he was coming out of the restaurant, where he had spent the last hour grazing the breakfast buffet. He was working a toothpick in his teeth.

"Romeo, Romeo, where art thou?" he said, slapping Purse on the shoulder. "Where hast thou been, my callow cockswain?"

"At the Stoneleigh. With Trieu. Anything happen I missed?"

"Well, not necessarily, my country Casanova," Aboy said, looking around the lobby for any reporters he might waylay with more juicy tidbits about Jimmy Dale and his personal aversion to taxes. "Although you would have enjoyed the movie last night. X-rated, I'd say."

"What movie?"

"Well, I call it 'A Big Hand for the Little Lady,' although it's actually a video of Jimmy Dale's debate debacle. He threw his arm across Purse's shoulder and escorted him toward the curving, red-carpeted stairway. "And, my good man, you play the love interest. If you've got nothing else to do, come on upstairs to the campaign room. I'd be happy to watch it again."

The debate war room was the Brazos Room on the mezzanine. It looked like the scene of a humdinger of a party the night before. Coffee cups, Coke cans, empty beer bottles and dirty paper plates were scattered about, and red Red posters and campaign signs were all over the floor and leaning up against the wall. Over in the corner was a TV monitor that had one of those newfangled tape players. Aboy plugged in the tape deck, punched the power button and they dragged over a couple of folding chairs and watched the debate, skipping over the dull parts at the beginning and some in the middle. Purse was ready to leave after Red made her closing remarks, but Aboy grabbed him by the shoulders and kept him in the chair. "Hang on, lover boy, you gotta see this," he said.

"See what?"

"Just keep watching."

So he did. And what he saw was himself. What he didn't realize the night before was that the camera kept rolling, even after the debate was over. It picked up everybody crowding around the candidates, Nabob trying to hornswaggle a swarm of reporters into believing that his man had won hands down, people milling around talking and heading toward the doors—and one curly-haired guy with his arms around an exotic, dark-haired girl, locked in a long, slow-motion kiss. Even when the credits began to roll, they rolled over Trieu and Purse still kissing.

He could feel his face getting hot, and he had no doubt his tell-tale cheeks were as red as a baboon's ass. When the image on the screen blessedly switched to snow, he heard applause. He hadn't noticed, but people walking through the room had stopped to watch the climactic love connection one more time.

"Way to go, Purse!" folks shouted. "Catch any zzzzz's last night?" somebody shouted

"Oh damn," he swore to Aboy. "I had no idea. And you're telling me that went out over the airwaves?"

"Every last thrust and moan, my boy."

What did Red say?"

"She just shook her head and laughed, said something about how she seemed to be losing her handsome brown-haired boy to another woman. Sue Bee got a little upset, but Red told her to get off her high horse. Said something about how her purse bearer deserves to get a little."

"She did not."

"Swear on a stack of my old daddy's memory tracts," Aboy said, holding up his meaty right hand. "Maybe she figured it'll help her with the queer issue in a subliminal sort of way, if you catch my drift."

They walked to the Trinity Room next door for a staff meeting, where he had to put up with another round of teasing. Joe Frank, humorless as ever, a cigarette dangling from the corner

of his mouth, handed out news clips from around the state. Not just the *Morning News* but every paper proclaimed Red the winner of the debate. Purse liked the *Star-Telegram* headline: "Sisco Spooked. A Long Fall Off a High Horse."

Sue Bee handed out the day's schedule. Mostly it was Red talking to reporters—print and TV, state, local and national. At noon, there was a big luncheon at the convention center for Take Back Our Streets from the Slime, an anti-crime group. Jimmy Dale was scheduled to be at the TBOSS luncheon too.

That evening, she was scheduled to cut the ribbon on the newly restored Big D Theatre downtown. After that, according to Sue Bee's memo, she would take a stroll through the beautiful auditorium and see the stars and clouds on the ceiling, the majestic Moorish columns on the side and then walk upstairs and tour the offices and rehearsal rooms and such. Then they would head home, touchdown 11 p.m. Trieu had told Purse she would catch up with him at the theater.

Aboy dropped him off at the Stoneleigh, where the king-size bed was still unmade. He changed out of his wrinkled shirt, the scent of Trieu on the shirt nearly sending him into a swoon. He grabbed a quick cab back to the Fairmount and hooked up with Joe Frank and Aboy. A couple of minutes later Sue Bee came down with Red. She seemed to be in a good mood.

Aboy drove them over to the convention center in the van. As they pulled up outside, crowds of people with Red signs waved and shouted and jiggled their signs up and down.

They made their way into the huge room, echoing with a thousand conversations. It was filled with round tables and milling people—a couple of thousand or so, at least—and music from a country and western band, "The Red-headed Outlaws." Purse told himself that was a good omen for Red.

The TBOSS folks believed in cops and guns. There were plenty of both in the room—small-town sheriff types in boots and big hats, big-city cops in blue uniforms, state troopers in their light brown with the blue trim. Behind the podium, draped with flags and bunting, was a huge banner—"OURS FOR THE TAKING," it said—and underneath it was a giant picture of a tall Texas Ranger with his hands on the shoulders of a little boy and girl. They were looking up and smiling at the man in the big hat.

Purse wasn't sure how comfortable Red was around this crowd, but maybe it helped with her toughness image, though he wondered whether any of these people would vote for a female anyway, this female in particular.

He helped her get seated at one of the head tables, spoke to Judge Young who had driven in from Floydada, then eased his way back through the crowd in the lobby to find Aboy. Red wanted Purse to tell him to bring the van around to the exhibition hall in the back of the convention center when the shindig was over. That way she could make a slightly quicker getaway.

When he came back in to the auditorium, he got caught up in the Jimmy Dale entourage, the bright lights of the TV cameras marking its passage between the tables. Along with the cameras and the media crush, the candidate had a bunch of blue-suited Dallas businessmen with him, including Calvin Locke, along with a couple of police chiefs in dark blue uniforms with a lot of gold braid.

Jimmy Dale had his left arm around the waist of a tall, blonde woman in a flowery dress. She had hair that stood up on her head like cotton-candy. She was about a head taller than Jimmy Dale, so his arm around her was more around her butt than her waist. Purse guessed she was the TBOSS chairwoman, Hunee Watts, an oilman's wife from Midland who was on a crusade against crimes committed by illegal immigrants. One time at Doc Driesan's Barbershop in downtown Elm Mott he had seen an article she had written for *Reader's Digest* with the title "Wet Backs, Sticky Fingers."

He could see Jimmy Dale's pet weasel, a.k.a. Nabob Slidell, sort of guiding his man slowly from table to table, his hand on Jimmy Dale's elbow introducing him to people, reminding him of names that might have slipped his simple mind. Listening to Jimmy Dale, you would figure they were all named "Hoss" or "Hoss Fly," as in "How you doin', you old hoss fly, you?"

Purse had no idea whether Nabob knew or cared who he was, even though he had seen him through the window of his speeding pickup that day in Junction. Fortunately, Nabob was too busy to notice. As they inched their way back toward Red's table, Jimmy Dale took his arm from around the waist of Hunee Watts, slowed Nabob down and leaned over to tell him something. Purse was close enough to hear him say, "Watch this."

With TV cameras whirring, still cameras going ka-chink, ka-chink and TV lights shining brightly, with newspaper reporters leaning in to hear what Jimmy Dale had to say, he sidled over to where Red was sitting between Judge Young and Judge Cleophas Steele, a black county commissioner from Dallas. Red glanced up, a smile on her face. She put her napkin on the table, Steele pulled out her chair for her and she stood up. She held out her hand for Jimmy Dale to shake, a loose gold chain dangling from her wrist.

Jimmy Dale ignored the hand. "I'm here to call you a liar today," he said, louder than he had to, so that all the TV reporters with their mikes could pick up his words.

Red's eyes got big, and she started to laugh, as if she thought it was a joke, but then she saw that ol' Jimmy wasn't joshing. Maybe it was his imagination, Purse was thinking, but it seemed the whole hangar-like auditorium suddenly got quiet.

"I'm sorry, Jimmy Dale," Red said, her hand still extended like a spurned beggar on Main Street.

"You've lied about me, and you've lied about my good friend Calvin Locke. I'm going to finish this deal today, and you can count on it," Jimmy Dale shouted over the din of the crowd.

Purse had no idea what he meant by how he was going to finish this deal, and Red didn't either. She stood there, a hint of a smile still on her face, but Jimmy Dale turned his back and sashayed toward his table, shoving his way through the mass of reporters gathered around him. Purse noticed he still sort of tippy-toed like he did the first time he had seen him, like his boots pinched his bunions. This cowboy thing was probably a bit of a stretch for him to pull off for any length of time.

"That's what I call a real major-league asshole," Judge Young said, watching Jimmy Dale and his entourage make their way to a nearby table. Nabob heard his deep, gravelly voice. He stopped and turned around, his squinty eyes like coin slots in his red face, but he didn't do anything.

"That little ol' white boy's runnin' scared," Judge Steele said.

"You can smell it on his little skinny white ass."

Red just smiled and looked down at her salad plate.

Later in the day Purse heard her tell a reporter, "Texas men just aren't like that. Texas men are very supportive. They're very encouraging. Their mamas brought them up to be gentlemen."

The theater celebration that evening was a rootin'-tootin' star-spangled event. Before they ever left the hotel, they could see the crisscrossing searchlights, like long, white fingers probing for the stars, back and forth, back and forth. Red and Aboy were still laughing about the luncheon.

"I thought he was going to say something in his speech about me," Red said, "but he didn't. I was surprised. He didn't even acknowledge my presence."

"Jimmy Dale's not one to deviate from his script, or rather from Calvin Locke's script," Aboy said. "Maybe that little incident was as spur-of-the-moment as the little pissant can get."

"I don't think he helped himself any," Red was saying as the van pulled up in front of the theater. She pulled down the mirror above the windshield, glanced at herself and then back at Purse. "Trieu gonna be here tonight?" she asked.

He felt his face turn red. "She's coming later," he said.

"Watch yourself," she said.

Aboy had to ease into line with limousines and cabs and Cadillacs and then creep along to avoid the happy crowd of folks all around them, some wearing tuxes and evening dresses. Horns honked and people shouted and clapped each time a famous face made an appearance.

"I remember bringing the kids here," Red said. "Years ago. Seems like we saw 'Around the World in 80 Days,' in Cinerama. With Cantinflas. Before your time, my child."

The crowd and Red's happiness got Purse to thinking about how it had been just a few weeks before, in Blooming Grove and Cumby and Athens and Junction, all those places in the heat of summer when they couldn't buy a crowd. No doubt about it, they had the Big Mo at their backs, and it felt fine.

Red hadn't said anything else about Trieu, much to Purse's relief. He hopped out of the van, and opened the front door. Red handed him her purse and stepped onto a red carpet, with maroon velvet ropes on both sides keeping the crowds at bay. She went right to the ropes, moving from one side to the other, shaking hands, hugging folks, kissing babies. Purse even shook a few hands himself. More than a few people mentioned to her how sorry they were the way she had been treated by Jimmy Dale earlier in the day. They had seen it on the 6 o'clock news.

Two smiling guys standing with their arms around each other's waists waggled their fingers at Purse. "Love your purse, ya handsome devil," they sang out in unison. He blushed, again, and said "Thank you."

Standing under the marquee, all lit up with hundreds of little white lights, the theater manager and the historic preservation woman were waiting to greet them, along with Mayor Wes Wisdom and City Councilman Tyce Lipscomb. Red was just one of several celebrities who would be there, although not Jimmy Dale. It was a little too high-toned, high-society for him, or at least for the image of himself he wanted to convey.

Purse was excited that Roy Rogers and Dale Evans were special guests. The theater was showing an old movie of theirs that had been an all-time-favorite Saturday matinee feature when the picture palace—that's what Aboy called it—was brand new. Purse was hoping to get their autograph. Only thing that would make it better was for his all-time hero, Hopalong Cassidy, to put in an appearance.

The theater people had a speaker's stand set up in the huge lobby, right in front of the concession stand. With the smell of hot popcorn and melted butter wafting around them, Red talked about how the city of Dallas was showing the world the definition of a real conservative, that fixing up and making new all over again was so much smarter than tearing down and putting up a parking lot.

"You don't get to be my age, with a face like this one, without knowing a little bit about historic preservation," she said. It was a good line, and everybody laughed. "What I'm hoping is the good people of this state are conservative in the same sensible way come

November. By God, I may not be as pretty as this lovely, old Big D Theatre, but I've got the experience it has. And like this beautiful facility, I'm ready to serve in Washington for a long time to come."

The crowd clapped, she cut a ribbon made out of an old curlicued length of film and the flashbulbs flashed and the news cameras rolled.

They started their tour, oohing and aahing over the auditorium, the stars and clouds on the deep-purple ceiling, the Moorish columns along the side walls like swirled taffy frozen in time, the blue-velvet seats and the Persian rugs down the aisles, the huge maroon curtain in front of the screen. Purse thought of the old movie house back home, The Orpheum, with its sticky concrete floors and ratty seats.

There were clowns, strolling musicians, jugglers. He took a deep breath and looked around, and in his mind he could hear his Uncle Clyde: "Boy, you're in high cotton now."

He followed Red and her gaggle of Dallas hosts, along with a herd of reporters and cameramen, up a broad carpeted staircase to the balcony and to the offices and practice rooms upstairs. Red was being shown the state-of-the-art projection room, and he happened to look down the stairs. He saw Trieu looking up from the mezzanine, looking for him. He waved at her, and she waved back. Just as she started up, he heard a familiar voice.

"Hello Wily."

He turned around again, and standing there in the flesh was Jo Lynne. He had never been so shocked. He could feel the hair on the back of his neck lift, his stomach feeling like it does at the top of a roller coaster. "Jo Lynne, what, what, what're you doing here?" he managed to stammer.

They just kept looking at each other, neither moving closer. She was holding a clear plastic cup of red wine. He shifted Red's purse from one hand to the other. He couldn't figure out what to do with it.

"Well, you've been so awfully, awfully busy lately," she said, finally, her voice sounding sort of higher than usual, and nervous. "I figured, I figured this might be the only chance I'd have to see you anytime soon, so I thought I'd drive up. Trudi offered to drive up with me, but I wanted some time to think. I figured we had some things to talk about, and I know you've been just awfully busy. It's a wonder you have any time to sleep, you're so busy."

"Sure," he said, looking for Red, watching Trieu still gliding up the stairs and catching the sarcasm in Jo Lynne's voice. "Sure, we can talk," he said, running his hand through his hair. He kept glancing about, sensing the approach of danger. "But remember I told you it was going to be this way, all the way through the campaign." Out of the corner of his eye, he saw the crowd clustered around Red slowly making its way out of the projection booth. They were coming his way.

"I know what you told me," she said, "but ..." She looked over her shoulder. She glanced back at him and then looked again. Trieu was coming toward them, a smile on her face. Jo Lynne saw her, and before Purse could say Jack Spratt she lunged at him. With her right hand, she grabbed him by the tie, while with her left she splashed the red wine in his face. He heard the crowd around Red go "Aaaaah!" "Wha'd he do to her?" he heard someone else say. The wine dripped off his eyebrows, burned his eyes.

"You son of a bitch," Jo Lynne kept saying in a low voice, "you asshole son of a bitch," all the while pulling on his tie and choking him. "You've been busy, all right. Busy with a trifling little Jap whore."

Like a yearling lassoed by a cowboy on a quarter horse, he had to move toward her, hoping to ease the chokehold she had on his neck, even as he tried to protect Red's purse. His white shirt and green suit coat were splattered purple. Over Jo Lynne's shoulder he saw Trieu headed back down the wide staircase. She was walking fast.

"Right this way, folks! Right this way," he heard a cheery voice say. A juggler in a tight black suit, bowler hat and red tennis shoes was trying to distract the curious crowd with three oranges he was miraculously keeping in the air. Bending back, still juggling, he was trying to lure the rubberneckers into a nearby classroom.

Jo Lynne pulled Purse into a broom closet. She was crying, kicking him in the shins, knocking over brooms and mops. In the tiny room he managed to get his arms around her and calm her down a bit. She was crying into his stained, wet shirt, and he was talking into her hair, curly and puffed up and smelling of hair spray.

"Oh Wily, I'm sorry, I'm sorry, I'm sorry," she was saying between sobs. "I'm so sorry, but I just couldn't take it anymore. I just couldn't take it."

He could hear the crowd making its way back down the staircase, and he wondered what Red had seen. "It's all right," he said, smoothing down Jo Lynne's hair, his other arm still around her. "It's all right."

He was just beginning to think how she looked really nice. She had on a tight turquoise dress with a high collar, red high-heeled shoes. The dress was sort of Oriental-like, he was thinking, when suddenly she started kicking him in the shins again with those sharp-toed red shoes. He tried to back away, but there was no place to retreat and Jo Lynne held on.

"What a chicken shit, you are," she said, looking up into his eyes. "Just a little chicken shit. Why did I ever think you loved me in the first place? When I saw that whore you were with on the TV last night, it was like scales dropped from my eyes. It all came clear. I told myself, that asshole's not a whit better than low-down Roy Towsen, and not any brighter either. Wily, you're nothing but a fool."

He hated like hell to be lined up with Roy Towsen, buckshot Roy Towsen, but he didn't say anything. He got her calmed down again and was trying to figure out how he was going to get out of this mess, when he heard a knock at the closet door. He opened it, and there was Sue Bee. "Wily, I need to talk to you downstairs," she said in her serious teacher's voice. "Immediately."

That set Jo Lynne in to crying again. She figured she had cost him his job. Purse figured she had too.

"I'll be back," he said, backing down the hallway. "No, wait a minute," he said. "Meet me in the lobby."

Downstairs, he and Sue Bee had to skirt a big crowd watching a white-hatted Roy Rogers twirl a lariat. Dale Evans, wearing boots and her own white hat, stood to the side smiling; she had just told a story about her beloved horse Buttermilk.

Sue Bee took him into the manager's office. Joe Frank was

already there, leaning against the back of the desk, a thick wreath of cigarette smoke around his head.

"Look at you, Purse. Just look at you," she said, once she closed the door on the crowd noise out in the lobby. "You used to be so reliable, so dependable, even when you were hanging around Aboy. I knew I could always count on you. What in God's name has come over you?"

"You know what's come over him," Joe Frank mumbled, his cigarette still dangling from the corner of his mouth. "The little shithead's thinking with his cock and not his brain."

Purse noticed a framed movie poster on the wall behind him. It was Humphrey Bogart in "The African Queen." Joe Frank looked sort of like a tall Humphrey Bogart. Purse wanted to be tough-guy Jimmy Cagney and smash the cigarette into his face, even though he knew Joe Frank was right about what he had said.

Sue Bee shook her head and ran her hand across her face quickly. "Never mind about that, Joe Frank. But Purse, surely, surely you realize how grave this unfortunate incident here tonight can be. You could have cost us the election with your antics. And that just can't happen. Too many people have worked too long and too hard to let something like this get in the way. I'm sorry, but something has to be done about it."

Purse could feel his arms and legs start to tremble. Out in the lobby, faintly, he could hear Roy and Dale harmonizing on "Happy Trails to You." Their voices sounded a bit wobblier than they used to.

"I'm sor...." he started to say, but his own voice wobbled. He wanted to say more, but he didn't know what, and he wasn't sure he would be able to if he did know. He noticed he was still holding Red's purse.

Sue Bee stood in front of him and put both her hands on his shoulders. She looked into his eyes. He could feel tears beginning to creep into the corners. He hadn't cried, as best as he could remember, since the death of Dooney, the beagle he had when he was ten. Dooney was the dog that followed him everywhere he went, once he got him to stop killing chickens.

"Purse, I like you. A lot," she said, still looking deep into his eyes. "Everybody likes you. You're a fine young man. But this can't go on. We have to do something. Now. I haven't had time to talk to Red and I know Joe Frank hasn't either, so I'm going to have to make a command decision."

Purse glanced over at Joe Frank who was now standing in front of the desk, his arms crossed, with what looked like a smirk on his face. Sue Bee's words echoed in his head, and he knew that whatever came out of her mouth in the next few seconds was likely to change his life totally. A dull roar filled his head.

"What I've decided to do," she was saying, "and this is for your own good and for the good of the campaign, you understand, is to suspend you. For one week. Without pay. That'll give me a chance to talk to the comptroller about your duties, and it'll give you a chance to get your personal life together. To get yourself refocused on what's important."

Purse couldn't believe it. That's all? To hell with the pay. He couldn't believe they were keeping him on.

"Now that's contingent on the comptroller agreeing with my decision. And I think she will. You know she likes you, Purse—she relies on you—but you know also you can't mess up anymore. We've got three weeks to go, and every minute of every day counts. We need you."

He hugged Sue Bee; he couldn't help it. He even walked over and shook Joe Frank's hand. He took a deep breath and turned back toward Sue Bee. "Thank you," he said. "I won't let you down."

"It's not me you'd be letting down," she said. "It's Red—and the people of this great state."

"That's not going to happen," Purse said, walking slowly toward the door. He opened it.

"Purse?" Sue Bee said. "The purse, please?"

Out in the lobby the crowds had cleared out. An old black man was pushing a flat broom across the marble floor, sweeping up popcorn crumbs and napkins and cups. The old man picked up a crumpled black-and-white photo of Roy and Dale before he got to it with his broom. When he saw Purse, his eyes red, his shirt stained, he stared.

"Boy, you all right?" he asked.

"Yeah, I'm okay," Purse said. He walked toward the front doors, then turned around. "Which way's the Greyhound station?"

★ ★ SIXTEEN ★ ★

Big D, little a, double l, little a, little s—that's spells Dallas, he remembered Pat Boone singing. The stupid song kept running through his mind, even though for him the Big D stood for Destruction, Damnation, Devastation. Hey pal, it could have been worse, he kept telling himself. And still could be, if some newspaper wanted to make a big Damn Deal out of the little set-to with Jo Lynne. He just wanted to get out of the place. Dallas, he felt, was sort of like Hunee Watt's big head of hair—stiff and uninviting.

Head down and sick at heart, he trudged back to the hotel, hoping he wouldn't see anybody from the campaign. He changed out of his soggy clothes into jeans and boots, grabbed his bag and checked out. Walking down Main Street, everything all lit up, people everywhere, he reached in his pocket to see what kind of money he had. He had decided he would take the bus home, but the money roll was thin.

He walked by Nieman Marcus. In the show windows, haughty mannequins, hands on their skinny hips, glanced back over their shoulders. On a leaf-strewn college campus—SMU or Harvard, maybe—they were wearing winter sweaters, mid-length wool skirts and white bucks Pat Boone himself might have kept in his closet. He had walked through Nieman's one Christmas when he was a kid visiting his aunt and uncle. The toys he saw looked too expensive for old St. Nick himself.

He passed the Carousel Club, with its gaudy neon sign of a big woman with Texas-size tits, wearing a cowboy hat and not much else. She twirled a yellow lariat above her head. At the door a guy with black, greasy hair combed back off his forehead, wearing a black suit and open-necked white shirt over a gold necklace, grabbed him by the arm. "Come on in, Slick," he said, trying to pull him toward the loud music inside. "We'll show you things you never imagined out there in hicksville."

He jerked his arm away and kept walking. That's the last

thing he needed. He waited for a red light and realized his shin hurt where Jo Lynne had kicked him.

The bus station was at the far end of downtown. He passed a brightly lit McDonald's, the french-fry smell wafting out onto the grimy sidewalk. Young black guys, talking loud and mock-fighting each other, were hanging around on the sidewalk out front. The Greyhound station was a block away.

The station itself was dingy, depressing. Cab drivers parked at the curb sat on the hoods of their cars talking to each other. An old woman pushing a grocery cart piled high with junk talked to herself.

The waiting room was lit up like a hospital waiting room. He read the schedule on the back wall. A bus headed south was leaving in less than an hour.

"How much to Austin?" he asked the woman behind the counter. "One way."

"Ten dollars and seventy-five cents," she said, never looking up.

He didn't have ten dollars.

"How far south can I go for five?"

"Four and a quarter to Hillsboro," she said. "You got that much, big spender?"

He glanced at the clock. 10:15. He sat on a hard plastic chair with other tired-looking passengers, crumpled shopping bags at their feet, clothes sticking out the tops of the bags. A lot of them were black folks, others were Mexicans on the way south, either to San Antonio or the Valley, maybe all the way to Mexico. Everybody looked weary, their minds far away from their bodies, especially the folks with crying babies. The room smelled like stale grease from the Burger King in the corner of the station.

He closed his eyes and nearly went to sleep sitting up. Over a crackly loudspeaker, he heard the droning announcement: "Now boarding in lane one, southbound bus to RedOakDe SotoWaxahachieItalyHillsboroWacoTempleBeltonAustin ... with connections to HoustonNewOrleansBatonRougeSan MarcosNew BraunfelsSan Antone and Brownzzz-ville. Allll aBOART!"

They shuffled onto the bus. He got a seat to himself in the darkness and tried to figure out how to make it all the way back to Austin. Then it hit him. He would just go stay with Mama a couple of days, maybe work a little around the house and then get on down to Austin. Maybe Aboy could come by and pick him up.

The bus lumbered out of the station and headed south across the old Trinity River bridge. He leaned his head against the window and tried to sleep, but the groove in the window sill dug into his cheek. His troubled mind, like a cockle burr to a cotton boll, stuck to thoughts about what had happened. He wondered where Trieu had gone. He wondered if he would ever see her again.

Every time he opened his eyes, he noticed an old man across the aisle staring at him. He was a heavy-set guy, bald, with a fringe of gray hair growing over the collar of a T shirt, one leg propped on the empty aisle seat beside him. He wore a pair of red suspenders, faded jeans and a pair of black tennis shoes. He had a wrinkled grocery bag on the seat. He looked like people Red had been talking to all over the state for weeks. Like she had been talking to, talking for, for years. Who knows whether he was the kind to go to the polls and vote.

Purse was too tired to talk, too caught up in his own trials and tribulations.

"Pardon me, son," he said. "But don't I know you?"

"Don't think so," Purse said. He closed his eyes again.

"Been visiting my boy up in Dallas," he said a few minutes later. "Got a furlough from the VA. Headed back home, back to Temple. Hospital's in Temple, you know. Can only take so much of that suburban lifestyle in the big city."

The man peered into his wrinkled paper sack, reached in and pulled out a sandwich wrapped in waxed paper. He held it out to Purse. "Half a baloney sandwich? Fresh 'maters on it. Little mayonnaise."

Purse told him no, thank you.

"Don't get me wrong," the old man said, biting into the sandwich, tomato seeds spilling down the back of his hand. Burt and Sue Ann are just good as gold. Burt's an optometrist, works hard. Sue Ann, she stays home with the kids. They even asked me to live with 'em. I told 'em, I said, 'No thank you.' What I didn't say, bless their souls, is too much church, too much TV, too—hey, that's where I seen you! On TV. Me and the kids was watching the big debate last night. You look just like that young fella I saw on the show. Had his mitts all over a young Oriental woman. Don't blame him. I tell you, she was a ring-tailed tooter."

"Don't think so," Purse told him. "I never been on TV in my life."

"I watch TV," he said between bites. "But most of what I see don't amount to much. Mainly people playing the fool, trying to convince theirselves they're more important than they really are. They don't realize that what they think's so all-fired important don't amount to a hill of beans. That's what I was like, back when I was full of piss and vinegar. Useta build pre-fab homes to beat the band up in Gainesville. Had myself a right-nice little businesss, but once you get old, you begin to see things different."

He took another bite of sandwich, wiped his mouth with the bank of his hand. "Come to think of it, maybe they do realize it. That's why they're so all-fired desperate to be on the gol-durn TV."

He reached in and pulled out the other half of his sandwich. "Sure you don't want a bite?" he asked.

The bus pulled into Hillsboro about midnight and stopped on the outskirts at the big truck stop that became the bus stop when the depot downtown on the square closed. He staggered on stiff legs into the bathroom and washed his face and hands.

Coming out, he scanned the brightly lit cafe, thinking he might see somebody he knew. Willie was playing on the Muzak. "Blue Eyes Cryin' in the Rain." He thought about asking one of the drivers sitting at the restaurant counter if he was headed south. He didn't want anybody else to turn him down on this night, so he decided not to.

Just as he headed out, he noticed an early edition of the Sunday *Morning News* somebody had left at an empty table. He picked it up, hands trembling, nerves on edge and took it outside. He sat down at the curb and started turning pages. Nothing about him, nothing about a fool for love losing control of his life at the Big D Theater, losing an election for Rose Marie Ryder.

What there was though was a front-page picture of Red, hand outstretched toward Jimmy Dale, at the TBOSS luncheon. Jimmy Dale, neck stretched out toward Red like an angry old turkey gobbler, Hoot Gibson hat pushed back on his head, looked like a damn fool. What that picture told him is what all of them already knew by now: If nobody got in the way, Jimmy Dale would beat himself.

He laughed out loud, and for the first time during that long night he felt a little better. It was a reprieve, maybe even a pardon, for Wily T. Foxx himself. He figured if the *Morning News* didn't pick up on his little escapade, nobody else would either. He left the newspaper atop a trash bin and took stock of his situation. It was cool and nice, except for the big, rumbling trucks parked on the station lot and the diesel smell.

He took off walking, like he was with Rufus Cuttrell again and they were headed out after dogs that had met their Maker, although about the only thing he saw that would have interested his old mentor was a dead armadillo. Only difference was, it was dark out. He took the overpass to get on the right side of the road, which was actually the left, and headed south down the access road. As soon as he got out of range of the floodlit truck stop, it was quiet and dark. The only noise was his boots trudging through the grass and the occasional passing vehicle on the interstate, sometimes a barking dog when he passed a farmhouse. It took him a while to get the hang of walking in the moonless night through the dry, scrubby grass without stumbling, but after a mile or so, he just kept churning.

Walking, it was cool enough that if he hadn't been on the move he might have needed a jacket. Trudging along, he kept thinking about his life, what was past, what was coming. He kept wondering whether he would ever see Red and Aboy and Sue Bee and Raenell again, wondering what he was going to tell Mama. He thought about Jo Lynne and what had happened at the Big D. He thought about what Uncle Amos said to him one time, after he got sent home from sixth grade for getting in a fight with Hocky Willis.

"You know what they say," Amos told him. "They say you cain't never bounce back til you've hit rock bottom."

For someone who had survived the Great Depression and two world wars, rock bottom was a place he was familiar with. Purse guessed he himself had hit rock bottom, although maybe the lack of a newspaper story meant he was bouncing back up.

It was past midnight. A road sign said Elm Mott 12 miles. At Abbott, he detoured off the access road to walk past Willie Nelson's small frame house, even though it was out of his way. Why, he wasn't sure, though he always admired how Willie had made the big time coming from a little no-count place like Abbott.

Purse got to thinking. Except for a fellow named Ellis "Split Tail" Taylor, a legendary cock fighter from Aquila, maybe a handful of others, Willie was one of the few people he had ever heard of from his part of the state who had actually made something of themselves. Aboy used to tell how he had seen him play years ago at the NiteOwl, the old beer joint he would soon be passing. In those days he was just a skinny, little guy in a suit who sang through his nose and wrote great songs that hardly anybody outside Central Texas had ever heard. If Red ever got elected senator, she was hoping she could get Willie to play for her swearing-in festivities in D.C.

The Nelson homestead was dark, and he kept walking. When he got to West, the little Czech community with the best kolaches in the state, the new day's sun was an orange stripe along the horizon of a purple sky. He thought about detouring into town to see if the Main Street Bakery was open. His stomach felt like Carlsbad Cavern, and a pint of milk and a prune kolache or two sounded great. But then he remembered, he had no spending money. Traffic was picking up, with huge semis passing by like they were going to blow him off the road. His pants legs were moist from the dew. His feet hurt inside his boots, and his bag was getting heavy. He was getting very tired. And very hungry.

The sun came up, and he kept on trucking. He passed a couple of "RED RYDER FOR TEXAS" signs in the front yards of a couple of farm houses. He saw some of Raenell's rosebuds alongside the morning papers. At the Aquila exit, he walked under a huge Sisco billboard. This one had Jimmy Dale sitting on his golden palomino beside a shotgun-armed prison guard on his own horse. They were watching guys in prison stripes bustin' rocks.

"THEY DON'T MESS WITH THE MAN," the sign said.

At the Ross exit, he left the interstate and headed down the two-lane farm-to-market road toward home. On both sides of the road, blackland fields of cotton had either just been picked or the withered leaves told you they were ready to be picked, last crop of the season. Now and then he would pass a corn field, the stalks dry and yellow and bent. Cows he would see occasionally beyond barbed-wire fences.

His mouth felt like he had been licking sandpaper. When he saw a windmill not far off the road, he ducked under the barbed wire fence. In a metal stock tank at the base of the windmill tower, ghostly, long-legged water bugs skittered across the surface. He dipped his hands into the cool, clear water and drank. The water tasted good, and the creaking sound the blades made as they turned in the morning breeze was a comfort.

Back on the road, his legs were beginning to cramp a bit. He thought about turning off at the Tours Road exit. He knew the Thompson family up the road a piece; they'd let him rest a while. Instead, he kept on walking.

A few cars and pickups passed, people on their way to work in town. He didn't hold his thumb out, just kept on. Nobody slowed down, until about 10 in the morning when he heard a car roaring up from behind, coming at a high rate of speed. He hopped across the bar ditch and moved closer to the fence row. He glanced back. Headed his way at the speed of light was a '63 Plymouth Fury, cherry red, fishtailing on an easy curve he had just passed, oversized rear tires whining and smoking as the driver down-shifted.

He knew exactly who it was behind the wheel, although he hadn't seen the car on the road in a couple of years. Lately, he had seen it parked, gathering dust, at the back of Crittenden's Trailer Court. With its full-race Mercury motor and dual cams, 275 horsepower, only one person in the world was allowed to drive that car. Weevil James. Jo Lynne's big brother was free at last.

Weevil roared past, a girl in the passenger seat beside him. Weevil kept on going maybe a hundred yards up the road, then slammed on the brakes, tires squealing, dust rising up behind him like a tornado as he slid toward the ditch. He slammed the Fury into reverse and backed up, almost as fast as when he zoomed by.

Weevil lurched to a stop beside Purse. A pretty girl with honey-blonde hair, white, white teeth and a scattering of freckles across her nose leaned out the window and smiled.

"Hello, Wily T.," Rae-Harvey Pierce said. "Where you headed?"

"Hello, Rae-Harvey," he said. "I'm just headed on to the house."

Weevil leaned over and shouted, "Well, don't just stand there you ol' cock-suckin' cock-sucker. Come on and get in." He reached across the seat and opened the back door.

Many thoughts passed through Purse's head as he stepped across the ditch. Mainly they concerned what Weevil knew about his problems with Jo Lynne. He never wanted to be on the wrong side of Weevil James.

Weevil had always been small for his age. To make up for it, he turned himself into the meanest, craziest son of a bitch in Elm Mott and environs, including Axtel, Elk and Prairie Hill. There was nobody he wouldn't take on, no matter how big. As far as Purse knew, nobody had ever bested him.

The first time Purse saw him was in the sixth grade. Standing on the top row of the bleachers at a football game one night, he looked back and down and there was Weevil. He had a guy a head taller than he was backed up against a tall chain-link fence. Weevil was wailing on him, the guy was crying and a crowd of gawkers was gathered 'round.

Purse had heard from Weevil's friend Malcolm Watson that's what he did in prison too. Stomped into a shower room naked as a jaybird except for his work boots and waded into a bunch of black guys who had been messin' with him because he was small, and white, ghostly white. With the water still running, he started kicking, swinging, biting, screaming. Like a maniac, like a rabid squirrel they couldn't swat away. They figured he was rabid, raving mad, and they let him alone from then on.

It was his mother who gave him the name. That's what Jo Lynne had told Purse. Homer Eloy, H.E., was his real name. Jo Lynne's mother had said that when he was a little bitty baby he just burrowed into her soft, white titty like a weevil burrowing into a bin of corn meal. The name stuck. He even sort of looked like what you would imagine a weevil to look.

Purse climbed into the back seat. The car smelled of mountain-pine air freshener and stale cigarettes. Weevil had had the tomato-red upholstery rolled and pleated, trimmed in white. It looked good. He reached across the seat and shook Purse's hand. "Good to see ya again, Senator. It's been a while," he said.

Weevil looked about the same as he had looked since he was 12 years old, even though he was close to 30. He had his blonde hair slicked back into a greasy duck's ass, a little curlicue on his forehead, blonde eyebrows so light they were almost white over ice-blue eyes. He wore a black t-shirt with a packet of cigarettes rolled up inside the right sleeve, just above a prison tattoo of a coiled cobra on a bicep newly muscled since he had been behind bars. As little as he was, Weevil still scared Purse.

Weevil reminded him of a Tasmanian devil. You never knew what he was going to do or what would set him off.

Weevil popped the clutch, laid yards of rubber on the asphalt road, speed-shifted into second, then third, then high, laying rubber each time. Purse took a deep breath. Despite the smell of burning rubber on the morning air, it felt good to be sitting, even if it was in a tricked-out Plymouth Fury with wildman Weevil James behind the wheel, even though he had a pint of Old Taylor between his legs. He took a quick swig whenever the car was on a straightaway.

Rae-Harvey tucked her left foot beneath her on the seat, so she could turn around and talk to Purse. Her tan face set off by a white, sleeveless blouse, she was still pretty, even though Purse could see up close that her stay in the women's prison at Gatesville had taken a bit of a toll on her. The first time he ever saw her—he was in the eighth grade, she was in the seventh—he thought she was the prettiest girl he had ever seen. Those freckles across a little, perky nose, her blue eyes, and a high-rising butt that jutted out like a young, healthy Bantu princess.

She had gained a bit of weight since he had last seen her, and her eyes looked tired, with tiny lines on each side like the lines on blotting paper. Like Weevil, she had been gone a couple of years herself, for shooting out the front door of her employer's house—former employer, that is—when she was working as a receptionist for a roofing company in town. Weevil had been driving; she was riding shotgun, literally. Jo Lynne had told him she had been out for about six months, was working as a dispatcher at Red Ball Freight.

"We saw you on TV the other night," she said, smiling in such a pretty way he was suddenly in the eighth grade all over again.

Purse's face turned red. "I'm sorry to hear that," he said.

"Who was that little chink?" Weevil asked, speed-shifting as the speedometer hit 70 on the narrow country road.

Purse knew he was walking into a mine field, however he answered. He looked out the window and saw a farmer plowing under cotton stubble. "Her name's Trieu. She's from Vietnam," he said.

"Friend of yours, huh?" Weevil asked.

"You could say that."

"You tell her about you and Jo Lynne?" Rae-Harvey wanted to know.

Purse looked out the window again. The fence posts were a blur. "Not exactly," he said.

"How come?" Rae-Harvey asked.

"I don't know. I just couldn't find the right time to sit down and talk to her about it. I've been really busy, what with the campaign and all."

Weevil took a curve a little faster than even he could handle. The Fury slid along the gravel shoulder at the edge of the ditch. Purse hung on to the door handle as Weevil downshifted and floored the Fury. Rae-Harvey didn't seem to notice his driving.

"How you think that makes her feel?" she asked.

"I know how she feels," he said. "She came to Dallas last night and told me, in no uncertain terms."

"She shoulda come to Dallas and shot you right between your banty rooster eyes," Weevil said in a low voice. "That's what I woulda told her if she hadda asked me."

Purse tried to see the expression on his face in the rearview mirror, to see if Weevil was messing with him. He was staring out the windshield. He didn't look like he was joking. Purse didn't say anything.

"You know what I'm thinking, Rae-Harvey?" Weevil said, glancing her way, a ghostly-pale eyebrow raised like he had just hit on a great, eternal truth.

"Whattcha thinkin', Hon?" she said.

"I'm thinkin' we've got a little, shit-eatin', sniveling two-timer in the back seat of this vehicle. I'm thinkin' he needs to be taught a lesson about how to treat women folk."

"Come on, Weevil," he said. ("Purse started to call him H.E., like his parents did, to show he meant no disrespect.) "This is between me and Jo Lynne. She may be your little sister, but she's big enough to take care of herself. We'll get it worked out."

"That's where you got it wrong, you curly-headed dick-twicker," Weevil said. "It's not between you and my kid sister. It's a matter of family honor. The way you was dry-humpin' that little Jap the other night, the way she was feelin' you up on national TV, is a matter of family honor. You besmirched the family name. The James family name."

"That's ridiculous, Weevil," Purse said. "It's got nothing to do with your family. (He wanted to ask, "What about you going to prison? Didn't that besmirch the family name?" He didn't.) "And besides, it wasn't on national TV. It was statewide TV."

"I don't care if it was on Elm Mott High School closed-circuit TV, you little pond-scum pansy. You made Jo Lynne James a laughing stock. Same as took the James family name and scooted your pimply ass all over it. The James family don't take that kind of treatment layin' down." He glanced back at Purse. "You may be dumb as a fuckin' stick, Wily, but I figure you've heard of Jesse James, me and Jo Lynne's great-great uncle. Am I right, shit-for-brains?"

"Yeah, Weevil, I've heard of Jesse James," Purse mumbled. ("Jesse James's somebody to be proud of?" he wanted to ask, but didn't.) "Now, why don't you let me out right up here at the corner, and I promise you I'll apologize to Jo Lynne as soon as I see her."

"Don't think so, you little pud-puller." He glanced at Rae-Harvey, who had been listening to their discussion sort of glassy-eyed, with a distant smile on her face. She seemed to be enjoying the drama of it all. Or maybe she was on something. "Don't we have something for our little two-timing amigo?" Weevil asked.

"Oh! You know, I think we do!" she said. She pulled out the ash tray and carefully laid her cigarette inside, then turned around on the seat. Leaning down toward the floorboard, she had one hand on the dashboard to brace herself while Weevil braked and shifted. With the other hand, she reached under the seat and came up with a double-barreled sawed-off shotgun, a shell in each barrel. She snapped the double barrels shut like she knew what she was doing. She twisted back around to Purse and propped the gun on the back of the seat. She had it aimed toward the back glass, a foot or so from his head. The safety was on, he noticed, but she had her crimson-nailed finger on both triggers. This time, she had a strange grin on her face, like she was in some sort of daze, like Weevil had her hypnotized.

"We're going to let you out, Wily T," Weevil said, slowing down at the Wilson Road intersection. "Fact is, we're going to give you a sportin' chance."

He skidded to a stop, and Purse opened the back door. He had one foot on the gravel before the car stopped sliding.

"Once you get over that fence there, shit-for-brains, Rae-Harvey here's gonna start firing at you just like you're a little quail she's flushed up out of the brush. She's been known to miss, a time or two anyway, so you got a chance." He gave a high-pitched giggle. "Just not much of one."

"Come on, Rae-Harvey," Purse said. "This is crazy."

"I'm sorry, Wily," she said. "I always sorta liked you. But this is for Jo Lynne. This is for all women everywhere."

Weevil had stopped beside a corn field. Purse got out of the car, walked to the barbed-wire fence and threw his bag over. He didn't look back, but he was scared to death Weevil would make Rae-Harvey shoot him in the ass while he was bent down between the two strands of fence.

She didn't. As soon as he straightened up, he took off running at an angle, like he was running a zig-zag pass route on the football field. He was hoping she would expect him to dart straight into the field.

He had run maybe 25 yards through the yellowed stalks before he heard the blast. He could hear pellets passing through dried leaves. He kept running, plowing straight through the stalks. She fired again. Again nothing. He heard her fire one more time, but by then he was deep into the field, and he couldn't see the red Fury on the road anymore, although he could hear both of them laughing. He figured they couldn't see him either, but he kept running anyway, even though his legs felt kinked up like a bike chain off its sprocket and he was blowing like a randy bull.

Up ahead, he could begin to make out the glint of the morning sun against the sheet-metal roof of a long, low chicken house, one of his dad's old brood houses before Pluckers Pride drove him out of business. Gasping for breath, hoping Weevil wouldn't somehow be waiting for him on the other side of the field, he headed in that direction. Just as he got to the door, he heard another blast and then hail-like sounds as shotgun pellets landed on the metal roof.

He opened the door and staggered into a roiling, noisy ocean of chickens covering the expanse of floor. Wading through the mass of birds was like wading through the surf at South Padre. After a couple of steps, he stumbled, fell, and went under, his body instantly covered over by thousands of squawking, flitting white chickens. It was hot, dusty and airless in his underchicken state, but he couldn't get up. He could feel gnarly chicken feet dancing maniacally over his body, like thousands of those electrocuted tic-tak-toe birds he saw once at the state fair. They were drawing blood on his neck and hands. On the dirt floor underneath the panicked birds, he gasped for air, breathing in the smell of ammonia and chicken shit. Death by a thousand pecks and scratches, he was thinking, just before he passed out. What a way to go.

He was out, how long? Ten minutes, maybe? An hour? He didn't know for sure. He just knew he was lying there, dead to the world, when two strong arms reached under his shoulders and lifted him to his feet. Two young Mexican guys draped his arms over their shoulders and half-walked, half-carried him outside into blessed sunshine and clean, fresh air. Leaning over, hands on knees, he coughed a couple of times, hawked up a bunch of dirt, then stood up straight and took a deep breath. He wiped his eyes and the back of his neck and came away with blood on his hands.

"*Necesite un medico, señor?*" one of the guys asked, his Indian-black eyes peering into Purse's.

Purse stood there trying to readjust to uncluttered air, swallowing and trying to open up his ears.

"*No,*" he said. "*No. Gracias. Estoy bueno. Muchas gracias.*"

They stared at him with looks of concern on their brown faces. And when he looked at himself, chicken shit all over his torn and wrinkled clothes, in his hair, his face streaked with dirt and sweat and wispy white feathers, the backs of his hands scratched and bleeding, he could see why they were worried. "*Estoy okay,*" he said. "*Gracias, señores. Gracias.*"

He had about a mile to go, up a little rise and across a weedy pasture, to get to the house. He wasn't sure he could make it without passing out again. He came into the back yard and Tramp, the old family collie, barked until she saw who it was.

He tried the back porch screen door, but his Mama had it latched. He knocked a couple of times and was about to trudge around to the front door when she heard her son. Coming out of the kitchen and across the back porch, her hand flew to her mouth when she saw the pathetic state he was in. Her hands trembled as she unlatched the door. She held it open, then put her arms around him.

★ ★ SEVENTEEN ★ ★

He woke up blind. At least, that's what he thought, until he pushed aside the wet wash cloth his Mama had laid across his eyes. He blinked and looked across the room at Little Beaver staring back at him from the wall across the room, an eagle's tail feather sticking up out of his head band. Of course, he had been staring back since Purse was 10 years old, since the time he got his autographed picture at the Heart of Texas Fair. He remembered being so disappointed that he wasn't a boy, that he was probably 40 years old and had hair on his chest and was about four feet tall. He probably wasn't even Indian.

The only difference in the room now was the condition of the wallpaper behind the picture. The pink roses on the paper his grandmother had plastered onto the walls when it was her house were faded and peeling. He was in his old room, in his iron-frame single bed. He vaguely remembered taking a bath, Mama dabbing "monkey blood" on his chicken scratches after he dried off. He remembered that it stung. He remembered falling atop the bed, sinking into blessed oblivion.

He had no idea how long he had slept, although he had some vague notion of a dream about riding in the back of a '52 Chevy pickup with Weevil behind the wheel and Jo Lynne in the passenger seat peering at him through the back window with a worried look on her face. He was naked, standing up like he was surfing, with nothing to hold on to. The wind blowing past him was cold and scary, and he knew it was going to blow him out the back of the truck, and he was reading Jo Lynne's lips, "Use your rudder, Wily, use your rudder."

He lay there for a minute trying to reconstruct the dream. Who the hell knew what it meant. "What time is it?" he called out, figuring Mama was in the kitchen.

"It's 10 o'clock, Wily. Monday morning," a soft voice answered from beside the bed.

He pushed the rag away and saw Jo Lynne sitting in a chair, a

Good Housekeeping magazine on her lap. "You've been asleep since yesterday."

He was stiff and achy, and weak, and he struggled to push a pillow up behind him and to sit up in the bed. He looked down to see if he was decent. No shirt, but he had pulled on a pair of EMHS gym shorts before falling into bed.

"How come you're here?" he asked, rubbing his eyes. "How long you been settin' there?"

"Just a little while," she said. She laid the magazine on the floor. "You want some coffee?"

"Yeah," he said. "But I can get it myself."

He swung his legs to the side of the bed, Jo Lynne's side, and sat there a minute trying to get his bearings. His hands looked like an Indian warrior's, what with the red dabs of medicine on them. He shuffled into the kitchen. Jo Lynne followed.

"You don't have to work today?" he asked, pouring a cup of coffee from the percolator on the stove. He poured a cup for Jo Lynne.

It's Monday," she said. "Beauticians and barbers don't work on Mondays."

Mama came in from the back yard where she had been feeding the chickens. She had a half-dozen or so brown-shelled eggs in her gathered-up apron. She put them in a bowl on the kitchen counter.

"I'd about given you up for dead," she said. "Almost called Doctor Boyd, see if he'd come by and check on you." She ran water over the eggs and dried them off with a dish towel.

"I'm all right," he said. "Just tired and achy from walking all night." He glanced at Jo Lynne. "Wanna go out on the porch?"

Jo Lynne took her coffee out through the front door, while he detoured by his room and pulled on a pair of jeans and a white T-shirt. He was feeling a little awkward with her, wondering how they were going to talk about what had happened the last couple of days.

She was in the porch swing, her feet crossed, gently rocking. The morning sun and the cool air made it a perfect morning. She wore a pair of khaki Bermuda shorts and a white blouse. She looked nice.

He didn't feel like sitting beside her, so he leaned against the porch column and took a sip of coffee. The smell of coffee was almost overwhelmed by the scent of honeysuckle entwined around trellises on both ends of the porch. The swing creaked.

"Your brother's crazy," he said. "He tell you what happened?"

"He didn't tell me, but I know," she said. "I haven't seen him the last few days, but Trudi saw Rae-Harvey. She told her."

"He's a menace to society, he and Rae-Harvey both," he said, tossing the coffee dregs into the packed-dirt yard. He looked up and noticed a wasp nest in the corner of the porch roof, the little brown-and-yellow creatures busily crawling in and out of the tiny gray compartments. "They're gonna kill somebody one of these days."

"You're right," Jo Lynne said. "They're crazy, both of them. And I'm sorry H.E's my brother. I'm sorry for what they did to you." She carefully placed her cup on the porch railing beside the swing. "But, Wily, what you and I need to talk about doesn't concern my brother and his hare-brained girl friend."

It was quiet and calm on the old home place. He could hear Mama puttering in the kitchen, katydids buzzing in the trees near the house. He looked out across the yard toward the gravel road. A car passed, and then it was quiet again. He thought about Austin and Dallas and where he had been the last few months. He wasn't sure he belonged here anymore. He wasn't sure he belonged anywhere.

"You had no right to do what you did in Dallas," he said.

"I know I didn't, but you had no right to be with that woman."

Jo Lynne looked down at her hands folded in her lap, then she looked up at him. "I knew what was going on, all along. I just didn't want to face it until that TV thing. That was just too much, Wily. Too much." Tears were welling up in her eyes, and she gave them a quick swipe with her fist.

He thought about going to sit beside her on the swing, but he couldn't make himself. Minutes passed. A couple of Hereford cows were grazing in the pasture across the road. "So what're we gonna do?" he asked, finally.

Jo Lynne looked out at the road without saying anything. Then she looked at him. "I know how you are, Wily," she said in a quiet voice. "You like to wait until the very last second before you decide anything, hoping you can squirm outta making any decision at all. So I don't know about you, but I know what I'm gonna do. I'm gonna make it easy for you, do what I have to do. I'm gonna get on with my life."

She put her feet flat on the floor to stop the swing, put her hands on her knees and stood up. She walked over to the screen door and peered in. "Mrs. Foxx, I'm going," she said. "Thanks for the coffee." Her voice was sort of trembly, but he didn't know if Mama realized it.

"Bye, Jo Lynne," she said. "Drop by anytime, you hear?"

Jo Lynne turned from the door and stood facing him. She looked up into his eyes, glistening tracks of tears on her face. She put both hands on his folded arms, and then put them down to her side. She looked down at the porch, and he couldn't see her face. "I'm sorry, Wily," she said. "I ...," and then she sobbed. She couldn't say anymore. She ran down the steps to her car and was pulling onto the road before he could even get off the porch. He stood there in the yard and watched her drive away, and then he went and sat down on the swing.

Mrs. Foxx cashed a check for him out of her egg money, and he headed to Austin on the bus the next morning. Despite what happened with Jo Lynne and despite making Mama unhappy, he was feeling better as the bus headed south, not only because his chicken scratches were scabbing over on his neck and hands—apparently he wasn't going to get the chicken pox or rabies—but mainly because of the front-page story in the newspaper he had bought that morning. Nothing about him, praise the Lord, but a lot about Jimmy Dale. The story quoted normal, everyday folks from all over the state saying Jimmy Dale had played the fool, that his little set-to with Red at the TBOSS convention was no way for a real man to act. "His mama should have taught him better than that," a woman from Clarendon commented.

Purse hadn't seen it, but apparently the paper had run a Sunday editorial saying the same thing. Even better, most polls showed Red pulling ahead past the margin of error. The campaign, it seemed, was doing just fine without Mr. Wily T. Foxx. He had mixed feelings about that.

Once he got to town, he took the city bus from the Greyhound station to Shady Grove, his trailer court across the river. Everything looked the same as when he had left it the week before. The Crusher was parked under the old pecan tree, the leaves beginning to turn a mustard shade of yellow, and Shoogy— he looked twice, three times at Shoogy. What he saw looked like a dusty, old baseball glove curled up in the sand in the corner of his cage. He wasn't moving, and Purse couldn't see his head, and when he rushed over he saw the bird's water bowl was empty. There was a sheet of lined paper from a Big Chief tablet on top of his cage, held down by a rock. He read it: "Mother's had an outbreak of soriasis. Had to go over to Henderson to check on her. Called the campaign office, but nobody could locate you. Hope your back soon." It was signed, "Your friend, Willis."

Willis Seymour always looked after Shoogy when Purse had to be away. In return Purse helped around the trailer park— replaced the propane heaters on the trailers, cut and edged the grass ever now and then. How long he had been gone Purse had no idea. Shoogy was still alive, but he was too weak to hold his head up, and his black eyes looked filmy. Purse got a water hose and filled his dish, then dunked his head in it. Shoogy shook the water off his comb and beak, but he still looked extremely puny.

Purse brought the bird inside, put him on the kitchen bar and turned on the radio. Sammy Redd and Bob Swit were talking about the Senate race. "Doncha just know ol' gals like that?" Sammy Redd was saying in his wheezy, fat-man's voice. They push ya and pull ya, and when you turn around right at the edge of the gol-durn cliff, when you turn around and stand your ground, tell 'em gol-darnit you've had enough, they go off squealing like a stuck pig. I tell ya, I've known women like that."

"I guess you have," Swit said, laughing. "Is this marriage number three or number four you're working on?"

"Don't matter," a peeved Sammy snorted. "You let a woman like that get her nose under the tent, let her amass a little power, and you've got a real problem on your hands. A real problem. It'll go to her head, and then you got hell to pay. I gotta a bad feelin' the people of this great state's about to make a bad mistake."

Swit rolled into a commercial about some kind of additive you could put in your gas tank and increase your mileage 40 percent, just like he had in his brand-new Ford pickup from Dentler's Ford and Mercury, on the Miracle Mile. When he and Sammy came back, they took a call from some rumbly-voiced fellow who called himself U.L.

"Bob, Sammy, top of the mornin' to ya," the caller said. "No offense intended, fellas, but you ol' boys are such ignoramuses, you're so ill-informed, you might as well be flyin' kites in Patagonia. Y'all can't smell the coffee brewing cause your noses are out of joint about a person of the female persuasion running things. Know what I mean? What you two shavetail chauvinists don't care to admit is that she took the campaign to him. The little woman did. She made him the issue, and for somebody as dumb and ill-prepared as Jimmy Dale that's a problem as big as your granny's goiter. A gargantuous problem!"—Sammy tried to break in, but U.L. talked right over him. "She broke through all the money, all the TV ads, the hidin' behind Calvin Locke's coat tails, and she said this; she said, 'Okay, Jimmy Dale, let's get it on!' Turns out the man was all hat and no cattle. You know I'm right, fellas: She unmanned him! Put the cuttin' tool to his private parts and positively unmanned him."

Sammy and Bob went to a commercial. Purse laughed and laughed. He knew exactly who "U.L." was.

He switched the station to country and western. Ferlin Husky was singing about champagne ladies and blue-ribbon babies. Shoogy Red seemed to be coming around a bit but still seemed weak. Purse was gathering up his dirty clothes from the Dallas trip when he heard the hornet buzz of a little sports car outside. He got a fluttery feeling in his stomach, a good feeling, although it made him a bit jumpy all over.

"Coast clear?" Trieu asked, peering in through the screen door. He opened the door and she jumped into his arms and wrapped her legs around his waist. He carried her that way, banging against the walls and shaking the trailer, down the hall to the bedroom.

★ ★ EIGHTEEN ★ ★

They were headed out of town in Trieu's Alfa Romeo, headed southeast toward Seguin and Trieu's trial. It was coming down to the end, she said.

"I'd love to go with you," he had told her, "but Shoogy's not doing too good. I need to stay here with him."

"Nonsense," she had said. "Bring him along. We can keep an eye on him."

So that's how they ended up headed southeast on Highway 71, Purse in the passenger seat and Shoogy in his pen in the trunk, the trunk lid propped up and tied down with twine.

"The fresh air will do him good," Trieu assured him. And that seemed to be the case. When they stopped at Smithville to get gas, Purse checked on him. He seemed positively perky.

They got to Seguin, and Trieu pulled up in front of the Oasis Inn, the roadside motel where she had been staying the past couple of months. It was strange; she had turned the shabby little room with its cement-block walls and linoleum floor into an Oriental space, with a statue of the Buddha atop the TV and a rice-paper screen in the corner. At the back door, outside, she had hung tinkling bells that sounded like those at her house.

He left Shoogy outside near the door, and two little girls who had been playing on a swing set ran over and squatted beside his cage. "Don't stick your fingers in," he warned them. About the only other people around were some construction guys who lived at the motel full time, and Purse didn't expect they would bother Shoogy once they saw he was too stringy to eat.

They went out for Mexican food at Lucita's, a hole-in-the-wall place Trieu had discovered. The trial, she told Purse as they drank margaritas and munched tostados, was not going well. The jury included a couple of Vietnam War veterans, and the district attorney played up the military angle every chance he got. He was making the point that the shrimper the young Vietnamese guy had allegedly killed was a veteran himself, a God-fearing man whose livelihood was threatened by the ungrateful Vietnamese who had been brought into this country. He even wore a flag tie every day.

The next day, she said, the defendant, Tran Kim Tuyen, would take the stand. They would be lucky, she said, to spare him the death penalty.

Purse was ready for bed, and he thought Trieu was too, so he was surprised when she said she had to go out for a while. She said she had to meet with Tuyen's attorney and plan for the next day. "I'll be late," she said. "Don't wait up."

He sat outside on the sidewalk for a while, looking at the stars and drinking a Tecate. Shoogy was in his cage beside him, apparently back to normal. He went to bed after midnight. He had no idea what time Trieu came in.

Sitting in the old-fashioned courtroom the next morning, Purse couldn't believe that the cold-blooded killer on trial for his life looked more like a 15-year-old boy. Smooth-faced, his lank, black hair neatly combed and parted, he might have been five feet tall. He couldn't have weighed more than a hundred pounds dripping wet. His clothes, a cheap gray suit, a tie and a dingy white shirt, looked like something from Goodwill that had belonged to a much bigger man.

Trieu looked fresh and confident, very professional. She wore a black suit with a white blouse and a small string of pearls. Her black hair shimmered as she turned this way and that. Sitting beside the young man at the counsel table, she glanced back at an older Vietnamese couple and gave them a confident smile. Tuyen's parents, Purse figured.

Tuyen's attorney, Lester Will, was from Houston. He glanced at Trieu. "Are you ready?" Purse heard him ask.

"Yes, Mr. Will," she said.

Judge Luther Sanders called Tuyen to the witness stand. Head down, the young man walked across the wooden floor as if it were a minefield. His pointy-toed black shoes squeaked with each step. The bailiff held out a Bible, and Tuyen put his hand on it as he raised his right hand. He took his seat in the witness box.

Trieu sat down just outside the box on a wooden chair dragged over from the defense table.

"What is your name?" Will asked. Tuyen bent to Trieu and whispered.

"Tran Kim Tuyen," Trieu said, her face serious and composed.

"How old are you?"

Tuyen who mouthed an answer. "I'm 35," Trieu said.

"And what is your occupation?"

"I have been a fisherman all my life," Trieu said after a low murmur from Tuyen.

"Where was your home before you came here?" the attorney asked.

Tuyen looked down at his hands. Purse couldn't hear what he mumbled to Trieu. "I come from a village on the coast," she said. "A fishing village near Da Nang. And I have always fished for a living, except when I was fighting with the Americans."

"You were involved in the war?"

Trieu listened and then turned to Will. "Yes. We were always on the side of the Americans. I served with them for almost a year. As did my father before me."

Purse heard murmurs in the courtroom, as people turned to each other and expressed their surprise.

"What did you do?"

"I was a diver. I became an expert in combat diving and demolitions. I worked with the Brown Water Navy, Navy Seals, until we had a misunderstanding."

"What kind of misunderstanding?" Will asked.

"Objection," the district attorney shouted, standing up at his table. He was a big man with bushy, gray sideburns, wearing a blue, western-cut suit and black boots. "This is totally irrelevant," he said in a deep voice.

"Overruled."

"How can any of this pertain to what happened in Minerva?"

"And I repeat, 'Overruled!'" Judge Sanders said, staring like a hawk at the big district attorney, who slowly sat back down.

To Purse, it seemed attorney Will and Trieu both were surprised. He knew people in the audience were. The whole trial had been going the prosecution's way. What had caused the shift?

Trieu, her voice clear, continued with Tuyen's answer: "Some new Seals came in. They didn't know us. Didn't know our work. They said we were traitors. They said we were warning the North Vietnamese about troop movements and locations."

It was the strangest thing. The longer the questioning went on, the more it seemed that the man on trial faded away. Trieu was the focus, and it wasn't just Purse who realized it. The jury looked to her, not Tuyen, when the time came for an answer. Purse's attention and everyone else's, including the judge, was riveted on her face and her clear, mesmerizing voice.

Tuyen leaned toward Trieu and whispered something.

"We didn't do it. We liked the Americans. When I was a boy, I worked at the PX. I had a shoeshine stand. I brought them fish from home. They taught me and my buddies songs. "Hang Down Your Head, Tom Dooley." They called us the Kingston Trio. I didn't understand what they meant, but we enjoyed being around them."

Suddenly Tuyen stood up from the witness stand, snapped his right hand to his forehead in a crisp salute, and in a high, thin voice began singing. In English. "Anchors away, my boys, anchors away. . . ."

The courtroom was shocked. So was Trieu, it seemed. The judge banged his gavel. "Sit down, Mr. Tuyen," he said. "Counselor, instruct your client there'll be no more singing, no matter how patriotic."

"Yes, your honor," Will said. Tuyen sat back down, and Will resumed questioning. "What happened after you were accused?"

"I had to run away," Trieu said. "I stayed in a fishing shack on an estuary I knew about, and then I went to Saigon."

"How did you leave Saigon?"

"My father had a small boat. We rounded up all our relatives— aunts, uncles, grandparents, cousins, brothers and sisters—and we set off for the Philippines. The boat was too small and we nearly capsized almost every day. We ran out of food and water. My aunt died the fourth day out. We were on the boat many days. Finally, we ended up in a refugee camp."

Purse could hear Tuyen murmuring, head down, leaning toward Trieu, but the words the jury was listening to came from the earnest young woman sitting beside him. She wasn't speaking loudly, but her voice was so clear and the courtroom was so quiet, you could hear her every word.

"Did you have any government help when you got to this country?" Will asked.

Trieu shook her head. "The church helped us, and our own people helped us," she said. "Not the government. All we wanted was a chance to work."

Will smiled slightly. "How did you get a boat?"

"I have a cousin in Lousiana. He has a donut shop in Algiers," Trieu said. "Cajun Bob's Donuts and Beignets. It's a franchise. I opened up for him every morning at 3. For four years. I got the hot grease boiling, got the coffee going. My cousin taught me to make donuts—glazed donuts, buttermilk donuts, cake donuts, maple icing donuts, vanilla icing donuts, cinammon twists, cinammon rolls, powdered-sugar donuts, apple fritters, beignets. . . "

"Thank you," the judge said. "Sir, you're making us hungry. Please move on, counselor."

"How did you buy your boat?" Will asked.

"After three years, my cousin opened another Bob's, in Slidell," Trieu said, "and I moved my family over there. My wife, once she got the kids to school in the morning, she would work behind the counter. That's how she began to learn English. She tried to teach me, but I am a slow learner. I didn't have to talk to people that much the way she did. So after four years we had money to buy an old fishing boat and fix it up and sail it to Minerva. My wife had an uncle who told us the fishing was good there. He said the small town was a good place to live. Like home, he said."

"And was it?" Will asked.

"We liked it," Trieu said. "Until we met Leonard Silsbee."

"When did you meet?"

"The first time I saw him he was marching in a parade in downtown Minerva. It was a parade of fishermen, but no Vietnamese. He was a big, big man, and he was wearing some kind of silvery fish costume. It had fish scales all over, and these pointy things, like fins on a dragon, from the top of his head to the tip of a long tail that dragged along the ground. It made me think of a movie I saw as a boy. At the PX. It was about a creature that lived under the water. 'The Creature From the Black Lagoon.' Leonard Silsbee looked like that creature."

The audience laughed. The judge frowned and banged his gavel.

"Who was marching with him?" Will asked.

"He had a bunch of men, fishermen. They carried a big sign. It said AGOG, in big letters. I asked my wife, 'What does that word mean?' She said it stood for Associated Guardians of the Gulf."

"Did he scare you?" Will asked.

"He didn't scare me, but he scared my kids. He was carrying a spear gun, and he walked over and shook it at them. They started crying."

"When did you meet Mr. Silsbee in person?" Will asked.

"We had been in Texas about three months," Trieu said, "and he came by the boat one evening just as we were docking. He had his spear gun with him, and he slammed it down on top of a crate. I couldn't believe how big he was. Like a giant."

"What did he say to you?"

"He asked me if I knew about AGOG. I told him I did. He said for me and all my chink cousins it stood for Ass-Kicking Guardians of the Gulf. He said if we got anywhere near his fishing spots he'd shoot us with his gun and use us for bait. He laughed and grabbed me around the neck with his big arm. He gave me, he gave me. . . ." Trieu hesitated, looking at Tuyen. "He gave me a noogie. It hurt."

The audience laughed, and Judge Sanders gaveled them quiet.

"After that," Trieu said, "things began happening."

"What kind of things?"

"We'd find our traps broken up, our nets cut. Someone threw burning tires in our front yard one night. A couple of boats burned. One morning we found a pelican carcass nailed to the front door of our church."

"A what?"

"A pelican carcass. Its mouth and gullet was filled with dead, smelly fish," Trieu said in a calm voice.

"How do you know Mr. Silsbee had anything to do with it?" Will asked.

"It was easy," Trieu said. "There was a cardboard sign attached to the pelican's foot. It said 'This town's filled up to here with VC. It's time for you all to fly away home. Or you'll end up like this dirty bird.' And it was signed: Leonard Silsbee, president of AGOG."

Trieu began to speak more slowly and directly to the jurors, hardly glancing at Tuyen. "He came by again one day. He told us that if we didn't leave the water, he was going to kill us. He said he would shoot us on the open ocean."

"Were there any witnesses? Did you make any complaints?"

Trieu shook her head. "We didn't know who to complain to."

"Did you continue to fish in the waters that Mr. Silsbee said were his?"

"No. We tried to stay away from him. We went to places where we were told there were no fish. But we caught fish anyway. More than Mr. Silsbee."

"Go on," Will said quietly.

"Three weeks before the shooting, Mr. Silsbee came to where we were crabbing in the mouth of the river," Trieu said. She listened intently to Tuyen, to his singsong murmuring in Vietnamese. "He started waving his spear gun," Trieu continued. "He said he'd run us through and pin us to the mast if we didn't stop fishing in his waters. He said he and his AGOG brothers would shoot all the Vietnamese they found and throw their bodies in the ocean if we didn't leave. After that, someone slashed the tires on my truck. We finally decided we had no choice. We would go back to Louisiana."

Trieu sighed and pushed back a lock of her jet-black hair. She clasped both hands in her lap. Will paused and looked straight at the jury. "Tell the jury about the day Mr. Silsbee died," he said.

Turning slightly to Tuyen, Trieu listened and then answered in a voice that was strong and direct. "My wife and I decided we would leave in a month. We needed to save our money and find a place to go. I wanted to fish, not make donuts, but I hadn't made any Louisiana arrangements. To save money, I let my crew go, and my two oldest boys became my crew. We found an inlet not far from the mouth of the river, and we were setting our pots out when Silsbee showed up on his boat. He was wearing his fish outfit. And he was carrying his spear gun. As best I could tell, he was by himself."

Listening to Trieu, Purse figured the members of the jury were having the same reaction he was having. Imagining that day on the water, it was Trieu he saw in his mind's eye, not the little guy sitting beside her. Glancing at the judge and the look of concentration on his face, Purse suspected he was feeling the same way.

"I shouted at him," Trieu said. "I said, 'What do you want with us? We're not bothering you."

Trieu paused and took a breath, then leaned forward and drank from a glass of water.

"Silsbee shouted at us, 'I thought I told you gooks to leave these parts. We don't want your kind around here. I've told you that for the last time.' He had told me that, but I thought I could stay away from him and mind my own business. Now I saw that I couldn't. The Gulf, I guess, wasn't big enough for both of us. I was scared. I was scared for myself, scared for my wife and kids."

"What happened next?" Will asked. He looked at the judge and then at the jury.

"Leonard Silsbee kept on yelling at us, shaking his fists, swishing that long tail. I got ready to pull up anchor and get away, but he had us blocked in. Then he picked up his spear gun. It looked to me like he was aiming it at my son. I didn't have a weapon on board, I don't have a weapon at all, so I picked up the first thing I could find before Silsbee shot my son with that spear gun."

"What did you shoot him with?" Will asked.

Trieu took a breath and looked at the jury again. The courtroom was quiet, as if everyone was holding his breath. Purse could hear the faint whir of the ceiling fans.

"I picked up a flare gun," Trieu said. "I pulled the trigger. I don't know how many times, but I saw a ball of flame hit Silsbee in the chest. He fell backward into the water, and his tail got tangled in the netting. We didn't know he couldn't swim. I was very frightened, and my wife and kids were crying. I would not have shot him, except I thought he was going to kill us all."

Trieu's eyes were glistening. She was silent. From the witness stand came another voice. Tuyen spoke, in broken English. "Sorry," he said softly. "Very sorry."

★ ★ NINETEEN ★ ★

It was Thursday, about noon, and they were talking poultry. Trial over, Trieu's duty done, they were headed down Highway 71 to Minerva. On the way out of town they had picked up the Colonel's finest, along with mashed potatoes, cole slaw and biscuits, and had just pulled up at a roadside park. It felt like fall, cool, sunny and crisp. In the field beside the concrete table where they sat, winter rye glowed like Oz.

They had hauled Shoogy out of the trunk and set his cage down on the grass near the table. Watching him strut, looking more pert by the day, prompted Trieu's question about Purse's poultry past.

He looked out across the field, remembering the browns and grays of the Foxx farm in the fall. Down here, he was thinking, with the old live oaks and well-filled stock tanks, the well-kept farms, it was prettier than up around the old home place.

"My daddy grew up on a farm," he told her, "and after the war that's what he went back to. This is the late '40s, you understand. Only thing is, his mother had died while he was serving in the Pacific and his daddy—a cold, mean man; that's the way I remember him—had married another woman, a woman with a bunch of kids. They'd all moved in, and there was no place for my daddy. He started wandering across the country—following the wheat harvest, picking cotton, digging ditches—you know, whatever he could find to do. Then his daddy's wife up and left him after all her kids were grown and out of the house, and the old man was left to batch it on the tired, old farm. My daddy went back home to help him out. And never left. When the old man died, Daddy inherited the place. For whatever it was worth. And then he married my mother."

Purse stopped to take a breath and a sip of Dr Pepper. Trieu took off her sweater and tied the sleeves over her shoulders. "Does any of that make sense to you?" he asked.

"Sure," she said. "I took American history. Your father lived it." She leaned back against the table, pulled her legs up to her chest and wrapped her arms around them.

"The way I got it figured," he said, "it was her idea, my mama's idea, to try chickens. She was listening to a radio preacher late one night on this station out of Del Rio down on the border—XIT, it was, a hundred thousand watts all the way to Canada—and one of his sponsors was a feed and seed company advertising chick starter."

"Chick starter?"

Purse grinned. "It's the little baby chicks that some hatchery somewhere hatched and raised for a week or so. Got 'em started, in other words. You send off for 'em."

"And how do you get this starter chicken?"

"Chick starter. They come in the mail, special delivery. I'm thinking Mama was thinking that maybe, just maybe, we could ride those chickens out of the endless rut that came with trying to make a living off 40 acres of worn-out blackland prairie. I think Daddy always felt like she was smarter than he was, more sophisticated. After all, she'd been a grammar-school teacher a couple of years before they met. So he'd do whatever she thought was best. One day a mail truck come out to the farm with a big cardboard box with holes on each side. I'm thinking it's some kind of birthday present, and I could hear these high-pitched cheeping noises coming from under the lid. We opened it up there on the porch, and there were a dozen fluffy little yellow creatures in little compartments just complaining to beat the band. And that's how we got started in the poultry business."

Purse glanced at Shoogy, and so did Trieu. "So you love chickens, right?" she asked in a soft voice.

Sitting on one end of the table, his feet on the bench, he looked down at her beautiful face. "I hate chickens, baby," he said. "I absolutely hate 'em."

Trieu looked shocked. A frown crossed her face, and she glanced over at Shoogy. "But Wily, why? You don't hate Shoogy, do you?"

"No, I don't hate Shoogy," he said. "He's different. Fighting cocks are a different breed of bird than the chickens I had to deal with every day of my young life."

He walked over to the iron pole holding up the roof of the roadside shelter, grabbed hold and stretched his shoulder muscles. "Sure, they're cute when they're these fluffy, little blobs of yellow, all bright and alert. But that don't last long. Pretty soon they're these stupid, long-legged creatures that don't know enough to get in out of the rain. They get all these diseases, pip and cholera and the avian flu. Or they stand out in the rain and catch cold. And they die. And first thing you know, we didn't have money to buy gas or new jeans for school. Because of some dumb-ass chickens. And here's Daddy going hat-in-hand to Mr. C. B. Lusker at Elm Mott State Bank—I'll never forget that name—asking for a loan to tide us over. I've seen it. I went with him one time. It was humiliating."

"But they don't always die, do they?"

"Not from disease they don't. But they were born to die. They were born to get their head chopped off and fried to a golden-brown crisp in the colonel's mystery batter."

He looked at the scratches on the back of his hands that still hadn't totally healed up. Trieu looked at the red-and-white cardboard box on the table. She closed the lid.

"Sorry," he said. "I didn't mean to make you lose your appetite. It's just that chickens are so stupid and so helpless. And so doomed. I used to get down in the dumps just thinking about it."

"Of course, Shoogy's not like that," Trieu said. "Just look at him. He's brave—and dignified."

"That's what attracted me to fighting cocks," he said. "They die in the end, sure, just like all of us do, but they go down fighting. Fighting hard. I admire that."

They were both quiet as they packed up the leftovers, threw away the trash and tied Shoogy's cage back into the trunk. Trieu tossed him the keys and he settled in behind the wheel.

"I'm exhausted," she said. She leaned back and got a pillow out of the tiny back seat. He watched her blouse stretch across her beautiful breasts. They were headed for Minerva.

Trieu was asleep in two minutes, and while they sped south in the little Spider, he kept going over what he had seen earlier in the day when they had driven into downtown Seguin. With the square around the courthouse packed with cars and people even before the sun came up, the side streets were gridlocked with traffic from out of town. TV trucks from Houston, San Antonio and Austin were pulled up behind the building, with cables snaking into the courtroom. It was a bigger media spectacle than some of Red's campaign events.

Mervin Lindsey, a white-haired TV reporter from Houston, was broadcasting live beside the giant concrete pecan that symbolized Seguin's most important cash crop. "It's the Vietnam War, Lone Star-style," he was saying in a loud voice. "It's a battle against the Asian hordes." He gave a big wink into the camera. "Leastways that's what some of the good folks down around Minerva are saying."

Inside, the courthouse lobby was packed and so was the courtroom. Not long after Purse found a seat, the jurors filed in. He tried to read their faces. They seemed indifferent to the defendant, cordial toward the D.A. The D.A. was one of them, even though he was from another town.

"Mr. Foreman, have you reached a verdict?" Judge Sanders asked.

"We have, your honor," the foreman answered. A middle-aged guy with a crew cut, he was one of the Vietnam War vets. He handed the verdict to the clerk, who gave it to the judge.

Judge Sanders adjusted his glasses and read aloud in a calm voice. "We the jury find the defendant not guilty."

Not guilty? NOT GUILTY? Purse couldn't believe it! He thought he must have heard wrong.

But Purse wasn't the only one dumbfounded. For a second or so, the packed room was speechless; then there were murmurs throughout the room and then shouts. Judge Sanders banged his gavel, but no one was listening. Purse heard somebody on the Silsbee side of the courtroom shout "No!" A guy behind him yelled, "That goddamn gook is guilty as sin!" The judge kept banging his gavel.

Sheriff's deputies led the jurors out. They looked neither toward Will and his client nor toward Trieu. They ignored the D.A. as well. The crowd seemed to be getting angrier, and the

Vietnamese in the courtroom seemed to have melted away, Purse noticed. He made his way toward Trieu.

"Let's get out of here," the attorney told Tuyen, who looked somehow less bewildered than he should. "Tell him he's free, Trieu, free to go."

Judge Sanders instructed his bailiff to stand guard until Will and Tuyen were safely in their cars. Trieu grabbed Tuyen by the hand, and Will hustled both of them out a back door, behind the judge's bench. Purse followed. A knot of young Vietnamese men stood across the street, watching. Tuyen wandered over, and they shook his hand and hugged him, laughing and talking in Vietnamese. He lit up a cigarette.

Trieu smiled and shook Will's hand. "Thank you for what you've done," she said.

"Thank you!" Will said. "We couldn't have done it without you." He leaned down and kissed her on the cheek.

Tuyen suddenly seemed as old as he really was. More mature. He escaped his friends and walked up to the attorney. He grinned and held out his hand. "Thanks, my man," he said in perfect English. "You done good."

Will was shocked. He stood there with his mouth open, still holding Tuyen's hand. Tuyen glanced at the courthouse crowd, most people making their way to their cars, to make sure no one but the small group of his supporters could hear him.

"Shocked, huh?" he said, chuckling. "Let me give it to you straight, bud. We figured our only hope was for me to keep my gook mouth shut and trust in Trieu, beautiful Trieu," he said. "Dig?"

"Jesus!" said Will.

"You ain't no Perry Mason, and this ain't no TV show, bro, so we gambled on Trieu. She's fuckin' mesmerizing, as I have a feeling you well know."

Tuyen flicked his cigarette onto the ground and gave Trieu a quick hug. She smiled and patted him on the back. He sashayed over to his friends in sort of a Michael Jackson moonwalk. "H-Town, here we come," he said, climbing into a late-model Chevy. "Y'all take care, you hear?"

As Trieu and Purse drove away, he kept asking some version of "What was that all about?" She didn't want to talk about it. An hour or so later, as they drove toward Minerva, she told him again what he remembered her telling him when they first met: "You do what you have to do to survive."

They pulled into Trieu's bayside hometown about four. She woke up on the outskirts, just as they passed lines of tall, swaying palms on both sides of the highway. The highway ended a couple of miles later, at the edge of the Gulf.

Purse idled the Spider for a minute and looked out over the water. The wind was light, but it was gusting enough to raise little white caps. Not far off shore, a rust-colored tanker with "Liberia" painted on the bow plowed through the waves toward Houston. There was a vague fishy scent in the air and the smell of dead sea weed; Purse realized he sort of liked it.

As he watched, a shrimp boat headed their way, winching in its nets as it bucked through the waves. He could barely see the black nets because of the wheeling, laughing crowd of gulls following the boat. The reflection off the silvery water made him squint.

Trieu had him turn left onto the beach road, which ran past row after row of shrimp boats. Squatty little boats, most of them, with nets hanging up on racks at the rear—at the stern, Trieu corrected him. They had names like China Sea, Miss Saigon, Bao Ngoc, Master Ricky, Miss Tran. A big one called the Lillie May had a green, fire-breathing dragon painted on the bow.

"That's my dad's," Trieu said. "It's a trawler. Named after my grandmother."

Purse pulled over and stopped. The Lilly May was truly an impressive vessel, the hull dark green, the upper part of the ship bright white. Huge black nets were hung out to dry.

"Are we going to see your dad?" Purse asked, a little apprehensive about meeting the man.

"I think he's in California," she said. "Visiting our relatives."

The boat docks were on one end of town. They drove through Minerva, with its small business district, its sandstone courthouse, and past a rambling frame beach hotel, painted white, with a huge grassy yard out front. A few folks were sitting in white rocking chairs, enjoying the ocean breeze and looking out at the water across the road.

"The Morris Hotel. It's very, very old," Trieu said. "My sister worked there one summer, in the kitchen. That's where they put the gooks, you know. In the kitchen."

Past the hotel was a run-down little subdivision of small, cheap-looking ranch-style houses, most of them brickfront with aluminum siding elsewhere. Vietnamese kids played in the small front yards or rode their bikes along the curving street. Except for the kids, it was drab and sort of depressing.

"Most of my people live here, in Little Saigon," Trieu said. "Or in the trailer court over by the Catholic church."

Purse drove slowly through the neighborhood, looking out for kids. Some of the houses had little aluminum fishing boats in the driveway, and in a vacant lot a rusty shrimp boat sort of keeled over. "Keep Out. Private Property," a homemade sign on the boat warned.

"Which one's your house?" Purse asked Trieu. The street through Little Saigon had curved back out to the beach highway.

"It's over there," she said, pointing to a two-story blonde-brick house situated by itself across the road. With palm trees lining a curved driveway and a big picture window near the front door, it was a whole lot nicer than anything in Little Saigon. It looked like nobody was home.

"We could stay there; I have a key," Trieu said, smiling mysteriously, "but I thought it might be more fun to stay on the water. Go left. We've got about a mile to go."

Purse had no idea what she had in mind. He hoped it wasn't camping on the beach. They drove down the highway about a mile, until they came to a narrow shell-paved road almost hidden by tall marsh grass. "Right here," Trieu said.

They slowly bounced along the rutted road for about a hundred yards before it came to an end at the beach. Small waves collapsed on a narrow sand beach. And anchored in the water at the end of a weathered wooden dock was a huge white yacht. "Trieu Bleu" was painted on the hull in big, blue letters.

"Wow!" Purse said. "Is this thing yours?"

"Pop's," she said, smiling. "Come on."

They parked the car and Trieu led him across a gangplank onto the boat. He had never been on a yacht before, but Trieu was right at home. "She's a beauty, isn't she?" she said, standing on the deck, hands on her hips. She glanced up at two tall chairs above them where fishermen sat when they were hauling in sailfish or blue marlin.

"Pop says she has the best rough-water hull he's ever seen, and he's a guy who knows his boats," she said.

She slid open a door, and Purse followed her down a narrow companionway into what looked like a living room. Trieu said it was the salon. It took up the whole width of the yacht. It had a big white couch that curved around two sides of the room, thick white shag carpet, a soft chair, a color TV, even a fireplace set into one wall. On the walls, he couldn't help but noticing, were black-velvet pictures of dogs—dogs playing poker, dogs shooting pool, dogs in a whorehouse with a saggy-jawed derby-wearing bulldog at the upright piano and pink-ribboned French poodles lying on couches.

"Daddy's little joke," Trieu said. "He loves those dog pictures. He collects them. He's hoping to find one of dogs at a cock fight. If he can't find one, maybe he'll commission an artist to paint him one."

She led Purse into the kitchen. "And this is the galley," she said, holding out her arm like a real estate agent. He looked around at the counter with a stove built in and little refrigerator underneath. Everything was all flush and tight. He suddenly understood what the term 'shipshape' meant.

Trieu slid open a paper-paneled door, and they stepped into one of the two bedrooms on the yacht. It had a kingsize bed with a big TV at the foot. Trieu flicked her hand at his chest and pushed him back onto the bed. As he lay back, she climbed atop, making little murmuring noises as she pulled off her clothes. "I've been waiting all day for this," she whispered, her tongue in his ear.

It was all a first for Purse: Making love on the ocean waves, on a big, beautiful yacht, with a lovely young woman who grew more mysterious each day they knew each other.

Afterward, they sat on deck chairs and watched the huge, fiery sun go down over the water. Far out in the Gulf he could see barges silhouetted against the sun. It was a beautiful sight.

Trieu had changed into a scarlet kimono with outlines of white cranes covering almost every inch. As she stretched her legs out and propped her feet on the railing, Purse noticed that the kimono matched the red of her brightly painted toenails. She had made herself a gin and tonic and opened a can of Lone Star for Purse. He had hauled Shoogy out of the trunk of the car, and out of his cage. He was strutting around the yacht where they sat, clucking and exploring little nooks and crannies.

Purse was telling Trieu about Aboy's cockfighting ideas. "He told me when I first met him they were Red's ideas," Purse said. "I don't know; maybe they were, but birds in booties and a Roosterama for Wichita Falls never came up during the campaign. It's a state thing anyway, not national."

Dinner was served by a large Vietnamese man with a big, bald head, his eyes and mouth mere gashes in his broad, flat face. He wore all black. Trieu called him Ngo; that's what it sounded like, anyway. Ngo never said a word.

After dinner they returned to the deck chairs, enjoying the evening breeze. It would be a perfect night for sleeping. Some minutes later, Trieu got up and walked to the railing. She stared out over the water, a dark, dark green now, with little white caps shining now and then in the light of the stars. Far out on the water, Purse could see the twinkling lights of a passing barge, across the bay the yellow glow of a giant refinery. Except for the water lapping against the boat, it wonderfully quiet, peaceful.

Trieu seemed restless. She walked back and forth as if she were thinking, then stopped and stared out at the water again. Purse watched her, thinking how beautiful she was, and how he really didn't know her. He thought about how it must have been when she was a young girl sailing across the China Sea, the long dangerous nights on the dark water, no idea what was in store for her. He was about to stand up and go to her, when suddenly she spun around and looked at him, her eyes glowing in the dark.

"You want to go somewhere, Wily? You want to do something different?"

"Sure," he said, "I guess. What did you have in mind?"

"We're going to a cockfight! Asian style."

They drove for half an hour on a country road away from the Gulf, although they kept crossing little bridges over what looked like a lagoon. "Alligators down there," Trieu said at one point. Purse glanced over at her. She had her hair up in a pony tail, a red ribbon holding it back. She wore a black T-shirt, black jeans, black US Keds. She looked like a young Vietnamese boy. Sort of.

Crossing one bridge, he could see fog beginning to roil up from the murky water underneath, and it wasn't long before the vaporous mist lay over the fields and the moss-draped live oaks. It was dark, extremely dark, especially after Trieu turned off the paved road onto a rutted shell trail. As she steered slowly through the fog and dust and dark night, her lovely chin almost atop the steering wheel as she leaned forward to see, their headlights began to pick up dim forms in the road, and they could see a blurry light through the ghostly trees. They passed cars and trucks pulled off to the side, and then people began to loom out of the misty dark as they walked toward a tall, ghostly-white building that Trieu said had been a fish cannery at one point. Many of the people they passed, mostly men—young, old and in-between—seemed to know Trieu. They shouted greetings, slapped the roof of the car, reached inside the open window and patted her on the shoulder. Trieu smiled and called many by name, in Vietnamese.

Trieu explained that a long-ago hurricane had destroyed the cannery operation, blown away many of the buildings, destroyed the wharves that reached out into what the locals called Dead Man's Lagoon. The sheet-metal main building had survived, although the cannery had never re-opened. Years later the concrete paving of the narrow road they were on had been broken up and taken away for riff-raff. They parked under ancient live oaks and joined the stream of people, all of them Vietnamese it seemed, headed toward the windowless, ramshackle building

Inside, whatever machinery there must have been had been taken away, and rickety-looking wooden bleachers on all four sides of the pit climbed almost to the smoke-blackened ceiling. Naked light bulbs burned hot and bright above the bleachers and a spotlight of sorts hung above the pit. The bleachers were packed with people, most of them men, although Purse noticed several young Vietnamese women, very pretty, wearing straight dresses with high collars, with deep slits along their shapely flanks. Other people were milling around behind the bleachers.

They pushed their way through the tightly packed crowd, with people happily giving way when they saw Trieu. A handsome middle-aged man in a white suit waved them over and made room for them on the second row. Trieu introduced Purse, who shook hands with the man but couldn't hear his name. It was pandemonium, with people shouting, arguing, betting in a language that sounded like high-pitched gibberish. Purse had never seen or heard anything like it. Not with the good ol' boys, and girls, in Elm Mott. Not in Oklahoma, when he used to drive up there. No place he had ever been with Shoogy or any other bird over the years. He estimated there were 500 people crammed into the building, every single one of them Vietnamese, except himself and two or three beefy, red-faced security guards.

The air was thick with tobacco smoke. A dead fish smell, along with the odor of sweat mixed with alcohol, and blood, was almost overpowering. The pit itself, like every one he had ever seen, was a square enclosure surrounding by a board wall about three feet high. A fight had just finished as they walked in, and the pitters were takng their birds from the pit. Both cocks appeared dead.

The next fight began. After the billing, the referee called out "Pit your cocks!" and the handlers turned the birds loose with their right hands. The fight lasted about 15 minutes, the crowd getting louder and crazier with every passing minute. It ended when one of the birds let out a long, bloodcurdling squawk and fell over dead, blood dribbling onto white feathers from a gaff wound in the chest. The referee called another break before the final fight.

The tension in the room was scary. Vietnamese men with angry, sweaty faces were shouting, arguing, waving wads of money.

A couple of fistfights broke out, but the off-duty cops rushed over and shoved the men apart. Trieu said something to Purse, but he couldn't hear her, even though she was right beside me.

"What'd you say?" he shouted.

She pulled him down closer to her mouth and shouted into his ear. "Let's match Shoogy."

He pulled back from her, a frown wrinkling his brow, shaking his head. Shoogy hadn't been pitted in a year or so. He wasn't in fighting trim. And besides, this was foreign territory. He wasn't sure he trusted the people running the matches or the rules. It didn't feel right.

Trieu pulled him down toward her again. "You know how much is riding on the next fight?" she shouted. "A thousand dollars."

He shook his head again.

"But Purse," she shouted. "Didn't you tell me that a bird like Shoogy is born to fight? That that's what they were meant to do? Don't let him spend the rest of his life cooped up like a withered old man in an old folks' home."

As she talked, Purse noticed that they were being surrounded by at least a dozen men, each with wads of money held tightly in his fist. Like so many others, they seemed to know Trieu. He glanced around the ring of men pressing in on them. Most were a little older than he was; some he couldn't tell how old they were. They all looked a bit menacing. He wondered if they had been Viet Cong. He looked at Trieu, who was smiling up at him. He wondered if this is what she'd had in mind all along. He felt like he didn't have much choice.

"Okay," he said. "I'll do it."

Trieu went off to enter Shoogy and to lay down their money with a guy sitting at a rickety wooden table, while Purse pushed his way through the noisy crowd and out the door. He took a deep breath. It was still foggy but cool and mercifully quiet. He could hear the deep mating call of bull frogs coming from Dead Man's Lagoon.

Purse walked over to the car and looked down at Shoogy, who glanced up at him through the wire cage. He thought about letting him out and walking back to town. He would catch a bus and head back to Austin, although he wasn't sure what he would do with the bird. But what would Trieu say about that? That he was chicken? That he didn't want Shoogy to live his fighting cock's life to the fullest? He took a deep breath, reached down and unlatched the cage, tucked Shoogy into the crook of his arm.

As they walked into the storm of noise, Purse could feel Shoogy tense. The bird's head bobbed, like he was looking for action, like he was alive again, like he knew exactly where he was and why. Purse made my way through the crowd to the pit. Trieu was there waiting for him, a smile on her face, her dark eyes glittering. She kissed him hard on the mouth.

Purse stepped into the pit and looked over at his opponent. He was a middle-aged man in a white, short-sleeve dress shirt and black slacks. He was holding a weird-looking bird, sort of green and yellow-colored with a bright-yellow Woody Woodpecker topknot and a tail like a feather duster. Some kind of Vietnamese breed, Purse figured. He saw the gaffs gleaming on the bird's gnarly legs.

"Pit your cocks!" the referee shouted. The crowd noise was so loud Purse could only read his lips, but Shoogy didn't hesitate. He shot out of Purse's hand and met the other rooster full speed in the center of the pit. The two birds flew up four or five feet into the air, dust and feathers flying off the whirling, interlocked creatures pecking and clawing at each other. Time after time they collided. Blood-spattered, they flew a little lower each time but they wouldn't give up. It was obvious that Shoogy had forgotten nothing, but then again he had never fought such an exotic creature, and such a game one.

Purse was accustomed to seeing Shoogy wade in to the worst of it, but he had never seen anything like this. The match went on and on. Purse was barely breathing. Stomach muscles clinched, gritting his teeth, a roaring in his ears, he wasn't sure how much more he could take.

And then it was over. Or he thought it was over. The two birds came out of yet another clinch, and Shoogy fell to the ground like he'd been shot. Purse stopped breathing, just stared at what was happening before his eyes. Trieu was gripping his arm, her nails biting into the skin. The noise around them reached an even higher pitch.

Shoogy lay there on his back, utterly motionless, both feet in the air, head to one side, his sliver of a tongue hanging out between his bloody beak. The referee leaped into the ring, got down on one knee and had his hand up in the air ready to call the fight when Purse felt a dark blur brush past. Suddenly Trieu was in the ring, pushing the referee out of the way, the crowd going crazy. Crouching down over Shoogy, she picked the lifeless bird up and cuddled him to her breast. She bent over and took Shoogy's limp, little head into her mouth. She inhaled deeply, leaned to one side and spit bloody mucous onto the dirt, then put his head into her mouth again and exhaled.

Purse could see Shoogy's breast rise, his legs scramble for the ground. His head popped out of Trieu's mouth, upright and alive, his bright eyes looking for the cock that had nearly killed him.

The referee signaled "fight on," and Trieu, her black t-shirt stained with bright-red blood, the knees of her jeans dirty, stepped out of the pit, put her arm around Purse's waist and planted a bloody kiss on his mouth, leaving the coppery taste of blood on his lips. The crowd noise resembled a hurricane, the roar bouncing off the old tin walls, as the birds went at it again. Three times more the birds got their gaffs tangled and had to be separated by hand. Purse could tell that both were exhausted. Shoogy's eyes were bloody, and the top-knot on the other bird looked like a lawnmower had run through it.

At the last scratch, the birds wobbled toward each other from opposite sides of the pit and struck, flying maybe a foot into the air this time. When they came down, Shoogy was on his back yet again, but obviously alive, his right gaff sunk in Woody's brain. After a few quivering death throes from Woody, Shoogy managed to crawl out from under his dead opponent and get to his feet. For the first time that night, the crowd was quiet. With the last ounce of his energy, with the last spurt of life force, he climbed atop the dusty, yellow lump that had been Woody Woodpecker, raised up his head and crowed. And then fell over on his side in the dirt, stone-cold dead.

★ ★ TWENTY ★ ★

He got home about noon on Friday. Trieu had offered to drive him back to Austin, even though she said she needed to be in Minerva a few days to take care of some family business. He told her he would get back on his own. What he didn't tell her is that he didn't feel like being with anybody, not even her.

He found a grocery bag for Shoogy, and Trieu drove him to the bus station, actually an all-night gas station and convenience store on the outskirts of town. She kissed him, told him again how sorry she was about Shoogy's demise and said she would see him in a few days. So instead of making love to a beautiful woman on a yacht that night, he found himself sitting on a cold, hard wooden bench drinking coffee and eating a Hostess cupcake with a quart carton of milk for breakfast.

There were times during that long night, say about three in the morning, when his butt was sore from sitting on the bench and he was stiff and cold, that he wished he had never left home. He wished he was still picking up trash with the highway department. Maybe by now he would have had a promotion, maybe driving an asphalt truck, patching holes on county roads.

He sat there from about midnight until six when the north-bound bus pulled in and he got on. There weren't many passengers, so Shoogy had a seat to himself. He still wasn't sure what he was going to do with his longtime companion.

With the bus ride, he had even more time to think—about Trieu and what he had learned about her during the week, and what he still didn't know, about how he really felt about her. About Shoogy's last battle. About Jo Lynne and how he really felt about her. About Red and the election and about his future in politics, if he had one.

When the bus pulled into Smithville and the driver announced a five-minute rest stop, he got off and bought an Austin paper. The lead story said the campaign was coming down to the end with Red a point or two ahead in most of the polls, basically a dead heat given the margin of error. He thought about the past six months, how they had traipsed around the state, to big towns and small, near and far, thought about all the planning, organizing and endless hard work, thought about how proud he was that he had been a small part of it.

The weather was supposed to be nice on election day, the story said, all across the state. Voters were expected to turn out in record numbers.

He slept most of Friday. When he woke up Saturday morning and spotted the roll of hundred-dollar bills on his dresser, he knew what he wanted to do with what was basically blood money. Shoogy's blood money. He had a little breakfast, tossed the bag with Shoogy in it onto the front seat of the Crusher and headed out South Lamar to what used to be a gas station when Lamar was still the main highway through town. A fellow he had met named Ambrose Kuykendall had turned it into a taxidermy shop. A wooden sign on the side of the building said "STUFF IT."

Purse parked in the runway where the gas pumps used to be. Kuykendall was an albino, a tall, skinny guy of indeterminate age—pink skin, thick glasses with flesh-colored rims, curly white hair. While he peered at Shoogy up close and fluffed up his feathers, Purse stood at the old wooden candy showcase he used for a counter and looked around at all the animal heads on the wall. Staring back were armadillos, a couple of javelina, a water buffalo and a stuffed herd of deer. In the candy case were a couple of coiled rattlesnakes, a pheasant, some quail. Beside him on the counter was a beautiful long-tailed roadrunner.

Kuykendall hefted Shoogy in his hands like he was a canteloupe and said, yeah he could do it. Initially, he was going to stage him with both feet on a wooden stand, but when Purse told him about Shoogy's life and career, he said there ought to be a way to have him in the air, talons out, wings spread, maybe connected to a clear plastic string Purse could hang from the ceiling. More life-like, he said. Realistic.

The taxidermist grabbed Shoogy by the feathers on his back, put his other hand under Shoogy's legs and sort of shook him at Purse, as if he were in fighting form. Purse hated to say it, hated to see it, but with his head drooped to the side, Shoogy looked more like a feather duster than a fighting cock.

Still, Purse trusted Kuykendall to bring Shoogy back to life, so to speak. He could see it: You would walk into the trailer and over in the corner of the kitchen you would see Shoogy just like in the old days, in full battle cry. Tap the string, and he'd be coming right at you.

Kuykendall said it would cost $200 for him to get started and $200 when he finished, in about 10 days. Purse peeled off a couple of the hundred-dollar bills and laid them on the counter. Kuykendall said he would make up a little wooden plaque Purse could hang on the wall, with a metal nameplate. Under the name would be the words, "RETIRED UNDEFEATED."

From Kuykendall's place, Purse drove across the river and met Aboy for lunch at Grungie's. He was already sitting at a booth nursing a Dr Pepper when Purse got there. "Aha," Aboy said, pulling the napkin out from his shirt collar and struggling up from the booth, "the prodigal son returneth."

Aboy gave Purse a hug and patted him on the back. "Missed you, little buddy," he said, as they both sat down. "I think Red did too."

"So what's going on?" Purse asked. Raymond came by with a menu, and he and Purse shook hands. Purse handed the menu back to him. "Cheeseburger and fries," he said. "And a root beer. You doin' okay, Raymond?"

"Can't complain," he said. "How 'bout you? You still seein' that little Tokyo Rose?"

Purse glanced at Aboy, who was looking at him from over the Dr Pepper glass. "Well," he said. "I guess we're taking a little break right now. We'll see about things later on. After the election."

"Boy, you don't let somethin' like that get away from you," Raymond said. "Ain't that right, Mr. Suskin? Now if you need any help, you just ask ol' Raymond. You know what they call me over on the East Side. I'm the Ebony Guru of Erotic Insight. The guru of love."

"So what'd I miss?" Purse asked again when Raymond headed off to the kitchen, chuckling.

"You must not've seen the story last week."

Purse told him he hadn't.

"Well, we thought we had a major crisis on our hands, but I think we dodged a bullet. It may even redound to our benefit."

"So what was it?"

"It seems that somebody tipped off Nabob about Red's mama. He got the *Morning News* on the story and started raining press releases about neglect of the elderly, parent abuse, about mental illness and a genetic component. Story came out Friday morning."

"Any idea about the damage?"

"No poll numbers yet, but by yesterday afternoon we had a response. Thanks to Sue Bee. I'll have to hand it to her. She did a great job. Just masterful."

"Wow!" Purse said. "It's Ewell Suskin his own self complimenting Sue Bee. What'd she do?"

Raymond brought their food, and Aboy attacked his cheeseburger. "Think about all those ol' biddies we've run into throughout the campaign," he said, chewing with his mouth open. "That little ol' rancher lady over in Junction. The one that flew over the water tower. The little ol' black lady down in Houston. I guess there were a half dozen, plus Eddie Owens herself. Anyway, Sue Bee got 'em all rounded up, got 'em all up here and they appeared with Red in a press conference in the House chamber. And they talked I'd say for a good half hour about what a caring human being she was and how they'd love to have a daughter like her."

"But what about her mamma? Is she still on the street?"

"Nosir. And this is where we could have used your help. Me and Raenell went out to Annie's Alley a couple of mornings ago and did a little friendly persuasion on her to come with us."

"How'd you persuade her?"

"Well, a quart bottle of Mogen David didn't hurt. That's her drink of choice when she can afford it. Anyway, Raenell got her cleaned up, bought her a new dress from K-Mart. She was at the press conference too. You could tell she was a ring-tailed tooter in her day. Standing up there on the speaker's rostrum, she gave Red a hug, said whatever problems she had were her own fault, not Red's. I even saw a couple of hard-ass reporters with tears in their eyes."

Purse salted his french fries, then stuck a knife in the ketchup bottle to get the flow going. Aboy reached over and grabbed one with his fingers.

"So how'd Jimmy Dale's people find out?" Purse asked.

"Classic case of loose lips sinking ships. Nearly," he said, taking a sip of Dr Pepper. "Who knows who blabbed. When you're dealing with Nabob Slidell, you just have to assume he's got rats in the woodwork, bats with radar ears. I don't care where you are. Maybe even right here. Hell, Raymond could be a Nabob agent."

"If he is," Purse said, "he's about the best I've ever seen at it. From what he's told me, he hates Jimmy Dale, just like he hates every other rich, white honky he knows. He told me that back in his heyday, he was a Black Panther. I'm not even sure, deep down, that he doesn't hate us, you and me."

"Well then, he'll appreciate tomorrow's headlines in the morning papers," Aboy said. "Thanks to yours truly, if I do say so myself."

Somebody had punched up Ferlin Husky on the jukebox, singing "From a Jack to a King." It could have been Aboy who picked the tune, since that's how he saw his life going at that very moment.

"So what is it?" Purse asked.

"Well, I got a call Tuesday afternoon from someboy I've never spoken a word to, a Republican, no less. A woman, no less. You know Jovita Starnes?"

"Congresswoman, right? From Dallas."

"Right you are, son. Anyway, she called, swore me to secrecy, said if I'd have a little look-see in the secretary of state's office, I'd find an interesting tidbit of information. Seems that when Jimmy Dale was having his bad year and couldn't afford to pay his taxes, he somehow scraped up $50,000 for the Calvin Locke for Governor campaign."

"What an asshole!" I said. "So who has the story?"

"*Morning News* for sure. I called everybody, so it just depends on whether or not they jump on it."

Jump on it they did. It was front page, above the fold, in the *Morning News*. Every big paper in the state carried the story. Red had an appearance that day at a labor function in Beaumont. A roomful of dock workers was the perfect place for her to comment.

"Last year was a bad year for truckers," she told the union guys, "but they paid their taxes!"

"Damn right!" her audience roared.

"Last year was a bad year for teachers, but guess what, they paid their taxes!"

"Damn right!"

"It was a bad year for state employees, but we paid our taxes! Now, you all know who didn't pay theirs."

"Jimmy Dale Sisco!"

"That's right, friends. My esteemed opponent just couldn't be bothered."

The union guys were on their feet, yelling, punching their fists in the air. "We want Red!" they shouted. Red just grinned.

On Monday, Red flew to Brownwood and Bowie and Wichita Falls. At every stop, she hammered the "bad year" line, and at every stop the crowds got bigger and louder. It was close to sunset when they trooped out to the plane for the trip home. Gene Ray Donovan stood by the door to help his passengers up the steps. He tipped his pilot's cap to Red. "I want you to know, Ms. Ryder," he said, "it's been a pleasure flying you. I wish you the very best."

"Thank you, Gene Ray," she said. "You're a real pro."

Gene Ray headed into the sky toward the Wichita Mountains of western Oklahoma and then banked back south, toward home. It was quiet on the plane headed back. Red even slept a little, and everybody on board, even Aboy, felt a little humbled, a little apprehensive, about what could happen in just a few hours.

It was a short flight. An hour after takeoff, Gene Ray was lining up the nose of the plane with the lights of the runway looming out of the dark. Purse watched the traffic on the interstate that ran beside the airport, and then they all started pulling things together. Red and Sue Bee worked on their makeup, everybody else straightened their ties and pulled up their socks. A boy shaped his hair.

Red handed Purse her purse, and as they taxied toward the charter-plane terminal, he glanced out the window. He saw bright-white TV floodlights and a crowd of people pushing out toward the plane, security guards barely able to hold them back. They were holding signs above their heads, they were jumping up and down. Purse couldn't hear them, but he could see the joy and excitement in their faces, and he could see Tex Thomas and the Dangling Wranglers playing up a storm.

Gene Ray cut the engines and unlocked the door. He went down the stairs first and was greeted with a wave of sound. Next it was Aboy, then Joe Frank, then Sue Bee, then Purse with Red's leather bag under his arm. They waited at the bottom of the stairs for Red herself, the crowd roaring, "We Want Red! We Want Red!" When she appeared in the doorway, the spotlights bouncing off her orange hair, a wave of sheer happiness washed over them all. The Wranglers were playing a country version of "My Love is Like a Red, Red Rose," as Red made her way down the stairs.

Red walked over to a bank of microphones, waiting briefly for a break in the din of jet engines revving up on the runway, and then shouted, "After tomorrow, this state will never be the same!" The response was deafening.

"All those attacks," she began hoarsely, "they weren't personal. I want y'all to know that. We're talking about improving people's lives, and that's a threat to a lot of people. We're talking about getting affordable health care. We're talking about seizing the educational system and shaking it up, allowing the teachers and the educators to take part in deciding what needs to be done. We're talking about equalizing opportunity. We're talking about the environment, about no longer allowing our air and our water to be poisoned by people from outside. We're talking about putting the jam jars down on the bottom shelf, so the hard-working people of this state can get to what they deserve from Washington."

A plane took off and Red paused. "Anything worth having," she shouted, "anything worth having is worth fighting for. This election is about opening doors. What is it Bob Dylan says? The first year we knocked on the door. The next year we banged on the door. And this year, this year I'm tellin' ya, we're gonna kick that sucker in!"

The crowd went crazy.

The next day was beautiful. Purse knew the weather made Red happy, because it meant a good turnout. Final polls, taken the day after Halloween, showed a 50.1 percent Ryder win.

Judge Young was still worried. "If she doesn't pull it out, it'll be 10 years, at least, before a woman can run here again for a major office," he told Purse over a paper cup of dirty-looking coffee, probably his tenth of the morning. "We're still gettin' calls saying, 'I just can't vote for a woman.' I think we're gonna do it, but the map's gonna be the craziest thing you've ever seen."

All over the state, get-out-the vote people were hard at work. Carl Castle had set up his lemonade stands to give out information his volunteers needed to turn out the votes in the central part of the state. Richard Zamora from Eagle Pass had labor organizers and *politiqueras* working Hidalgo County and other voter-rich counties down south. They dropped the last of 75,000 leaflets they had begun handng out over the weekend. Aboy and Purse manned one of the sound trucks after they went to the polls themselves. They motored over to Smithville, then to Bastrop, on over to Taylor. Teams of walkers knocked on doors, and every phone line in the Valley was humming. In Houston, the Washington brothers were lining up rides to the polls, and Eddie Owens was calling black preachers all over the state.

They had people combing the swing precincts for Ryder voters and goading them to the voting booths. Republican women were calling each other for courage and going to the polls, sometimes together, to do something they never thought they would. Some slipped out of the house and drove to the polls in secret while their husbands were at work. A week before the election, a poll had found that 23 percent of Republican women remained undecided, while 11 percent said they would vote for Ryder.

That afternoon Red put on sunglasses and an Astros baseball cap and sneaked out to the movies with Axel and Sue Bee. They saw "McCabe and Mrs. Miller."

About 5, they drove over to Ralph Wayne's office, where Sue Bee and Joe Frank joined them. At the campaign office a couple of hours later, people milling around waiting, talking, passing along rumors, the numbers slowly began coming in from election officials in the field. The county clerk would call and Ben Hurr or someone standing next to him would take the numbers down and pass them along. This meant they were getting results almost as fast as the secretary of state over in the capitol building got them. Every few minutes Sue Bee or Joe Frank would phone to ask, "Where are we now?" At half past eight, Red and Sue Bee and Joe Frank abandoned Ralph's office and drove over to Ryder headquarters.

They trooped upstairs to surround Ben, who sat at a messy folding table in the middle of the room, voting tabulations tossed all around him. He had unbuttoned the top button of his light-blue dress shirt and loosened his tie. Full moons of sweat darkened his beefy underarms.

Red stood looking over his shoulder as he filled in the empty column next to the list of counties and projected numbers on the sheets laid out on the table. He would write in a new set of figures, and the comparison with the projections might show that Red was two votes off on overall turnout and one on how many people would vote for her candidate. An hour passed and then an hour and a half. Every once in a while Ben would let out a manly whoop and Red would say, "What do you mean by that?" But then he was quiet for a while, and Red asked him what he meant by that.

"Nothing really," he said. "Only, we're not seeing the returns from those counties over in the northeast—Paris, back over in there. More of 'em should be in by now."

Still, it was looking good. About 9:30, the hotel called to say the crowd was unruly and likely to riot unless Red got there soon.

"What do you think?" she asked Ben. He looked at her. He was feeling confident, but he also knew—as did Red—that as soon as she got there the networks would go live and she would be on statewide TV. He made his way through the crowded room to the water fountain and downed a couple of aspirin. "Now I know what a stroke feels like," he said to Aboy, out of Red's earshot.

"I'm not going over there, Ben, unless you tell me to," Red said. "I'm not going til you tell me I'm going to win. Yes or no? I need to know. Am I going to win?"

Everyone was looking at Ben. He took a deep breath and ran both hands through his brush-cut hair. "There's still those East Texas votes out, Red, and some from South Texas, but it sure looks to me like you're going to win."

They shouted for joy. Red grabbed Ben around his big shoulders, gave him a big hug and headed toward the front door.

"You sure as hell better be right," Bill Young said over his shoulder to Ben, following Red down the stairs.

Axel was waiting for them in the van. Raenell had even gotten Red's mother ready. She was on her medication, wearing a new dress. She looked a little dazed at everything going on around her, but she seemed happy. Red's kids piled into cars behind the van, along with Judge Young and Ben Hurr and Sue Bee, in what became a makeshift caravan. Everybody in Red's van was strangely quiet, maybe a little stunned. Campaign scenes kept flashing across Purse's eyes—that cafeteria in Paris, those steelworkers out on the highway, Nabob Slidell's pickup truck out west in Junction.

People on the sidewalks waved and yelled as they drove down Rio Grande Street and crossed the bridge to the hotel. Inside the hotel, the security men had started moving in on the peripheries of the Ryder crowd. With Red in the lead, she and her entourage came in through the back way, howdying and thanking their way past a giddy gaggle of well-wishers. They walked into the kitchen, where Red shook hands with cooks and busboys before making her way to the back entrance of the ballroom.

When they finally opened the big door onto the storm of noise and craziness and light, Purse almost started crying he was so happy. He looked at Raenell. She was crying. Red's mother stood beside her, a strange, little smile on her brown, wrinkled face.

Red handed Purse her purse and started up the ramp to the platform. Joe Frank, who had some kind of mobile phone with him, held back and jammed it to his ear. He put his hand over the other ear. A second later, he held the phone to his chest and looked for Sue Bee. "It's Calvin Locke," he shouted once he had spotted her right behind Red. "Says he wants to talk to Red."

"Shall I get her?" Sue Bee mouthed back.

"No," Joe Frank told her. "I'll tell him she'll call back."

Purse heard him deliver the message and then listen to Locke's reply. Joe Frank responded. "Fuck you!" he said and threw the phone against the wall. Purse went over and picked it up before it got stepped on, while Joe Frank told Aboy what happened.

"He said they're not conceding," Joe Frank said. "He said there were too many votes still out."

Aboy rubbed his chin, then looked at Purse. "They're gonna try to steal it," he muttered.

Red was on the platform by now, the crowd going wild. Almost 15 minutes passed before they were quiet enough for her to speak. They went off again when she held up a white T-shirt somebody in Houston had given her. Across the chest it read, "A WOMAN'S PLACE IS IN THE DOME!" superimposed over the Capitol in Washington.

Standing behind Red on the platform, Purse scanned the happy crowd, wondering where Trieu was. Off to the side, he noticed Joe Frank back on the phone, leaning over, a finger in his ear trying to hear. He saw Purse and motioned him over. "Tell Red to wrap it up," he shouted. "We've got a problem."

Purse waited until Red came to a stop in her remarks and while the crowd cheered, he touched her on the arm. "Joe Frank says we have a problem," he shouted. "He thinks you need to break it off."

A frown passed over her face, but when she looked back at the crowd she was smiling. She raised her arms for quiet. "Okay, folks, we may be in for a long night, so take a little break and don't go anywhere. I love you all."

The crowd cheered again as she backed away, still smiling and waving. As she was leaving the stage, Purse happened to notice Ed Small, the cattle association lobbyist, and a dozen or so fellow fat-cat lobbyists make their way through the crowd to an exit. In the holding room moments later, Purse was watching coverage of the Sisco campaign party in a hotel ballroom a couple of blocks away. Standing there in camera range were Small and his friends. Lobbyists, it seemed, were having a hard time picking a pony to ride. Trying to hedge their bets, they had made a split-second decision to abandon Red, at least for the moment, and to show their faces among the Sisco crowd. They would make sure, Purse had no doubt, to shake the hand of Calvin Locke.

While Purse watched the TV screen, Joe Frank, Sue Bee, Aboy and Ben Hurr were huddled around Red in the center of the room. All of them had worried looks on their faces. She bore into Ben. "I thought you said we had it in the bag," she said. "What in hell's going on? Did you fuck up?"

Ben's big, round face turned a bright red and tears sprang to his eyes. "Something's wrong, Red," he said, "but I'm not sure it's us. The South Texas precincts came in and they don't make sense. About half of them went for Jimmy Dale, and those were votes we were counting on."

"You know what they're doing, Red," Aboy said. "They're hoarding the count until they see how many they need. It's happened before."

"Goddamn, I know it's happened before Aboy, but I thought we had that covered," she said, looking at Joe Frank and Sue Bee for confirmation. Just then Joe Frank's phone rang. He answered, and they were quiet while he listened to Ralph Wayne. The clanging of dishes and the shouts of cooks and waiters were the only sounds. Then Joe Frank looked at Red. "CBS just called it for us," he said.

"Fantastic!" Sue Bee said. Ben took a deep breath and wiped his eyes.

"I don't trust it," Aboy said. "I don't want to be a killjoy, but they may be relying on the same projections we were."

Less than five minutes later Joe Frank's phone rang again. He listened without saying anything, then looked at Red. "CBS has backed off," he said. "Now they're saying it's too close to call."

★ ★ TWENTY-ONE ★ ★

Purse dragged himself home about three that night, that terrible Tuesday night. Most of the crowd had trudged out of the hotel ballroom several hours earlier. His footsteps echoed as he walked past the piles of trash, the saggy red, white and blue balloons that had drifted down from the ceiling, the smudged and wrinkled bunting that had fallen to the floor, the larger-than-life photos of Red. At home 20 minutes later, he lay in bed listening until about five to the low drone of the radio before he finally dropped off to sleep. He expected to wake up the next morning—hoped to, at least—hearing that all the votes had been counted, that Rose Marie Ryder had squeaked by, that the state had a new U.S. senator.

It didn't happen that way. The sun coming in through the window woke him up about nine, that and the sound of a trash truck mashing down its load in the alley. The radio was still on. Bob Swit and Sammy Redd sounded like two yahoos from the sticks who had won a teddy bear knocking over wooden bottles at the Heart of Texas Fair. "You see her out on that stage?" Redd was saying. "Thought she had it in the bag. In the bag."

"In the purse, you might say," Swit said. "In that Needless Markup purse of hers."

But it's not Nieman-Marcus, Purse wanted to say. It's from the outlet mall near San Marcos. He held his breath, waiting to hear she had lost.

"So she's out there lapping it up last night," Sammy Redd was saying, "and then here comes that curly-haired kid telling her, 'Uh oh, sweet mama, maybe you better climb back down off your high horse.' Soooweee, that was sweet! So what's the count now?"

"I just checked the wires," Swit said. "Secretary of State's still got her ahead, but her lead's down to about 200 measly votes. Out of a little less than a million counted."

"Don't that beat all? And from what I hear, there's still a whole passel of votes out there left uncounted. Apparently there were computer glitches all over the state," Sammy Redd said.

"Thank the good Lord for glitches," Swit said. "That's what I say." He segued into a pitch for burial insurance, "for as little as $9.95 a month, for when it's that time."

Purse shut off the radio and wandered into the kitchen. He put a piece of bread in the toaster, poured himself a glass of orange juice and almost went out to feed Shoogy. He pulled on a pair of jeans and a sweatshirt and walked barefoot to the office to buy a paper, scanning the headlines as he walked back to the trailer. "UPSET IN THE MAKING," big letters screamed, above a photo of a smiling Red at the podium just a few hours earlier. "Ryder Leads in History-Making Squeaker."

He loved looking at it, even though he had an empty feeling in the pit of his stomach that things were not breaking their way. Maybe it was the naturally suspicious nature he had inherited from his mama, the inclination to keep your head down because you never knew when a hail stone, or worse, might be headed your way. He remembered what Judge Young had said the night before.

He drove to campaign headquarters about an hour later and had to park six blocks away. On the sidewalk out front, TV reporters were doing interviews and stand-ups. Inside the jam-packed front room, supporters, campaign workers and politicians milled about as best they could, desperate for something to do, for something they could do. Desperate for something to happen that would change-settle-ease the sky-high tension. Purse had never seen anything like it.

He knew exactly what they were feeling—frustration, anger, excitement. He wanted to saddle up and ride, storm the Bastille, Remember the Alamo. Nabob Slidell, the smug little bastard who tried to toss him out of a pickup, he wanted to squash him like a bug. Jimmy Dale Sisco, all hat and no cattle, he wanted to slap him silly. There's no way he could be going to Washington.

He sidled through the buzzing, angry crowd to Joe Frank's office in the back, where Judge Young was still the voice of doom. "They're stealing votes over in East Texas," he was saying, a cigarette in one hand and a paper cup of coffee in the other. "By God, they're stealing votes down in the Valley."

The judge and Joe Frank and Aboy were hunched over a cluttered foldout table in the middle of the room, ragged piles of printouts with vote totals scattered everywhere. Aboy had opened a box of Shipley's Spudnuts and had eaten at least half of them. All three were wearing the same clothes they had been wearing the night before. Their faces looked as wrinkled as their clothes. None of them looked like they had slept.

Purse stood at the table listening to their conversation while keeping an eye on the TV in the corner of the room. He poured himself a cup of coffee and took a sip. It was cold, from the night before. The phone never stopped ringing.

"How we gonna stop it?" Joe Frank mumbled, a cigarette in the corner of his mouth. "Call in the Rangers? Get the FBI down here?"

"This is war," Young said. "We need to call out the troops. That means the Rangers, the FBI, hot-shot lawyers from Washington. Goddamn-it-to-hell, we need everybody we can think of."

"How 'bout the lawyers from the national committee? Aboy asked.

Ralph called 'em last night," Joe Frank said. "They'll be in about lunchtime."

"Where's Red?" Purse asked.

"She's supposed to be at home," Aboy said. "Getting a little sleep, I hope."

"It's just like '48," the old judge growled, "and before that '41. You fellas are too young to remember, but there's a lot of old timers that won't never forget how, by God, they came up with all those names and those extra votes after the polls had closed. Some of these little inbred precincts over in the Piney Woods. Meskins down in the Valley, their *cojones* in hock to the *patrones*. There's no telling what they're going to pull."

That was Wednesday morning. By late Wednesday afternoon, Red had won—again. The Election Bureau declared that she was leading by 149 votes with only 40 more ballots from a Valley precinct left to count.

"It ain't over 'till it's over," Jimmy Dale declared on the 6 o'clock news. "I just have a feeling that my opponent will stop at nothing, and all you folks who know me, you know Jimmy Dale won't take it lyin' down. Jimmy Dale Sisco will not—repeat, will not—concede."

An angry Rose Marie Ryder, her eyes flashing the way Purse had seen them when she got mad at Aboy, went on national TV. "I'm not inclined to tell my opponent what he ought to do," she told Dan Rather, "but the good people of this state are telling him. They're telling him loud and clear. They're telling him to fold up his tent and go home. It's time to get on with the people's business."

Thursday morning: The 40 votes from the Valley were finally totaled up. Red got most of them, but that was really academic. She had won the election by a total of 175 votes.

Jimmy Dale still wouldn't concede.

"I am absolutely sure that Jimmy Dale Sisco is your next U.S. senator," he told an early-morning news conference in the lobby of a Dallas hotel. Calvin Locke and a bunch of dark-suited lawyer types stood in a semicircle behind him. "When all the votes are in, I will be senator," Jimmy Dale said. "Sure as shootin'."

"That goddamn little piss ant," Bill Young mumbled. "Somebody oughta mash him into the ground."

By Thursday noon, Jimmy Dale had the votes he had been counting on. Election officials in Hopkins County reported they had come across a mistake. Compared with the Election Bureau's figures for "Box 7" in their county, there was a difference of 200 votes. An official reported that someone had misread a 9 as a 7, which changed the total from 965 for Jimmy Dale and 317 for Red to 1,165 for Jimmy Dale and 317 for Red.

"We're satisfied that a mistake was made, and we have since

corrected it," the county election official told reporters. "We have certified the new total."

Two hours later the Election Bureau also certified the new totals. Jimmy Dale Sisco was declared the winner. The fix was in.

★   ★   ★

Raenell told Purse she happened to be at Red's house delivering a batch of Western Union telegrams that had come in from around the country and that Red pitched a fit when she heard. Of course, as Raenell said, who could blame her? Everyone around her had come a long way since the campaign had begun nearly a year earlier. She had traveled her whole life to this moment and was about to see it snatched away.

Raenell said she picked up a shot glass of Maker's Mark that Axel was sipping and threw it at the living room wall, just missing Sue Bee. Raenell said she couldn't stop watching the light-brown liquid slowly dripping like syrup down the wall.

She said Red stormed across the room, opened the sliding glass doors onto the upstairs deck and screamed into the night for about five minutes. Wouldn't let anybody come near her. Axel was afraid she was going over the wall, where she would have landed on the rocks and the scrub cedar below. He finally was able to coax her back inside the house. By the time she got downtown about an hour later, she seemed composed.

"We wuz robbed," she told a gaggle of reporters Thursday night outside campaign headquarters, a huge crowd of supporters looking on under the bright, white TV lights that spilled into the street. "Let me correct that. The people of this state were robbed. And we owe it to them to do everything in our power to make sure that their voices are heard. Not the whining, sullen voices of the fat cats. Not the belligerent bullies of this state. Not the plutocrats who'll stop at nothing to make sure they prevail. I'm not talking about you people—the hard-working, tax-paying, law-abiding decent folks of this state."

The supporters went crazy, shouting, pumping fists, cursing Jimmy Dale. It went on for four or five minutes.

"At this point, what can you do?" Glenn Roy Smith from the *Chronicle* yelled out when the crowd calmed down a bit.

"We're going into court tomorrow to make sure the so-called official results of this election are overturned," Red told him.

Jimmy Dale and his people beat her to it. They went into state court that very night to make sure that Hopkins County officials couldn't change the late-reported figures. At the same time they went into federal court to stop any kind of federal investigation. Calvin Locke held a press conference of his own outside the federal courthouse in Austin, live for the 10 o'clock news. He claimed the Sisco campaign had evidence of voting irregularities in other counties, irregularities in Red's favor, that would give Jimmy Dale a majority even without Box 7. Purse heard that and thought of Aboy, but he quickly realized that even Aboy couldn't pull off something like that, even if he had tried.

"Where's Jimmy Dale?" an El Paso reporter shouted.

"Home on the Jimmy D," Locke said. "That's where he always goes to recharge his batteries. Back to the land. He's also meeting with a host of high-level officials over the next several days who'll be assisting in the transition. He wants to be up and running on Day One."

Red decided to go back to where it all began, back to Hopkins County and its county seat, Sulphur Springs. On Friday morning, Red, Joe Frank, Sue Bee and three lawyers from Washington flew to Tyler. Aboy and Purse had gotten up at 5 and gone on ahead in the van. They were waiting at the airport when Gene Ray brought in the plane. It was another 60 miles to Sulphur Springs, and the conversation all the way over was about legal precedent, legal strategy, legal maneuvering. It was not a happy crew in the van that morning.

They started seeing clumps of people just before they got to the railroad tracks that ran through downtown Sulphur Springs. They were waving Texas flags, American flags. Cheering. Throwing kisses and tossing red roses in the street as Red and her entourage drove by. Sulphur Springs may not have been Red Country last

August, but it sure was now, Purse was thinking. Even the dogs were frisky this time.

"Stop the car," Red told Aboy. They were a couple of blocks from the courthouse square. "Let's go, Purse," she said, handing him her purse.

Before anybody in the van could say anything, she had the front door opened and was stepping onto the street. The people around the car seemed as surprised as Red's people were. She walked over to the curb and shook hands with a man in baggy jeans and a gimme cap. Just a few minutes earlier he had been raking leaves in his front yard. People began crowding around her, and it was hard for Purse to stay close.

Up the street a ways, the old man Red had helped back in August stood on the curb grinning from ear to ear. He had on a red plaid cap, the flaps pulled down over his ears, and he had a little rosebud in his hand. Red saw him and called out to him. "Mr. Simon," she said. "I hope the sheriff kept his promise and you got your furniture back."

"I know who you are, now," he said. He handed Red the rosebud, and Red gave him a hug.

"I've got to get on to the courthouse," she said, smiling, and two boys on bicycles, maybe about 12 years old shouted out, "We'll take you!" Slowly they rode in the center of the street cutting a path for Red and Purse through the crowd. Folks were shaking her hand, shouting out encouragement, laughing, waving signs and flags. Purse glanced back and saw the van engulfed in people. Aboy couldn't move, and Purse could barely hear himself think inside the happy maelstrom.

People would look at Purse, the curly-haired guy with the purse, and they would shout out, "Go get 'em, boy!" Suddenly from back in the crowd somewhere, the sounds of people singing "The Eyes of Texas" wafted across the crowd, and soon everybody was singing, loudly and joyfully, "The eyes of Texas are upon you, all the livelong day, the eyes of Texas are upon you, you cannot get away...." Purse started crying. He couldn't help it.

TV crews with their satellite trucks had the handsome, old red-sandstone courthouse under siege, parked crossways over most of the head-in spaces on the square. Purse walked past an old man who must have been the town's parking-meter reader. He was fuming about the parking to a member of the camera crew from Houston, who just shrugged his shoulders and kept on setting up equipment. Yards and yards of black cable snaked around and underneath the trucks.

The crowd spilled onto the courthouse grounds and made way for Red to walk up the sidewalk toward the steps where she'd given her speech three months earlier. Reporters ambushed her. "What do you hope to accomplish here today?" a reporter from a Houston TV station shouted, sticking a microphone in her face as she walked.

She slowed down a bit but kept on walking toward the courthouse steps. "We're here on the people's business," she said, looking very businesslike herself in a blue pinstripe skirt and jacket, yellow scarf, white blouse and high heels. "We want to have a look at those ballots."

As she spoke to reporters, Aboy, Ralph and Sue Bee walked up. Aboy had parked the van on a side street and they had walked the last two blocks.

Purse took a good look at who was waiting for them at the courthouse door. It was Jim Ned Moody himself. Hands on his hips, legs spread shoulder-wide like he was ready for a gun duel at the OK Corral, the old Hossman wore a white western-style shirt with a silver badge pinned to his broad chest. He had his khaki pants stuffed into shiny brown boots. With his white Stetson pushed back on his broad forehead, he reminded Purse of Big Tex, the 40-foot-tall cowboy dummy that welcomed everybody to the state fair in a deep recorded voice.

Red led her team up the steps. Reporters with their tape recorders and camera equipment scrambled up behind them. Chin up, she walked briskly over to the sheriff and held out her hand. "Sheriff Moody," she said. "Good to see you again."

"Yes ma'm," he said, looking past her shoulder at the crowd of reporters trailing her. He looked like he wished he had a fire hose and could sweep them like autumn leaves down the steps and out of town. He pretended not to see her outstretched hand.

"Sheriff, we'd like to see the tally sheet," Red said.

Moody kept surveying the crowd. Purse glanced at Red. He

could tell from the little throbbing vein in her left temple that she was having trouble controlling her temper. He thought about the shot glass from the day before. Of course, she had been in similar situations as comptroller collecting taxes from stubborn business owners, although the stakes had never been so high.

The sheriff finally deigned to look down at the red-haired woman standing before him, but before he could say anything the sound of horses' hooves on brick streets caught his attention. Coming into the courthouse square in two columns were a parade of golden palominos, ridden by men in Stetsons and yellow dusters, all of them carrying flags and banners like they were Cowboy Lancelots. Lettering on their bridles and saddles said something about the Association of Southwest Sheriffs. One of the riders carried a yellow flag with red lettering: "ASS KICKERS"

As the riders reached the courthouse grounds, each column wheeled in opposite directions, riders interweaving, until they had encircled the grounds and then formed a column from the street to the steps. They sat at attention on their horses, flagpoles held straight up, the handsome horses standing stock still, never once making that horsey sound they usually make when they blow air through their lips. The crowd buzzed, in awe at the spectacle.

As everyone watched, a loud beating noise that instantly transported Purse back to Vietnam came from the sky and, suddenly, coming in over the sandstone tower of the courthouse, a black helicopter hovered like a huge, awkward praying mantis over the grounds between the building and the magnolia tree. Men grabbed their hats and women the hem of their dresses as the chopper hovered and then set down amidst a swirling dervish of dust.

The blades began to slow, and a door opened. A black-suited Nabob Slidell got out first and then waited, hunched over, while silver-haired Calvin Locke climbed out. The blades stopped turning and Jimmy Dale himself popped out. He snapped off a salute to the horseman holding the Texas flag, waved his ten-gallon hat as he looked around at the crowd and then shouted "God Bless Texas!" and "How y'all doin'?"

The three men walked briskly up the steps to where Red and her people were standing. Jimmy Dale shook hands with the sheriff, then walked over to Red, gave a little bow and took her hand. Smiling to the cameras, he muttered words out of the side of his mouth that only those nearby could hear. "It's over, you dyke bitch," he said. "Mark my words."

Red wasn't smiling. "Jimmy, I feel sorry for you," she said, shaking her head. "But most of all, I feel sorry for the people of this state. They don't deserve the likes of you."

The microphones got what she said. She turned to Locke. "As I was saying to the good sheriff here when y'all walked up, we want to see the tally sheet." She turned back to Moody. "How 'bout it, Sheriff?"

Moody glanced at Jimmy Dale, then at Locke. "Well, that's not gonna be possible, Miss Ryder," he said, in a voice that made Purse think of an 18-wheeler idling at an all-night truck stop. "We're always happy to have you here in our community, but I'm afraid you've made the long trip for nothing."

"Whatta you mean it's not possible?" Ralph Wayne asked him, stepping up to stand beside Red. His tasseled cordovan loafers reflected the noonday sun.

"I said what I mean, and I mean what I said," Moody said in a John Wayne sort of way. His right hand hovered near the pistol on his hip. His trigger finger twitched.

"But they're part of the public record," Wayne said, his face flushed, his voice squeaking a bit. "You have to let us see them."

Moody folded his arms across his chest and looked down at Wayne. "Sir, I don't have to do nothin'. Not a gol-durn thing," he said. "Specially when some lily-livered liberal from north of the Mason-Dixon tells me I have to."

"This is highly irregular," Wayne said. "Highly irregular. I'm inclined to believe that a federal judge will help you see the light, sheriff."

"Miss Ryder, I'm about to lose my Christian temperance and forbearance. You better get this little pip-squeak out of my sight, or else..." the sheriff was saying, when the courthouse door opened and a stocky, middle-aged man in a light-gray suit stepped out and stood beside the sheriff. Purse suddenly realized it was the same fellow they had seen last summer when Red was trying to help the old geezer whose furniture had been pilfered. It was the Chamber of Commerce guy who had made fun of the old man.

A friendly smile on his face, he looked up at Moody, put a hand on the sheriff's folded left forearm and stood on tiptoes to whisper in his ear. Then he turned toward the crowd and held out his hands, palms down, like he was the Pope blessing the faithful in St. Peter's Square. "Now let's don't get excited," he said, glancing up at Moody again and then smiling in the direction of Red and Jimmy Dale. "We are a reasonable people here in Hopkins County, and I think we may be able to accommodate everyone's concerns."

"And you are?" Joe Frank asked.

"Please forgive my thoughtlessness," the man said. "I should have introduced myself. I'm J. Paul Greathouse III. Hopkins County district attorney for the past dozen years, a veteran of the Korean conflict and a lifelong resident of this fair city." He shook hands with Red, Sue Bee and Joe Frank, then with Jimmy Dale, Nabob and Calvin Locke.

"What I would suggest, Ms. Ryder, is that a trusted member of your entourage, someone of your own choosing, come inside the courthouse with me and our elections officer, and we'll go into the vault and inspect the election papers together. Including the tally sheet. And Mr. Sisco, I extend the same invitation to you. Now, I hasten to add, there won't be any note-taking, and your representatives won't be able to bring anything out, but we'd be more than happy to let them peruse the papers."

Greathouse looked up at the sheriff, who gave a grunt and a slight shrug of his broad shoulders.

Jimmy Dale and his people huddled on one side of the courthouse steps, Red and her people on the other. Red looked at Ralph Wayne and Joe Frank and Sue Bee, first one, then the other. "Whatta you think?" she asked.

"May be the best deal we can get for now," Joe Frank said. "'Til we can get the papers subpoenaed."

"I'd say go for it," Sue Bee said.

"I'm inclined to agree," Red said.

Locke told Greathouse that Jimmy Dale objected, and while Locke and Ralph Wayne were arguing, Purse suddenly thought of something. "Ma'am," he said in a quiet voice, sidling over to Red. "You know who you oughta send in there, since we can't take any notes or anything, is Aboy. Aboy's got a memory system his daddy taught him when he was a little boy."

"What do you mean, a memory system, Purse? Some kind of secret tape recorder?" The impatient tone of her voice and the frown on her face told him she had no patience for fooling around.

"No, it's his own memory. From studying the Bible. His daddy taught him how to memorize the whole thing."

"Where is he?" Red said.

Purse noticed Aboy at the bottom of the steps talking to an attractive young female reporter from a Dallas TV station. Joe Frank caught his eye and motioned him up. He put a hand on the reporter's shoulder, then turned and headed up the steps.

Red looked at Aboy, who was huffing a bit from the quick climb. "Can you do it, Ewell?" she asked.

"Power and MIGHT—M-I-G-H-T," he said, grinning, trying to break the tension at the top of the stairs. "My dear old Pappy's never failed me yet. Come to think of it, neither has my pappy's Pappy, with whom I'm in frequent prayerful intercourse." He patted Red on the shoulder. "Send me in, Coach. I'm ready."

And she did. Red chose Aboy, Jimmy Dale picked Nabob, and Greathouse escorted the two men inside. While everyone waited, two women in ankle-length dresses—twins, they appeared to be with long, straight hair and no make-up—sang "What a Friend We Have in Jesus" and other gospel favorites. The sheriff explained to the crowd that they were from his church, Sulphur Springs Primitive Holiness Church of God.

Aboy would have enjoyed the music, but he was otherwise occupied, and from the looks of things when he and Nabob emerged 20 minutes after they went in, Christian brotherhood wasn't on the agenda. His tie was yanked out from beneath his jacket and pulled down from the collar. His face looked flushed.

Nabob looked worse. At first Purse couldn't tell what was different about him, but then he realized that he wasn't wearing his glasses. He had them in in his hand and one lens was shattered. His left cheekbone seemed splotchy and swollen. Aboy had a priestly smile on his face. Nabob didn't. His glasses broken, Nabob had to be helped down the steps by Calvin Locke.

What Aboy told Red half an hour later, as the two of them conferred in a jury room on the second floor of the courthouse, confirmed their suspicions. He had seen at least 200 names added to the list, the election-day list that had been kept from 7 in the morning until 7 at night. They were in a different colored ink and a different handwriting than the others. And they were in alphabetical order.

"There's one other thing," he told her. "The certification of the vote's been changed. It's as plain as the wart on old Aunt Wilhelmina's chin. Somebody went in there and changed what had been a 7 to a 9. All they had to do was give it a little loop, make it a 9. And that's what they did."

What's more, Aboy told her, he managed to memorize several dozen names—names that might come in handy in an investigation. Sue Bee took down the names while they drove back to Tyler. The fact that they were in alphabetical order made Aboy's chore even easier.

"What happened to Nabob's glasses?" Purse asked him on the way back to the Tyler airport.

Aboy laughed. "Well, the young man went just a little beyond the bounds of civic decency," he said. "I caught him leaning over the tally sheet, pen in hand. Where he got it from, I have no idea, and what he was doing with it I couldn't tell. Have you no decency, sir? That's what I said, and when I saw that fellow in there with us wasn't going to do anything, I took the situation into my own hands. Let's just say we had a bit of a tussle."

Back in the capital on Friday evening, Red and her lawyers made their appeal to the state Supreme Court, using Aboy's findings as evidence. The court issued a ruling promptly at 10 a.m. Saturday morning after an extraordinary late-night conference.

"There is ample evidence to suggest palpable fraud and irregularities in the recently concluded election," the chief justice himself wrote. "Therefore the results will be held in abeyance until a thorough examination can be made by an arbiter of this court's choosing."

That arbiter, as it turned out, was none other than Judge Luther Sanders of Seguin, Texas. Whether that was a good omen or not, no one could say, although Purse thought he might be able to find out.

A little before noon on Saturday, he drove to Trieu's house on the hill above Town Lake. He hadn't seen her since she had dropped him off at the bus station in Minerva in the dead of night. Hadn't talked to her either. If anybody could tell him what to expect from Judge Sanders, she could.

The gleaming red Alfa Romeo was nowhere in sight, and when he pulled the string that rang the bell at the old wooden door, no one answered. He went around to the back of the house, looked through the cedar trees at the houses on each side, and when he didn't see anybody, jumped up and got a handhold atop the thick, limestone wall. Boosting himself up, he dropped into the backyard. The rice-paper blinds were pulled down, and nobody answered when he knocked on the glass back door. At the front of the house, the gold fish that had been in the little pond near the door was gone, either gone or hibernating, whatever gold fish do when it starts to get cold. The mouth of the stone frog was empty. No front door key. He got the feeling she hadn't been home for several days.

A strange feeling came over him, just for a second, a feeling that Trieu had never really existed. Maybe she was a dream, a fantasy. Maybe he had made her up. Maybe it was some kind of post-battlefield stress syndrome from his time in Vietnam. Only he hadn't been in any battles to be stressed about.

He drove to campaign headquarters but couldn't stir anything up, drove by Raenell's place but couldn't find her. He dropped by Otto's Biergarten looking for Aboy, but he wasn't around. The football game going on in the stadium just a few blocks away was on national TV, which explained why even the streets were empty. It was strange to see the game on the screen and then step outside and hear the crowd noise and the bands from just up the street.

Red, he knew, was conferring with her lawyers. Shoogy was gone, there was no more campaigning. He felt lonely, at loose ends. He thought about driving to Elm Mott but decided against it. He could get a call from Red at any time.

No call came. He wondered what was next. What else could she do to take the office that was rightfully hers? Lying in bed that night, he wondered, for the first time in weeks, what Jo Lynne was doing.

He spent most of Sunday morning sitting at his little kitchen counter and catching up on his newspaper reading. He figured reporters were happy about the temporary lull, maybe the calm before the storm; they could finally catch their readers up on the amazing string of events during the last few days. An editorial in the *Star-Telegram* took a poke at Red for not conceding. "The people of this state don't need a long, drawn-out process," the paper wrote. "What they need is a U.S. senator. Ms. Ryder, for the good of the people, should graciously concede."

The *Abilene Reporter-News* reported that Hunee Watts was under consideration for a position in a Sisco administration, maybe head of a citizen's task force on illegal immigration. She was said to be in favor of calling up the state national guard and posting them every 50 yards on the border as a first line of defense against invading hordes. They would be backed up by an armed citizens militia, "SOS," she called them, "Sons of Sam," as in Sam Houston. Jimmy Dale said he would give the idea prayerful consideration.

The San Antonio paper had a profile of Judge Sanders, about how he was known for his probity, had been on the bench for 20 years, was a family man and a deacon in the Seguin Lutheran Church, Missouri Synod.

About four on Sunday afternoon the phone rang. He was taking a nap. It was Aboy. "What're you doing?" he asked.

"Nothing much. Just reading the papers, thinking about going to get some Mexican food over at La Reyna."

"How soon can you get down here?"

"Get down where?"

"To Minerva," he said. "Down on the coast."

"I don't know. Three hours or so." He got a funny feeling in his stomach, like he was about to be pulled into something he didn't want to be a part of. "What's going on?" he asked.

"Never mind what's going on. Just come on down, if your car's up to it. When you get to Refugio, stop and call me and I'll give you directions on in."

"Aboy?"

"Yes, son?"

Does this have something to do with Trieu?"

"Never you mind," he said. "Just get yourself on down here."

He threw a change of clothes and a jacket in the back seat, filled the Crusher with gas at a station on the corner of South Lamar and headed south on 290 toward the coast. He was thinking about Aboy's voice, how there was no hint of the foolishness he almost always heard.

What he was driving into he had no idea. He was sure it had something to do with Trieu, although being in Minerva, as he got to thinking, it could have something to do with the trial and with Judge Sanders. Of course, that would involve Trieu too. Musing about all this, he almost didn't notice a stoplight and skidded to a stop halfway into an intersection on the outskirts of town. A gravel truck came on through, its air horn blasting. "Get ahold of yourself, Wily," he told myself. "You'll find out soon enough."

Two hours later, it was getting dark and quite a bit cooler. Thunder clouds were building up toward the south. He stopped in Refugio at a gas station and called Aboy on a pay phone near the road. "*El Corral*," a Mexican-sounding male voice answered. Purse almost hung up before he realized Aboy was calling from some bar where he didn't want to be seen.

"I'm calling, uh, Aboy?" he said.

"*Quien es?*" the man said. He could hear the clink of beer bottles near the phone and *conjunto* music in the background. "*Oh, si, si. El gringo grande. Un momentito, por favor.*"

"You ever been down here?" Aboy asked.

Purse told him he had.

"There's a Mexican nightclub just after you make the turn off 290 to go downtown, right there at that Y in the road," he said. "I want you to meet me there. How soon you think you'll be here?"

"I don't know. Maybe an hour," he said.

"Don't tarry," he said. "You need to get here quick. Looks like a storm's coming up."

A little less than an hour later, he pulled into the crushed-shell parking lot of El Corral, a low, white-stucco building on the edge of a cotton field. Aboy's white Caddy was one of the few cars in the lot. Inside, it took him a second for his eyes to adjust to the gloom. He saw a couple dancing to a slow Mexican ballad near an empty makeshift bandstand; revolving colored lights from the jukebox made rainbow colors on the concrete floor. He spotted Aboy, sitting at a table near the back with a young Asian guy in a Houston Astros baseball cap. Aboy introduced him as Mike.

"Mike's gonna take us on a little expedition this evening," Aboy said. He pulled out a roll of bills and peeled off a five. "Mike, why don't you go over and sit at the bar for just a minute while I talk to my friend here. We'll be ready to shove off in about 10 minutes."

The kid took the money, shoved back his chair and strolled over to the bar.

"What's up?" Purse said, taking in Aboy's attire. It was sort of a two-piece Miami Beach leisure ensemble—baggy, baby-blue swim trunks, a matching short-sleeve jacket and blue canvas loafers. A low-crowned straw hat he might have plucked off the head of a Caribbean plantation owner was on the seat next to Purse.

Aboy stared at Purse without saying anything. It made him nervous, but he waited for his friend to speak.

"Son, how well do you know Trieu?" he asked.

He immediately thought about how well he knew her in the Biblical sense, and he felt his face blush. Fortunately, it was too dim in the bar for Aboy to see. "I don't know," he said. "We've spent quite a bit of time together."

"And a good time was had by all, I'm sure," Aboy said. "Unfortunately, you didn't know her as well as you thought you did. Lot of other people didn't either."

"I don't get it."

He took a swig of his Lone Star and wiped his mouth on the back of his hand. "I'll explain as best I can," he said, "but we don't have a whole lot of time. For one thing, her name's not Trieu. It's Alma Barbero. For another, she's not Vietnamese. She's Filipino. Oh yeah, she's also 35 years old."

Suddenly, while the whiny, haunting voice of Freddy Fender sang "Wasted Days and Wasted Nights" on the jukebox, *en espanol,* Purse seemed to be seeing Aboy through the wrong end of a pair of field glasses. His voice sounded like he was in a barrel. Purse couldn't make sense of what he was hearing, and he could feel his hands start to tremble.

"Are we talking about the same girl?" Purse said, trying to keep his voice from trembling too. "We're talking about the girl that came up and asked you to dance back at the Wagon Wheel?"

"One and the same," he said. "Little Miss Tokyo Rose herself."

Aboy reached into his jacket pocket and pulled out a newspaper picture of Trieu at some kind of social function in Los Angeles. ArtSpace, a gallery on Melrose, the caption said. She had her hand on the arm of an older man, some Fernando Llamas look-alike with slicked-back gray hair who had a drink in his other hand. The picture identified her as Alma Barbero.

"Now, her husband's Vietnamese," Aboy said, "but usually she uses her maiden name. Although maiden is not exactly what comes to mind when you think of Alma Barbero."

What he had discovered, Aboy said, was that Trieu's husband—that is, Alma's husband—Ly Tong Nguyen was an LA businessman, or drug-running gangster, depending on who you talked to, who financed several Vietnamese big fishing operations along the Gulf Coast from Brownsville to Pensacola. He was a close associate of Calvin Locke, and Jimmy Dale's campaign was the beneficiary of many thousands of Nguyen dollars. So was young Mr. Tuyen, the guy who got away with murder back in Seguin. Nguyen's money helped cover up the fact that he was involved in a low-level drug deal gone wrong. Judge Sanders was no doubt in on the take.

"We've been suspecting for some time that Jimmy Dale had a plant in the campaign," Aboy said. "There were just too many coincidences, too much insider information they were privy to. You couldn't chalk all of it up to Nabob Swindell's evil genius."

"So you're sure it was Trieu?" Purse said, still not wanting to believe what he knew in his heart was true.

Aboy looked at Purse like he was a pathetic little dunce. "Not Trieu, Purse. Alma Barbero," he said. "Filipino bar girl. Gangster's wife. Undercover agent for Nabob Swindell. Or maybe I should say under-the-cover agent who found her way into young Mr. Foxx's Fruit of the Looms. Whatever you want to call her, she's the one who nearly wrecked this campaign. She's mighty adept at what she does, partly because she's done it before out in California. And as hard as it may be for you to believe, she's sure not Trieu."

"But why me?" Purse said. "I'm nobody, I'm ..."

Mike walked up, and Aboy interrupted him. "We've got a little undercover work of our own to do," he said, "and Mike here's going to help us."

Aboy took a last swig of Lone Star and tossed a twenty on the table. He put on his planter's hat, and they walked out into the evening gloom, the dark clouds casting a greenish glow over everything around them. Aboy went to his car and got a camera out of the trunk, and then walked over to Mike's battered Toyota pickup. On its back bumper, a faded sticker read, "My Child is a * (star) at Fondren Elementary." The three men squeezed into the narrow seat.

"There's a little party going on over on Santa Lucia Island," Aboy said as Mike drove down a shell-paved road toward the water. "You and me are gonna play paparazzi, if we're not too late." He looked through the view finder on the camera he had slung around his neck and pressed a button to make sure the battery was strong.

They left the truck in the parking lot of a place called Sunny Ray's Bait Shop and Grocery and followed Mike to a little 14-foot johnboat he used when he worked as a fishing guide. "Go back and get those two plastic buckets in the back of the truck, if you don't mind," Aboy said. "We have to look like we're avid shell collectors. From what I hear, there's more shells on Santa Lucia beaches than any place on the Gulf Coast."

Purse ran back to get the buckets. They clambered into the boat, and Mike yanked on the cord a few times before the motor barked to life. "How far is it?" Purse asked Aboy as they puttered away from the dock.

"You can almost see it from here," he said, nodding toward the south. "'Bout a 10-minute ride." The wind blew his hat off, but he had a string around it, so he just kept it on his back.

✦

CHAPTER FOUR

Making Things Smoother for the Touch Dominant Child

If your own child is touch dominant, or if you are in frequent close contact with someone else's touch dominant child, you now understand the difficulties that child will face. This chapter will offer some practical strategies you can follow to help with those difficulties, no matter what your personal sensory dominance may be. Let's begin by looking at Scenario Four.

Scenario Four

Clare Wilton looked at the report cards in her lap and sighed, wishing there were some *good* way to handle the situation. It was the same every time. All three boys would bring home their report cards and stand there waiting while she looked them over. The two older boys would have good marks—mostly As; she'd be able to tell them how pleased she was and send them on out to play. But nine-year-old Adam would have only Cs and Ds, in every subject except physical education, where he could count on a B. She would have to talk to him about it and explain that he ought to do better, in spite of his obvious misery. She *hated* it, but what else could she do? If Adam had been a child with low intelligence or some kind of handicap that held him back, it would have been easier; it wasn't like that.

"Oh, Adam," she said sadly when his brothers were out of earshot. "You've done it again, you know that?"

The little boy nodded his head, his face white and pinched; he stared at the floor, with his hands clenching and unclenching at his sides.

"What are we going to do with you, honey?" Clare asked him.

"Throw me out of the house, I guess," he muttered.

"Adam!" Clare was shocked. "Is that how you feel? Like we're going to just kick you out?"

"Why <u>not</u>? I can't do anything right. I'm <u>stupid</u>! You'd all be glad to get rid of me."

Clare bit her lip; she didn't know what to do. She agreed with her husband and the teachers: Adam was an intelligent child who could do much better. It was important to make him understand that and to let him know that people expected him to live up to his potential. She agreed that it wasn't good for him to be allowed to slide through everything doing only the minimum necessary to keep from failing. But it broke her heart to have him stand there and tell her he thought he was so worthless that his own family would be glad to get rid of him. Surely *that* couldn't be good for him either!

"Adam, honey," she said gently, "we <u>love</u> you, no matter <u>what</u> your grades are!"

"Oh, yeah?"

"Yeah," she said.

"So, are you saying it's okay?"

"No," she said slowly. "You know it's not okay. You can do <u>better</u>, Adam, if you'd only try harder. But I <u>am</u> saying—"

"Hey, Mom," he interrupted, looking up at her with that tough, closed expression she dreaded plastered on his face. "I don't care about any of it, okay? Just ground me, or whatever you're gonna do, and get it over with."

"Adam, <u>please</u> don't act like that!"

She could remember, only a year ago, when he would have looked away, but not anymore. He stared at her without flinching, even with the tears welling up in his eyes, doing a pretty good imitation of a street punk, and waited.

Clare was ready to cry, too; she remembered very well how it felt to be the child who always got extra chores for her grades while everybody else got dimes for Bs and quarters for As. *Shape up*, Clare! she told herself sternly. *Do you want him to have the same kind of rough time you had all the way through school, just because you haven't got any backbone?* She pulled herself together and spoke as firmly as she could manage, given the way she felt like a hypocrite doing it.

"All right son," she said. "I don't have to put up with that face you're making. You go to your room, and when Daddy gets home we'll work out what we ought to do about this."

Adam turned his back and marched away from her and up the stairs, stamping his feet, being just as obnoxious as he thought he could get away with being.

Not until Clare heard the door to his room slam and the thud of his books hitting the floor did she let herself start crying.

◆

What's Going on Here?

It would be easy to say that what we have here is a defiant and uncooperative little boy headed for big trouble, and a mother with weak parenting skills and a tendency to spoil her youngest. But before leaping to such conclusions, it's always wise to take a close look at the *language* in an interaction. Even when the most negative judgments about the actions and attitudes of the people involved turn out to be *correct*, the chance for improvement in the situation almost always depends on how well they can communicate with one another.

In this case—no matter what else may be going on—it's important to realize that we have a touch dominant mother and a touch dominant child. They share their sensory preference, and this woman *could* be very helpful to her son. Unfortunately, her own difficult lifetime experience has left her with no confidence in her own opinions. Despite the sympathy she feels for Adam, and her own memories of what it was like to be a child who is always in trouble, she's afraid to question the judgment of his teachers and her husband. They tell her Adam is just an "underachiever" who doesn't work hard enough, and insist that she must take a firm hand with him and demand better performance; Clare is doing her best. The problem is that unless things change, this little boy very likely *is* headed for big trouble; it appears that he's going to handle his problems by going along with the adults' worst predictions for his future.

It doesn't have to be this way. There are a number of things that Clare and the others can do to help Adam. They need to start doing them while he is still a small child and not yet deeply set on the path to failure or delinquency, or both. Let's move on to those helpful strategies.

What You Can Do to Help

There are three strategies adults can use to help touch dominant children over some of the bumps and barriers that might otherwise hold them back: awareness; talking touch; and supplementing with touch. We'll take these up one at a time.

Awareness

✦ Always keep in mind that these children are touch dominant, and be sure *they* know you're aware of it.

Never forget that the child is touch dominant. I don't think it's possible to emphasize that too strongly. It's especially important when the negative reports—"This child doesn't try," "This child won't pay attention"—and the labels—"slow learner," "hyperactive," "underachiever"—start coming your way.

Children do have different levels of ability. Some are slower than others; some make friends easily while others have to work hard at it; some behave badly. Some children have physical and emotional problems. All these things are common, and it's always possible that the label proposed for your child is accurate. But before accepting it, ask yourself: Could the real problem be touch dominance? A touch dominant child often feels discouraged and frustrated, as would a sight dominant child who had to manage school and play while blindfolded. That discouragement and frustration can lead to behavior that *looks* as if it goes with one of the labels.

If we had strong scientific evidence for touch dominance as a problem, and pages full of statistics from research studies to back it up, this would be more easily dealt with. Parents would then be able to go to the child's school and say, "My daughter isn't a slow learner, she's touch dominant." Teachers would be able to call parents in and say, "I don't think your son is a bad child at all—I think he's just touch dominant." But no one has yet done the research and the controlled studies that would provide that evidence, and without it such a strategy is unlikely to be useful. You *can* use the term "learning style," however, plus plain English. You can say something like this:

> "As you know, children have different learning styles. I think the main reason Jennifer seems a little slow learning to read is that she learns best when she can get in there with both hands and <u>do</u> something. Learning to read doesn't offer a lot of chances for hands-on activity, and that's slowing her down."

The child also needs to hear this explanation, with your words tailored for his or her level of sophistication. Suppose your small child has come home complaining, "I'm just stupid! Everybody <u>else</u> can do stuff, but I can't! I'll <u>never</u> learn to read!" (Or to do fractions, or whatever.) Your best move is to say firmly, "Of <u>course</u> you're not stupid. You're just as smart as anybody else. And I will help you with your reading." To an older child you can be more explicit and say, "I think this is hard for you because you have trouble learning things using just your eyes and ears. You need to use your hands. But you'll be able to do it—I'll help you."

Finally, it may happen that the touch dominant child also has another problem, perhaps one that requires expert attention, such as dyslexia or impaired hearing. In that case, touch dominance is an *extra* complication that may make the other problem an even greater burden, and that must be kept in mind. The most important thing is to be sure the child knows that *you* understand what's going on, even if many other people don't, and that you're prepared to lend a hand.

None of this means that you should coddle the child and let touch dominance become an excuse for every difficulty. Not at all. It just means that before leaping to conclusions (or accepting the conclusions *others* leap to) you should go through one extra step. Take the time to stop and ask yourself: "Is it possible that the reason for this behavior is at least partly touch dominance?" And then take that into account as you decide what to do next.

Talking Touch

✦ In your conversations with the child, try to use touch mode yourself whenever possible, and to scale down your use of sight and hearing mode.

You can be sure that touch dominant children will never suffer any lack of eye and ear language in this society; they will be surrounded with it as fish are surrounded with water. This makes it absolutely safe for you to use as much touch language with the child as you can manage.

Making Things Smoother for the Touch Dominant Child

This sensory mode matching technique will be helpful to the child, especially in situations of stress. If you're eye or ear dominant yourself, you may find it hard to do at first, but you'll quickly get the hang of it. Throughout this book you'll find lists of touch mode words and phrases that you can substitute for the eye and ear vocabulary you would ordinarily use, like asking "Do you get what I'm saying?" instead of "Do you see what I mean?" and "Does that feel right to you?" instead of "Does that sound right to you?" You can make an effort to remember that the child won't take much interest in the *appearance* of things and will have to be reminded to pay attention to colors and other visual data when that's important. And you can do your best not to fill every other sentence you say with "look" and "listen" and "see" and "hear."

The basic rules for this technique are very simple:

RULE ONE: Match the child's sensory mode.

RULE TWO: When you can't follow rule one, try not to *clash* with the child's sensory mode.

That is, if the child says, "I feel like going outside," say, "As soon as you get your homework done you can do that." And if an appropriate touch mode sequence doesn't come readily to your mind, avoid all sensory vocabulary. To "I feel like going outside," say, "I think that's a good idea, as long as you finish your homework first."

What About All Those "No Touching!" Rules?

There will be many times when you have to pass along the antitouching rules to the touch dominant child. That can't be avoided. We let babies and tiny toddlers do a lot of touching, but that's a temporary tolerance; by about the age of three we start to limit touching privileges severely. But you can be careful to do this without making the child feel that

65

touching is *inherently* nasty and disgusting and forbidden and dangerous.

You don't have to word these messages as "Don't touch!" and "Keep your fingers to yourself!" and "Get your hands off that!" You can say "It would be better not to touch that" and "I'd rather you didn't touch that" and "Touching that is against the rules." And you can be *very* careful to use the same voice you'd use to tell the child you'd rather he or she didn't eat so many potato chips. We tell a child "Don't look!" or "Don't listen!" only in emergencies (or when it's part of the rules of a game); "Don't touch!" should be reserved for similar situations.

Supplementing with Touch

✦ Add plenty of touch data to the eye and ear information that surrounds the child, especially when something has to be learned, and in stressful situations.

All children, no matter what their sensory preference, should be given abundant information from *all* the sensory systems. The more different ways information is presented, the better it will be learned, and touch data is important to every child. But because so much of the information in our culture is directed at eyes and ears, touch dominant children often don't get as much touch data as they need. This is something you can easily help with.

Encourage the child to take part in strongly tactile activities such as sculpture, pottery-making, weaving, dance, carpentry, needlework, playing musical instruments, contact sports, and so on. This doesn't have to be expensive. There's plenty of touch information in playing with mud and weaving on a cardboard loom and pounding on empty tin cans. If you can send the child to take dance lessons from a professional, that's wonderful; but there's nothing wrong with learning to dance from a videotape or from a relative. You can buy expensive kits for making collages and doing all sorts of paper art; you can accomplish the same thing by giving the child the junk mail you ordinarily throw away (to be torn up and folded and crumpled and crushed) plus some paste or glue to stick it together with. Beans and seeds are cheap. The adult who is eye or ear dominant can easily find the child lots of things that it's okay to touch and handle. The problem is more likely to be resisting the constant temptation to say "Why don't you go watch television?" or "Why don't you find a nice book to read?"

When the child is having trouble with a school subject—and especially with the basics—you can help him or her understand and learn and remember by reinforcing the information in touch form as well as touch language.

- To help with reading, write letters and words on a sheet of paper with glue and shake ordinary salt or sand over the page. This will make a raised surface the child can follow with his or her fingers, to provide a *tactile* shape to go along with the shape the child sees and the sound. (You can also do this for numbers and maps and charts and other visual information.)

- To help with math, give the child lots of things with interesting *textures* to use for counting and for addition, subtraction, multiplication, and so on. Not only smooth pieces of plastic or wood, although those are better than just lines on a page. A supply of twigs with the bark still on, rocks with nice rough surfaces, strips of different kinds of cloth, like wool and corduroy and velvet—all these are more helpful to the touch dominant child than textureless items are.

- Writing, fortunately, is something we do with the hands! Just remember that how the writing *looks* should not be your major concern. If the child's writing is big and sloppy and crooked on the page, that's okay; what's important is to make writing a pleasure instead of a dreaded chore. Encourage the child to make books and illustrate them; never mind how "messy" they are.

For subjects like social studies and history, do everything you can to "translate" the information the child needs into touch form. Encourage the child to make models of forts and castles, to act out battles and coronations and sea voyages, to put together collections of rocks and bugs and leaves.

Anything that takes eye and ear information and gives it a shape for the hands and body to learn from will help. When that can't be done, talking about the eye and ear information in touch *language* will help. In every case, whatever the subject or skill, ask yourself, "What could this child do that would give the information a tactile form? What would be a hands-on presentation of this data?"

Your goal isn't to *replace* the eye or ear form of the material. You want the child to be able to cope with eye/ear information; that's a critical skill in our society. And you know that all the sensory systems should get as much information as possible. Your goal is to provide not a replacement but a supplement.

Special Problems of Touch Dominant Girls

Biological gender differences do not seem to me to be very significant for TD children except that by early puberty most boys are beginning to be taller and stronger than most girls. But differences due to socialization—to the way children are *raised* in our culture—do have consequences even for very young children.

Most normal toddlers want to operate hands-on. They want to play with mud and blocks, they want to use fingerpaint, they want to take things apart and handle everything that doesn't bite or sting. They like to hug people and crawl up into laps and roll around on the ground; they are most definitely not "sedentary" creatures. This is true for both girls and boys. But tolerance for such behavior tends to be much lower for girls than for boys, and the difference increases as the child grows older. She is expected to "grow out of" this, in a way that boys aren't. Even when a little girl's parents don't feel that "sugar and spice and everything nice" behavior is obligatory for their daughter from about the age of three on, she's sure to run into disapproval and negative messages from others. Children will call her a "tomboy." Adults will do the same, and add that she is a "rowdy little girl." In today's society, homosexuality is a matter of intense controversy, and penalties for it can be severe; worried parents may, as a result, bend over backward to curb even the slightest tendency toward "boyishness" in a little girl. Alternatively, they may decide that if their daughter wants to be a tomboy they should support her in every way possible, and then go too far in the opposite direction.

The eye and ear dominant girl may find it easy to give up rough and tumble behavior for dolls and coloring books and sedate pastimes. For the touch dominant girl, however, this will be tremendously frustrating; she may find that everything she most enjoys doing is only considered suitable for boys—who often won't let her join their play even when there are no adult objections to her doing so. Adults should be prepared for this development and take active measures to help out.

Many people divide touch dominant persons into at least two subgroups; the terminology used varies widely. Roughly speaking, they set up a "tactile" group—for whom what matters most is the opportunity to touch and handle and manipulate things—and a "kinesthetic" group, who place the highest value on whole-body movement and activities. Most of the time I don't believe that this division is important; certainly it's not something that has to be worried about where touch *language* is concerned. It can be a useful distinction, however, when you are trying to help a TD girl find suitable pastimes.

I want to emphasize that—for *both* subgroups—tactile and kinesthetic activities will be more helpful than those that rely on the eye and the ear; that's an absolutely reliable principle. Beyond that basic fact, however, it's useful to match the child's tactile/kinesthetic preference when you can. A strongly tactile little girl may not find much pleasure in the gymnastics classes that would thrill a kinesthetic little girl. Similarly, the kinesthetic girl is not going to be as pleased to get a nice weaving loom for her birthday as the tactile little girl would be. Your own common sense and adult experience will make these distinctions obvious: Just ask yourself, "Is this a tactile [primarily for the hands] pastime or a kinesthetic [involving much more of the body than the hands] pastime?" and act accordingly.

If relatives and friends insist on giving your daughter eye and ear toys and games, fill that gap for her with hands-on alternatives. Be sure she has a pet that she can stroke and carry and groom to her heart's content without being criticized for it, if that's at all possible. If she's interested in sports, encourage her (but don't leap to the conclusion that touch dominant kids always *are* fond of sports). *And find a way for her to join the activities of other little girls,* especially at the age where the little boys are passionately opposed to letting her join their play. Although TD girls won't care much about how their Barbie dolls *look,* the tactile little girl will enjoy dressing and undressing the dolls (and should have doll clothes with buttons and snaps and zippers, not just Velcro strips), and the kinesthetic little girl will enjoy having a toy stage on which she can move the dolls around and act out stories with them. If adults have bent over backwards to encourage the "tomboy" role, a child may feel that they'll disapprove if she takes part in activities traditionally associated with girls. She may feel that she has to pretend to find them boring, even when she'd really like to join in. She needs to know that you will do your best to follow her lead instead of locking her into some stereotyped pattern.

Adults can usually figure out a way to fit touch dominant girls into the play of the sight and hearing dominant ones if they are aware of the problem and will take time to think about it for a minute.

Special Problems of Touch Dominant Boys

Touch dominant boys don't have the same problem the TD girls have. If they want to spend their time with building sets and toy cars and trains, no one will disapprove; if they want to play football and climb trees and roughhouse with other boys, that will be accepted both by adults and by their peers. The strongly kinesthetic little boy may become the athlete that almost everyone looks upon as a hero; the strongly tactile little boy is likely to be the one who builds the gizmo that wins the Science Fair prize. Problems like the ones the girls face don't usually come up until adulthood approaches, when the brilliant youngster's parents who have their hearts set on sending him to law school discover that he is flat-out determined to be an auto mechanic. But there is a different problem that can have equally grave consequences.

Many people assume that a touch dominant adult is going to do a lot of touching of other people. In my experience, this is sometimes true of women, but rarely of men, especially if they are large and strong men. Why? Because of the way they were brought up. As young boys they were constantly warned never to touch others "because you'll *hurt* somebody"; as older boys it became unmistakably clear to them that any such touching they did would be taken as potentially sexual or potentially violent. The result is an adult male who is so sure that all attempts at touching others will be misunderstood or do actual damage that he might as well have his arms tied to his sides. And since he so rarely has any practice touching people, when he *does* try to do so his awkwardness almost guarantees the very misunderstanding he has been taught to be so afraid of.

71

It's very important to help the touch dominant boy learn the difference between acceptable and unacceptable touching—*off* the playing field—so that this won't happen to him. One of the best training devices for this purpose is a carefully chosen dog. The little boy who is responsible for the care of a dog (or who helps care for it while he's really too little to do it alone) will learn how to caress and hold and hug without hurting. He'll have the dog to pet and carry; he'll have the dog to run and play with. And the dog will give him not only acceptance but unconditional love. I can think of nothing more useful to the touch dominant boy than a dog, or any other animal that will provide affectionate companionship and that will *enjoy* being touched rather than be harmed by it. If you live in a small city apartment, it may be hard for you to offer this option, but do it if you can.

If the little boy is noticeably larger and stronger than his playmates, you should be prepared for the times when he will come home hurt and baffled because when he tried physical behavior *that all the other kids were engaged in* everybody got mad at him and told him he couldn't play. The prohibition may have come from the other kids, or an adult may have jumped in and told him, "Hey! You're too big to do that, you'll hurt somebody!" or both. It will happen, and he won't understand. He will say, "I was doing the same thing everybody else was doing! It's not fair!"—and he'll be right. Nevertheless, it will happen. The only thing an adult can do in such a situation is explain what's going on, in a way suitable for the age of the child, and provide enough love and support at home to ease the pain.

There's nothing "wrong with" the touch dominant child. There's a good deal wrong with a world that makes touch dominance, natural and normal as it is, *seem* wrong. Unfortunately, the child will have to learn to function in that world, however unfair and difficult it may be. With the strategies described above, you can help make that happen, and make it as easy as possible.

Now let's close this chapter by going back to Scenario Four to see how it might have gone differently if the mother in the scenario had been familiar with the information in this chapter.

Another Look at Scenario Four

It's reasonable to assume that if the mother had known about touch dominance Adam would not have *become* the sullen, miserable child we saw in the original scenario. Since Clare is also touch dominant, she would have found it very easy to stay aware of the problem, to talk touch with her son, and to add plenty of supplementary touch information and opportunities to his life. That might have meant that his grades would have been much higher; the situation shown in the scenario might never have come up. But let's not go that far; let's assume that Adam has brought home a report card that's mostly Cs and Ds and that he and Clare are going to talk about it. Here's a likely revision.

Clare: "Adam, you've got some grades on this report card that I expect you don't feel too good about."

Adam: "Yeah, Mom . . . I know. I got a lot of Ds again."

Clare: "You got a C in math, though—that one went <u>up</u>, honey. And you got a B-plus in phys. ed. You can pat yourself on the back for those two."

Adam: "Thanks, Mom."

Clare: "You're welcome; you've got it coming. Now, these other classes . . . which one is the hardest for you?"

Adam: (With a long sigh.) "Language, Mom . . . I just don't get any of it. Mrs. Taylor's always chewing me out about it."

Clare: "Maybe if we put our heads together we could figure out some way to make that one go better. What do you think?"

Adam: "I don't know, Mom. It's really <u>hard</u>. And who cares about all that old dumb stuff <u>anyway</u>?"

Clare: "I care. Daddy cares. The people you'll be working with when you get to be a grown-up will care."

Adam: "I've got to learn it, even if it's dumb. Even if I hate it! That's what you're laying on me, right?"

Clare: "Right."

Adam: (He sighs again, and looks down at the floor.)

Clare: "Let's make a deal, Adam. Let's make a deal that we'll get that language grade up to a C. You can do it. And I'll help you all the way. Okay?"

Adam: "I guess. Okay, Mom."

Clare: "Good enough! Now, you go on out and play, honey."

This revised scenario isn't a fairy tale. It doesn't make Adam into a scholar; it doesn't turn him into a perfect child. But it shows this mother and child communicating *successfully*. Clare doesn't feel forced to back Adam up against a wall; Adam doesn't find himself in a predicament where the only way he knows how to deal with the hurt and shame he feels is to put on a tough-guy act. This is a significant improvement.

If you are a sight or hearing dominant person, your most probable reaction to the dialogue in this revision is that these two speakers make much too heavy use of "get" and "feel" and "do." That's precisely the problem; it's a reaction based on fashion rather than on logic or facts. "Get" and "feel" and "do" are perfectly good verbs, for one thing. For another, if you were to put a voice-activated tape recorder in your pocket for a few hours and later count up the number of times you said "see" and "look" (or "listen" and "sound"), you'd be surprised. The repetition in the scenario seems odd and catches your eye (or ear) only because it's not from *your* preferred sensory mode.

The way Clare talks in the revision comes naturally to her; she doesn't feel awkward talking that way. It might be harder for you, if you're not a touch person, but you can do it. It just takes a little practice, and the realization that it gives you a way to help a child you care about.

Workout Section Four

◆

1. If all our children started learning American Sign Language (ASL) as tiny kids, the benefits would be substantial. Not only would they be bilingual, which is an advantage in itself, but their second language would be one they could use without making any noise at all if they liked. That's not likely to happen anytime soon; for touch dominant children, however, learning ASL is *such* a good idea that parents should do all they can to make it possible. You can get a complete catalog of absolutely reliable ASL materials—books, games, videos, teaching guides, even videos with stories like *The Little Mermaid* and *Cinderella* presented by native signers—from DawnSign Press, 9080 Activity Road, Suite A, San Diego, California, 92126. Their phone number is 619-549-5330, and their fax number is 619-549-2200.

   There's also a very short American Sign Language sampler on pages 155–163 at the end of this book, just to give you an idea of what ASL is like.

2. Many educators have now accepted Howard Gardner's claim that there are at least seven different *kinds* of intelligence, one of which is being "body smart." You can get information about "body smartness" from the Teaching for Multiple Intelligences Network. Write to David Lazear, Facilitator, 729 West Waveland, Suite G, Chicago, Illinois, 60613, or call him at 312-525-6650.

3. Many of the books for children that have "touch" (or a related word) in the title turn out to be disappointing. I've seen a number of them that offered *pictures* of things to touch; apparently the eye and ear dominant authors and editors don't grasp the fact that all the pictures have exactly the same slick, smooth texture—boring and uninformative to the touch. Even the ones that do try to include textures put in only a few, usually in tiny patches. For a

varied and much more useful source of touch books, write to Science Products, Box 888, Southeastern, Pennsylvania, 19399, or call them at 1-800-888-7400 and ask about their "Tactile Books" list.

You can make any children's book tactile by doing any of the following:

- Glue on appropriate patches—a patch of synthetic fur on a pictured animal, for example, or tiny feathers on a pictured bird.

- Use a squeeze bottle of glue to outline illustrations or text or both; the raised lines will be useful to a TD child.

- Put a thin layer of glue over an appropriate picture and shake salt, sand, or another textured material over the glue to make a textured area.

4. Make a texture *collection* for a child. Get pieces of different fabrics, textured papers, and the like and glue them on, one to a page; put the pages in a three-ring binder. Or, for a smaller collection, glue the samples to index cards and put them in a card box. Older children should be encouraged and/or helped to do this for themselves.

5. A collection of sculptures and carvings would be great for a TD child, but is likely to be a more difficult (and more expensive) project than the texture collection in #4. You can get around that by calling it a collection of "handleables," which will then include pebbles and wood scraps and shells and other textured items that can be found for free. And remember—hard as it may be for you to do so if you are sight dominant—that it's far more important for the child that the little figure of a person or animal be interesting to *touch* than that it please your educated adult eye. The kind of cheap trinkets and figurines that strike you as tasteless kitsch are often perfect for a collection of handleables. The way they *look* is irrelevant to how "feelsome" they are.

6. If the children you interact with *aren't* touch dominant, keep in mind the fact that exposing them to lots of touch materials will make it easier for them to get along with the TD people in *their* lives. You don't want to push a texture or handleables collection on a sight dominant child whose passion is collecting beautiful postage stamps or a hearing dominant child who wants to collect cassette tapes. But children who find touch resources interesting should always be strongly encouraged to follow that interest; it will be valuable to them in later life.

Touchpoints

1. "The haptic system is the system of information that comes from our skin, the movement of our joints, and the movement of our bodies through space. It is the tactile and kinesthetic modes combined. . . . Although the haptic system is activated whenever there is body movement, it functions at a higher level when we block out visual sensory input by closing our eyes."

> (Barbara Meister Vitale, in *Unicorns Are Real,* on p. 39. She goes on to list some activities for children to be done with the eyes closed, such as writing words or numbers in the air with the hand, recognizing words or numbers written on the child's skin by another person, etc.)

2. "Tests of 14 children who had normal hearing but who learned sign language because one or more of their parents were deaf showed that they had considerably better word mastery than children who just learned spoken English, said Marilyn Daniels, a speech communications expert at Pennsylvania State University. The children ranged in age from just under 3 to 13 years."

> ("Sign Language," *Orlando Sentinel,* August 22, 1993.)

3. "[W]e found, not surprisingly, that one of the most effective interventions with crying newborns was to pick them up and hold them close to the shoulder. What we did not anticipate at all was that this intervention, in addition to soothing the infants, almost invariably made them bright-

eyed and alert and caused them to scan their surroundings. . . . The reason we got excited about this was that we were predictably producing the state that many investigators believe is the one most conducive to the earliest forms of learning."

> (Anneliese F. Korner, Ph.D., "The Many Faces of Touch," pp. 107–13, in Brown 1984, on pp. 107–8. These investigators were interested in learning exactly *what* it was in this "intervention" that had the alerting effect on the babies. They discovered that it was the *combination* of lifting and holding, and note on page 108 that "When the investigator embraced but did not lift or move the infant (contact alone), it produced no more alerting than would have occurred by chance.")

4. "There are individual differences in parents' feelings regarding physical contact with their infants, differences that become manifest when an infant is frightened or apprehensive and attempts to approach the parent. Under these conditions, a majority of parents adopt an open posture and gladly accept the infant. . . . But others adjust their bodies so that the infant is barred from access, or actively turn the approaching infant's body . . . or simply push the infant away."

> (M. Louise Biggar, Ph.D., "Maternal Aversion to Mother-Infant Contact," in Brown 1984, pp. 66–73; on p. 66. The study found that the more infants were physically rejected by the parent, the more *anger* they showed as they got older. On page 69 they say that "the more the mother had shown an early aversion to physical contact with the infant, the more frequently the infant struck or angrily threatened to strike the mother in relatively stress-free situations." Studies like these tend to focus on mothers, by the way, not

because they feel that mothers are the only parent but because women are more likely to be available to come to the research lab with their babies than men are.)

Talking Touch

1. When you understand a situation, you may . . .

   have a good grasp of the problem

   be in touch with all the facts

   put your finger on what matters most

   go straight to the heart of the matter

   have all the information on the tip of your tongue

   have all the facts at your fingertips

   really put your back into it

   be on solid ground

   get right in there with both hands

   jump in with both feet

   have a gut feeling that you're right

   get to the bottom of it quickly

2. When you don't understand a situation, you may . . .

   not have a leg to stand on

   get a sinking feeling

   feel a shiver up your spine

   shrug it off

   make waves

put your foot in it

be on a slippery slope

bend over backward to avoid mistakes

get your feet knocked out from under you

have both hands tied behind your back

be unable to get a grip on the problem

be up against a stiff penalty

have your back to the wall

go under

get bogged down

lose your balance

3. A difficult experience can be . . .

a rough and bumpy ride	a rough row to hoe
too heavy to bear	a heavy load to haul
back-breaking	off the beaten path
more than you can handle	an uphill climb
too hot to handle	touch and go
a tight squeeze	a slippery slope
only skin deep	hard to get out of
like walking on hot coals	like a fist in the gut
a pressure cooker	like shoving molasses

CHAPTER FIVE

◆

Making Things Smoother for the Touch Dominant Adult

Scenario Five

"Look, Kenneth," said Mason Lassiter, "it's clear to me that this is just a communication problem. But you have to at least try to see it from the patient's point of view."

"Oh, yeah? Why?"

"Why?" The administrator leaned forward and glared at his sullen surgeon. "Because she is going to sue you, and this hospital, if you don't—that's why!"

"She's got no case, Mason. She's a nut!"

"That may be," Mason said patiently; he was used to this kind of scene with Kenneth Trask, and he knew that patience—lots of patience!—was required. "But even if she loses, it will cost us; there's no such thing as a free lawsuit, Doctor!"

"If she wants to complain, she knows how to get to my office."

Mason Lassiter shook his head. "Kenneth," he said, "I don't think you understand this situation. According to her attorney, every time she sees you, you <u>insult</u> her. You can't ask her to come to your office and be insulted <u>again</u>. Can't you see that?"

The doctor slouched down farther in the chair and folded his arms over his chest.

"No," he said bitterly. "No, I can't. I'm a good surgeon— I'm the best surgeon you've got, and you know it. What difference does it make what comes out of my <u>mouth,</u> as long as my <u>hands</u> save people's lives? If that Crandall woman wanted somebody to coddle her little feelings and make pretty speeches at her, why'd she hire a surgeon? That's not what surgeons are <u>for</u>!"

Mason sighed, and wished he knew what to do with this man—it was what he *always* wished. How anybody so brilliant and so skilled could be such an impossible person was a mystery; what was even more baffling was the doctor's seeming inability to understand what he was doing *wrong*, no matter how many times it was explained to him. Sometimes Mason thought it had to be an act Dr. Trask was putting on just as a way of being even *more* impossible. But Kenneth was one of the top surgeons in the country, and neither Blakeley Hospital nor his patients could manage without him.

"Kenneth," he said, "let's just look at the list of things Miss Crandall claims you said to her and see if we can't—"

"No WAY!" Kenneth stood up, shoving the chair back so hard that he had to grab it to keep it from turning over. "Before I got my hands on Crandall she couldn't even breathe, and now she's on her feet and strong as a horse! She oughta be down on her knees giving THANKS for what I did for her, instead of SUING people! And I've got surgery in ten minutes, Lassiter—I'm <u>out</u> of here!"

He was, too; he turned and rushed from the room, shoving his way out the door in a rage. Mason was grateful that it was the kind of door that can't *be* slammed. He rubbed his forehead, thinking for the ten thousandth time that he ought to be paid extra for every session he had to suffer through with Dr. Trask, and he opened his desk drawer to hunt for the bottle of aspirin.

◆

What's Going on Here?

This is a typical communication breakdown caused by touch dominance. It illustrates both the on-the-spot trouble the touch dominant adult has in talking to others and the trouble caused by the strategies such adults build up over the years for dealing with constant negative reactions. In Scenario Five the TD adult is a brilliant surgeon whose hospital considers him indispensable, which gives him options that other TD adults may not have. Nevertheless, most of Dr. Trask's interactions with other people—in both his personal and his professional life—are like this one: disastrous.

How we ordinarily deal with people like Dr. Trask in our society depends on the relationship we have with the person. If the TD adult is someone we run into briefly once or twice a year, or may never see again, we ignore the problem. If the person is someone we often have to deal with, we can't ignore it; we struggle along as best we can, frustrated and tense and often in despair. When the "impossible" person is someone who has power over us or someone we love deeply, we may go to a great deal of trouble to try to maintain the relationship—as in Scenario Five, where the hospital administrator would be very upset if he lost the touch dominant doctor, or when the person is our spouse or child or parent.

In all these cases (and the multitude of possible variations on them) we tend to make the same mistake: We take it for granted that the source of our difficulty is the character and/or attitudes of the TD individual; we call it a "personality problem." We assume that the only way we could make things better would be by *changing the person*. Because that is one of the hardest tasks there is, we either don't try it or we try it and get nowhere; most of the time, we end up like the hospital administrator, needing an aspirin.

This is unfortunate. It doesn't have to be this way. It's not *easy* to set up pleasant relationships with many TD adults, because they, like you, are set in their ways. But it's possible, and it will repay your efforts. The first step is always to drop the assumption that the problem is in the person and deal with the *language*. That is, set aside the idea that the person is obnoxious or impossible or uncooperative or hostile or deliberately troublesome in any way. That may be it—but it should be the assumption you make last, not first. First, you need to assume that changing the language (rather than changing the person) is the way to a solution. Let's consider what that would mean.

What You Can Do to Help

Touch dominant adults have already gone through the process of growing up in an eye and ear dominant society. Whatever labels they have acquired are firmly attached, and their consequences are already in place. Touch dominant adults have either worked out ways to cope with these problems (like the belligerence and rough defensiveness of Dr. Trask) and have succeeded in spite of them, or the outcome has been more negative—in which case they may have *additional* problems. At this point, they come into your life as your spouse, your colleague, your employee or employer, your friend, and so on, and you must now interact with them.

There are four strategies you can use to make things go more smoothly for touch dominant adults and everyone around them: awareness; talking touch; supplementing with touch; and improving the language environment.

Awareness

✦ Always keep in mind the fact that the person is touch dominant.

The reason this is so important is that it makes it possible for you, when you find yourself irritated by a TD person, to put that irritation on hold while you investigate the possibility that the problem is in the language. Think about how you react when you have a problem with someone who obviously doesn't speak English very well. You don't leap to the conclusion that the difficulty is deliberate obnoxious behavior; you think, "Maybe he/she doesn't understand." Staying aware of someone's touch dominance will give you that same sort of detachment.

When you find yourself reacting to the touch dominant person negatively, *stop* for just a minute. Ask yourself: "Is he really being uncooperative, or am I reacting to his touch language?" "Is she really unable to get along with anybody in the department, or are we just reacting badly to her touch dominance?" "Is he really yelling at our kids because he's mean, or is his touch dominance making it hard for him to get his meaning across?" "Is she really refusing to talk to me because she doesn't love me as much as she used to, or is she just having trouble talking because the tension is locking her into touch mode?"

Often this practice, *all by itself,* goes a long way toward removing the rough spots in relationships. The fact that *you* don't react with immediate annoyance often makes it possible for the touch dominant person to relax. Remember: Touch dominance is usually a problem for adults only in situations of tension and stress. With decades of rejection and misunderstandings behind them, TD adults tend to *anticipate* a negative reaction, to recognize it instantly when they run into it, and to conclude on the spot that things are going to go badly from then on. This can make almost *every* interaction with another human being stressful for them. Your demonstration that a negative reaction isn't inevitable will improve matters, and may head off many otherwise likely disagreements and arguments.

Talking Touch

✦ Use touch mode when you talk with a touch dominant person, if possible—and avoid sight and hearing mode.

Using touch mode in your language interactions with touch dominant adults, and carefully avoiding eye and ear vocabulary when possible, will help tremendously. (If you find it hard to think of touch mode vocabulary, use the lists in the workout sections of this book, along with any good dictionary, as a resource.) This may strike you as so simple and so trivial that it couldn't possibly make any difference; try it, all the same. It's free, it cannot do any harm, and it may work wonders. It can be especially useful when you are in a very close relationship with the person . . . when you have a touch dominant spouse, for example. If it doesn't seem to help, you can drop it anytime.

In my files I have scores of letters like this one (from a reader who asked to remain anonymous):

"There's a woman at my office that I'd always thought just loved to argue for the sake of arguing. Everything, no matter how trivial, turned into an argument when I had to deal with her. I had decided that she was a thoroughly obnoxious person, someone that I had to tolerate but that I would do my very best to avoid as much as possible. Then I read your description of touch dominance and realized that it <u>fit</u>! The next time I had to discuss something with this woman I made an effort to use all the touch language I possibly could—and the result was astonishing. Suddenly I was talking to someone just as reasonable, just as easy to get along with, as anyone else I work with. I have to admit that I only tried this out because I was desperate, but I'm so glad I did. It works every time; I just wish I'd known about it sooner."

Supplementing with Touch

✦ Provide touch-related resources.

Adults are long past the stage when you can be helpful by giving them your junk mail to play with. However, giving a touch dominant person something that emphasizes touch—equipment for doing a handicraft, for example, or a small carving or sculpture, or a scarf with a specularly interesting texture, or a class in one of the "bodywork" fields—is an excellent idea. The response to such a gift may surprise you; often the person will have wanted a gift of that kind for many years without ever having felt free to *ask* for it. And anytime you have the responsibility of choosing some object for the use of a touch dominant person, remember that they place high value on textured things and choose accordingly.

✦ Use lots of body language when it's appropriate and you feel comfortable doing it.

When it's appropriate to let a touch dominant person touch *you*, do so; it helps. Obviously, this isn't an option for you if you are someone who dislikes being touched; in that case, *tell* the TD person: "I'm one of those people who just doesn't like being touched; I want you to know that. It isn't anything personal. I'd feel the same way if you were the Prince [or the Princess] of Wales."

And remember that for many touch dominant people, *touching, much of the time, is only ordinary communication; don't leap to conclusions.* That is, before you conclude that what you're dealing with is a sexual overture, or sexual harassment, or even physical violence, ask yourself: "Am I misinterpreting this? Am I really facing sexual touch or violence, or is this just a touch dominant person having a hard time communicating?" You can still object to the behavior as strongly as you want to. But the way you feel *toward* the person should be different. For someone to deliberately come at you with unwanted sexual touch or with violence is one thing; for someone to use the same body language in an attempt to communicate is another. The distinction is important.

Touch dominant adults tend to divide into two groups with respect to touching other people. One group, in the opinion of the mainstream society, does far too much touching (and uses far too much body language, in every way). If you can do it without too much difficulty, it may help for you to explain to such people that their body language can be misinterpreted. The other group does almost no touching at all, behaving as if they were frozen or made of stone. This usually means that every attempt they made to touch others as they were growing up got an immediate "Keep your hands to yourself!" reaction, and they have concluded that it is *never* safe to touch. This pattern is especially common in big, husky males whose parents may have been forever cautioning them to be careful not to *hurt* people. The fact that they don't touch others doesn't mean that they don't want to; it means that they're afraid to. When such people *do* touch others, especially in a public place, it may indicate that they are under severe stress. In a situation like that, proceed cautiously.

Improving the Language Environment

We would all *prefer* to carry on our language interactions in a warm and pleasant atmosphere; that's only natural. For touch dominant adults, however, a good language environment is particularly helpful. Because as long as they aren't tense and under stress, their touch dominance won't get in their way, and they'll usually be able to use (and understand) sight and hearing modes easily. There are a number of techniques you can use to reduce stress and tension in language interactions. Matching sensory modes (and using nonsensory vocabulary when you can't find a match) is one that you already know. Let's take a brief look at another, quite similar, technique— using the Satir Modes.

Using the Satir Modes

Just as people communicating under stress tend to fall back on a preferred sensory mode, they tend to lock into one of *another* set of language behavior patterns, the Satir Modes. (These patterns come from the work of therapist Virginia Satir.) And just as you recognize a sensory mode automatically, you will recognize the Satir Modes once you read their descriptions; you, and everyone around you, use them all the time. Here are the characteristics of each Satir Mode, followed by a few example of utterances in that mode.

Blaming

Blaming has three major characteristics: an overall impression of anger; a heavy use of the personal vocabulary ("I, me, you, this department"); and extra emphatic stresses on words and parts of words. In addition, Blaming makes heavy use of words like "every, always, never, everybody, nothing." The body language that accompanies Blaming words is appropriately threatening; it includes frowning, glaring, pounding fists, jabbing index fingers, and so on. *Examples:*

"WHY don't you ever think about ANYbody but your-SELF?"

"You could at LEAST get to work on TIME once in a while!"

"You ALways try to make me look STUpid, DON'T you?"

"What's the MATTER with you? Can't you do ANYTHING RIGHT?"

"If THEY think that I'M going to put up with THIS garbage, THEY are in for a surPRISE!"

"NObody EVER wants to do anything I want to do!"

Placating

Like Blaming, Placating uses a lot of personal language and puts extra emphatic stresses on words and parts of words. The person who uses Placating may also rely heavily on the "always, every" words. The overall impression, however, is not anger; it's apology and a desire to please. Placating body language is deferential and apologetic; Virginia Satir said it reminded her of cocker spaniel puppies. *Examples:*

"Whatever everybody ELSE wants to do is okay with ME. ... YOU know me—I don't care!"

"Oh, I wouldn't THINK of picking the restaurant! Wherever YOU want to go is ALways okay with ME!"

"I'm so sorry, I KNOW this is a stupid QUEStion; but I really DO need to know—when do YOU want to leave?"

"You KNOW I'd never tell you what to DO, but you'll be sorry for the rest of your LIFE if you don't go to COLlege!"

Computing

Computing is very different from either Blaming or Placating. It uses as little personal vocabulary as possible, as little body language as possible, relies heavily on generalities and abstractions, and puts very *few* stresses on words and parts of words. The tone of voice, the gestures, and the facial expressions will be kept carefully neutral. (Think of Mr. Spock on *Star Trek*.) *Examples:*

> "There is undoubtedly a good reason for this delay."

> "Many people dislike green vegetables."

> "Lawyers sometimes fail to consider the wishes of clients."

> "People who forget to turn in their taxes should expect to have problems."

Distracting

Nothing new has to be learned for Distracting: it's a cycling through the other modes. A sentence of one, a sentence or two of another, with body language changing right along with the words. *Examples:*

> "WHY can't you EVer follow even the SIMPlest diRECtions? Not that I care how long it takes to get to the party—YOU know ME, I'M always happy if YOU'RE happy! But ANYbody knows better than to start out for the SUBurbs without EVen taking a MAP! People who do that are sure to get lost."

Leveling

Leveling is what's left over; it's the simple truth, with the feeling and the words and the body language all in harmony. If someone communicating under stress isn't using one of the other four Satir Modes, the language is Leveling. *Examples:*

> "When you don't follow instructions, it bothers me."

> "I like you, but I don't like your methods."

"My appointment was at six and it's six-thirty now; I'm going home."

The *words* used in Leveling can be identical to the words used in any other Satir Mode, but the tune they're set to (something that standard English punctuation conveys very badly) will be different. Compare these sentences:

1. "Why do you watch violent movies?"

2. "Why do you watch violent movies?"

3. "WHY do you watch VIolent MOVies?"

The words are the same in all three examples, but the tunes—*and therefore the meanings*—are quite different. Example #1 comes from someone who wants the answer to the question but feels neutral about it. Examples #2 and #3 aren't neutral. The extra emphases on "why" and "mov-" and "VI-" signal the emotional messages that are being added to the words, and we would hear them clearly in speech. The more such extra stresses there are, the more the emotional content; and the switch from underlining to capital letters indicates greater *intensity* of emotion. For English, here's the basic principle to remember:

> Almost all utterances that use the personal vocabulary and also contain extra stresses on words and parts of words are *hostile* language. (The exceptions are announcements and emergency messages, like "YOU just won the SWEEPstakes!" and "Look OUT! You're going to FALL!")

Language interactions are *feedback* loops: if you feed them, they will grow. Responding to hostile language with more hostile language will increase the hostility every single time. By carefully choosing your Satir Mode—instead of letting the choice be a matter of habit or just a knee-jerk reaction to

94

someone else's language—you can greatly decrease the tension in the language environment around you. All you need to know in order to make good choices are the usual consequences of Satir Mode loops, as follows:

- Blaming back at Blaming guarantees a fight.

- Placating back at Placating guarantees undignified delay ("YOU pick!" "Oh, no—YOU pick!")

- Because both Blaming and Placating are hostile language, Blaming back at Placating (or vice versa) is going to create a hostility loop, always.

- Computing back at Computing also means delay, but it's a dignified delay.

- Distracting loops are panic feeding panic.

- Leveling back at Leveling is the simple truth going both directions.

Unlike your sensory mode preferences, which are pretty much a permanent characteristic by the time you're five, your Satir Mode preferences change with your situation. You may prefer to handle tension and conflict by Blaming when you're at work but by Placating when you're at home, for example, or the other way around. Many people react to tension in interactions with doctors by Placating but routinely switch to Blaming when the health professional is a nurse. We have far more control over our Satir Mode choices than over our sensory modes. To keep the tension and stress low in your language environment, as a way of helping the touch dominant adults who are present, follow these simple rules:

1. Avoid hostility loops.

2. When you're not sure which Satir Mode to choose, go to Computer Mode and stay there until you have a good reason to change.

You will be amazed at how much easier communication with touch dominant persons will be when you use the sensory mode and Satir Mode techniques. It's well worth the effort involved.

What About That "Official Translator" Role?

You'll remember that touch dominant adults often have someone serving as a sort of translator for them—following them around trying to smooth over the rough patches they've created, explaining and apologizing, telling other people, "He doesn't mean any of those awful things he says," or, "Don't pay any attention to the way she talks, it doesn't mean a thing."

You may *have* to take this role; sometimes it's necessary. But do it as little as possible. It's not *good* for touch dominant people. They either take excessive advantage of it and become overly dependent on you for the service (instead of making an effort to learn to cope with social interactions themselves) or resent it and feel that you're treating them as if they were inferior or impaired. When it *must* be done, keep it as *positive* as possible. It's just as easy to say "Allen sometimes sounds a little harsh, but he usually has the best of intentions" as it is to say "I know the way Allen talks is horrible, and it embarrasses everybody who knows him, but he can't help it, and he doesn't really mean it."

You can also do some translating in the *opposite* direction. If your relationship with the touch dominant person allows it, explain what touch dominance is and what its typical consequences are. You can suggest reading this book, or talk about its contents. And you can go over unpleasant incidents in which touch dominance has interfered with communication and help to straighten them out, without preaching or being patronizing. Like this, in touch mode:

"Remember when you talked to Mrs. Hepplewhite this morning and she got so chilly and sort of walked out on you? I have a feeling that it was because you told her that her proposal was 'like a kick in the gut.' There must be another way to put that if it ever comes up again. How about, 'Your proposal wasn't exactly what I was expecting'?"

It's typical for touch dominant adults to know very little about what it *is* in their words and body language that has offended someone or made the other person uneasy. If you had a French-speaking friend whose English was a little shaky, and you were present when those weak English skills caused an unpleasant confrontation that left your friend distressed and mystified, you wouldn't hesitate to explain. *You would tell your friend that the English used had been understood to mean something other than what was intended.* Explanations of communication breakdown due to touch dominance are exactly the same thing, on a smaller scale.

However, you may discover that your explanations and translations only cause resentment, even when you bend over backward not to be patronizing or judgmental. Long experience with rejection makes some TD adults overwhelmingly "touchy." In that case, it's best not to struggle; offer help only when the TD individual has asked you for it.

It's very important to resist the idea that touch language is *"wrong"* because it's "crude" or "ignorant" or "uneducated" or "colloquial" or anything else of that kind, for at least these two reasons:

- A touch dominant person with a Ph.D. or a medical or legal or engineering degree is just as likely to use this sort of language as one who didn't finish high school. Highly educated TD adults may have a larger vocabulary and far more knowledge about what words and phrases are considered "elegant," but their decisions about when to put that knowledge to use are still personal ones. (Remember Dr. Trask in Scenario Five.) And in a crisis they may lose track of their coping strategies altogether.

The idea that a word or phrase that's unfashionable is therefore "wrong" is a distortion of the facts. It's not only not *morally* wrong, it's not grammatically wrong either. For someone to say "I tree the climbed" instead of "I climbed the tree" is a grammatical error; saying "I get it" instead of "I understand it" is only a fashion error. There's no logical or scientific reason for such preferences, any more than there is for preferences in hemlines or necktie styles.

This is far from a trivial matter. It's not a digression from our topic. Whether anyone should consider another person inferior because the individual *is* crude or ignorant or uneducated is a subject for a different book entirely. But these negative labels get attached to touch dominant persons *on the basis of language alone* even when they are totally unjustified, and that can create major misunderstandings.

The sight and hearing dominant majority needs to understand that, and to realize that although formality and "usage" may be *their* basis for choosing between "I can't put my finger on the problem" and "I can't identify the source of the difficulty," TD adults may choose the former simply because it's touch language. Understanding this is especially important when the TD adult has long since *accepted* the negative labels and truly believes that his or her touch vocabulary is something to be ashamed of. Those who are in frequent interaction with such people need to be able to make it very clear that this is a misconception and that it's not a prejudice they share.

Sight and hearing dominant adults rarely find touch dominant adults easy to deal with, and vice versa; relationships between the two are often rocky. But knowing what the problem is—instead of assuming that the other person is deliberately being uncooperative or malicious or

98

obnoxious—usually improves matters substantially. And the strategies described in this chapter will always help.

Are There Special Touch Dominance Problems Linked with Gender in Adults?

The gender-linked problems faced by touch dominant adults are basically more intense versions of those that emerged when they were children. Boys are more likely to have their touching misinterpreted as violent or erotic than girls are, but touching by girls is still disapproved of and may be misunderstood; this is even more true for adult males and females. The "mannish" woman faces the same sort of social quandaries and potential rejections as the "tomboy" girl; the "rough" man has the same sort of problems as the "rough" boy. By the time touch dominant people of either gender reach their teens, they usually know these problems well and can anticipate to some extent what they will be like in adulthood.

Negative or uneasy reactions to homosexuality are so prevalent in our society today that people have become hypersensitive. Same-sex touching that no one would have thought twice about in previous generations is very risky today for those who are *not* gay—but that problem is only slightly more awkward for men than for women. Two young women who hold hands in public are just as likely to be assumed to be gay as two young men. *Elderly* women can still do far more touching than young ones (and far more touching than elderly men), but it's often unwelcome, especially across the generations.

I believe that the problems touch dominant adults face because of their sexual gender alone differ only in degree, at least at the present time.

Now, suppose the hospital administrator in Scenario Five had been familiar with the information in this book. Could he have used it to make his encounter with the touch dominant surgeon less disastrous? Let's explore that possibility.

Another Look at Scenario Five

Remember Mason Lassiter's opening? He said, "Look, Kenneth, it's clear to me that this is just a communication problem. But you have to at least <u>try</u> to see it from the patent's point of view." That utterance has four sight mode items: *look, it's clear, see, point of view*. It's overwhelmingly sight dominant language. Using it when he's involved in a tense interaction with someone he already knows he has difficulties with is a strategic error. Let's rewrite it in touch language (or nonsensory language) and then go on with the rest of the dialogue in the scenario in the same way.

Mason: "Kenneth, I feel sure that this is just a communication problem. But you have to at least make an effort to perceive the situation the way the patient does."

Kenneth: "Oh? Why?"

Mason: "Because she is going to sue both you and the hospital if you don't, Kenneth."

Kenneth: "She doesn't have a case, Mason. She's a nut!"

Mason: "That may be. But even if she loses, it will cost us. I know you understand that there's no such thing as a free lawsuit, and I know I can count on you to pull your weight and help us out of this rough situation."

Kenneth: "Couldn't she come to my office so we could go over all this and try to straighten it out?"

Mason: "Well, what's your feeling about that? How have you and Mrs. Crandall gotten along in the past?"

Kenneth: "I guess I always rub her the wrong way, Mason."

Mason: "According to her lawyer, she feels like you always insult her."

Kenneth: "Mason, I don't get it. Before I got my hands on Marta Crandall she could hardly breathe, and now she's back on her feet and strong as a horse. How come what comes out of my mouth matters more to her than *that* does?"

Mason: "Maybe you went a little over the line, Kenneth."

Kenneth: (Sighs.) "I guess I did. I'm sorry. I didn't *mean* to hurt her feelings."

Mason: "I know you didn't."

Kenneth: "Well, what do you want me to do?"

Mason: "I've got a list of the things that seem to have set her against you, Kenneth. I'd like to go over them with you and find out exactly what you were trying to get across to her. Maybe then I could meet with her and do something to smooth things out a little. Okay?"

Kenneth: "I've got surgery in ten minutes. Can we do it this afternoon . . . about four?"

Mason: "That's fine with me."

Much better. And there may be some hope of heading off the lawsuit after all.

Mason Lassiter used several wise strategies in this rewrite:

1. He used touch mode when possible and avoided sight and hearing mode at all times.

2. He was careful to keep his language neutral and to avoid either Blaming or Placating. Notice: In both versions he told Kenneth that the patient was likely to sue both the doctor and the hospital—but in the rewrite he got rid of the extra emphatic stresses and other body language that would signal hostility and make Kenneth more tense.

3. He made an effort, in touch language, to express his own support for Kenneth, in "I know I can count on you to pull your weight . . ." and in agreeing with the doctor's claim not to have intended to be insulting.

The messages the administrator had to deliver were no less negative in substance than in the original version, but he found ways to express them that made the discussion with the surgeon less stressful for both of them and made it possible for them to take the useful step of setting up an appointment to discuss the problem together. This is a major improvement.

Workout Section Five

◆

1. You've been building a database of information about touch dominance, either because you are yourself TD or because you need it in your interactions with others who are. I suggest adding to it a set of pages like this:

TOUCH DOMINANCE INCIDENT LOG

Date: _____ Time: _____

Place: _____

People Involved: _____

_____

Situation: _____

_____

Touch Language That Was Used: _____

_____

What Was Said Next: _____

_____

_____

_____

_____

_____

[Repeat this line as many times as necessary.]

The Outcome: _____

_____

_____

What I Might Do Differently If This Happens Again: ____

_____

_____

Comments: _____

_____

_____

Whether you are the touch dominant speaker in these incidents or the person talking *to* the TD speaker, keeping a record of them is useful. It's easy to lose track of exactly what happens in cross-dominance interactions; a written record is your best move.

(It's also useful to have a record of the same kind to keep track of incidents involving the Satir Modes, even when touch language isn't directly involved. Just change "Touch Dominance" and "Touch Language" to "Satir Mode.")

2. Make a list of (a) the two or three dozen key words that you use most frequently in your work, and (b) the dozen or so sentences coming up most often in your work that frequently lead to tension, verbal confrontations, and the like. Then find touch mode equivalents for them if that's possible (it may not be, especially for technical terms!) and learn them, so that you'll have them on the tip of your tongue when they're needed. When no touch equivalent seems to exist, try to find a phrase or sentence you could use to explain, or to work around, the problem.

3. Sight and hearing dominant people often tell me that they find it hard to believe that they'll be able to spot touch dominant speakers. They say, "Won't it be a pretty subtle effect?" It's not subtle, and the more tense the TD speaker is, the more obvious it will be. I came home one day and found the following message on my answering machine:

"I've got your book and I feel like it's really what I need, but I'm having a hard time getting my hands around some of the material. Maybe you could give me a call? I wouldn't mind letting some of my co-workers in on it, I want you to know." When I returned the call, this person—instead of "My secretary isn't here"—said, "I haven't got my secretary here—can you hold on?" and then, "Reading the stuff is okay, but I feel like what's important is *doing* it, and that's kind of *hard*."

This is typical communication from a touch dominant adult who is uneasy or under stress. It not only isn't hard to spot, it's hard to *miss.*

4. The April 11, 1991, issue of the *New York Daily News* carried a story reporting that St. Luke's Hospital, on the city's Upper West Side, has more than seventy-five "Baby Holder volunteers." The Baby Holders are adults of both genders and all ages, from all walks of life, who come in to the hospital to help hold and carry and touch infant patients. (Under staff supervision, of course.) The program was founded by Virginia Crosby, director of volunteer services at St. Luke's. If your city has a Baby Holder program, you might join it; if it doesn't, consider contacting a local hospital about setting one up. Given the evidence that babies who don't get enough human contact fail to thrive, and the limited time hospital staff members have for such contact, there's a real need for volunteers to help out—and it's good for the volunteers as well.

5. The human brain is not able to distinguish between a sensory perception from "outside in the real world" and an imagined one, if the imagined one is vivid enough. That's why imagining that you are biting into a raw lemon and slowly swallowing the lemon juice makes your jaw ache. Your brain can't distinguish between a "real" experience of biting into a lemon and an "imaginary" one, and it sends out the same neurological messages in both cases.

The technique of using vividly imagined perceptions for relaxation, stress reduction, and healing is called "creative visualization" (notice the sight-bias in the term) or "creative imagery." Typically the instructions for the technique are heavily sight dominant, with just an occasional reference to other sensory systems; the only tool we have for constructing such perceptions is language. Touch dominant people often lose out on this powerful technique and say "I can't do that; I can't see pictures in my head!"

Here are four sets of instructions I use to show how the imagery technique can be adapted for the touch dominant. All have been thoroughly tested, and I am told that even people totally convinced that they "can't DO that!" find that they can do these with ease. The instructions are brief, and users should feel free to add many more details, from any of the sensory systems; the more details they contain, the more vivid they are.

a. *You're walking a tightrope between two trees, about six inches off the ground (so there's no need to be afraid of falling). Feel your feet on the rope as you move along. Each time you set a foot down or lift it up, be aware of the sensation(s) you feel in the foot and the adjustments your body has to make to stay balanced. Go back and forth as many times as you like.*

b. *You're swimming—having a wonderful time—through a substance that you find pleasing: warm or cool water; blackberry jam; baby powder; sand; your choice. You don't have to worry about breathing or effort, you just swim along through it easily and gracefully. Put your attention firmly on the way the substance you chose for your "sea" feels on your skin, all over your body, as you swim.*

c   *You're going to be carrying a "phantom" bowl on your head, filled with anything you want to put into it. (If you'd rather carry a basket, pitcher, or other container, that's fine.) Feel the items you fill it with as you*

106

put them into the bowl . . . fruit, flowers, stones, liquids, little carved figures, foods, anything that pleases you. Notice their weight and shape and temperature and texture. When the bowl is full, lift it up and settle it on top of your head, so that it's comfortable. Be aware of its weight on your head; be aware of the adjustments you make with your head and neck and body to keep it balanced as you walk or carry out other activities. . . . When you're ready, take the bowl off your head and "unpack" it for next time.

d. *You are a broad ribbon of velvet, draped over the back of your favorite chair (or a limb of your favorite tree, or any other support that pleases you). You are absolutely relaxed and absolutely safe and totally comfortable. . . .*

Touchpoints

1. "Rosalind Gefre, a certified massage therapist in St. Paul, Minnesota, finds that many of her clients come to her with psychological aches as well as physical ones. 'People are skin-hungry,' she says. 'They need to be touched.' . . . Besides being a bodyworker, Gefre is also a nun. Her clients call her Sister Rosalind."

> ("Bodywork and Soul," by Barbara Grace-Pedrotty, *In Health,* January/February 1995, p. 26. Sister Rosalind is a member of the National Association of Bodyworkers in Religious Service; for information, contact M. Wamhoff, NABRS, 7603 Forsyth Boulevard, Suite 214, St. Louis, Missouri, 63105. Another source for information on various systems of bodywork is Somatic Educational Resources, 1516 Grant Avenue, Suite 220, Novato, California, 94945; among other things they publish "Somatics: Magazine-Journal of the Bodily Arts and Sciences.)

2. "Most striking of all is the discovery that the cells on the surface of our skin, once thought to be a purely passive defense against the outside, play a major role in the functioning of the immune system. . . . We now know that the skin is both a key element in the immune system and a chemical conversion factory that rivals the liver."

> ("More Than Skin Deep," by Albert Rosenfeld, pp. 15–17, *Science Illustrated,* August/September 1988; on p. 17. The headline for this article reads, A RASH OF NEW EVIDENCE INDICATES THAT OUR HIDES ARE HOTBEDS OF VITAL CHEMICAL AND IMMUNOLOGICAL ACTIVITY; we learn that there's a new medical field called "immunodermatology.")

3. "The word *touch* and its common synonyms, *feel* and *contact*, refer to a complex set of sensations that can be narrowly or broadly conceived. Although touch often refers to cutaneous sensations aroused by stimulation of receptors on the skin, sensations of the muscles and joints (proprioceptive sense) and sensations of movement (vestibular sense) are closely linked. Moreover, the experience of touch is complex, encompassing as it does separate sensations of warmth, pressure, pain, weight, location, and so on."

("Preterm Responses to Passive, Active, and Social Touch," by Susan A. Rose, Ph.D., pp. 90–100, Brown 1984; on p. 90.)

Talking Touch

1. When you've done something well, you may:

feel ten feet tall	feel ten pounds lighter
be full of joy	get carried away about it
go off the deep end	give it another go
feel that it's a load off your shoulders	feel you've made a powerful impression

2. When you don't want to do something, you may . . .

wiggle out of it	fail to put your mind to it
put it off	put it out of your mind
put it aside	feel like you're in a vise
let it slide	try to get it off your back
not be up to it	feel like you're in a bind
refuse to tackle it	chew it up and spit it out

run away from it	push yourself to do it
take a walk	wish it were out of your hands
grit your teeth and do it	try to put a different spin on it

3. When people argue with you, you may . . .

feel they're being heavy-handed	cut them off
break off the conversation	feel choked up
let it run off your back	throw up your hands
try to make a strong case	feel boxed in
try to get around them	stick to your position
feel on edge	feel pushed around
get hot under the collar	freeze up
draw a line in the sand	stand your ground
wish you could get along	be in a tight spot
handle them with kid gloves	clench your fists

4. Japanese has a wonderful touch word: *sukinshippu*. (The English is of course "skinship.") It's a term for the intimate touch of skin on skin, especially between mothers and children; it's found in Kittredge Cherry's *Womansword: What Japanese Words Say About Women*, Kodansha America, Inc., 1987. I know no reason why we could not "borrow" it back and extend its use to fathers and to others.

CHAPTER SIX

✦

Making Things Smoother if *You're* Touch Dominant

In the first five chapters of this book, the "how to do it" sections have all been addressed to people who are not themselves touch dominant. Now I'm going to turn that around. The "you" in this chapter is the touch dominant reader, and I will be doing my best to put the information down *in touch mode* everywhere that that's doable.

Scenario Six

Cynthia had worked hard to get ready for this morning's presentation, leaving no stone unturned. She had gathered every chunk of information she could possibly need. She had carefully worked out all the opposing positions the others might take; she had made sure there were no rough edges in her arguments. She was determined to get her message across and win them all over to her side.

She waited patiently until they were all seated around the table. Lenny and Maria from the sales department; Steve and Phil from marketing; and Howard, representing management. Not exactly an easy group to win over, but better than what she'd been up against in the past.

"Okay if we get started?" she asked.

"Sure," Howard said, and the others nodded.

"You've all got information packets in front of you," she told them, "but if there's anything you can't find, just let me know. I'm all set to answer any questions you've got."

And then she took a deep breath and started telling them why they really *needed* a company newsletter, what it should have in it, and why they should let *her* put it together. She didn't get far.

"Where's your dummy issue, Cynthia?" Maria asked her, about four sentences into the presentation. "I'll understand this a lot better if I can see what you have in mind."

"It's in your infopack," Cynthia answered.

"Where?"

Cynthia leaned across the table, pulled the sheet of paper out of Maria's folder, and handed it all back. "Here," she said, patting the sheet. "Right here."

Darn, she thought as they all started hunting for their copy of the page she'd given to Maria. *I'll have to start over once they're all settled down again!*

"This is it?" Howard held up the sheet of paper between his thumb and index finger. "This is all you have to show us?"

Cynthia's heart sank. It happened every time. She would plan what she was going to say right down to the second, polishing it until it was perfect, and then, when she got into the meeting, people kept breaking into her talk and getting in her way.

"Everything's there, Howard," she said, trying not to sound as cross as she felt.

"This is just <u>notes</u>, Cynthia," he snapped. "We need to see a prototype, not a page of vague ideas and doodling."

"I can explain every word on that sheet," she protested. "I

was getting ready to expand on it when Maria cut me off! And if you'd let me—"

"Wait just a minute," Howard said, interrupting her again. He turned to the others. "What about the rest of you? What do you think? Can we discuss this project without seeing at least one sample issue?"

"Howard!" Cynthia was angry now, and she didn't feel like trying to hide it any longer. "You don't need anything else! I'm going to take up each one of the sections that's on that sheet and give you all the details about it. . . . Come on— nobody told me I had to put a sample together! Give me a chance!"

"Cynthia, I'm sorry," Lenny said. "I have to agree with Howard, and I think I'm speaking for all of us. We really do have to see what you're planning, or this is all a waste of time."

"You don't know that!" she shouted at him. "You didn't even let me get started! You're not being fair!" And she slammed her stack of notes down on the table so hard that half of them fell off onto the floor.

That was a mistake; she knew it the minute she did it. She'd been so hurt that she'd forgotten about staying cool. The looks she hated so much were on everybody's faces now . . . the ones that told her how crude and melodramatic she was, how low-class, how un*couth* by comparison with their high-and-mighty majesties. . . .

Give up, Cynthia, she told herself. *Just give it up. They all get too big a kick out of putting you down to ever level the playing field for you.* She felt so stupid . . . why had she made a fool of herself *again?* She said nothing; there wasn't anything to say that wouldn't have just dug her deeper into the hole she'd gotten herself into. And she was quite sure that she was meant to hear Steve's jab as they were filing out through the door: "How could she possibly not have known she needed to show us a sample? Does she spend all her time under a rock, or what?"

He was right, she thought; she should have known. It was *stupid* of her; anybody else would have known, that was obvious. But why couldn't they just let her *tell* them, and get some kind of agreement, before she went any farther? Why did they have to be so picky and domineering? Why was there never any way to do anything except *their* way?

◆

What's Going on Here?

Cynthia's Perceptions of the Situation

Cynthia is touch dominant, with hearing as her second choice; how things look is absolutely unimportant to her. She put a lot of effort into getting ready for the meeting in the scenario; she worked hard, and she feels that she deserved a chance to demonstrate that. And she feels that she's been given a rough time by a group of rigid, stuck-up people who don't like her and will go out of their way to make things hard for her. It seems to her that they waited till they got to the meeting, hunted through the folder until they knew what was in it, and then demanded something *else*—not because it was anything important but because they knew they could use it to break off the meeting and put her down. In Cynthia's opinion, what matters is what would go in the newsletter and how it would affect people; what difference does it make how it would *look*? She wasn't suggesting that they let her do a *fashion* magazine, after all!

Cynthia probably won't try to go any farther with this; it's too painful and too risky, with the deck so obviously stacked against her.

Her Colleagues' Perceptions

The people Cynthia wanted to persuade perceive the world very differently; before they can take her newsletter proposal seriously, they really *do* have to see a sample issue. Furthermore, they consider that so overwhelmingly obvious that they are genuinely unable to believe it wasn't obvious to Cynthia, too. It seems to them that the problem is laziness—that she doesn't want to go to the trouble of creating a prototype issue until they've committed themselves. They can understand that. Sure, *anybody* would like to have people solidly behind them without being forced to go through the preliminaries! But that's not how it's *done,* and they resent Cynthia's wasting their time trying such a childish trick. They're not about to go into another meeting with her—she can get somebody else next time. And they wonder . . . what on earth makes someone like Cynthia think she can write a newsletter, anyway?

You've been there, right? You've done that. Maybe you haven't been in exactly Cynthia's situation, maybe you haven't made exactly the mistake she made—but the rest of it is familiar. And you will be wondering . . . why couldn't those other people have cut Cynthia a little slack? There was plenty of time to work out the format and graphics for the newsletter; somebody could have given her a hand with that. Why didn't they let her finish what she had to say before walking out on her?

You're right. They *should* have done all those things. The problem is that Cynthia rubs them the wrong way and always has; they go into any meeting with her *expecting* it to go badly, and of course they find what they're expecting to find. If Cynthia didn't have skills that are truly valuable to the firm, she would have been replaced long ago, because the perception is that she makes *no* effort to get along with other people. Because they "know" in advance that Cynthia will go out of her way to be irritating and difficult, they never give her the sort of help and courtesy they would routinely give someone else. And every time something like the mess in the scenario happens, it locks this pattern more tightly into place.

You can't turn into the person that sight and hearing dominant people want you to be, nor is there any reason why you *should*. There are things you can do, however, that will help you avoid getting into a rut like the one that is about to swallow up Cynthia and her career forever. In what follows below we will go over some of them, to find out how you can put them to use in your own life.

Making *Your* Life Go More Smoothly

If you are a touch dominant person, get a firm grasp on the information in this book and put it to constant use. (You already know all about what it's like to *be* touch dominant, of course; but most of the other material may be new to you.) You have at least five ways to make the information work for you: awareness; deliberate strategic use of sensory modes and Satir Modes; explaining; using Miller's Law; and supplementing with touch.

Awareness

The problem you're up against in your contacts with eye and ear dominant people—who make up the majority of the population in the United States today—can be boiled down to this: OFTEN, YOU RUB THEM THE WRONG WAY. Not because of any of the things that you may have thought were responsible. Not because of your physical appearance or the way you dress, or the car you drive, or your social status, or your educational background. You rub people the wrong way because your language behavior differs from theirs and they find it hard to understand and perceive you accurately when there's tension in the air—which, in today's society, is far too much of the time. It's much like the problems some people are burdened with because they speak English with an unfashionable *accent*. You need to keep this firmly in mind at all times.

When you find yourself facing irritation or a chilly pulling away from you in others, your first reaction is likely to be one of these:

- *"Something's wrong with me!"*:

  "Oh, yeah ... it's because I'm overweight" or "because my grammar's not good" or "because I'm short" or "because I didn't go to college."

- *"Something's wrong with her (or him)!"*:

  "Oh, yeah ... it's because he thinks he's better than anybody else" or "because she gets a kick out of picking on people" or "because they think they're superior to anybody who doesn't make as much money as they do" or "because he's a creep."

You need to make a new rule for yourself: that before you leap to such conclusions you will stop just for a second and ask yourself: *"Is this person reacting negatively to my touch language? Is that what's causing the problem?"* And remember that language isn't just your words: It's everything you say or do that transmits a message. When you think, "It can't be anything I'm saying—I haven't even opened my mouth yet!" remember that in English more than 90 percent of all emotional information, and more than half of *all* information, is carried not by words but by body language. When it's not your words, it may be the expression on your face, or a gesture you've made, or the way you're sitting or standing, that triggers the uneasy reaction.

It may also be that you've done more touching than the other person finds acceptable. Many touch dominant people touch *before* they talk—they grab a shoulder, or put their hand on an arm, for example. Sight and hearing dominant people are often put off by this before a word is spoken, and they may misinterpret your touch as a sexual overture or an attempt at physical force. You may feel that this is ridiculous; you may be *right*. But the fact that you don't mean anything by it when you do this sort of casual touching is irrelevant if your goal is improved communication. Because other people will base their behavior toward you on what they *think* you mean, regardless of your intentions; and they can't read your mind.

It's also important to remember that the most powerful part of body language is *tone of voice*. Your words may be completely innocuous. You may have bent over backward to be careful that the rest of your body language is restrained. Nevertheless, if your tone of voice makes other people think of physical contact . . . if it sounds pushy and overbearing, or sensual or intrusive . . . it becomes a kind of *touching at a distance*. This can be an advantage when you're talking to someone who welcomes your touch, but that will be a small set of people; much of the time it will put people on their guard against you.

You may find it useful (with the permission of the people around you) to tape an hour of your conversation and listen to yourself; if you have the equipment to *videotape* yourself in conversations, that's even better. You may feel that people who consider your body language too intimate are imagining the whole thing—but when you see and hear yourself in a video, you may suddenly realize that they're picking up cues you didn't know you were handing out.

I once had a client who was a paramedic, and whose problem was that he *scared* his patients. He was very careful to speak gently and to use only nonthreatening words and phrases. Nevertheless, when he moved to put people on a stretcher to take them to the ambulance (or do any other of the physical tasks he needed to do for them), he could tell that they were alarmed. They would pull away from him or put their hands up to fend him off—or worse. "What am I doing *wrong?*" he wanted to know; he was completely baffled.

He wasn't doing a single thing "wrong." However, when we watched and discussed a videotape of him in action, he understood why he was having this difficulty. With very little help from me he grasped the fact that he moved toward people too quickly and too abruptly and with too much force. He *loomed* over people. He held his body—especially his shoulders and arms—like a fullback just about to knock another player flat. When his hands were at his sides they were frequently in fists; when he wasn't talking his face was often set in a frown. And this was all a surprise to him! He hadn't known he was doing it, and he didn't *feel* threatening or scary in any way. It took a lot of hard work for him to unlearn his "dangerous thug" style of body language so that his patients would trust him instead of fearing him.

You need two kinds of awareness. First, be aware that negative reactions in others may be for no other reason than your touch language; check that out. If the reaction is really due to something more serious, you'll find that out soon enough, but don't make it your *first* conclusion. Second, be aware that the majority of other people have never heard of touch dominance and may be as baffled by their reaction to you as you are. Often when I'm called in to do communication troubleshooting and touch dominance is involved, people say to me, "I don't know what it is about him [or her]! Every time I'm around him [or her], I get upset—and then afterward I realize that he [or she] didn't do anything!"

Deliberate Strategic Use of Sensory Modes and Satir Modes

Your choice when talking with others who are sight or hearing dominant is always simple: either stay in touch mode or switch to the sensory mode the other person prefers. Let's go over both choices.

Stay in Touch Mode

This choice is just fine. But remember that, except in casual communication, it will bring certain consequences with it. Set firmly aside your tendency to anticipate negative reactions and to read them into everything you see or hear. Be prepared to make an extra effort to get your messages across. You may have to do more explaining than seems reasonable; you may have to repeat yourself. You may need a good deal of patience. As long as you don't let this make *you* tense and uneasy, which would lead you into a hostility loop in most cases, it's no big deal; you will be able to communicate effectively. The problems come up when you blame the communication breakdowns and misunderstandings on the people talking instead of on their language—don't let that happen.

Switch to the Other Person's Preferred Sensory Mode

When you're under a lot of pressure, this may strike you as much too heavy a burden. Unfortunately, it's when you're under pressure that you're most likely to *need* to make this modification. You can do it—it's just a matter of getting yourself prepared and putting in some practice time.

Before you speak, ask yourself: "How would an eye or ear dominant person put this? What eye or ear words could I use in place of the ones I have on the tip of my tongue right now?" Sit down and make a list of half a dozen stressful situations that come up in your life over and over again—ones you know you'll have to keep dealing with over time. Write down the kinds of things people say in those situations and rewrite them using eye or ear language, so that you'll have lines ready to use when you need them. This will feel awkward at first, but remember: *Every item in the verbal and nonverbal vocabulary of sight and hearing is part of your own grammar of English, too.* You can do it, even under stress, more easily than you may think.

Many people in the United States use one dialect of English at home and another (usually "Standard" English) in the workplace; many speak an entirely *different* language, such as Spanish or Laotian or Navajo, in their private lives. Every single one of us uses several different registers (ways of talking tied to a particular role) in our lives. The ability to make these language changes—called *code-switching*—is one of the most valuable communication skills you can have. It means that *you* choose, on the basis of your own needs and goals, how you will speak in a given situation, and that you are equipped to make that choice and carry it out. Moving from one sensory mode to another is just another type of code-switching.

Satir Mode Choices

Where the Satir Modes are concerned, your best move will be obvious. Remember that what turns a minor tendency toward the use of touch language into a position of being *locked in* to touch language is tension and stress. Remember that one of the most common causes of tension and stress is hostile language. When you make deliberate strategic choices among the Satir Modes, using them to reduce tension and avoid hostility, you are taking a major step toward a language environment in which you're able to use all the sensory modes with equal or nearly equal ease. This will level the playing field for you and improve matters tremendously. You can use all of the Stir Mode material in this book to help you increase your skills with this technique.

Explaining

Remember the little boy in Scenario Two who told his sight dominant playmate that he needed to *hold* the game in his hands while he listened to the instructions for playing it? And said, "I need for you to go slow enough so I can do it while you're telling me, okay?" You can do that. When an interaction seems to be taking a wrong turn, say, "I don't feel like I've gotten my message across very well. Let me try again." With people you're close to, say, "I think what's getting in our way here is my touch language; I'd like to get around that if I can. Let's try it again." *Before* things get sticky, particularly in an interaction that you know will probably be stressful for those involved—a job interview, a request for a loan or a promotion, a personnel evaluation, a meeting that requires intense negotiation—explain. Say, "I'll be using a lot of touch language as I talk, because touch is the sense that works best for me and the one I rely on in tight spots. When it sounds strange to you, just say so—I'll try putting it another way." There'll be times when Leveling like that is unsafe or inappropriate; your own common sense will tell you which ones they are. When it *can* be done, however, it's useful.

Finally, don't hesitate to explain when someone has misunderstood you and the interaction has *really* gone wrong! When someone has obviously taken your touch (or touch language) as erotic or threatening, you risk being accused of sexual harassment or violence. Say, "I think I've offended you. I'm sorry; I didn't intend to do so. When I'm tense, I sometimes forget how other people feel about touch. Please accept my apologies." Keep your voice neutral and calm: Your goal is to explain, *not* to make excuses or to grovel. And above all, *back off!* You may feel that you can't get your message across unless you get very close, or unless you hang on to the offended person's arms or hands. Don't give in to that feeling. Step back, take a completely neutral position, and *change the subject.* Say, "Now, what time were you planning to schedule the meeting this afternoon?" That is, acknowledge your error, apologize calmly and briefly, and move on immediately to something else. It was no big deal; don't turn it into one.

Using Miller's Law

Psychologist George Miller once said something so important to good communication that I call it *Miller's Law.* He said:

"In order to understand what another person is saying, you must assume that it is true and try to imagine what it could be true of."*

We tend not to do this in our society; in fact, we tend to use what can only be called "Miller's-Law-in-Reverse." When we hear someone say something that strikes us as outrageous, we assume that it's *false* and we try to imagine what's wrong with the speaker that accounts for it having been said. This makes communication breakdown almost inevitable; it's a blueprint for misunderstanding. We need to get into the habit of using Miller's Law (and this is true for *all* of us, not just for the touch dominant).

Suppose you're a man who's just met a visiting company executive—a woman—at a reception where she opened the evening with a brief talk. You like her very much; you find her sharp and effective and interesting; and you seize the opportunity to tell her so. Suppose you say, "You're a knockout, you know that? You really got *to* me with that speech!" But instead of the smile and warm "Thank you" that you're expecting, she gives you an icy look and says, "You're wasting your time; I don't find that sort of thing appealing." Now what?

Now apply Miller's Law. Assume that what she said is true—she doesn't find that sort of thing appealing and you're wasting your time offering her that sort of compliment. What could that be true of? The answer will be obvious to you: It's true of a sight or hearing dominant person to whom touch language seems crude and threatening. Say, "I'm sorry; let me put that another way. Your speech was excellent; I enjoyed it tremendously." And then—unless she says something welcoming like "I'm sorry if I seemed hostile; I'm afraid it's been a very long day"—excuse yourself and move on. Remembering three things: that her initial reaction was not to *you* but to

*In Hall, Elizabeth, "Giving Away Psychology in the 80s: George Miller Interviewed by Elizabeth Hall," *Psychology Today*, January 1980, p. 46.

your language; that you understand what happened and why; and that when you encounter her in the future you'll know how to avoid a repetition of the unpleasantness.

Supplementing with Touch

The need you feel for touch data from your environment is natural and should be attended to. If you take care to fill that need you will be more at ease in the world, and that will make you easier to get along with. It's a very good idea to surround yourself with textures and shapes, with things that move and things that can be handled. I recommend taking up an activity that's heavy on touch, if you haven't already done so; this is especially important if you put in most of your time doing tasks for the eye and the ear.

When learning something is hard for you, try to find a way to input the same information in tactile form; if that's not possible, try for input through sound. Sound is closer to touch than sight is, and may prove helpful. One very simple strategy is to write down what you need to remember, in longhand; then, still in longhand, write it down in a touch language "translation." What you're trying to do is put a touch index in place in your memory for this particular set of data. Using touch vocabulary will help you do that, and the process of writing it out in longhand—a genuinely hands-on activity—will also help.

I want to close this section with one crucial point: The language behavior of touch dominance, though currently unfashionable, is in no way "wrong." It is extremely valuable. Our culture needs more, not less, emphasis on touch; we need to be in closer contact with our world and other people. Nothing that I have said in this book should be taken to mean that touch dominance is something to get *rid* of. On the contrary.

Remember that one of the most useful skills in this world is the skill of *code-switching*, the ability to switch easily and voluntarily from one variety of language to another and back again. The very direct style that's most comfortable for you is one code; the more distant style that's fashionable and approved of today is another. Using the language that is being used around you is no different than wearing clothing enough like what those around you wear to keep you from being conspicuous or offensive, something you do without giving it a second thought. Code-switching doesn't mean *abandoning* one sort of language for another, and it doesn't mean that one is better than the other. It's just a way to make deliberate strategic choices as to what will best achieve your goals in particular circumstances. The more different styles of communication you're good at, the more tools you have to communicate with. When you're able to switch easily in and out of all the sensory modes, using whichever one is most *handy* at the time, you have a valuable communication advantage.

Another Look at Scenario Six

In a perfect world, Cynthia's colleagues, knowing that she is a touch dominant person, would have made absolutely certain that she knew what had to be done instead of taking it for granted. One of them would have told her, straight out, that she could not expect to get and hold their attention for her presentation unless she arrived at the meeting with a sample issue of the proposed newsletter. In the less than perfect world we're stuck with, it's up to Cynthia to remember that *she's* the one who perceives the world differently from the majority and take steps to find *out* what she needs to do. Well in advance, she should go to two or three of the people who are coming to her presentation and *ask* them: "What do you need to have before you at the meeting? What can I bring for you to look over that will help you make a decision about my proposal?" And then she must follow through on the advice she gets.

It would also be wise for Cynthia to use all the sensory modes as she talks instead of relying so heavily on touch mode. Making a presentation is by definition stressful, and she may find it hard to use sight and hearing mode—but it would be wise for her to try. She can sit down in advance of the meeting, write down a list of the things she plans to say there, and write out sight and hearing mode translations that she can keep in mind.

Let's suppose that Cynthia has made these preparations. We can then rewrite the dialogue at the beginning of the scenario to reflect the change:

Cynthia: "It looks like everyone's here. Shall we start?"

Howard: "Please."

Cynthia: "All right. As you can see, each of you has an information packet. I tried to make those packets complete; you'll find all the background figures and statistics, some graphs, and a sample copy of the newsletter I believe we need."

Maria: "Great! Okay if we look at that while you talk?"

Cynthia: "Sure. Just remember that it's only meant to give you a rough idea of how it would look; it's not intended to be in final form. I'll be filling in the details as we go along. If anything's not clear, just tell me and I'll try to fix it. Now . . ."

This is better. Although Cynthia's right that the dummy issue is only a rough draft (and that's all it *should* be at this point), her sight dominant colleagues are far more comfortable when they have it there to look at. And the more comfortable they are, the better the chances for effective communication between them and Cynthia. She doesn't care how wide the margins are going to be or how much space will be between the columns of print or what the typeface will be; she cares about the content. But without those other items, she won't get to *do* the newsletter at all.

Finally, Cynthia is in a very good position in one way. If she were sight dominant, she might feel a strong attachment to the choices she made about the newsletter's appearance, even at the dummy-issue stage. Since she is genuinely indifferent to such things, it will be easy for her to accept the inevitable suggestions her colleagues will make about *changing* the looks of the newsletter. That will make them feel that she is cooperative and willing to consider their ideas as well as her own, and that's a plus—it will increase her chances for getting their final approval for her project.

Workout Section Six

◆

1. Go through all the "Talking Touch" sections in this book and turn them right around: Find a sight or hearing mode equivalent for each touch mode item. When it's possible, find both. (This is one time when *you* have the advantage, by the way. You've spent most of your life immersed in the eye and ear environment. It won't be nearly as hard for you to do this as it is for eye and ear people to move from sight and hearing modes to touch mode!)

2. Join the Touch Dominance Network™, which is located at the Ozark Center for Language Studies, P.O. Box 1137, Huntsville, Arkansas, 72740-1137 (or, by E-mail, ocls@sibylline.com). Consider setting up a local or regional chapter. The Network was founded in May 1994, and has two goals: to restore a more wholesome attitude toward touch in our culture, and to make things go more smoothly both for the touch dominant and for those who interact with them. It has a newsletter—the *Touch Dominance Quarterly;* by the time you read this it may have a computer network as well.

3. As a resource for describing and discussing wines, wine tasters can use a wheel created by Ann Noble, who teaches sensory evaluation at the University of California at Davis; it has 132 descriptive terms. The innermost part of the circle is divided into nine basic categories: *fruity, vegetative, earthy, chemical, woody, caramelized, microbiological, floral,* and *spicy.* Then each of those terms is divided into subcategories, which divide again, and so on out to the outside of the wheel. (If you'd like to get a close look at the wheel, it's on page 74 of the October 1985 issue of *Science.*) "Spicy," for example, is subdivided into "mint," "licorice," "black pepper," "cloves,"

and "cinnamon." We need a similar system for sorting *textures;* so far as I've been able to find out, none exists.

In the Spring 1995 issue of *Touch Dominance Quarterly* a first stab was made at setting up a "texture wheel," for which the innermost circle of categories would hold these ten terms: *smooth, sticky, patterned, irregular, slippery, rough, yielding, dry, hot, sharp.* What do you think of that set? Would you add others? Take some out? Make other changes? How would you subdivide each of the categories? The Touch Dominance Network would be very interested in getting your comments and suggestions.

4. Get a copy of the latest edition of Ashley Montagu's book titled *Touching: The Human Significance of the Skin,* published by Harper & Row. This is the most useful book for the general reader, and it will give you roughly five hundred pages of detailed information and references for further reading on the subject of touch. In the "Touchpoints" section below I have included several quotations from the third edition, and you will find others elsewhere in this book; I know no better basic source on touch, or anything that even comes close.

5. Many public libraries have on their shelves copies of the episodes of *Masterpiece Theater* shown on public television. Ask your library for a copy of the episode called "Glory Enough for All," which is the life story of Dr. Fred Banting, the discoverer of insulin. I have no way of knowing whether the real Banting was touch dominant; I *do* know that the human being in the dramatization is a perfect example of a touch dominant person.

6. One of the things you may find hardest to do is to learn a body of material that has no touch content. Like what you find in most books of philosophy, for example. As an experiment, choose something of that kind that you would like to learn and remember (something fairly short), and sit down and copy it out *in longhand* from be-

ginning to end. For many touch dominant people this process involves the body deeply enough in the information being written down to bridge the gap between sight/hearing data and the sense of touch. It will strike eye and ear people as an unbearable task because of the time and effort required, but for TD people it's often the *shortest* path to the goal.

Touchpoints

1. "Diverse qualities of touch may be viewed as symbols in a language of touch, just as word symbols create a verbal and written language for communication and shared meaning. . . . Six major tactile symbols . . . appear to create the language of touch. These six tactile symbols are: duration, location, action, intensity, frequency, and sensation. The symbols in no way attempt to define the circumstances surrounding the occurrence of touching, but rather define the act of touching itself as an independent channel of communication."

   ("The Language of Touch," by Sandra J. Weiss, pp. 76–80, *Nursing Research*, March/April 1979; on p. 77.)

2. "The child soon realizes that the culture does not trust body experiences; his education focuses on cultivating intellectual capacities, but his teachers insist that he control body impulses that are likely to 'break out' if not closely monitored. . . . For these reasons, the individual is likely to view his body as having alien qualities and to entertain numerous irrational notions about it."

   ("Experiencing Your Body: You Are What You Feel," by Seymour Fisher, *Saturday Review of Science*, July 8, 1972, pp. 27–32; on p. 28. I recommend asking your library to get this article for you if possible; it's worth the effort.)

3. "Actually there are several tactile senses, which are together subsumed under the term *touch:* these are often difficult to define. . . . We do, however, know of the elements that enter into touch, such as pressure, pain, pleasure, temper-

ature, muscle movement of the skin, rubbing, and the like; then there is the information we receive from our muscles, through the skin, when we move. The term haptic is used to describe that mentally extended sense of touch which comes about through the total experience of living and acting in space."

(Montagu 1986, pp. 14–15.)

4. "Consider: as a sensory system the skin is much the most important organ system of the body. A human being can spend his life blind and deaf and completely lacking the senses of smell and taste, but he cannot survive at all without the functions performed by the skin. . . . Among all the senses, touch stands paramount."

(Montagu 1986, p. 17.)

5. "The tactually failed child grows into an individual who is not only physically awkward in his relations with others, but also psychologically, behaviorally, awkward with them. Such persons are likely to be wanting in that tact which the *Oxford English Dictionary* defines as the 'Ready and delicate sense of what is fitting and proper in dealing with others, so as to avoid giving offense . . . the faculty of saying or doing the right thing at the right time.' "

(Montagu 1986, p. 286.)

6. "I recently surveyed virtually every medical school in the English-speaking world and discovered that only 12 of 169 gave any training whatsoever in touch beyond that needed for pulse-taking, palpation, and the like. With the excep-

tion of the University of Otago . . . no school allotted more than two hours in the entire curriculum to touch as a healing agent. . . . I believe that our doctors will be better healers when they are more skilled at, and more comfortable with, touch."

> ("Epilogue: Touch in All Ages," by Jules Older, Ph.D., pp. 155–62 in Gunzenhauser 1990; on p. 158.)

7. "From the alarm clock a spherical shock wave traveling at Mach 1 starts growing outward, spreading and spreading till it hits the wall. Some of the energy it carries causes the curtains over the window to heat up from the friction of the onslaught; much of the rest rebounds back, enters the ears of two sleepers, and finally rouses them awake.

   "There's a rolling of eyes and a stirring of head, then a female hand gropes out from under the security of the comforter, fumbles on the bedside table, finds the alarm clock, and clacks down the button on top to turn it off."

   > (David Bodanis, on p. 11 of *The Secret House: 24 Hours in the Strange and Unexpected World in Which We Spend Our Nights and Days,* Simon & Schuster 1986. I cannot recommend this book too highly; it's one I read again and again and never get tired of. Its wonderful pictures make it a treasure for sight dominant people, of course; but for the TD person, this book fills a unique function. It takes hundreds of phenomena that we ordinarily perceive as things to see and hear and turns them, miraculously, into *touch* phenomena.)

◆

CHAPTER SEVEN

The Special Problem of Touch Dominance in the Intimate Relationship

Scenario Seven

Jeanine lay with her head on Bryan's chest, still breathing hard. "That was wonderful," she said softly. "Thank you, love."

When he said nothing back, she raised her head to look at him. "Is something wrong?" she asked.

Bryan stared straight ahead, and although his arm was still around her, his voice was chilly. "Why should anything be wrong?"

Jeanine didn't answer. After all, what could she say? *I gave you a compliment, now I think you should give me one?* She knew how childish that would sound.

"Well," he said, "I'm late already, Jeanine. If you'll excuse me—"

135

She sat bolt upright, clutching the sheet around her. "If I'll EXCUSE you! What kind of a line is THAT?"

"Sorry!" he said abruptly, almost leaping out of bed, headed for the shower. But Jeanine wasn't willing to let him get away with it this time.

"Bryan!" she said. "You wait a minute!"

"Hey, I'm really late for—"

"I don't care what you're late for! This is the fourth or fifth time after we've made love that you've given me a cold shoulder like this ! I want to know what's wrong! What are you MAD at me about?"

Bryan stopped, but he kept his hand on the bathroom doorknob and he kept his back to her. "I don't want to talk about it, Jeanine," he said.

"Well, I do want to talk about it! Please!"

"I just wish . . ." He paused.

"You just wish what?"

"I just wish that when we're in bed you could try to be a little bit more . . ."

"Well?"

"A little bit more ladylike!" he snapped, and he was through the door and had closed it behind him before she could say a word. She heard the snap as he locked the door . . . as if she couldn't be trusted to respect his privacy.

Jeanine sat on the edge of the bed, trying not to feel the hurt, but it was no use. With tears pouring down her cheeks, she got up and pulled on her robe and went to the window; at least if he came out now he wouldn't know she was crying! *He sounds like my mother,* she thought miserably. It seemed to her that every third sentence from her mother, her whole life long, had been, "Jeanine, can't you at least try to act like a lady?" And now, when they'd been married only three months, she was hearing the same line from her *hus*band! *What am I going to do?* she wondered. *How can anybody be ladylike when they're making love? And since when is it out of line for a woman to be passionate with her husband??*

◆

136

What's Going on Here?

This is perhaps as wide a communication gap as anyone could imagine. Here we have two people who loved each other enough to marry and set up life together, but in their most intimate moments they are miles apart—and they're having no luck in their efforts to bridge the gap by talking about it.

The scenario shows us a touch dominant woman married to a man who is sight or hearing dominant and who finds her too aggressive in bed. There are three other likely versions of intimate sensory mode mismatch:

- Bryan is the touch dominant one, and Jeanine finds *him* too aggressive in his lovemaking, perhaps even perceives him as brutal and hurtful.

- Jeanine is touch dominant as in the scenario, but has learned such a strong personal "NO touching is safe!" rule that even when making love with Bryan she is unable to relax and move naturally—so that she is perceived as cold and uncaring, even frigid.

- Bryan is the touch dominant one, but after years of hearing "Don't touch! You'll <u>hurt</u> somebody!" he is unable to set the constraint aside even when making love with Jeanine—and *he* is the one who seems to have no interest in their sexual relationship.

When people are in the "honeymoon" stage, still deep in romantic love, they usually find one another perfect. It's not so much that they're willing to tolerate flaws as that they quite literally don't perceive any. But this stage is temporary! And when it's past, the shock of finding out that the beloved is human and has human failings can be severe. Touch dominant individuals of either gender may have serious problems in intimate situations, because their eye or ear dominant part-

137

ners consider them either too aggressive or too wooden. Behavior that seems like the most enthralling passion—or the most charming shyness—through New Love's rose-colored glasses may inspire distaste or resentment or even disgust after the glasses come off, as they inevitably will. And rejection that might be shrugged off when it comes from an acquaintance or a stranger is going to cut *deep* when it comes from an intimate partner.

This book is not a manual on improving sexual relationships; I will leave that topic to those who are authorities on the subject. What I *can* usefully take up here, however, is the relationship in which sexual difficulties like those described above are made worse—or impossible to solve—because the two people involved are unable to talk about the problem together and negotiate some sort of mutually acceptable solution. What the Bryans and Jeanines do in bed is not my field or my concern; how they use language in touchy situations like these *is*. Language (both verbal and nonverbal) is the only tool they have available for solving their problem, or at least improving matters enough to keep their marriage intact.

What You Can Do About It

You would think, from reading current fiction and watching today's films, that men and women can and do discuss every last detail of their sexual activities with complete ease and no inhibitions. It may be true that they can do that when they're talking about *other* people, but when they talk to their own sexual partners about their own sexual performance and practices, it's false. This is especially true when one person in the couple has negative feelings about the bedroom behavior of the other. It's not just a matter of being able to talk frankly or of not being prudish. Even the "hippest" lover knows that when you do a negative sexual critique of someone else's partner, you don't have to live with the consequences of the pain and embarrassment you cause; when it's your *own* partner, all the unpleasantness is part of *your* life. This is just as valid when the source of the problem is one partner's touch dominance as when it's physical appearance, disagreements about what is and what isn't "kinky," staying power, or any other of the many possible reasons for sexual discontent.

If you are part of a couple like Jeanine and Bryan, there *are* things you can do, steps you can take, in order to discuss your sexual difficulties frankly without doing one another irreparable harm. Let's go through a list of them and explore each one briefly.

✦ Begin by building a foundation of trust *outside* the bedroom.

If you spend your time together outside the bedroom tiptoeing uneasily around each other, always expecting something unpleasant to happen, always on guard, you can't possibly hope to discuss a subject as emotion-fraught as your sexual relationship. Before you do anything else, use the techniques in this book to decrease the tension and hostility between you, to build rapport, and to learn how to talk together successfully. *Then* take up the sexual issues. (There are rare couples whose only intimacy is sexual, who treat each other like acquaintances the rest of the time, and for whom this *works;* but they are people whose relationship is based upon sex. They won't be having bedroom problems.)

Sometimes the problem with communication in the home is the feeling that you don't *have* to make any effort in that environment. People will say things to me like "Listen, she's my wife—she loves me no matter <u>how</u> I talk!" and "I don't have to worry about how I talk when we're together—he's my husband. He <u>has</u> to talk to me" and "Hey, home is the only place I can just kick back and be myself!" As long as the two of you are passionately in love, as long as every word your partner says fascinates you just because it's coming from your partner's mouth, you may be able to get away with that attitude. When problems surface, however, it will fail you. One of the most amazing things about divorces in this country is the frequency with which people tell you that until the very instant when their partner said "I want a divorce"—or just up and left, without warning—they had no idea there was a problem. When two people in a couple are able to communicate with one another successfully, that cannot happen.

Use the techniques presented in this book. Match your partner's sensory modes. Use Miller's Law when your partner says things that strike you as outrageous. Respond to your partner's Satir Modes (and choose your own) according to the rules on page 95. These techniques, together with ordinary courtesy and the affection you feel for one another, will establish a foundation of rapport and trust that you can then use to tackle even the most delicate subjects.

◆ Write a letter, or make a cassette tape, that explains your feelings to your partner.

One of the problems with intimate discussions between couples is the problem of *face*. For men, the fear of not being perceived as The World's Best Lover is most likely to be the issue; for women, it's the fear of rejection, of not being perceived as The World's Most Irresistible Woman. Even when both know perfectly well that they can't claim those titles, having to be present when the other one comes right out with that judgment means an intolerable loss of face. It's easier to accept even very tender criticism when you can read it (or hear it) all by yourself.

There are other advantages to this method of communicating difficult messages besides the obvious fact that the letter or tape can be attended to in privacy. It can be gone over as many times as may be necessary for understanding. The person it's addressed to doesn't have to think of something to say *back* at a time when emotions are running high and talking may be dangerous. The letter or tape is concrete evidence that the sender cares enough and is concerned enough to make a real effort to set things right. All this is helpful.

However, there is *one* advantage that can also be a hazard. Spoken messages are often *mis*perceived, so that they turn into arguments over what, exactly, was or was not said. This isn't a problem when a permanent record is available on paper or tape—but if the message is badly done, it's *still* permanent. You handle this by following three guidelines:

1. Use Leveling or Computing only, without exception. Blaming and Placating have *no* place in messages of this kind.

2. Comment only on the *specific item of behavior* that you'd like to have changed—*not* on the person. Don't say, "You're too rough with me," or "You're so aggressive that I don't feel like I have any choice at all about what we do." Don't say "When we make love, you act like a [n] _____" or "when we make love, you make me feel like a [n] _____" unless what goes in the blank is something complimentary, like "the world's greatest lover" or "the world's most desirable woman." Say "It's scary [or distracting, or embarrassing] when you hold my shoulders so tightly that I can't move." (Or whatever item of behavior it may be that you feel distressed about and that is affecting your sexual relationship negatively.)

3. Write your letter (or record your tape) and go over it until you're sure it says what you want to say. *Then put it away for at least forty-eight hours, and go over it again before you pass it along to your partner.* If you've gone too far, if you've used language that you would regret later, if you've just put your case badly, this waiting period will provide you with the detachment you need to spot your errors and fix them.

✦ Make an *appointment* with your partner to discuss the problem in a neutral setting and at a neutral time.

This means that you approach your partner when you're both at ease—not in the middle of an argument or a sexual encounter—and you say, "I'd like to talk to you about a problem that's worrying us both; I'd like to try to straighten it out. How about tomorrow night?" and suggest the place and time. Since you know it will be a difficult discussion, don't try to hold it in a crowded restaurant or any other public place. Go for a drive while you talk, on a road where there's little or no traffic. Go for a walk in the woods together. Have a picnic— and take fast food, so that there's no chance of your meeting turning into an "I spent two HOURS fixing all this food and NOW you won't even EAT any of it!" argument. You know your own environment and circumstances; choose a place well away from the bedroom itself, a place where you and your partner can talk at length and in private, and choose a time that you both feel willing to set aside for this purpose.

People tell me that they don't dare have this discussion. That's up to them. But the consequences of not talking about it, even if they and their partners stay together, are almost certainly that they will grow more and more apart as time goes by. Sometimes the response to the explanation is going to be "I'm sorry you don't like my doing that, but you'll just have to learn to put up with it." In that case, you know where you are. But a great deal of the time the response will be "That's not important to me at all, honey; I just wish you'd told me sooner, so we could have avoided all this tension" or "I didn't even know I was doing that; if you'll remind me about it, I won't do it anymore."

The touch dominant partner in an intimate relationship can't stop being touch dominant; that's not under voluntary control. Nor can the partner who is eye or ear dominant voluntarily become more interested in touching and body things. It's important for the other partner to remember that and not to fall into the trap of believing that if their spouses "*really* loved me they wouldn't *want*" to do or say whatever is being perceived as offensive or as evidence of coldness. But

142

much of the time such problems, between people who love each other, are associated with a small number of specific items of behavior that *are* under voluntary control and can easily be changed. The touch dominant partner can't read minds, and will often have no idea what's causing the reaction; it has to be made clear.

If the touch dominant partner's coping strategy for not being sure *when* it's okay to touch has been to internalize the rule "*Never* use touch!" the most important thing to get across to him or her is that the rule doesn't apply when the two of you are alone together. And then you must be patient, because years and years of following that rule can't be set aside overnight. Your partner will be afraid that if he or she trusts you and moves naturally, you will be disgusted or frightened; it will take time to overcome that fear. If you don't *tell* your partner, however, nothing will *ever* change.

This is not an easy problem. But it can be solved, and when a relationship matters to you it *should* be solved. The key to the solution is not in one partner being a martyr and maintaining a miserable silence; it's not in endless fighting over all sorts of things that have little to do with what's really causing the friction. The key to the solution is in good communication based on a solid foundation of mutual trust.

Another Look at Scenario Seven

Suppose we consider only the language and nonerotic body language Jeanine and Bryan use—what would a knowledge of the facts about touch dominance tell us about their situation? Let's go through the scenario section by section to find the trouble spots and suggest changes.

1. Jeanine lay with her head on Bryan's chest, still breathing hard. "That was wonderful," she said softly. "Thank you, love."

When he said nothing back, she raised her head to look at him. "Is something wrong?" she asked.

Bryan stared straight ahead, and although his arm was still around her, his voice was chilly. "Why should anything be wrong?"

Jeanine didn't answer. After all, what could she say? *I gave you a compliment, now I think you should give <u>me</u> one?* She knew how childish that would sound.

Unless Bryan wants to discuss his complaints right then and there, he should respond to Jeanine's compliment and thanks by saying, "Thank *you*, honey," with a caress . . . stroking her hair or some such thing. This is courteous, and costs him nothing. The more courteous he is at this point, the more likely it is that when he talks to Jeanine about what's troubling him she will be courteous in return.

On the other hand, Jeanine is choosing a bad moment to try to force the issue. If Bryan's failure to answer her opening line indicates to her that there's a problem, she'd be wise to ask him about it some other time.

2. "Well," he said, "I'm late already, Jeanine. If you'll excuse me—"

She sat bolt upright, clutching the sheet around her. "If I'll EXCUSE you! What kind of a line is THAT?"

Jeanine is right to be distressed. "If you'll excuse me" is something you say to a stranger or an acquaintance, not to a lover. The way Bryan uses it here sends a message—a deliberate message—that he is feeling trapped and imposed upon. It's rude and hurtful; he shouldn't do it. "I have to get going, honey—I'm late for work" is enough. But Jeanine's immediate response in open Blamer Mode is also a serious error, and a way of feeding a hostility loop. She'd be far wiser to say, "Of course; you go ahead," and take it up with him later at a less strained moment.

3. "Sorry!" he said abruptly, almost leaping out of bed, headed for the shower. But Jeanine wasn't willing to let him get away with it this time.

   "Bryan!" she said. "You <u>wait</u> a minute!"

   "Hey, I'm really late for—"

   "I don't <u>care</u> what you're late for! This is the fourth or fifth time after we've made love that you've given me a cold shoulder like this! I want to know what's wrong! What are you MAD at me about?"

This is the fight that is the expected result of a hostility loop. It should not have happened, but when Jeanine attacked Bryan in the previous section she backed him against a wall. In this situation he felt he had to either fight or flee, and he chose flight. If Jeanine had given him half a chance he would not have said anything more about the issue; if he had been wiser he would have said, "Jeanine, we'll talk about it later; this isn't a good time for it," and gone straight on to the shower, no matter how vigorously she protested. But he didn't. . . .

4. Bryan stopped, but he kept his hand on the bathroom doorknob and he kept his back to her. "I don't want to talk about it, Jeanine," he said.

   "Well, I <u>do</u> want to talk about it! Please!"

   "I just <u>wish</u> . . ." He paused.

   "You just wish <u>what</u>?"

   "I just wish that when we're in bed you could try to be a little bit more . . ."

   "Well?"

   "A little bit more <u>ladylike</u>!" he snapped, and he was through the door and had closed it behind him before she could say a word. She heard the snap as he locked the door . . . as if she couldn't be trusted to respect his privacy.

This is what happens when, in a moment of severe stress and emotion, you force your partner to explain his

145

or her feelings with no time to think about how that should be done. Bryan certainly knows that Jeanine has spent much of her young life hearing that she's "not a lady"; he knows she's sensitive about that line of talk. But she has forced him to make a statement, with predictable results. Locking the door—which says, "If you try to pursue me any farther I'll do whatever it takes to keep you away"—rubs salt in the wounds; nobody has to lock a "lady" out of a bathroom. It's a cheap shot; unless Bryan knows from previous experience that his wife really is capable of following him straight to the shower and insisting on continuing the argument, he should have enough self-control not to do this. But he badly wants to make it clear to her that what he perceives as her forcefulness and aggressiveness is distressing to him, and they haven't been able to talk about it together. His ostentatious locking of the door is one eloquent way of transmitting that message, in a situation where he feels justified by the conviction that she's forced him to say things he would have kept to himself if she'd given him the choice.

If this sort of thing keeps happening, Jeanine and Bryan will soon have a high barrier between them made up of all the negative words and actions that they will have come to associate with their lovemaking. It's a very poor way to handle the problem, and they would both be wise to make a sincere effort to improve matters.

Workout Section Seven

◆

1. Read the article "Metaphor In Action: Using a rope to untangle relationships," by Bunny S. Duhl, pp. 49–51, *Family Therapy Networker,* November/December 1993. Duhl is a family therapist who gives couples in conflict a rope, asking them to pull on it "with the amount of tension they each experienced in their relationship. Then I asked each, *at a moment of his or her own choosing,* to let go." (On p. 49.) On p. 51 she notes that "The body in action does not lie. When answering verbally, one can mask words with voice tone and incongruent body behavior, but when responding on a physical level, it is hard to mask low energy and make believe that it is high, or vice versa. A person's dynamic intent shows physically."

2. There is a medical (primarily nursing) technique called "therapeutic touch"; oddly enough, it doesn't involve touching the person directly. Instead, the touch is directed to the energy fields that surround the body. I know a number of couples who have learned the technique for use when one of them has some discomfort. You will find a large literature on the subject at your library, and some sources are listed in the bibliography at the end of this book; among the authors to look for are Delores Krieger and Janet F. Quinn.

3. Another area to investigate is the theory of metaphor coming for the most part from the University of California at Berkeley; the theory claims that metaphors have their roots in direct bodily experience, as with the metaphor "Understanding is grasping." A good first source is the book *Metaphors We Live By,* by George Lakoff and Mark Johnson, University of Chicago Press, 1980.

Touchpoints

1. "People, it seems, have a special pathway of nerves that send pleasure signals to the brain when the skin is gently stroked. The pathway is present at birth and may help human infants distinguish comfort from discomfort. . . . It had been believed that all human nerves involved in touch send their signals to the brain at a fast speed, 200 feet per second. . . . But these fibers—there are more than 1000 fibers in each nerve—sent their message at three feet per second . . ."

   > ("Slow path for touch discovered: Research explains pleasure of caress," by Sandra Blakeslee, *The New York Times,* November 26, 1994. This is a report on research by neurophysiologist Hakan Olausson of Sweden.)

2. "Early in our lives we lose the ability to move freely and spontaneously. . . . I remember, as an adolescent, trying to figure out how to walk. Suddenly something was wrong with allowing my body to do what it naturally did—partly because what it now naturally did was vaguely awkward. . . . I remember feeling clumsy until my late 20s—not because I was, necessarily, but because I had encountered so much law about how to move one's body that there seemed to be no possibility of moving correctly, let alone freely."

   > (*A Kinesthetic Homiletic: Embodying Gospel in Preaching,* by Pamela Ann Moeller, Fortress Press 1993; on p. 21.)

3. "Rather than being given the freedom of our bodies, we were taught how to bludgeon them into order. Part of the

fault lay in dualistic theology obsessed with subjugating the body; the body was at best a container for the mind and the soul."

> (Moeller 1993; on p. 22. If you suspect that problems in your relationship as a couple may come from religious attitudes one or both of you have learned that carry negative messages about touching, I recommend an audio program called "The Spirituality of Touch," by Robert Gervasi, Ph.D., available from St. Anthony Messenger Press, 1615 Republic Street, Cincinnati, Ohio, 45210.)

4. "Emotions, like colds and flus, are contagious. . . . For example, researchers now know that the transmission of moods occurs via split-second mimicry, when one person unconsciously imitates the facial expressions, posture and tone of voice of another. It's through the mimicry that the person comes to *feel* as her model feels."

> ("Spread The Mood," by Jennifer Kaylin, pp. 126–27, *Self,* May 1992; on p. 126. You might also take a look at the work of Robert B. Zajonc, whose controversial theory is that facial expressions come *before* the emotions they signal, so that putting on a happy face—or someone else's happy face—actually makes you feel happier.)

5. "Sexuality was not quite what we think it was even during the buttoned-up Victorian era of the mid-19th century. . . . But gradually, during the second half of the 19th and early 20th centuries, forms of physical touching formerly regarded as signs of sentiment and affection were sexual-

ized and privatized, and came to be regarded as sexual foreplay."

> (Robert Taibbi, in a review of Stephanie Coontz's *The Way We Never Were* titled "Burning Images: Debunking Nostalgic Myths About the Family," pp. 63–66, *Family Therapy Networker*, November/December 1993; on p. 64.)

6. "The true language of sex is primarily nonverbal. Our words and images are poor imitations of the deep and complicated feelings within us. Unsure of touching as a way of sharing with others, we have allowed our fears and discomforts to limit the rich possibilities for nonverbal communication. . . . In the profoundest sense, touch is the true language of sex."

> (Montagu 1986, p. 204.)

7. "The roughness with which many men will handle women and children constitutes yet another evidence of their having been failed in early tactile experience, for it is difficult to conceive of anyone who has been tenderly loved and caressed in infancy not learning to approach a woman or a child with especial tenderness. The very word *tenderness* implies softness, delicacy of touch, caring for . . ."

> (Montagu 1986, p. 222.)

8. "At all ages the female is very much more responsive to tactile stimuli than the male, and more dependent upon touch for erotic arousal than the male, who depends more upon visual stimuli. The difference seems to be, at least in

part, genetic; but cultural differences undoubtedly also play a role in the development of tactual responsiveness as between the sexes."

> (Montagu 1986, p. 233. Surveys have demonstrated beyond all question that many women, if forced to choose between giving up sexual intercourse itself or giving up tender holding and cuddling, would unhesitatingly hang on to the holding and cuddling. This seems to have come as a harsh shock to many men.)

Talking Touch

If you are part of a couple who are both touch dominant, you probably have no problem using touch language in your intimate moments. For couples in which only *one* person is touch dominant, however, intimate communication can be a minefield through which they have to pick a very nervous path that is inhibiting and that can hold back their sexual relationship.

Such couples need to work out, *together,* a way of talking during intimate activities that they can both live with and that won't set off alarms in either one. If there are particular touch words and phrases (and particular touches or body language) that one of you finds distasteful, you need to know that. You need to be able to talk about it; you need to know what words and phrases can safely be used instead. If there are particular aspects of touch and of touch language that will enhance pleasure, you need to know that also.

This isn't a task a book can carry out for you. It's a project that you have to get into with both hands and struggle through together, paying the most meticulous attention to keeping your personal egos and vanity out of the discussion until you have a large enough shared database of information set up to make negotiation possible.

CHAPTER EIGHT

◆

Conclusion

We have come to the end of our exploration of touch dominance and its effects on the lives of every single one of us. I am sure that means you now understand many things (and perhaps many people!) that have puzzled you in the past; I hope it means that your life will now go more smoothly and evenly than it did before.

Our society's attitude toward touch is in no way logical or rational. It's coming closer all the time to being an attitude that truly deserves the term *paranoia*, in which even the lightest and most casual physical contact is perceived as potential violence or a sexual act. We have lost our trust in one another, and we do not seem to know what to do to get it back.

That way lies loneliness and bitterness and sorrow; with all my heart, I hope we can do better than that. This book is my effort to take a first step forward; by reading it, you have joined me on what will surely be a long and burdensome path. Thank you.

—SUZETTE HADEN ELGIN

‧

An American Sign Language Sampler

American Sign Language (ASL) is a foreign language, just like French or Chinese or Cherokee, and would be learned in the same way. All I want to do in this brief section is give you a feeling for what ASL is like, so that if you find it interesting you can go into it further. You'll find many ASL grammars and teaching videotapes available; often you can find an ASL course at a local college or on one of your television channels. You can have a lot of <u>fun</u> with ASL without becoming an expert—and it's the handiest language I know of.

Let's begin with just four handshapes, from which we can get all the others. You make your signs in front of your body, roughly in the space where you'd hold your glass at a party.

A-Hand: Make a relaxed fist, without curling your thumb over your other fingers or tucking it under them. (This is "A" in fingerspelling.)

B-Hand: Hold all your fingers straight up together; now fold your thumb over your palm. (This is "B" in fingerspelling. When the thumb isn't folded over, this is called an "open B-hand.")

O-Hand: Make an open circle by touching your thumb and fingertips together around a circle of air; now flatten it just a little, so the circle is an oval. (This is "O" in fingerspelling.)

1-Hand: Hold your index finger straight up; fold your other fingers down against your palm; fold your thumb over your fingers. Like a teacher trying to get a class to pay attention. (This is the number 1 in ASL.)

Now we can move on to learn some signs. Because most people are right-handed, I'll give right-handed instructions; if you're left-handed, just switch left for right, and vice versa. *Always go back to the basic shape before trying a new sign.*

From the A-hand

SORRY: Put the A-hand against your chest, palm toward you, thumb pointing toward your left arm. Move your hand in a circle about the size of a saucer, two or three times. (If you do this with an *open* hand instead of a fist, it means PLEASE.)

NOT; DON'T: Put the tip of your right thumb under your chin; your palm will be facing left and your knuckles pointing up. Move the A-hand forward quickly so that your thumb flicks the underside of your chin.

FAST; RIGHT AWAY: Put both A-hands in front of you, palms facing and knuckles pointing ahead. Now tuck your thumbs under

156

your folded index fingers and flick them up, fast—just like shooting marbles.

WOMAN; GIRL; FEMALE: Put your right thumb on your cheek near your jawbone, back toward your ear; move it forward along your jaw to the side of your chin. This sign comes from the hand movement women once used to tie the strings of a bonnet. (When you do this sign and then clasp both hands in front of you, right hand palm down, left hand palm up, it means WIFE. If you do it with your fingers open and extended, it means MOTHER.)

From the B-hand

GOOD: This takes both hands. Hold the left B-hand in front of you, palm facing up. Put the right B-hand fingertips against your lips, palm toward you, fingers pointing up. Now lay the right B-hand down, palm up, in your left palm. (If you do this with your right hand palm down, it means BAD. If you sign GOOD and then clap your hands once, it means CONGRATULATIONS.)

KNOW: Touch the fingertips of your right hand, palm toward you and fingers pointing up, to your forehead—roughly just above the middle of your right eyebrow.

WILL: This is the "will" of future time, as in "I will go." It uses what is called the "open" B-hand, meaning that the thumb is not folded over the palm. Put your right B-hand beside your face, palm toward your right cheek and fingers pointing up. Now move your hand forward and up, away from your face, in an arc.

HELLO, HI!:
Hold your right open B-hand up, palm out and fingers pointing upward, beside your right forehead. Move your hand out to the right just a bit.

MY; MINE:
Put your right open B-hand, palm toward you and fingers pointing left, against your chest. (If you turn your palm out toward the person you're signing to, this means YOUR or YOURS; signed toward someone or something else, it means HER(S) or HIS or ITS or THEIRS.)

THANK YOU; YOU'RE WELCOME:
Put the fingertips of both B-hands, palms toward you and fingers pointing up, against your lips. Then move your hands forward, like throwing someone a kiss.

BIG; LARGE:
This sign is made with both hands. Let your thumbs drop and extend straight out sideways. Put both hands in front of you, palms down, *thumbtips touching*, other fingers pointing straight ahead. Now move your hands apart to each side. The farther apart you move them, the bigger whatever you're referring to is.

158

LATER:

Put your left open B-hand in front of you, fingers pointing up and palm facing right. Let the thumb of your right B-hand drop and extend; put your right thumbtip in the center of your left palm, with fingers pointing up. Now, using your right thumb like a pivot, move your right hand forward till your right fingers are pointing straight ahead.

FATHER:

Unfold your thumb and let your fingers spread apart. Put the thumbtip of your right hand on your right forehead, with your palm facing left. Now move your hand out and down away from you just a little bit.

FINISH:

Using both B-hands, unfold your thumbs and let your fingers spread apart. Put both hands against your upper chest, fingers pointing upward. Now turn your hands over and out, ending with both palms facing down and your fingers pointing forward. (This sign is used in ASL to indicate past time, like the "-ed" ending in English. "Went" in ASL would be GO plus FINISH; "I ate" would be I plus EAT plus FINISH; "I didn't eat" would be I plus NOT plus EAT plus FINISH.)

LOVE:

Cross your open B-hands over your heart, palms toward you, fingers pointing up. (Also done with A-hands.)

TOUCH: Touch the tip of the middle finger of your right open B-hand to the back of your left hand.

From the O-Hand

HOME: Touch the fingertips of your right O-hand first to the right corner of your lips and then to your upper right cheek.

PRETTY; BEAUTIFUL: Put the fingertips of your right O-hand against your chin, palm facing down. Now move your hand in a circle around your face to your forehead and back to your starting point. As you move your hand, let your fingers open wide and then close again to end with the O-hand at your chin. The bigger the circle, the more beautiful.

EAT: Put the fingertips of your right O-hand almost touching your lips, palm toward you. Move your hand a little bit away from your lips and then back again, two or three times.

IN; INSIDE: Put your right O-hand in front of you, palm toward you, fingers pointing left. Make a left O-hand and put all your fingertips (and thumbtip) inside the right O. (If you do this and then move the left hand out again, it means OUT or OUTSIDE.)

MAN; BOY; MALE: Put your right O-hand at your right forehead, palm down, fingertips pointing left. Move your hand away

160

from your forehead and down, just a little bit. This sign comes from the old-fashioned gesture men made tipping their hats. (If you do this and then clasp both hands in front of you, left palm up, right palm down, it means HUSBAND.)

I; ME: Fold your right thumb over the other fingers of your O-hand and raise your little finger straight up. Now put the thumb edge of your hand against the center of your chest, palm facing left, fingers pointing up. (If you do this sign by touching your right shoulder instead of your chest, and then moving the hand across and touching your left shoulder, it means WE or US.)

From the 1-hand

SAY; TALK: Put the index finger of your right 1-hand in front of your lips, palm down. Now make a small circle forward and back in front of your mouth. (If you make a big and vigorous circle, it means COMMAND.)

EYE; EAR; NOSE; MOUTH: Just point to the body part with the index finger of your right 1-hand. (The sign for EAR also means HEAR.)

THINK: Use your right 1-hand, palm toward you. Make a little circle with your fingertip on your right forehead, above your eyebrow. (If you do this with your extended index, middle, and ring fingers, holding your little finger down with your thumb, it means WONDER.)

UP; DOWN; THERE:

Just point!

PAIN:

Put both 1-hands in front of you, palms toward you, with your index fingertips facing and almost touching. Now jab the index fingertips together several times.

GO:

Put both 1-hands in front of you, palms toward your chest and index fingertips facing each other. Now circle one index finger around the other several times, moving away from you. (If you do this moving *toward* you, it means COME.)

THIRSTY:

Move the tip of your right index finger down your throat from top to bottom, with the palm of the 1-hand toward your chest.

WHAT:

Your left hand should be in an open B, thumb relaxed beside the fingers. Now draw the index fingertip of your right 1-hand across the open palm of your left hand, from thumb edge to little finger edge.

WHO:

With your right 1-hand, palm toward you and finger pointing up, make a little circle around your lips.

WHERE:

With your right 1-hand at the right side of your nose, palm facing left and finger pointing up, move your hand out and down away from your face in an arc. (If you start this sign from roughly the middle of your lips and make a small arc, it means TRUE or SURE.)

TO ASK QUESTIONS:

To ask a question in ASL, you use a "question face"; raise your eyebrows and look curious. You can also draw a big question mark in the air in front of you with the index finger of your right 1-hand.

ASL (also called Ameslan) has its own grammar rules, and they're not identical to the rules of English. Word order is very different, for example. (When English word order is used—as is done in some schools in this country, but not in the deaf community—the result is called "Signed English" or "Siglish.") For information on ASL grammar, you'll need to go to the books and videos or to a teacher or native signer. As is true for English and all other living languages, different dialects have different rules; don't be surprised if your sources fail to agree on every detail.

◆

Curlylocks
and the Three Bears
(a touch dominant version)

Once upon a long-ago time, there were three bears. There was a great big furry fuzzy Papa Bear, and a middle-sized fuzzy furry Mama Bear, and a tiny little Baby Bear with fur as soft and feelsome as velvet. And they all lived together in a cozy little house with smooth stone walls and a rough shingled roof, tucked down under the big tall trees in the deep woods.

One cool summer morning the three bears got up feeling *especially* happy. The Papa Bear wrapped his arms around the Mama Bear and gave her a big hug, and said, "I feel *won*derful!" The Mama Bear gave the Papa Bear a big kiss—first on the left cheek and then on the right cheek—and said, "I feel wonderful, *too!*" And they both put their arms around the Baby Bear and nuzzled him with their cool damp noses, and they said, "We love you *enor*mously, Baby Bear, and we feel *won*derful!"

"Well, you know what?" said the Baby Bear, hugging them

right back, "I feel like going for a walk in the *woods!*" And so they did—and they went off in such a hurry that they didn't even finish their breakfast.

Now, while the bears were out in the woods taking their walk, along came a little girl named Curlylocks. She made her right hand into a fist and knocked on the door softly—but nobody came. She made her left hand into a fist and knocked on the door *hard*—but nobody came. So she turned the doorknob all the way, gave the door a push till it opened wide, and went right on in.

The first thing she found in the three bears' house was their breakfast, with the three bowls of oatmeal not quite empty, and the three mugs of milk not quite empty, and three spoons waiting.

Curlylocks stuck her thumb in the Papa Bear's big bowl and popped her thumb right into her mouth, to get a taste. "OH!" she said, quick as quick. "That's too HOT!" She stuck her thumb in the Mama Bear's middle-sized bowl and popped her thumb right into her mouth, to get a taste again. "OH!" she said, quick as quick. "That's too COLD!"

And then she stuck her thumb in the Baby Bear's little tiny bowl and popped her thumb right into her mouth, to get a taste just one more time. "Oooooooh," she said, slow as slow, "that's perfect!" and she licked all the oatmeal off her thumb for starters, and when that was all gone she picked up the Baby Bear's spoon and finished every last little bit in his bowl, too, and she topped it all off by drinking up every last drop of milk in the Baby Bear's little tiny mug.

The next thing Curlylocks found in the three bears' house was the three chairs where the bears always sat when they were tired. She sat down in the Papa Bear's big chair on the Papa Bear's big cushion, and popped right back up again quick as quick. "OH!" she said. "That's too HARD!" She sat down in the Mama Bear's middle-sized chair on the Mama Bear's middle-sized cushion, and popped right back up again quick as quick. "OH!" she said. "That's too SOFT!"

And then she sat down in the Baby Bear's little tiny chair,

on the Baby Bear's little tiny cushion. "Oooooooooh," she said, slow as slow, "that's perfect!" And she made up her mind to sit right there and think things over. But suddenly . . . Ker-WHACKety WHACK! . . . the little tiny chair broke! And it split, and it cracked, and it disINtegrated! And it dumped Curlylocks out onto the floor, KerTHUMPety THUMP!

Curlylocks was so shaken up from falling out of the chair that she felt like lying down for a while. She found the Papa Bear's big bed and stretched herself out on top of it on the thick wool blanket that Mama Bear had made with her own two hands. "OH!" she said, jumping back up quick as quick. "That's too SCRATCHy!" She found the Mama Bear's middle-sized bed and stretched herself out on top of it on the patchwork quilt—some squares satiny and some squares puckery and some squares with little bumpy flowers and leaves all over them—that the Mama Bear had made with her own two hands. "OH!" she said, jumping back up quick as quick. "That's too mixed UP!"

And then she found the Baby Bear's little tiny bed and stretched herself out on top of it on the soft small puffy comforter that the Mama Bear had made with her own two hands. "Ooooooooooooooooh," she said, slow as slow as slow, "that's perfect!" And she snuggled down and cuddled down and curled herself up, and fell fast asleep.

Pretty soon, here came the three bears home from their walk in the deep woods. Down the path and through the door they came, still feeling wonderful! But then . . .

"Woah!" said the great big Papa Bear. "Somebody's been sticking her thumb in my *oat*meal!" And "Woah!" said the middle-sized Mama Bear. "Somebody's been sticking her thumb in *my* oatmeal!" And "Woah! Woah!" said the little tiny Baby Bear. "Somebody's been sticking her thumb in *my* oatmeal, *too,* and she ate it all *up,* every last bit!" He took a big breath and added, "And she drank up all my milk, too, while she was at it!"

And "Woah up!" said the great big Papa Bear. "Somebody's been sitting in my *chair!*" And "Woah up!" said the

167

middle-sized Mama Bear. "Somebody's been sitting in *my* chair!" And "Woah up! Woah up!" said the little tiny Baby Bear. "Somebody's been sitting in *my* chair, *too,* and she smashed it all to SMITHereens!"

And "Woah up all OVer again!" said the great big Papa Bear. "Somebody's been sleeping in my *bed!*" And "Woah up all OVer again!" said the middle-sized Mama Bear. "Somebody's been sleeping in *my* bed!" And "Woah up all over again and WOW!" said the little tiny Baby Bear. "Somebody's been sleeping in *my* bed, *too*—and there she IS! WOW!"

Well, all that WOWing made so much commotion that it woke Curlylocks right up. She opened her eyes wide, took one look, jumped right off the Baby Bear's bed and out through the open window beside it, and ran through the woods and over the fields and down the road all the way home, not looking back even once to find out if the bears were running behind her!

And Curlylocks *never ever* went into anybody's house without being invited . . . or tasted anybody's oatmeal without being invited . . . or sat in anybody's chair without being invited . . . or lay down to take a nap in anybody's *bed* without being invited . . . ever again!

And that's the end of this story, and it's all over.

THE END

References
and Bibliography

Articles

Baldwin, J. G., Jr. "The healing touch." *American Journal of Medicine* 80:1 (1986), pp. 76–80.

Barnett, K. "A Theoretical Construct of the Concepts of Touch As They Relate to Nursing." *Nursing Research,* March/April 1972, pp. 102–10.

Bauman, M. "The Dangerous Samaritans: How We Unintentionally Injure the Poor." *Imprimis,* January 1994, pp. 1–5.

Bigger, M. L. "Maternal Aversion to Mother-Infant Contact." In C. C. Brown, ed., *The Many Facets of Touch* (Skillman, N.J.: Johnson & Johnson, 1984), pp. 65–73.

Blakeslee, S. "Slow path for touch discovered: Research explains pleasure of caress." *The New York Times,* November 26, 1994.

Davis, L. J. "The Next Panic." *Harper's Magazine,* May 1991.

Douglas, C. "The Beat Goes On." *Psychology Today,* November 1987, pp. 38–42.

Duhl, B. S. "Metaphor in Action: Using a rope to untangle relationships." *Family Therapy Networker,* November/December 1993, pp. 49–51.

Fisher, S. "Experiencing Your Body: You Are What You Feel." *Saturday Review of Science,* July 8, 1972, pp. 27–32.

Goleman, D. "Studies Point to Power of Nonverbal Signals." *The New York Times,* April 8, 1986.

———. "The Experience of Touch: Research Points to a Critical Role." *The New York Times,* February 2, 1988.

———. "Researchers Trace Empathy's Roots to Infancy." *The New York Times,* April 28, 1989.

———. "A Feel-Good Theory: A Smile Affects Mood." *The New York Times,* July 18, 1989.

———. "Sensing Silent Cues Emerges As Key Skill." *The New York Times,* October 10, 1989.

Grace-Pedrotty, B. "Bodywork and Soul." *In Health,* January/February 1995, p. 26.

Greenbaum, P., and H. Rosenfeld. "Varieties of touching in greetings: Sequential structure and sex-related differences." *Journal of Nonverbal Behavior* 5:13 (1980), pp. 13–25.

Gunzenhauser, N. "Appendix: Research Issues and Directions." In N. Gunzenhauser, ed., *Advances in Touch: New Implications in Human Development* (Skillman, N.J.: Johnson & Johnson 1990), pp. 163–67.

Gup, T. "Adventures (and misadventures) of Watson Fellows." *Smithsonian Magazine,* September 1994, pp. 68–80.

Harrison, L. L. "Effects of Tactile Stimulation on Preterm Infants: An Integrative Review of the Literature with Practice Implications." *The Online Journal of Knowledge Synthesis for Nursing* 1:6 (1994).

———. "Early Parental Touch and Preterm Infants." *Journal of Obstetric, Gynocologic, and Neo-natal Nursing,* July/August 1991, pp. 299–306.

Jones, E. E. "Interpreting Interpersonal Behavior: The Effects of Expectancies." *Science,* October 3, 1986, pp. 41–46.

Jourard, S., and J. Rubin. "Self-Disclosure and Touching: A Study of Two Modes of Interpersonal Encounter and Their Interrelation." *Journal of Humanistic Psychology* 8 (1968), pp. 39–48.

Juni, S., and R. Brannon. "Interpersonal Touching As a Function of Status and Sex." *Journal of Social Psychology* 114 (1981), pp. 135–36.

Kaylin, J. "Spread the Mood." *Self,* May 1992, pp. 126–27.

References and Bibliography

Kochakian, M. J. "Those Youngsters Out of Synch." Gannett Suburban Newspapers, May 18, 1992.

Korner, A. F. "The Many Faces of Touch." In C. C. Brown, ed., *The Many Facets of Touch* (Skillman, N.J.: Johnson & Johnson, 1984), pp. 107–13.

Kutner, L. "Knowing When to Touch." *The New York Times,* June 29, 1989.

Lubove, S. "People Talk Thin but Eat Fat." *Forbes,* July 10, 1992, p. 307.

Lynch, J. J. "Interpersonal Aspects of Blood Pressure Control." *Journal of Nervous and Mental Diseases* 170 (1982), pp. 143–53.

Major, B., and R. Heslin. "Perceptions of Cross-Sex and Same-Sex Nonreciprocal Touch: It is Better to Give Than to Receive." *Journal of Nonverbal Behavior* 6 (1982), pp. 148–62.

McCorkle, R., and M. Hollenbach. "Touch and the Acutely Ill." In C. C. Brown, ed., *The Many Facets of Touch* (Skillman, N.J.: Johnson & Johnson 1984), pp. 175–83.

Older, J. "Teaching Touch at Medical School." *Journal of the American Medical Association* 252 (1984), pp. 931–33.

————. "Epilogue: Touch in All Ages." In N. Gunzenhauser, ed., *Advances in Touch: New Implications in Human Development* (Skillman, N.J.: Johnson & Johnson 1990), pp. 155–62.

Rose, F. E., Jr. "Weasel Words." *Forbes,* December 23, 1991, p. 184.

Rose, S. A. "Preterm Responses to Passive, Active, and Social Touch." In C. C. Brown, ed., *The Many Facets of Touch* (Skillman, N.J.: Johnson & Johnson 1984), pp. 90–100.

Rosenfield, A. "More Than Skin Deep." *Science Illustrated,* August/September 1988, pp. 15–17.

Quinn, J. F. "Building a Body of Knowledge: Research on Therapeutic Touch, 1974–1986." *Journal of Holistic Nursing* 6:1 (1988), pp. 37–45.

Sauder, D. "Immunology of the Epidermis: Changing Perspectives." *Journal of Investigative Dermatology* 81 (1983), pp. 185–86.

Selzer, R. "The Art of Surgery: Trespassing on Sacred Ground." *Harper's Magazine,* January 1976, pp. 75–78.

Sharp, D. "Aristotle's Garage: A Mechanic's Metaphysics." *Harper's Magazine,* March 1981, pp. 91–93.

Smith, D., et al. "Success and Interpersonal Touch in a Competitive Setting." *Journal of Nonverbal Behavior* 5 (1980), pp. 26–34.

Stier, D. S., and J. A. Hall. "Gender Differences in Touch: An Empirical and Theoretical Review." *Journal of Personality and Social Psychology* 47 (1984), pp. 440–59.

Taibbi, R. "Burning Images: Debunking Nostalgic Myths About the Family." *Family Therapy Networker,* November/December 1993, pp. 63–66.

Tucker, W. "Foot in the Door." *Forbes,* February 3, 1992, pp. 50–52.

Weiss, S. J. "The Language of Touch." *Nursing Research,* March/April 1979, pp. 76–80.

Zajonc, R. B. "Emotion and Facial Efference: A Theory Reclaimed." *Science,* April 5, 1985, pp. 15–20.

Items With No Byline

"Sign Language." *Orlando Sentinel,* August 22, 1993.

Books

Ackerman, D. *A Natural History of the Senses.* New York, N.Y.: Random House, 1990.

Argyle, M. *Bodily Communication.* London: Methuen, 1975.

Beattie, G. *Talk: An Analysis of Speech and Non-Verbal Behaviour in Conversation.* Milton Keynes, England: Open University Press, 1983.

Bodanis, D. *The Secret House: 24 Hours in the Strange and Unexpected World in Which We Spend Our Nights and Days.* New York, N.Y.: Simon & Schuster, 1986.

Bolinger, D. *Intonation and Its Parts: Melody in Spoken English.* Stanford, Calif.: Stanford University Press, 1986.

Brown, C. C., ed. *The Many Facets of Touch.* Skillman, N.J.: Johnson & Johnson, 1984.

Cherry, K. *Womansword: What Japanese Words Say About Women.* New York, N.Y.: Kodansha America, 1987.

Dillard, A. *The Writing Life.* New York: Harper & Row, 1989.

References and Bibliography

Ekman, P., et al. *Emotion in the Human Face.* New York, N.Y.: Pergamon, 1972.

Gunzenhauser, N., ed. *Advances in Touch: New Implications in Human Development.* Skillman, N.J.: Johnson & Johnson, 1990.

Hall, E. T. *The Silent Language.* New York, N.Y.: Doubleday Anchor, 1959.

———. *Beyond Culture.* New York, N.Y.: Doubleday Anchor, 1977.

Henley, N. *Body Politics: Power, Sex and Nonverbal Communication.* Englewood Cliffs, N.J.: Prentice-Hall, 1977.

Key, M. R., ed. *The Relationship of Verbal and Nonverbal Communication.* The Hague: Mouton, 1980.

Krieger, D. *The Therapeutic Touch: How to Use Your Hands to Help or to Heal.* Englewood Cliffs, N.J.: Prentice-Hall, 1979.

Lakoff, G., and M. Johnson. *Metaphors We Live By.* Chicago, Ill.: University of Chicago Press, 1980.

Lynch, J. J. *The Language of the Heart: The Body's Response to Human Dialogue.* New York, N.Y.: Basic Books, 1985.

Martin, E. *The Woman in the Body: A Cultural Analysis of Reproduction.* Boston, Mass.: Beacon Press, 1987.

McClure, V. S. *Infant Massage: A Handbook for Loving Parents.* (Revised edition.) New York, N.Y.: Bantam Books, 1989.

Moeller, P. A. *A Kinesthetic Homiletic: Embodying Gospel in Preaching.* Minneapolis, Minn.: Fortress Press, 1993.

Montagu, A. *Touching: The Human Significance of the Skin.* (Third edition.) New York, N.Y.: Harper & Row, 1986.

Moroni, G. *My Hands Held Out to You: The Use of Body and Hands in Prayer.* (Translated by Paul Burns.) New York, N.Y.: Paulist Press, 1992.

Vitale, B. M. *Unicorns Are Real: A Right-Brained Approach to Learning.* Rolling Hills Estates, Calif.: Jalmar Press, 1982.

Other

Elgin, S. H. *The Touch Dominance Quarterly.* (Newsletter of the Touch Dominance Network™) Huntsville, Ark.: OCLS Press.

Gervasi, R. *The Spirituality of Touch.* (Audio program.) Cincinnati, Ohio: St. Anthony Messenger Press.

Index

Index